THE FAERIE VORTEX

BOOK 5 THE PARANORMAL CASEBOOKS OF SIR ARTHUR CONAN DOYLE

VAUGHN ENTWISTLE

The Faerie Vortex, Book 5, The Paranormal Casebooks of Sir Arthur Conan Doyle

E-book edition: ISBN 978-1-8381568-6-2

Print Edition: ISBN 978-1-8381568-2-4

Second edition: June 2023

❦ Created with Vellum

A SUMMONS TO THE BRITISH MUSEUM

Oscar Wilde skipped up the steps of the British Museum, swept through the heavy bronze doors, and plunged from sun-drenched summer streets into a cool and gloomy corridor lazed by sleeping shadows. Here he paused to scratch a Lucifer and puff one of his Turkish cigarettes to life, then followed his own echoing footsteps into the circular expanse of the library Reading Room. Seated at the radiating spokes of the readers' tables were dusty men and dusty women perusing dusty tomes taken down from dusty shelves. A studious hush filled the great domed space—a quiet disturbed only by the licking of index fingers and the susurration of turning pages.

But on this particular day, the Irish wit had come neither to write, nor to idle away the hours with a casual morning's read. Instead, he scanned the downcast faces seated at the blue leather topped tables, searching for the author of the telegram that had summoned him here. He flinched as a hand touched his arm and a voice spoke so close to his ear he felt warm, stale breath wash the side of his face:

"A friendly reminder, sir, no smoking in the Reading Room."

Wilde turned to find the owner of the voice lurking at his shoulder —a tall, rather desiccated figure in an *out at the elbows* suit and round spectacles. Undoubtedly a librarian: the fellow had the constipated face and unnaturally long index fingers of a man born to *shusssssshhhhh!*

"I'm afraid you'll have to put that out," the librarian insisted.

After a momentary wobble, Wilde regained his equilibrium with the alacrity of a seasoned tightrope walker.

"I'm sorry? Ah, the cigarette. For a terrible moment, I thought you were referring to my genius, which is inextinguishable." He flashed his mossy teeth, counterfeiting affability.

The smile failed to mollify the librarian, whose spectacles caught the light from the high windows and bounced it back, hardening into opaque white disks. "You know the rules, sir . . ." The librarian shook his head so that dandruff blizzarded down upon the shoulders of his mousy jacket. " . . . no smoking in the Reading Room."

At the reprimand, the Irishman's long face drooped into a parody of itself. "Oh, really? Must I? As you might note the cigarette is Turkish, rather expensive to obtain in England, and only recently lit."

The librarian's lips puckered in a moue of displeasure. "Sorry, sir, but rules are rules."

"Ah. Very well, then." Wilde huffed an exasperated breath and extinguished the cigarette on the inside of his silver cigarette case and then slid it beneath one of the elastic holders. He would save it for later. He bowed his head and threw a gesture of obeisance at the librarian. "Thank you, noble guardian of the printed word . . ." he said, adding in an under-the-breath-mutter as he waltzed away, " . . . for saving me from the meagrest particle of happiness."

The British Library Reading Room was a temple devoted to books. The library stacks, three tiers high, groaned beneath the collective genius of Literature's greatest writers. As Wilde perambulated the circular room in a counter clock direction, the literary canon unwound in reverse alphabetical order: Zola, Wilde (he could not suppress the urge for a quick glance at the shelf which held a single copy of his notorious novel, *The Picture of Dorian Grey*). Moving on past Tennyson, Shakespeare, Poe, Melville . . . unalphabetizing until he reached the D's where he found his friend, Arthur Conan Doyle, sitting (appropriately) at the reading table at the end of C-through-E.

It was the height of summer and Wilde was sportily kitted out in a white linen suit with a straw boater and cane. By contrast, Conan Doyle was overdressed for the heat in his work-a-day tweeds. He looked up as Wilde stepped to the reading table. If anything, the Scotsman's dour expression was even gloomier than his dress.

"Whatever's wrong, Arthur? You have the face of a man unfashionably late for his own funeral."

"Sit, Oscar. I have something of grave importance to share with you."

"*Grave* importance? Oh, very good, Arthur," Wilde chuckled at the unintended pun but did not sit down, eyeing the straight-backed chair with clear reservation. "For once I prefer to remain standing. I was playing horsey-rides with the boys last evening and believe that I have ruptured my spleen or one of those equally obscure organs that somehow performs a vital function."

Conan Doyle brushed his walrus moustache with his thick fingers, a "tell" that Wilde recognised as an unequivocal sign of agitation.

"I recommend you take a seat, my friend. What I have to say will soon make you forget your back ache." Conan Doyle snatched open his leather satchel and drew out a familiar leather-bound book held closed by a strap and miniature lock. "You know what this is?"

"Of course," Wilde replied, settling gingerly into the chair opposite. "One of your *Casebooks*." He drew off his straw boater and tossed it onto the table, set down his walking cane next to it, and smoothed back his chestnut-colored hair. The long wavy curls of his aesthete days had been trimmed by a recent visit to his barbers, and these days he wore his hair short and brilliantined into place.

"Look at the cover, Oscar."

"That is precisely where my eyes are pointing."

"Take special note of the number."

The Irishman frowned and hunkered forward, eyes asquint. "*Casebook Number Five*," he read aloud. "Is that all? Can we go now? I am quite famished, and your telegram lured me here with the promise of standing me breakfast."

"I'm afraid it will have to be lunch."

"Breakfast," Wilde insisted. "I arose from my bed this morning at the crack of 11:30, a full hour earlier than usual. Just in time for breakfast."

"My telegram requested you arrive here at ten," Conan Doyle pointed out in a peevish voice: "It's now almost one o'clock."

Wilde laughed dismissively. "That's as may be, but clocks are mere mechanical contrivances prone to error. Whereas, the Wildean stomach is the most reliable chronometer I own and it informs me that is still breakfast time."

"Very well, breakfast it is. But first I must read the contents of this Casebook to you."

The Irish wit's eyes widened in alarm. "Now? The entire book? Surely not? Could we not adjourn to the Savoy where you could synopsise over oysters on horseback and a chilled bottle of *Perrier-Jouët*? I was never one for idling in libraries, particularly this one, where I am jostled by the ghosts of literary giants criticising my punctuation and mocking my abhorrence of the semicolon."

Conan Doyle held up the Casebook again. "Read the full title, Oscar. All of it."

Wilde sighed and leaned forward, peering. "*Casebook Number Five: The Faerie Vortex*. Yes. Very nice. A spanking good title. Has a definite ring to it."

Conan Doyle set the Casebook down and drummed his fingers atop the cover. "Do you remember a year ago when you and I went on a little adventure to the southwest of England? Our visit to a picturesque old village named *Wyrme-Hallow*?"

Wilde pursed his generous lips and knitted his brows, nonplussed. "No, I confess I have no such recollection."

"Come now, you must remember staying in a rustic inn with a thatched roof?"

Wilde's frown deepened. "If I did, it quite escapes me."

"So you don't remember us going down there to investigate the mysterious disappearance of two young girls?"

Wilde unleashed an exasperated sigh. "Examine my face, Arthur.

This is the most puzzled expression I can make without straining a muscle."

"Then you don't remember fishing for trout in a stream?"

Wilde laughed musically. "Now you *are* being ridiculous. Fishing is one of the many manly outdoor pursuits Oscar Wilde does not participate in—and with great enthusiasm, I might add. When it comes to the pursuit of fish, I prefer my catch to arrive on a plate, poached, with a slice of lemon and a tureen of hollandaise sauce."

"So you don't recall posing for this photograph?"

Conan Doyle flipped open the Casebook, turned it around, and slid it across the table. Wilde studied the photograph glued into its pages and his mouth dropped open. There, rendered in sepia tones, was the most famous playwright of his generation in hip waders, standing in the middle of a stream, an enormous trout dangling from the line of his fishing rod.

Wilde's eyes widened with bemusement. "What? I don't understand. I never . . ." He trailed off mid-sentence and cast a suspicious glance at his friend. "Is this some kind of clever prank, Arthur? I have read that there are ways of altering photographs. Is this a new hobby you've taken up? Are you now dabbling in *trick* photography?"

But Conan Doyle's face looked anything but prankish. "No tricks, I'm afraid. I am in deadly earnest." He took a deep breath and shudderingly released it. "You know I keep my Casebooks behind a hidden panel in my writing desk?"

"Yes, and if you die before me I am to remove them and find a similar safe hiding place. The books can only be made public five years after the last one of us dies. That is our agreement."

Conan Doyle nodded. "Yesterday, I opened the secret compartment —there was something I wished to refer to in the second Casebook . . . a name I had forgotten. That was when I discovered the book you see before you—Casebook Number Five. Like you I was baffled. I have written four Casebooks to date. I certainly do not remember writing a fifth. But the handwriting is undeniably mine. Plus, there are a number of telling artefacts pasted into its pages: stubs of train tickets, photographs, newspaper clippings, and even a tattered and antique map. And yet I have no recollection of any of it. No recollection of the train journey. No recollection of visiting the rustic hamlet of Wyrme-Hallow. No recollection of you posing for the photograph . . ."

The Scotsman hesitated and glanced down, gathering himself before looking his friend in the eye and adding, " . . . and no recollection of you being arrested for murder."

At the words spoken aloud, all colour drained from Wilde's already pallid complexion. "Murder? A-a-arrested? Oh, this is all a joke is it not? It is, isn't it? Wu-what are you saying? It's quite impossible!"

In reply, Conan Doyle flipped to a newspaper cutting pasted into the pages of the Casebook and held it out for Wilde to examine. The clipping was from a small, local paper: *The Darvington Recorder*. The playwright read the headline and recoiled: IRISH FIEND RUN TO GROUND. Accompanying the article was a reporter's sketch—drawn looking in through the bars of a prison cell—of a forlorn and disconsolate man sitting slouch-shouldered on the end of a wooden cot. The face in the drawing bore an unmistakable likeness to the face that Wilde's barber dragged a razor across each morning.

"I have read the article," Conan Doyle went on. "It describes the arrest of one Oscar Fingal O'Flahertie Wills Wilde for the suspected abduction and murder of two village girls."

Wilde jumped up from his seat, fidgeting with distress. "Stop this, Arthur. You're frightening me."

Conan Doyle looked up at his friend with bloodshot eyes that testified to a sleepless night of pummelled pillows and bedclothes wrestled into knots. "You are right to be frightened, Oscar." And then he added in a voice torn to rags, "Because I, too, am frightened."

Oscar Wilde looked into his friend's face—a face that always held a calm, resolute certainty. But now the expression of hopeless uncertainty Wilde found there chilled the summer sweat on the back of his neck. The Irishman's knees buckled, and he sagged back into his chair.

"Are you still in a hurry to dine?" Conan Doyle asked mildly.

"No. My appetite has fled. What is it all about, Arthur?"

"That I cannot begin to fathom. I have grappled with this hideous discovery all night long. Just before you arrived, I came to a rather unsettling conclusion. As I have written in my Sherlock Holmes stories, "Once you eliminate the impossible—"

"Yes-yes . . ." Wilde interrupted, finishing the quote. " . . . whatever remains, no matter how improbable, must be the truth. But what does that mean in this case?"

Conan Doyle's shoulders heaved as he sucked in a deep breath and launched into an explanation. "It means that, a year ago, you and I had an experience that has somehow been erased from our minds. We must find out what that experience was, and why we have no recollection of it."

For a long, long time Wilde sat in a stunned, mind-wracked silence. When he finally spoke, his voice was as brittle as the dangerously thin ice on a winter skating pond. "Bu-but how do we even begin to go about such a task?"

Conan Doyle slid the Casebook back from his friend and turned it around, opening to the first page. "First you must become familiar with the story. Or, at least, the story thus far."

And then Conan Doyle began to read aloud the words he had no recollection of writing.

AN INCIDENCE OF FAERIES

"Faeries at the bottom of the garden?" Wilde chortled. "Surely that is a music hall song?"

Conan Doyle glumly regarded the large Irishman seated across from him in the first class carriage. It was a fine, blue-sky day and the two friends were on a train steaming across England, heading from London to the coast of Wessex. But whereas most of their fellow passengers were holidayers traveling to the seaside resorts of Minehead and Ilfracombe to escape the gritty summer heat of London, Conan Doyle and Wilde were hot on the trail of a mystery worthy of Sherlock Holmes himself.

"She did send proof," Conan Doyle countered, and turning to the first page of a brand-new Casebook, he rustled through the pages of a folded letter and plucked loose a photograph printed on heavy card, which he handed across to his friend.

Wilde took the photograph and held it up to catch the light from the window, squinting at a sepia-toned image that depicted a remarkable scene:

A young girl, only just into her teen years, sat with her knees tucked beneath her on a picnic blanket spread out in the shade of a large tree. Evidently, the girl was hosting a tea party. As at any good tea party, tiny cups and saucers for four were set out upon the blanket. Occupying the guests of honour spot were two dollies—one a yarn-haired rag doll, the other a bonneted baby with a chipped porcelain head. Also in attendance was a battle-scarred teddy bear with a chewed ear and a missing button eye. Sprawled beside him in a doll-size rocking chair was a Pagliacci clown with large teardrops daubed upon its cheeks. Most remarkably, the young lady was entertaining some rather more unusual picnic guests, which consisted of six or seven winged sylphs who frolicked about her knees, or perched in the nearby flowers.

"Faeries!" Wilde blurted.

"Wings and all," Conan Doyle noted. "Now do you believe?"

But Wilde answered with a sceptical scowl and, after perusing the photo for several long minutes, cleared his throat with a noisy harrumph and handed the photograph back. "Paper cut-outs," he opined, "posed in the grass. A rather crude hoax."

At the response, Conan Doyle swallowed hard and ground his molars, unable to conceal his irritation at Wilde's summary dismissal. "At first glance I thought the same. But take another look at the faeries, Oscar. A much closer look."

The author of Sherlock Holmes handed back the photograph and this time and, in an appropriately Holmesian gesture, drew a large magnifying glass from his bag and handed it to Wilde by its scrolled silver stem. "In particular, study the faerie figure that appears to be perched in the flower."

The corners of the Irishman's mouth drooped in a doubting frown, but he did as he was bade, and directed his attention to the sylph-like creature that appeared to have alighted upon the stalk of a petunia, tromboning the large lens back and forth until the image snapped into sharp focus. This time, Wilde gave a little gasp and threw a wide-eyed glance at his friend. "It appears to be transparent. See-through. The leaves of the flower are plainly visible through the faerie's body!"

"Precisely!" Conan Doyle said, his voice bursting with enthusiasm. The fairy figures are semi-transparent, and yet nothing else in the frame is. I have carefully scrutinised every inch of the photograph: the base of the oak tree, the young girl, the teddy bear and the dolls, the picnic hamper—everything is solid *except* for the faerie figures. Through my connections with the Society for Psychical Research, I have examined many so-called 'spirit' photographs that purport to have captured the image of a ghost or spectre on film. Most of these prove to be fakes: trick photographs produced by what is called a "double exposure." For example, a photograph is taken of a female medium sitting in a chair against a black or dark background. A second exposure is then made of a puff of white smoke or a figure dressed in a bed sheet, using the dark, unexposed area of the same negative. When a print is made, the two exposures appear to have been made contemporaneously. Ergo, the ghostly apparition seems to float above the head of the medium."

Wilde shook his head in bafflement. "So you contend that these faeries could not be the result of your so-called, double-exposure?"

"Not as far as my knowledge of photography extends. The faeries are not set against a dark background. Which means that the figures were indeed transparent, or an even more intriguing explanation . . . they were moving. In the photograph, they appear to be dancing. In other words—"

"They were animate creatures?"

"But there is even more compelling evidence contained in the letter that accompanied the photograph. Listen to this." And with that, Conan Doyle unfolded the letter and began to read the tiny, but graceful handwriting:

Dear Doctor Doyle,

I am writing to you as my last resort. I am the mother of two young girls, Wilhelmina (age 12) and Philomena, (age 8). My husband is the Reverend Aloysius Shepherd. When we moved into the rectory two years ago the girls would come in from the garden telling fanciful tales of playing with faeries. Both girls are bright children with active imaginations and such fanciful notions are not unusual in the young. However, the stories persisted beyond the usual period such a mania possesses an immature mind. In an attempt to curtail the fanciful stories, my reverend husband leant the girls his camera and challenged them to produce proof of their faerie visitors. You can imagine our surprise when my husband developed the plates and discovered a number of startling images we are at a loss to explain. Aloysius was convinced of the girl's trickery but I have full reason to believe that our household has come under some kind of supernatural influence. My husband went missing a year ago under strange circumstances. Then, two weeks ago, the girls went out to play in the garden and vanished. The Darvington Police have made a thorough search of the entire village, but to no avail, and yet my girls remain missing. I understand you have children of your own, so you can understand the depth of my heartbreak. I find myself utterly bereft and sob myself to sleep every night. And so, Doctor Doyle, I turn to you as my last resort. From what I read in the London newspapers, you seem to be a kind man with a mind that can both ravel and unravel mysteries. Also, I have read of your courageous acts in helping other people in dire circumstances. I only pray you will agree to help me in mine."

A hitch came into Conan Doyle's voice as he read the last line and his eyes were gleaming when he looked up at his friend. "The letter is signed Mrs. Delphinia Shepherd, of *The Old Rectory*, Darvington."

Wilde said nothing for a moment, tapping his steepled fingers against his generous lips before noting, "Poor lady. Although I must say, losing one family member is a calamity. Losing three family members strikes me as the height of carelessness. Were I a neighbour I should not lend the lady so much as a tea infuser."

Conan Doyle made a pained face at the remark. "That sounds like a witticism from one of your plays."

"Not yet, but it soon will be," Wilde answered, taking a small, leather-bound notebook from his breast pocket and beginning to scribble in it, "It is so difficult not to quote oneself. After all, I am quite the wittiest fellow I know."

"Don't you see the importance of this, Oscar?" Conan Doyle interrupted Wilde's fevered jotting by waving the photograph under his companion's nose. "I hold in my hand physical proof of the existence of supernatural beings . . . faeries . . . call them what you will." He settled back on the cushion, bursting with restless enthusiasm. "I believe that we are on the brink, Oscar. The brink of a new epoch when the great mysteries of life will be revealed: the afterlife, the existence of the soul, the nether realms of the faerie . . . all will become known."

In response, the Irish wit raised a sceptical eyebrow. "You certainly seem to be on the brink, Arthur."

Conan Doyle huffed in exasperation and muttered, "Yes, very droll, Oscar.

But Wilde went further. "My mama, Lady Wilde, is an avid collector of faerie lore and regaled me with tales of the Fey since I was in short britches. Even as a child it struck me that, for all their magic and insight into the future, the Fey invariably make terrible choices when it came to property. It seems their kingdoms invariably sink beneath the waves—Lyonnesse off Cornwall, Cantre'r Gwaelod in southern Wales, and Tyno Helig off Conwy, to name a few. There are times when I complain that my home in Chelsea is rather damp. I cannot image what it must be like living at the bottom of the sea. Although every story ends with the tolling of church bells coming from beneath the waves."

Wilde's flippant skepticism always riled Conan Doyle, who was about to respond when the carriage door flung open and a figure barged in calling out brusquely: "Tickets! Tickets, please."

Both men reflexively looked to themselves: patting their pockets, rummaging their bags, searching for their first-class tickets.

Wilde drew his ticket from the breast pocket of his blazer and absently held it out to the conductor. "Well, Arthur, I'm afraid it will take more than one photograph to convince me—and the world in general."

The conductor took his ticket, punched it and handed it back.

Conan Doyle continued to search but was having difficulty locating his ticket. He set the faerie photograph down on the cushion beside him and rummaged his pockets. Eventually, he decided that the ticket must be in his coat pocket. He stood up and turned around to start searching in his overnight bag sitting on the overhead luggage rack when he remembered securing the ticket in his inside breast pocket. He fished it out and dropped back into his seat, holding it aloft for the conductor who snatched it from him and punched it.

"The letter mentioned that the girls had gone missing . . ." Conan Doyle continued, ". . . abducted by faeries . . . thank you," he said as the conductor handed the ticket back. As he glanced up to receive his the ticket, Conan Doyle noticed the conductor's hands. The man had the most extraordinarily long fingers, almost as if they possessed a third knuckle joint. But then the conductor muttered a "good day," and whisked out of the carriage.

"If these girls have disappeared," Conan Doyle continued, "then it marks something terrible and mysterious."

Wilde released a mocking breath. "I know young children. From time to time, they are wont to run away from home. The tragedy is that a disappointing number of them return. And usually by the time supper is served. As a young and rather sensitive child, I often threatened my parents that I would run away from home. I stopped threatening when my father, Dr Wilde, graciously offered me the use of the pony and trap and promised to drop me anywhere in Ireland I desired."

The carriage door banged open a second time and a figure stepped inside.

"Tickets please."

Both men looked up in surprise.

"But you just punched our tickets!" Conan Doyle protested.

The conductor, a rather worn-looking man in a worn railroad uniform, eyed both friends sceptically. "Wot you on about? I just started me rounds. I ain't been in 'ere before."

"Nonsense!" Wilde said, "Not a moment ago you popped in here and asked for our tickets. Here is my punched ticket as proof." He rummaged in the pocket he had secreted his ticket in, and, to his shock and surprise, pulled out a large green leaf. "What the devil!" he uttered.

Conan Doyle plumbed his pocket and produced a similar leaf. "What the deuce?" Both men looked at one another in disbelief. Conan Doyle was baffled. "Did you see the first conductor? Is this the same chap?"

Wilde shook his head. "I cannot say. I barely glanced at the fellow."

The conductor's eyes narrowed suspiciously. "Oh, I get the picture. Trying to scrape by without buying a ticket, eh?"

Conan Doyle jumped to his feet. "Now see here, my man. We have been taken advantage of by some kind of trickster!"

The conductor nodded his head in an *I've-heard-this-story-a hundred-times-before* fashion.

"The rascal must be on the train somewhere," Conan Doyle added. "He was dressed—" He shot a desperate look at Wilde. "Did you see how he was dressed, Oscar?"

Wilde shook his head. "If I did it never registered." He turned to the conductor and complained, "My good man, do you know whom you are addressing? We are not a pair of scallywags. I am Oscar Wilde, world-famous wit, rake and raconteur. And my friend here is Arthur Conan Doyle, author of the Sherlock Holmes mysteries."

The conductor's moustache was not dense enough to conceal his wet-lipped scowl. "Izzat right? Then maybe your friend can use his detective skills to fathom out where his bloomin' ticket went!"

Wilde screwed up his face in umbrage, "Now see here, my man! Your response bears all the hallmarks of sarcasm."

The conductor was running short of patience. "Listen, I don't give a baboon's bright blue arse who either of you two gents is. You could be the Duke and Duchess of Kent for all I care. No one rides without a ticket. There's a ten-pound fine."

The argument continued for another five minutes and grew ever more contentious, but in the end, and to their intense chagrin and annoyance, the two friends were left with the option of being issued a fine and ordered off the train at the next stop, or paying again for two first-class tickets. But the conductor had no sooner collected their money, issued them with new tickets and slammed out of the first class compartment when Conan Doyle made another, even more galling discovery.

"It's gone!" he uttered in shocked tones.

Wilde paused in lighting one of his Turkish cigarettes and cocked an eyebrow. "What's gone? Our self-respect, or the last shreds of our dignity?"

"The photograph!" Conan Doyle said as he jumped up from his seat and began agitatedly pawing at the seat cushions, riffling through the pages of the open Casebook and his leather satchel. But to no avail. The photograph had vanished. "He must have taken it!" Conan Doyle exasperatedly breathed. "The cheeky blighter who took our train tickets. I set the photograph on the seat beside me. Did you see him take it?"

Wilde released a mouthful of smoke and shrugged his shoulders helplessly.

Conan Doyle jumped up and began to ransack his satchel, but at that very moment, the train lurched violently, throwing him back in his seat. The train's brakes squealed on, and the carriage resonated as the steamer began its rumbling deceleration. A moment later the *Darvington* station sign slid past the windows and the train shuddered to a halt at platform 2.

A LESS-THAN-HEROIC ARRIVAL

Conan Doyle was still banging on about the missing photograph as they stepped down from the train onto the platform.

"I am ashamed to say," he admitted, "that I do not possess my consulting detective's powers of observation. I never so much as glanced the fellow's way. I remember having a vague impression of someone wearing a railroad uniform, but I could not swear to it in a court of law."

"Me neither," Wilde agreed.

Conan Doyle shook with irritation, unable to drop the subject. "I never saw his face, but if I ever run into the blighter again, I'll recognise him by those fingers. They were of the most extraordinary length."

"Perhaps he is part of a lost tribe of pianists," Wilde suggested. "You could single him out by shaking the hand of every man in Darvington—a simple process of elimination."

Conan Doyle grunted bad-temperedly at Wilde's jest and took notice of his surrounds for the first time. The Darvington station was tiny, with only a single, double-sided platform and a ticketing booth the size of a large wardrobe. But on the far side of the platform, the trees had been cut back and the ground levelled as a small army of navvies swarmed about, swinging pickaxes, shovelling gravel, laying shiny new rails while in the distance another work crew armed with saws and axes were busy hacking a path for a new railroad line through the woods beyond the end of the platform.

Wilde removed his boater and fanned his face with it. The day was warm and sunny. The air carried a tang of salt water and the blue skies above were flecked with the white confetti of keening seagulls circling in thermals. At Wilde's insistence, Conan Doyle had surrendered his smothering tweeds, and both men were dressed in linen trousers, light summer blazers (Wilde's had green stripes, Conan Doyle's had red stripes) with straw boaters and canes. As always, Conan Doyle carried a battered leather satchel (containing a brand new Casebook) slung over one shoulder while his free hand gripped a small wicker suitcase.

"But where is your baggage, Oscar?"

"Still in the baggage car, I expect."

"I expressly advised you: just the one bag on this trip. You promised, remember? One bag. We are only staying overnight. At the most, two nights."

At that moment, the train they had just stepped down from blasted its whistle and jetted plumes of steam from its side. When the swirling white clouds had dissipated, they noticed a large leather suitcase waiting on the platform.

"Ah, I believe that is my baggage now," Wilde said.

Conan Doyle looked, and his face broke out in a smile. A single leather case stood waiting to be claimed. "Oh, well done, Oscar!" He shifted his small wicker case from one hand to the other to pat his friend on the shoulder. "It is perhaps the largest piece of hand luggage I have ever seen, but you were true to your word." He set off walking briskly to retrieve Wilde's baggage. "Come, Oscar, let's collect your bag and then see if we can hail a cab."

But Wilde tugged at his friend's arm, trying to hold him back. "No, no, Arthur. Let's hail a porter."

Conan Doyle frowned at his friend. "Don't be ridiculous. It's only thirty feet to the end of the platform. We can carry your bag that far. Let's not waste time."

"Really, Arthur, I think it best if—"

"Nonsense!"

Conan Doyle snatched up the handle of Wilde's suitcase and tugged with all his might, only to let out an agonised howl as a lightning bolt of pain shot from his neck and shoulder, radiating all the way down the sciatic nerve of his left leg and into his foot. His hand reflexively unclenched the suitcase handle, and he took two staggering steps, grasping at his arm, which tingled with pins and needles.

"By all the gods!"

"I did try to stop you, Arthur."

"What on earth do you have in that bag? Surely a dead jockey still sitting astride his horse!"

Wilde shook his head innocently. "Ju-just the essentials," he stammered.

Disbelieving what he had just experienced, Conan Doyle once again grasped the bag by its handle with both hands and heaved. The leather of the case stretched, but Conan Doyle was unable to lift it free of the ground. He let go with an explosive wheeze of breath and stumbled away, once again rubbing at his throbbing arm. "Is this some kind of prank? It feels as though it's been nailed to the platform!"

In the end, it took a porter, straining alongside Wilde and Conan Doyle, to heave the bag's crushing weight onto a luggage trolley so it could be wheeled down the platform to the road. Wilde tipped the porter generously, but the man could be heard to mutter the word "rupture" as he wheeled his trolley away, limping slightly.

The two authors looked about themselves as they stood on the High Street. Like many seaside towns, Darvington had been built on a hill overlooking a small bay below. The cobbled road descended in a steep curve so that the bottom of High Street vanished from sight, masked by shop fronts.

"So this is Darvington," Conan Doyle said, eyeing the rather paucy line of businesses. "It's not exactly Paris, is it?"

"Nor London," Wilde replied sourly. "I am already nostalgic for our capitol: the smoke, the filth, the stench; a beggar on every street corner, a dead climbing boy in every chimney."

"I must say," Conan Doyle added. "The town does look rather down in the mouth."

Wilde sniffed at the remark. "When I visited the American West, I passed through ghost towns more vibrant."

It was an accurate observation as many of the shops were boarded up, or the windows had been plastered with newspaper to show they were out of business. The black paint of the iron gas lamps lining the street was scabrous with rust. The few businesses still open boasted paint-peeling facades and faded shop signs squealing to and fro on rusty iron brackets. Darvington's main thoroughfare had the disheveled air of a grand dame who, once beautiful, had aged badly and fallen upon hard times so that she had been forced to flog off the family heirlooms, and whose once fine gowns had grown tattered and embarrassingly out of fashion.

Conan Doyle gazed up and down a high street largely uncluttered by shoppers or strolling holidaymakers. Although it was nearly midday, the only sign of life was an unenthusiastic street sweeper sulkily stirring the dust with his broom. After several minutes, the Scotsman stroked his moustache and conceded, "I'm afraid our chances of hailing a cab seem rather slim."

But just then a pony and cart appeared at the bottom of the High Street, slowly climbing the curving rise of the road toward them.

"Ah, look," said Wilde, pointing with his cane. "There's a cab or carriage of some fashion approaching. Let's flag them down." He snatched a handkerchief from his breast pocket and began to wave it, but then Conan Doyle grabbed his sleeve and dragged his arm down.

"Not so fast, Oscar. I am certain that is no cab as you shall soon see."

When the cart grew closer, Wilde saw that a tall man on foot preceded it. He was dressed in the rough clothes of a navvy and walked waving a red flag on a short stick. The cart driver hunched over the reigns was similarly roughly dressed, with a face barely visible behind an enormous moustache, a cloth cap pulled down low over his eyes. Lashed to the cart behind the driver were a great many wooden crates. Riding atop the stack of crates was a young man barely in his teens. From the way he was gripping the ropes securing the crates, it was apparent that the young man's job was to see to it that none of the crates shifted, or came loose and tumbled from the cart.

At sight of the cart, the few pedestrians perambulating the streets hastily dodged into shop doorways or plastered themselves against the brickwork, while home dwellers in the act of stepping out their front doors, took one glimpse and hurriedly retreated back indoors, slamming the door fast shut.

"What on earth?" Wilde remarked.

As the cart reached them and swung into the station, a navvy foreman drew out a whistle on a chain and gave a long, loud blast upon it. The navvies laying the new rails dropped their picks and shovels and hurriedly backed away from the tracks, retreating as far as the bordering trees would allow.

As the cart passed by, the two friends noticed for the first time the black lettering stencilled on the sides of the crates that read "DYNAMITE."

"Now do you see why I did not think you would care much for a ride on that cart?" Conan Doyle asked.

"My heavens!" Wilde exclaimed. "Dynamite? Most of my entrances involve fireworks of a kind, but that is a little too incendiary, even for me."

As the wagon passed by, the young man riding the crates tipped his flat cap to the two friends, flashing a toothy smile and a jaunty wink.

Conan Doyle chuckled. "What a cheek. No doubt the young scamp earns an extra shilling for danger money and is proud of his temerity."

Wilde released a pent-up breath as the cart safely passed by. "Typical of youth—convinced of its own immortality."

The wagon rumbled the length of the platform and disappeared from view into the slot in the forest that had been cleared to make way for new railroad lines to be laid. The navvies who had drawn away for safety now sauntered back to the rails, snatched up their abandoned tools, spat on their palms, and the air soon rang with the driving of spikes and swinging of picks.

"So what do we do now?" Wilde asked. "Walking is so deleterious to the constitution."

At that moment a rag-bone cart rounded a corner and the broken-backed nag pulling it clop-clopped toward them. The bundle of rags hunched over the reigns had a Methusulan beard that would have put an Old Testament prophet to shame. The unidentifiably rumpled hat jammed upon his head was pulled down low over his eyes, the peak held up by a bulbous nose strawberried with gin blossoms.

"Rag-booone . . . rag-booooooone . . ." he called out at intervals, apparently for his own amusement, or the benefit of the few ragged-winged seagulls scavenging the gutters as sight of the dynamite cart had swept the streets clear of its few shoppers, and the citizens of Darvington were still cringing inside their domiciles.

As the rag-and-bone cart approached, Conan Doyle stepped into the road, raised his boater, and waved down the driver.

" Oh no!" Wilde complained. "Now that's going too far, Arthur."

As the cart pulled up, he eyed it petulantly. "Moi? Ride on a dust-cart? Surely you jest. I'd rather ride on the dynamite cart—at least it has the cachet of danger. Did Alexander enter the cities he conquered riding upon a dustcart? I think not. Likewise, would Oscar Wilde make an entrance perched upon the seat of rag-and-bone cart?" He visibly shuddered. "Unthinkable."

"Not as comfortable as a hansom," Conan Doyle admitted, "but it's preferable to walking . . . or would you rather carry your own bag?"

Wilde's long face drooped comically, and he responded with a huff of mortification.

Moments later Conan Doyle's small suitcase and Wilde's crushingly heavy juggernaut had been heaved onto the back of the cart, and the friends found themselves sitting on the bum-polished seat next to the rag-and-bone man, who Conan Doyle promised a sixpence to convey them to the return address on the faerie letter.

As the horse and cart clop-clopped through the empty streets,

Conan Doyle turned to the aged driver and asked, "The streets of the town are nigh empty. Where is everyone?"

"Aarrrrr," the rag-and-bone man answered in a phlegm-gargly voice. "The old town, she be dying on her feet—ever since the new railroad link opened to Minehead and cut an hour off the trip from London. Nowadays, no poor bugger comes to Darvington no more."

"Ah yes," Wilde agreed. "When we alighted from the train we noticed the new line under construction. Evidently, an attempt to redress the balance?"

The rag-and-bone man made a liquid hawking sound and then turned his head and with a *phwutooo*, spat a quivering oyster at the road. "New railroad?" he chuckled. "That's a larf, that is. Third time they tried. Mark me, this time won't be no different. Just loik afore it'll end in blood and tears."

"*Third* time?" Conan Doyle repeated. "What happened the first—?"

His words were drowned out by a thunderous BOOOOOOOM! that struck like a punch to the solar plexus. Startled, the two friends looked back to see a thick black pall of smoke mushrooming into the sky above the chimney tops of the Darvington High Street.

"That's coming from the railroad station!" Conan Doyle said.

The rag-bone man chuckled softly. "Woods beyond the station, more like. They be blastin' through the rock, at's all. You'll hear a lot of that. But won't do 'em no good. There's a reason why no one's never built nothin' in the gorge."

"Why is that?" Conan Doyle asked.

The rag-and-bone man flashed a wicked grin and said, "Cause' the Fey folk don't like us bein' there."

At that piece of news, Conan Doyle and Wilde exchanged a look of consternation.

A LITTLE GIRLS' TEA PARTY WITH SHOTGUN

The cart followed the narrow winding road as it climbed a shallow gradient from the lower-lying High Street. The lanes hereabouts were deeply shaded by the sinewy boughs of mature trees stretching overhead. Here and there they passed by pretty stone cottages with thatched roofs arranged like freshly risen loafs set out upon a table to cool. Up ahead, glimpsed now and then through breaks in the trees, poked the squat stone spire of a small church. As the cart turned a bend in the road, Conan Doyle spotted something and pointed, saying, "That's the house we're looking for: *The Old Rectory*. Pull up, if you would, my good fellow."

The cart rattled to a standstill outside a charming red brick house, old but not quite as ancient or rustic as the farmer's cottages they had passed, and the two friends climbed down. Conan Doyle handed the driver the promised sixpence, and he accepted it with a gap-toothed grin and tugged the brim of his battered hat in thanks. Conan Doyle then paid him another sixpence to deliver their baggage to the Claremont Hotel, where they had booked rooms for the night. As the horse and cart clopped away, Wilde scanned the modest house.

"So this is *The Old Rectory*, eh, Arthur? Another of your Holmesian deductions, I take it? You noted the arched windows, evocative of the ecclesiastical, and the stained glass lantern above the front door?"

"Not exactly," Conan Doyle responded as he slung the strap of his leather satchel over one shoulder. "I noticed that small wooden sign next to the front gate." He pointed with his cane. "The one that reads: *The Old Rectory.*"

"Ah." Wilde replied in a deeply disappointed voice.

Conan Doyle could not hide a crafty smile as he lifted the iron latch and the gate squealed open to his push. The two friends followed a path of intricately laid bricks to the front door. Large, mature trees crowded about the house so that filtered sunshine dappled the paths with light and arboreal shadow. The trees harboured many birds, and the air was rapturous with bird song. The front garden was of the English Country variety and was ablaze with a riot of colourful wild-flowers. Large flower baskets also hung from the eves and were busied by droning bees. With the garden flowers and the rose bushes clambering the trelliswork surrounding the front door, the air was drunk with perfume.

The front door echoed the windows with its Norman arch shape and was a spectacular piece of woodwork. Conan Doyle seized the ring that swung in the mouth of the lion's head doorknocker and clapped it down sharply upon the striker three times.

"What an idyllic spot," Wilde mused as they awaited an answer. "A home in the English countryside. While I am very much a city mouse, I do see the attraction of living the bucolic life in such a peaceful and tranquil—"

He was interrupted by a shrill scream that shattered the peace and flushed the birds from the trees. The two friends shared a look of alarm.

"That sounds like a young girl!" Conan Doyle said.

"Yes," Wilde agreed. "It seemed to be coming from the back garden."

Just then the first screaming voice was joined by another girlish shriek, even louder.

"*Two* young girls!" Conan Doyle said. "And it sounds as if they are being murdered!"

Without another word, the friends abandoned their vigil at the front door. Flinging aside a willow gate, they dashed into the side garden.

"Quickly, Oscar!" Conan Doyle urged as they trampled through flowerbeds overflowing with nasturtiums, crashed through an apple tree's clattering tangle of low-hanging limbs, knocking loose fruit, and leapt over a green push mower abandoned in the overgrown lawn. They raced around to the back of the rectory, where the property opened out onto a large and attractively landscaped garden. Long, screening hedgerows and topiared bushes in various shapes sprouted in profusion. A wrought iron park bench had been positioned at a strategic location for viewers to idle upon while enjoying the view of the gardens, which sloped down to a stand of oak trees of great age and height. Beyond the oaks, the flash and sparkle of moving water marked the furthest limits of the garden. *A river*, Conan Doyle thought.

Both men stumbled to a halt. Panting. Looking. Listening.

But the screaming had ceased.

"There!" Wilde said, pointing at a flicker of motion. Conan Doyle followed his point to see a young girl running pell-mell through the trees. She erupted into shrieks as another girlish form flitted from the topiared bushes. Both were screeching as if being pursued by all the demons of hell. The lead girl, the smaller and younger of the two, suddenly weaved around a topiary swan and nearly bowled into the two friends.

The girl, who looked to be all of eight years old, stopped short, mouth agape, breathing hard. She looked up at the two friends, cheeks flushed pink, her intense blue eyes wide with surprise.

"Don't be afraid, little girl—" Conan Doyle started to say when the girl interrupted him: "I know who you are," she said breathlessly.

"You do?" Conan Doyle replied, momentarily taken aback.

"Yes, of course, silly," the little girl said in a breathless lisp (she was missing her two front teeth). "You're the wizards who've come to release the dragon from his cave."

The two authors shared a patronly smile, their alarm of a moment ago subsiding. It seemed that the girls were merely playing a game and were not in imminent danger of being murdered.

"And what adventure are you playing, little miss?" Wilde asked. "A game that involves dragons and wizards?"

The little girl pouted vexedly and spoke with the patronising tone used by children when correcting adults, "It's not a game. We are being chased by elves. They are very naughty elves and keep tying knots in my hair. See." And as proof, the little girl lifted one of her long blonde braids, which was, indeed gnarled and knotted.

A moment later and they heard the pounding footfalls of running feet. Then a second girl, a brunette both older and taller, burst from behind the hedgerows and stumbled to a halt when she saw the two men with her sister.

"Philomena," the older girl scolded. "Come away, this instant. You know Mama does not encourage talking to strangers."

"They're not strangers, you ninny," the young girl said, wiping her runny nose on the sleeve of her pink dress. "They're the wizards we've been waiting for."

"Yes, quite correct," Wilde put in. He had composed many fairy tales for his boys, Vyvyan and Cyril, and was anxious to join in the girls' fun. "We are the wizards who've come to slay the dragon."

"No, no! You must not *slay* the dragon," the young blonde corrected in a cross voice. "The giant Wyrme is imprisoned beneath the ground. You must free him to save the village."

"Oh, I am sorry," Wilde apologised, raising his boater and bowing slightly. "It appears I have the wrong end of the stick. Perhaps you can tell us how the story should go?"

Both friends had instantly recognised the older sister as the girl in the faerie photograph: she had a wildly extravagant mane of brunette ringlets piled upon her head and tumbling down about her shoulders. The hair had been fastidiously fixed in place with a number of jewelled combs, but after her frenzied dashing about she had shaken several strands free, and her cheeks were red and flushed. The girl showed not the slightest sign of self-conscious reticence in the presence of two strange men, and fixed her attention upon Conan Doyle. "Well then," the brunette said with remarkable composure for one so young coming upon two strange men in her garden. "You gentlemen must be guests at our tea party, and we shall tell you all." She boldly stepped forward and slipped her small hand inside Conan Doyle's.

The younger sister took Wilde by the hand and the two men allowed themselves to be led down the sloping garden toward the immense oaks.

As they walked, Conan Doyle muttered to Wilde, "So it seems the Shepherd girls have not been abducted, after all."

"No," Wilde agreed, "Either that, or they managed to escape their faerie captors."

The girls led them to the same oak that had appeared in the recently purloined photograph. Just as in the photograph, a large blanket was spread in its shade and a doll's tea party laid out. Beyond the oaks' writhing splay of muscular roots, the garden terminated in a stone bank bounding the narrow and fast-running river.

As Conan Doyle and Wilde settled themselves on the blanket, the brunette girl said, "Shall I be mother?" and filled tiny china cups with lemonade poured from a tiny teapot. My name is Wilhelmina," the brunette girl said, handing Conan Doyle a cup. She poured a cup for Wilde and added, "My sister's name is Philomena. She is rather foolish, but it is a fault of her age, so you mustn't take mind of all the nonsense she talks." Wilhelmina opened the picnic basket and lifted out a large round plate covered with a white dishcloth. She whisked away the cloth to reveal a heaped mound of cucumber sandwiches, the crusts of which had been neatly cut off. Conan Doyle's stomach clenched at the sight. The London train had lacked a dining car and the only thing he had eaten that day was a soft-boiled egg for breakfast. Playing the perfect host, Wilhelmina passed around small plates, and then the two authors fell upon the pile of sandwiches and began to devour them voraciously.

"Mmmn," Wilde drawled around the sandwich he was chewing. "Cucumber sandwiches. Quite my favourite."

"Yes, we know," piped up Philomena, who was rocking the Pagliacci clown in his miniature rocking chair. "That's why we had Aggy make them."

"Aggy is our housekeeper," Wilhelmina explained.

"She is an elf," the blonde girl blurted.

The brunette wrinkled her nose at her sister's interruption. "She is not an elf, Philomena. Do not talk such nonsense. She is a dwarf."

"Same thing," her sister insisted.

"It is not!" Wilhelmina snapped and looked at the two men for support. "As I said, she is young and very foolish."

Wilde shot Conan Doyle a puzzled grin, but he merely shrugged as if to say; *the imagination of the young* and when he had finished chewing his mouthful, asked, "And what is the name of your teddy bear?"

"Conan," Wilhelmina said in a matter-of-fact voice which made Conan Doyle splutter and spit crumbs.

"Conan?" Wilde chortled. "Did you hear that Arthur? The bear is named Conan, how apropos."

And what is the name of your sad clown?" Conan Doyle asked.

Philomena was shyly nibbling the edges of her sandwich, but she stopped and said, "His name is Oscar."

"The sandwich in Wilde's mouth turned to glue and he choked it down with difficulty, blinking away tears. He fixed his face in a look of bemused merriment and commented, "He looks a very glum clown. Why, might I ask . . . why is he crying?"

The little girl answered carelessly, "Because, one day, all his friends will forget him, and he will be very sad."

The avuncular smile on Wilde's face collapsed. His body visibly shuddered as if someone had stepped over his grave. He threw a look at his Scots friend to see that, he too, wore the same look of perplexity. Naming a teddy bear "Conan" might have been an amusing coincidence, but naming a sad clown doll "Oscar" seemed disturbingly portentous, as if, beneath the sisters' veneer of girlish innocence, something sinister lurked.

The spell was broken when Wilhelmina noticed that only crumbs remained on the sandwich plate and brightly announced, "We have cake!" She lifted out of the wicker hamper a clear glass dish burdened with slices of jam roly-poly. Fresh cream and strawberry jam oozed from the whorls and looked stickily delicious. A dusting of sugar crystals sparkled in the light. But Conan Doyle was more struck when he saw what the dish had been concealing. Within the hamper sat a squat black box: a camera! Conan Doyle (who was a photography enthusiast) even recognised the make and model: a Midg quarter plate.

"Now we must reveal to you girls that we know who both of you are," said Conan Doyle hoisting the tiny cup and saucer, which seemed Lilliputian in his large hands. He paused to take a sip and smack his lips. It was remarkably good lemonade, sweet and nicely tart. "Your mummy sent me a letter and a photograph of you taken with . . . faeries."

At the mention of the word, Wilhelmina's eyes grew guarded and she looked away rather guiltily. Conan Doyle and Wilde shared a crafty look and a grin. They had not anticipated being able to question the girls without their mother present.

"My friend Arthur and I should so like to meet the faeries," Wilde ventured. "I do hope they approve of wizards?"

"Silly," the younger sister said, in between bites of jam roly-poly, "The faeries will only come out for us. They don't like grown-ups."

Wilde looked hurt, and offered contritely, "Ah, I am sad to say that, even as a wizard, I can do nothing about my age."

The little girl took a huge bite of cake and a blob of strawberry jam dropped onto the front of her pink dress. She tried to wipe it away with a pudgy hand, but only succeeded in smearing it.

Her older sister gasped with dismay and cried, "Philomena!"

Conan Doyle was burning to find out more and used the interruption to his advantage. "Wilhelmina," he began in a warm voice, "Is that, by chance, your papa's camera?"

The brunette seemed to guess where the question was leading and replied guardedly, "Yes. Daddy let us borrow it."

"Of course he did," Conan Doyle replied, and then asked, as casually as he could, "Do you think you could take a photograph of the faeries for us?"

A frown pulled the corners of Wilhelmina's mouth down. "I don't think my mummy would like that."

"Oh, I'm quite sure your mummy would have no objections once we explain to her."

The little girl suddenly pointed a finger at something over Conan Doyle's shoulder, saying, "No. I am sure mummy is rather upset."

Before either man had chance to so much as turn their heads to look, there was a loud metallic clunk and both men tensed at the unmistakable sound of a shotgun being snapped shut. And then a women's stern voice addressed them from behind. "Both of you . . . stand up and step away from the girls."

Both men sprang to their feet. Facing them was an attractive, if rather zoftig, woman of perhaps thirty years. From the glorious celebration of brunette curls piled atop her head and by her comely looks, no doubt the mother of the two angelic girls. The woman was striking, but what was what even more striking at that moment was the double-barrelled shotgun she had trained on them.

"Arthur," Wilde muttered sotto voce, "why is it when I accompany you I invariably find myself being chased by gangs of brutes or staring into the maw of a shotgun? This never happens with my other acquaintances."

"Who are you?" The woman demanded. "Why are you in my garden, molesting my girls?"

"Wu-we heard screams coming from the back garden," Conan Doyle stammered to explain. "We ran around the side of the house fearing someone was in distress."

"We did knock on the front door," Wilde added, "Rather loudly."

The woman's eyes lowered slightly at that. "I was sleeping," she conceded, but then raised the muzzle of the shotgun, pointing it straight at Wilde's face and demanded. "Who are you? Tell me your names."

Wilde removed his straw boater and threw the lady a courtier's bow. "I am Oscar Wilde, playwright, wit, and raconteur."

Wilde's announcement stunned the woman's eyes wide, and her startled gaze turned to Conan Doyle.

"And I am Doctor Arthur Conan Doyle, novelist. You might have heard of Sherlock Holmes. He is my invention."

The woman's mouth worked soundlessly at forming words, but then her eyes fluttered and closed, the shotgun drooped in her slackening grip and her knees buckled as she fell into an apparent swoon.

"Oscar!" Conan Doyle shouted in warning. Lunging forward, he was just in time to catch the woman with an arm about her waist before she fell, while Wilde grabbed the shotgun and snatched it away.

AN ATTACK OF THE VAPOURS

"Where shall we put her down? The settee?"

"The settee? Are you mad?"

"Why ever not?"

"The lady is wearing a purple dress and the settee has a green and yellow floral pattern. It will clash horribly."

The two men had asked the girls to wait in the garden as they carried the unconscious mother between them, Conan Doyle with a grip beneath her armpits, Wilde by her legs, one thigh splayed on either side of each hip, an unseemly way to carry a lady, but necessary under the conditions.

"Come, Oscar. Decide. We must put her down somewhere."

"You should complain! The lady has an hourglass figure and most of the sand has settled in the end I'm carrying."

Wilde looked about the room with clear distaste, dithering. "Ugh, chintz cushions with waffle pattern china. Doilies and bric-a-brac and Hummel figures and candy dishes. It's all too, too much. This isn't so much a décor as an attack of the vapours. Just the thought of such a violent clash will have *me* falling into a swoon."

"What about the leather Chesterfield?"

"Ah yes, a somewhat oversized piece given that the rest of the furniture appears to have been purloined from a rather low-rent doll-house, but needs must suffice."

At that precise moment, the parlour door opened and a diminutive woman in a white pinafore bustled in: no doubt Aggie, the dwarf maidservant the girls had mentioned. When Aggie saw two strange men holding the sagging and unconscious form of her mistress, she froze on the spot, mouth open, eyes wide and then fled from the room, banging the door behind her.

"Oh, dear," Conan Doyle remarked, "I cannot imagine what that must have looked like."

"Perhaps she has gone to fetch smelling salts," Wilde offered hopefully.

"More likely to fetch the local constabulary."

Conan Doyle's arms were beginning to ache. He eyed the oxblood leather Chesterfield in the corner. "There?" he suggested.

"As the only masculine object in the room, not an ideal choice, but as this warrants an emergency good taste will have to take second place to good sense."

They carefully laid the woman down on the Chesterfield, and Conan Doyle took the time to tug down the hem of her dress and arrange her knees together for the sake of propriety. Both men now stood over her, studying her face, relaxed and unconscious. Mrs Shepherd was a pretty woman with a fine, upturned nose. Conan Doyle could tell that, in her salad days, she had likely been the town beauty. But with the years her chin had doubled, and her features had softened and were turning to plump. Not surprising given the large number of cake stands and candy dishes festooning every horizontal surface so that the parlour smelled of icing sugar and cream.

"Shall we try to awaken her?" Conan Doyle asked.

Wilde frowned. "Perhaps we should first search the house for more firearms and hide them."

"The shotgun wasn't loaded, Oscar. I checked. No harm would have come to us."

"You fail to consider, Arthur, the ten years the incident has subtracted from my lifespan. I call that harm. And the fact that I very nearly ruined a brand new pair of trousers."

Conan Doyle lifted the woman's limp arm and began to chafe her wrist in an attempt to revive her.

Wilde asked, "Do you have a hip flask on you, Arthur—mine's empty?"

Conan Doyle shook his head. "She's unconscious, Oscar. I rather think smelling salts are called for."

"I was asking for myself," Wilde replied. "After the drama with the shotgun, I, too, am in need of a restorative."

Just then the woman's eyes flickered open and she looked up at them from a mind still swathed in dreams. "The woman lurched up in the chair and glared at them. "Who are you? What were you doing to me?"

"You swooned, Madam," Conan Doyle hurriedly explained. "We carried you inside and set you upon the chair."

A waist-long long strand of hair had come loose, and now it draped across the woman's face. She paused to tuck it back into place before saying. "I . . . I did not swoon, sir. I, I have an ailment. Strong emotion causes me to fall asleep. Often without warning."

Conan Doyle shot a sideways look at his friend and whispered sotto voce, "Narcolepsy?"

"I am Delphinia Shepherd," the woman said, "My husband is the Reverend Shepherd. She sat up shakily, and spent a few moments rearranging her hair, straightening her dress, and composing herself.

"But where are my manners?" she said. Once satisfied with her attire, Mrs Shepherd reached for a small china bell sitting on the side table, picked it up and tinkled it. "We shall have tea, and then you must explain why I am entertaining two famous London gentlemen."

The parlour door opened into the room, and Aggie entered, nervously wiping her hands upon her starched white pinafore. "Yes ma'am?"

"A pot of tea for our guests, Aggie, if you please."

The tiny woman curtsied and scurried off on her errand.

"A loud shriek, followed by girlish laughter came from outside, and

Conan Doyle's eyes were drawn to the window overlooking the garden. He was in time to see the older girl run past, followed a moment later by her younger sister, who was chasing her with something. It looked like a garden gnome, but they flashed past so quickly he could not accurately discern what.

A few minutes later, they were all sipping tea from china tea cups so garishly feminine and almost as tiny as the girls' tea party china that Conan Doyle's large fingers would not fit through the handle, and he had to grip the handle gingerly for fear it would snap off.

"That's better," said the woman, having had a long, reviving sip of tea. She turned her china blue eyes to the two large men who were jammed hip-to-hip upon a tiny loveseat extravagant with doilies, fringed arm towels and other fripperies. "As I said, my name is Delphinia Shepherd. Now you gentlemen must tell me what has caused two august literary figures to descend upon my little household."

"Why, the letter you sent me," Conan Doyle explained.

The rector's wife frowned at his words. "Letter?"

"At her obvious puzzlement, Conan Doyle began to sweat inside his blazer. Perhaps this had all been a hoax. A prank. "Yu-yes, the one about your daughters and their encounter with the faeries. You included a most intriguing photograph." He started to rummage in his pockets for it but then remembered he no longer had the photograph. Instead, he drew out the letter from his jacket pocket and handed it across to her, and then awkwardly folded his large hands in his lap.

Wilde and Conan Doyle sat silently watching the woman read the letter, her eyes following the lines of writing, her expression betraying a visibly rising unease.

"Wickedness," she burst out finally and threw the letter to the floor. "Pure wickedness!"

Wilde leaned close to his friend's ear and whispered. "Is she describing you, me, or the contents of the missive?"

She watched as Conan Doyle bent to collect the letter, a strange expression on her face.

"But I don't understand, Mrs Shepherd. The letter mentions the extraordinary photographs your daughters have taken and claims they were abducted by faeries."

"No!" the woman snapped, "that is the one part of the letter that rings true, both my daughters have been abducted."

Wilde laughed, thinking that she was making a joke. "But we have just met your two beautiful girls in the garden."

At the Irish wit's words, Mrs Shepherd leaned forward, her demeanour hardening so that her eyes burned lambent, and the teacup in her hand chinked loudly against its saucer as she hissed, "The two creatures in the garden are not *my* girls."

The friends sat silent for a moment, utterly flummoxed. "I don't understand," Conan Doyle put in. "You mean they are your husband's children through a previous marriage? Or are they adopted—"

"No. I mean they are not children of this earth, Doctor Doyle. They are changelings!"

There was another long silence, interrupted only by another girlish whoop and burst of giggling from the garden. The girls were evidently back at their chase game.

"Changelings?" Conan Doyle repeated.

"A changeling," Wilde explained in his most didactic voice, "is a faerie child swapped at birth for a human child. The faeries steal human children and replace them with a faerie child, who then grows up. A sort of cuckoo in the nest." He leaned forward and addressed Mrs Shepherd in a conspiratorial voice. "My dear mama, Lady Wilde, is an avid collector of faerie tales and Irish folklore."

"But what on earth would make you believe such a thing?" Conan Doyle asked. "We have met your girls. They are sweet, innocent, young things—"

"Pah!" The woman snarled. She leaned back into the Chesterfield and her eyes narrowed as she muttered, "They know things. Things young girls should not know of. Things a married woman of my age would blush at."

"Politics?" Wilde fliply opined.

Conan Doyle shot his friend a censorious glare to let him know that now was not an appropriate time to display his wit and quickly put in, "I must assume you are speaking of—to be delicate—those things that transpire between a married man and his wife in the privacy of their bed-chamber."

"But how do you know?" Wilde put in.

The woman's pretty features hardened uglily. "I have overheard them. I happened to be passing the children's bedroom one night and listened to their conversation."

"You mean, you eavesdropped?" Wilde could not help but comment.

Delphinia Shepherd's steely gaze pinned the Irishman to his seat like a moth to a mounting board. "They are children, sir. Wilhelmina is twelve. Philomena is but eight years old, still a babe. And yet the things they spoke of." She released a gasp of umbrage. "The profanities they used."

Wilde leaned forward and smiled reassuringly. "But children are like sponges at such an age. Every day when my boys come home from school, there is always a newly acquired vice my wife wishes me to spank them for. Many weeks the rugs in our house receive fewer beatings."

Mrs Shepherd's voice grew yet harsher. "Mister Wilde, my girls are schooled by myself. At home. Precisely to avoid such . . . contamination." She gasped with remembered horror and put a hand to her bosom. "And the filthy talk? Such that sailors would blush at! They learned none of this under my roof, I can assure you. Plus there is also craftiness, insubordination, dishonesty . . ."

She shook with irritation. "I did not write that letter to you, Mister Doyle. Although it is in my handwriting, I am sure that Wilhelmina forged it. The girls are old beyond their years—in an unnatural way."

Conan Doyle digested that statement and then cautiously ventured, "I do not wish to be indelicate, Mrs Shepherd, but might I ask about your husband, the Reverend Shepherd? The letter mentioned that he disappeared under strange circumstances."

"Self-preservation," Conan Doyle heard Wilde whisper beneath his breath and jabbed an elbow to silence him.

The reverend's wife grew tearful; she turned and lavished her gaze upon a framed photograph standing on a nearby table. The photograph showed a man of seventy-or-eighty-plus years, with a huge vortex of grey beard and enormous winged eyebrows. The man wore a clerical collar and glared out at the camera with a stern, Old Testament look.

"Good lord," Wilde muttered sotto voce, "the reverend is a giant grey owl."

"I'm sorry, did you say something, Mister Wilde?" Mrs Shepherd inquired.

The Irishman made a show of massaging his temples. "Merely that I feel a headache coming on."

"Is it the closeness of the room?" she asked.

"No. I rather think it is the willow pattern china. I was never an enthusiast."

Conan Doyle repeated his question; "You were about to tell us about your husband's disappearance?"

The woman gulped down what she was about to say and swallowed with some difficulty. It took her several attempts before she finally prised the words loose from her throat. "Although my husband is a man of the cloth, he has a weakness for the drink. Many times a day he would go out into the garden to check on the girls or to develop his photographs—he has a shed in the garden that he turned into a darkroom. At first, I thought I could smell the photographic chemicals on his clothing. Only after some time, when his behaviour became quite erratic, did I realise that it was strong liquor I could smell."

"A most unexpected *development*," Wilde quipped.

At the awful pun, Conan Doyle threw a sour look at his companion and hurriedly put in, "Your husband, Mrs Shepherd, he was fond of the girls?"

A bittersweet smile creased her lips. "Oh, he doted on them. Long after I was asleep, he would steal from his bed to check on them. I pretended to be asleep, but I heard him."

Conan Doyle felt Wilde stiffen on the seat beside him. Both men knew exactly what the other was thinking—the Unthinkable.

"And when did your husband's, ahem, mania begin?"

"About a year ago. Last summer."

"When did the girls first begin to take the fairy photographs?"

"About a year . . . " she trailed off, her eyes widening at the realisation. "About the same time. It had never struck me before. But around the same time."

"And your husband never believed in the girls' story?" Wilde asked mildly, "About the faeries?"

"Oh no, he was very sceptical. He believed the girls were playing a trick. As a man of the cloth, he, of course, was opposed to the notion of faeries and other such wickedness. He honestly believed—"

"Wait! Shush!" Conan Doyle suddenly interrupted, raising a hand. He cocked his head to one side, listening intently.

"What is it, Arthur?" Wilde asked. "What do you hear?"

"Nothing."

"And we should be alarmed by that?"

"The girls have been making a constant racket since we arrived. As a father myself I know that when children fall silent they are invariably up to something." Conan Doyle tried to get up from the love seat but he was wedged in tight. "Oscar," he urged. "Up. Get up!"

It took two attempts, and when the two friends finally rocked to their feet, the tiny loveseat came up with them. They pried their backsides loose and hurried to the garden window, with Mrs Shepherd following close behind.

Conan Doyle snatched aside the lace curtains and peered out. "I don't see them!"

"Surely they're just playing somewhere," Wilde suggested. "Another game of hide and seek?"

Moments later the three of them spilled out of the house into the garden, the mother calling loudly for her girls: "Philomena. Wilhelmina. Girls, where are you?"

But after ten minutes of frantic searching and calling, there was still no sign of the sisters.

"I'm certain they're just hiding," Wilde said. "If we go back inside they'll become bored and pop out from their hiding—"

He was interrupted by Mrs Shepherd's shrill scream. Both men shared a look and then dashed off to find her standing in the shade of the picnic oak. The doll's tea party was still in place, but now the mother was leaning with one hand against the tree and staring fixedly at the glistening river.

"What is it?" Conan Doyle asked.

The mother said nothing. She covered her mouth with one hand and pointed at something with the other—something in the water. Conan Doyle narrowed his eyes against the glare of sunlight coruscating on the rippling waters. Eventually, he made out the shape of a small body half-submerged among the riverweed.

"Dear God, no!" Wilde cried.

Conan Doyle frantically searched the riverbank and found a large branch deposited by an earlier flood. He snatched it up and heaved its quivering, waterlogged weight into the air. Fishing with the improvised pole, he finally snagged the floating shape and lifted it dripping from the water.

The teddy bear named Conan. Waterlogged.

"It's just the stuffed bear!" Wilde gasped in relief.

"But how did it get into the water?" Conan Doyle asked aloud, depositing it on the grass beside the tea party picnic blanket. He shot an interrogative look at the vicar's wife, who stood on the bank, wringing her hands with trepidation. "The girls wouldn't go into the water. Would they?"

The vicar's wife's face twisted in a look of terror. "I have scolded the girls a thousand times not to play so close to the river!"

Conan Doyle tossed aside the branch and gripped the woman's hand. "We haven't a moment to waste. We need to make a thorough search."

"Oh, dear!" Mrs Shepherd exclaimed, pulling distractedly at her hair. "It's happening again." Her hands fidgeted with one another as her agitation increased. "It's happening again!" She stopped short, her head tremoring atop her neck as she fixed Conan Doyle with an almost demented look and hissed, "They've been taken."

"Taken where?" Wilde asked. "And by whom?"

"This time they've been murdered. Just like the rest!" She started to say more but her words dissolved into an unintelligible slur of consonants.

"Oscar!" Conan Doyle shouted to Wilde, who was the closest. "Grab her!

But it was too late, for at that moment, Delphinia Shepherd's eyes rolled up into the back of her head, her knees buckled, and she swooned to the ground.

THE SHEPHERD GIRLS VANISH!

After, once again, depositing the unconscious Delphinia Shepherd in her parlour, Conan Doyle and Wilde set out to search for the girls. The garden and grounds of *The Old Rectory* proved rambling and surprisingly expansive and the two friends spent the best part of an hour scouring them. At every turn they expected to hear a burst of held-in laughter, a girlish giggle, and see the sisters spring from their hiding places. But after searching a mazework of secret gardens, goldfish ponds, topiaried bushes, and tall hedgerows, they discovered only a bare vegetable plot and a mossy garden shed that contained the earthen smell of dirt and humus, and a clutter of empty-flowerpot-strewn benches swarmed by ghostly white spiders.

A short distance away stood another shed, this one painted black.

"A second gardening shed?" Wilde observed.

"I think this might be the darkroom the Reverend's wife spoke of. Notice the window is painted black from the inside."

"Should we not search it?" Wilde suggested hopefully, but then frowned when he noticed the bulky padlock swinging from a hasp. "Ah, but it appears to be securely locked."

Conan Doyle grasped the padlock and gave it a moment's study. "I am familiar with this type of padlock." He looked up at Wilde and flashed a crafty smile. "It is a cheap padlock from an inferior manu-facturer."

Wilde smiled in response and said, "And do you have your lock picks upon your person?"

In answer, Conan Doyle dipped a hand into his inside breast pocket and drew out a small leather pouch. "I never leave home without them," he smiled. He sorted through his set of lock picks and then inserted one in the lower half of the lock while he jiggled the topmost pick. A moment later the lock snapped open.

They both stepped into a gloomy, windowless space that reeked of chemicals. The Scots author found a lantern hanging above a work bench and lit it with a match. By its pulsing light, the two friends stood looking around.

"No young girls lurking inside," Wilde said.

"No, but perhaps a search will reveal something about the good Reverend Shepherd."

Conan Doyle dabbled in photography and had his own dark room. The Reverend Shepherd's dark room looked pretty much like any other.

Atop the work bench was a selection of trays used to hold devel-oping chemicals, which had now dried to ugly stains. Beneath the bench a long shelf held a scatter of smoke brown bottles stoppered with corks. White lettering on the side of each bottle identified its contents: Developer, Fixer, etc, but at the base of each was an ominous depiction of a skull and crossbones with the appellation, "POISON."

Conan Doyle grabbed the nearest bottle, marked *Developer*, yanked the cork, and brought it to the base of his walrus monstrance as he sniffed at the open neck. He threw a quick look at his companion, flashed a grin, and then lifted the bottle to his lips and began to take a swig.

"Arthur! No!" Wilde cried and grabbed his friend's arm to prevent him drinking further. "Are you mad? The bottle's marked Poison!"

"I think it depends upon your opinion of what constitutes a poison." Conan Doyle offered the bottle to his friend and urged, "Go on, Oscar, take a whiff."

Wilde looked doubtful but took the bottle from his friend and hovered his nose above the bottle's open neck in a cautious sniff. His eyes widened, and he shot a look at his friend. "Smells remarkably like a good whiskey. Is that what they use to develop photographs?"

"Developing photographs, no. Developing cirrhosis of the liver, yes. And to quote you, Oscar, 'Alcohol, taken in sufficient quantities, produces all the effects of drunkenness.'" He nodded at his friend. "Go on. Try a swig."

Wilde cautiously put the bottle to his lips, took a swig, savoured the mouthful, and then threw a devilish look at his friend. "Rather a good whiskey," he grinned. "Top drawer stuff. I think we now know the cause of the Reverend Shepherd's mysterious disappearance—too much photography."

The two authors continued to search the darkroom, but found little else of interest, although both men made a point of refuelling their hip flasks before they left.

"Well, that was an interesting diversion," Conan Doyle said as he snapped the padlock back onto the shed door. "But it didn't assist us in finding where the girls are hiding."

"*If* the girls are hiding. Assuming that something dire hasn't befallen them."

A jolt of concern rippled across Conan Doyle's face, but then he shook his head. "I am quite sure this is all mere hi-jinks. The Shepherd girls are clearly high-spirited, and quite precocious."

"There is definitely a spark of deviltry in them, especially the eldest — " Wilde stopped short as something in the distance caught his eye. "Ah, look, there's the church we saw earlier. I didn't realise it was so close. Could they be hiding in there?"

In the near distance, beyond a small apple orchard that bordered the property, stood a squat stone church of great antiquity judging by the simplicity of its architecture and absence of a steeple.

Conan Doyle squinted at the holy building. It was the closest structure bordering the rectory property. "The girls would have had sufficient time to walk there," he pointed out.

"Yes," Wilde agreed. "The two little minxes could definitely be hiding there. Let's find out, shall we?"

The two authors passed through a wooden gate in a fence that separated the garden from the apple orchard. The apples had not been harvested, and they kicked their way through windfall fruit abandoned on the ground to rot. The air around them buzzed with the somnolent hum of bees and wasps devouring the ruined fruit. Beyond the orchard rose a stone church wall low enough that they could just glimpse the tops of gravestones and burial monuments. A foot-worn path through the grass led to a Lych-gate. The rough iron latch lifted beneath Conan Doyle's thumb and they stepped through into an overgrown churchyard dizzy with tilting tombs and toppled grave markers. A path of up-heaved paving stones wandered to the church's ornately carved Saxon door. At that very moment, the church door opened and a man in a cleric's white surplice stepped outside.

"Good day!" Conan Doyle shouted.

The cleric visibly started. He looked momentarily heavenward, as if he had just received a rebuke from his employer, but then noticed the two friends standing at the gate. Fixing his face in an amiable smile, he strolled toward them, hiding his clasped hands within the long sleeves of his vestment. Up close, he was a large, soft man with the pinkish complexion of a freshly unearthed mole and a wispy halo of white hair that spoke of a life of quiet contemplation spent indoors. To add to his appearance of being a village vicar, he had a simple wooden cross hung around his neck on a stout hemp cord.

"Good day and God's blessings to you, both. I am the Reverend Troutt," he said, and added, "That's Troutt with two t's." The curate spoke in warm tones and affected the kind of calming and beatific smile that all Church of England curates are required to master. "I'm sorry if you've come to look at our Anglo-Saxon Church, but I've just locked up. However, we will be open again for evensong."

Both friends had plainly witnessed the fact that the curate had not locked the church door, but Conan Doyle figured the man had his reasons for dissuading visiting tourists. "Actually, we haven't come to see the church," he explained. "We're looking for two young girls who've gone missing. The youngest is but a child of eight. Blonde. Very fair. Blue eyes. The eldest girl is a brunette, around twelve years. They've run off and we're concerned they might be hiding in the church."

The curate's milky blue eyes lit with recognition. "Ah, you are enquiring about the Reverend Shepherd's girls?"

"Yes, they were playing in the rectory garden one moment, and then they suddenly vanished."

The curate's face was unreadable behind his sheep's-head smile. "Again? Oh, dear."

"It is not the first time?" Wilde asked.

"No. It is not the first time." The curate's smile faltered. "It pains me to speak ill of a fellow clergyman, but Reverend Shepherd—the girls' father—has fallen. Spiritually, I mean. I was brought in by the diocese as his temporary replacement. I'm afraid the Shepherd family is in much distress."

"I understood the Reverend Shepherd has fallen from the spiritual into strong spirits," Wilde quipped. "Whiskey and such?"

Troutt nodded. "Sadly, it is true."

"And when did this fall from grace begin?"

"Long before I came to this parish. Around a year ago." No, I'm wrong. It would be more than a year. I believe it was just before the previous Christmas. It caused some disruption of the usual Christmas services."

Conan Doyle tried to sound casual as he asked a very pointed question. "Did something happen? Some sort of tragedy, that prompted his drinking?"

A look of distress momentarily troubled the shallow waters of the curate's face, who answered haltingly. "Darvington. This parish. Our little Flock. Has been under a cloud for some time."

"A cloud?" Wilde asked. "I trust you are speaking metaphorically and not meteorologically. What precisely do you mean by cloud?"

The curate answered with obvious reticence. "A number of young girls from the village have gone missing."

The news, coincident with the Shepherd girls' sudden disappearance stunned both authors into momentary silence.

"Missing?" Conan Doyle repeated. "Do you mean—?"

The curate's smile remained beatific. "*Missing*. Simply that. We do not know of their fate, although I pray daily for their safe return."

"Exactly how many girls?" Wilde enquired.

"Three, or rather four. The first a year ago. The second and third, six months ago. And then—just last month—a fourth."

Conan Doyle tried not to betray his growing sense of unease. "So the disappearances began around the same time Rev Shepherd began drinking?"

The curate looked surprised. "Why, yes, I suppose it was around the same time. Oh, but I cannot believe that the Reverend Shepherd had anything . . ." He trailed off. Shook his head. "No, I cannot believe he could be possibly be implicated."

"Yet he suddenly took to drink for no apparent reason?" Wilde pointed out.

The curate licked his badly chapped lips. "I am sure the Reverend Shepherd had his reasons, but they are between him and his God. We may never know. He himself vanished from the parish shortly after."

At the news, Conan Doyle blinked with surprise and said, "The girls who disappeared . . . they were never found?"

"Vanished," the curate repeated, shaking his head resignedly. "Simply vanished. Of course we searched. But nothing. It is as if they were spirited away."

He noticed the dire look that Conan Doyle and Wilde shared and hastened to add, "Oh, but I do not think the same will be true for the Shepherd girls. They have run off before, but they always return. Sometimes a day later. Sometimes two days."

"And no one knows where they go?" Wilde pressed.

The curate was about to say something when the church door behind him opened and a small girl stepped outside. With a burst of sudden hope, Conan Doyle quickly scanned the figure, but she was an intensely freckled, carrot-haired girl of around twelve, awkward and cowed-looking, with none of the missing girls' willowy grace. Definitely, not one of the Shepherd sisters.

"Looks as if you didn't lock the church after all," Conan Doyle couldn't help but point out.

"Oh, dear," the curate chuckled with embarrassment. "And a good thing, too. I had quite forgotten about Tilly. She stays behind to clean the church. The money helps her family, who are amongst the poorest of our flock."

The girl looked about uncertainly, spotted the reverend, and called out in her thin girl's voice, "Reverend Troutt, I've finished sweeping the church. Is there anything else you wished me to stay behind for?"

Conan Doyle noticed that Tilly wore the same simple wooden cross around her neck as Troutt.

"Er, no, Tilly. You may go home now . . . and thank your mother for the loaf of bread."

Troutt looked back at the two friends and bashfully explained. "The girl's mother bakes the most heavenly bread. I use it in the harvest Thanksgiving." He shifted his feet, clearly anxious to leave. "Well, I must lock up. In truth, I don't know why I bother locking the church door. Nothing ever goes missing in a small town like Darvington."

"Except young girls," Wilde observed drily.

The curate had been about to walk away, but he paused, visibly stiffening at the Irish wit's sarcasm. He flashed his sheep's smile once again and nodded to them, muttering, "Blessings be upon you." His smile seemed to hang in the air behind him—Cheshire cat-style—as he ambled back toward the church, his hands clasped together, still hidden in the folds of his cassock.

Both friends were quiet and reflective as they strolled through the orchard on their way back to the Shepherd house.

"I can't quite say why," Wilde said, as he paused a moment to spark up one of his Turkish cigarettes. He puffed the cigarette to life and tossed the match away, "but I didn't care much for that curate fellow."

Conan Doyle nodded. "Me neither. He gave us his blessing but did not make the sign of benediction, as if reluctant to show us his hands."

"Perhaps he is another of your tribe of long-fingered piano players?"

Conan Doyle chuckled. "I did feel as if the Reverend Troutt with two t's was hiding something."

"Troutt, indeed?" Wilde echoed, the corners of his mouth twitching in a smirk. "He rather struck me as a cold fish."

Conan Doyle snorted a laugh and said, "Are you trying to *bait* me, Oscar?" joining in on the punnery.

"I am sure the good Curate Troutt is dedicated to saving *soles*."

"Come, Oscar, let us leave this *plaice*, before we pun again."

After Wilde puffed his cigarette into piquant life, the two authors resumed their stroll, snickering like naughty schoolboys playing pranks behind teacher's back. As they passed through one of three secret gardens, Wilde gestured at his friend with the cigarette and said, "What is going on in that mind of yours, Arthur? I can hear the purr of greased gears."

The Scotsman shook his head. "I confess I find this whole affair most perplexing. We are lured down here by the report of two girls abducted by faeries, only to find the girls all hale and hearty. I was then excited to think we would interview the girls and hear tales of faeries and the supernatural, but then the mother tells us that she did not write the letter to me and that the girls are not her true daughters but imposters. Moments later, the girls vanish before our very eyes."

Wilde added, "And now we discover the disappearance of yet more girls from the village."

"Exactly. Events seem to take on an ever more sinister aspect with every turn. I find my mind whip-sawed by the dizzying turns of fortune."

Wilde pondered upon that and then added, "I am perhaps most discomfited about the shocking story Mrs. Shepherd told us—the girls speaking about adult matters, and using the coarsest of language. That suggests to me something deeply unhealthy happening in the Shepherd household."

"Yes. I don't know what to make of that. It could be true. Although there is something of the hysteric about the poor woman."

"And in her sense of décor? All that chintz and willow pattern? Doilies and dishcloths and cake stands and fripperies?" The aesthete made a face and shuddered visibly at the memory.

"I want to question her further, Oscar. I am not entirely certain whom I believe. Or if I believe anyone."

The two friends paused again. Stood stock-still. Looked. Listened. Both still half expecting to hear a suppressed giggle, a titter, the trill of girlish laughter. But there was nothing but the restless hiss of the breeze stirring the treetops.

Without the girls' laughter, the garden seemed dreadfully empty. And so the friends set off again, but had walked no more than a dozen feet when Wilde suddenly stopped, grabbed Conan Doyle by the sleeve and pointed at something with his cane. "Look at that, Arthur!"

"What?"

Conan Doyle followed the point and finally saw what his friend was pointing at something set into the base of a nearby oak tree.

"It's a door."

"A faerie door, as my mama, Lady Wilde would say."

"Yes, I am familiar with faerie doors. There are a number in the park near my home in Norwood."

"Well don't you see? There's our answer—the girls must be hiding inside!"

Wilde rushed over to the tree. Conan Doyle trailed behind, already convinced this discovery would lead nowhere.

The large Irishman crouched down, rapped his knuckles on the door and called out, "Miss Philomena, Miss Wilhelmina. Come out at once, girls."

"No, Oscar, faerie doors are merely decorative doors nailed to the trunk of the tree. A bit of whimsy people like to indulge in. They are not actual *doors*, per se."

"Nonsense!" Wilde said. He gave an experimental tug on the tiny door handle and to Conan Doyle's surprise and chagrin, the door swung open, revealing a roomy hollow in the tree's base with ample room for two small girls to crouch.

Wilde got up from his knees, wiping his hands. "For once, Arthur, you were wrong and I was right. Although the two girls are not inside at the moment."

Conan Doyle pointed to a pair of small footprints, side by side in the loosely scuffed earth. "No, but look at those footprints. Our two little ladies have hidden in there at some point." He looked up and scanned the surrounding undergrowth, suddenly pointing with his cane. "And look there—a path trodden through the bluebells! They came this way and hid inside the tree, and fairly recently."

"Then there's our answer, Wilde said. "All logically deduced as if by your Sherlock Holmes fellow. Come, Arthur, let us return to the rectory post haste. I'm sure the Shepherd girls will be waiting for us when we return."

"No doubt," Conan Doyle replied in a voice bursting with happy conviction.

But when they reached The Old Rectory, the girls were not there. Instead, waiting for them was a huddle of strange figures that marked the beginning of the London authors' troubles in Darvington.

BACK IN THE BRITISH MUSEUM
READING ROOM

The two friends still occupied the blue-leather topped reading desk in the British Library Reading Room, where Conan Doyle had only just begun reading aloud from his mysterious Casebook number 5.

"And that was when the Shepherd girls vanished?" Wilde asked. "A sorry trail of events which led to me being arrested for their abduction and murder?"

Conan Doyle nodded. "Apparently so."

"And the girls were never found?"

The Scotsman brushed his moustache with his fingertips and sadly shook his head. "We haven't reached that point in the narrative yet."

"And you intend to keep me on tenterhooks? Good Lord, Arthur! You would have been discharged from the Spanish Inquisition for cruelty."

"The story builds, as you will soon see. If I reveal to you now what and how events progressed—out of chronological order—it will only confuse you."

"I could hardly be less confused. If you wish to continue at this pace, you will have to lend me your cuticles, for I will have already chewed mine to the quick."

Conan Doyle continued, "To risk getting ahead of myself, apparently, we searched for the Shepherd girls at a village named Wyrme-Hallow."

Wilde made a face. "Wyrme-Hallow? Does such a place exist?"

"That presents one of the many enigmas about the case. I have consulted the best maps of England in the library's possession."

"And?"

Conan Doyle shook his head and frowned. "None of them show a village called Wyrme-Hallow."

"So, does it exist?"

Conan Doyle opened his Casebook to a page where an old and time-yellowed map had been pasted in. "This is a section of an antique map we purchased in Darvington. It dates back to 1729. Here is the River Wyrme. The river starts in the hills to the east of Darvington and runs past *The Old Rectory*, to Darvington Bay. If you follow the river upstream, you eventually come to a small village, which by the quaint, hand-lettered script is identified as *Wyrme-Hallow*."

Wilde's generous lips puckered in a moue of puzzlement as he studied the map.

Conan Doyle carried on. "Judging by the olde-worldy script, I would say the village no longer exists, or at best is just a ruin."

"What do you mean?"

"The village we supposedly visited is no longer there. Modern maps show only a small lake on the former site of the village. And as you no doubt know, the word 'Wyrme', in all its various spellings, was another term for dragon." He drew forward a book of modern maps that had been propped open to a specific page. "As I said, the village is not shown on any modern map. I have read the narrative of events in the entire book and they are all shockingly fantastical."

"Fantastical?" Wilde challenged, "Even more fantastical than what you have already grudgingly revealed to me?"

The Scots author shrugged his shoulders. "Fantastical in the strange events and the descriptions of the unearthly denizens of Wyrme-Hallow."

Doubt crinkled the corners of Wilde's eyes. "Arthur, are you sure this is not one of your *scientific romances* you scribbled one evening—perhaps after an intimate encounter with that top-drawer brand of Scotch you favour?"

"Not all amnesia requires alcohol, Oscar."

"True," the Irishman conceded, "only the good kind."

Conan Doyle sighed wearily, "I profoundly wish that were the case. But as I've noted there is ample physical proof pasted into the Casebook: photographs, an ancient and time-faded map of Darvington and its environs, train ticket stubs, the article from the Darvington Recorder describing your arrest—they are all very real. Plus, I am sure I pasted them into the journal precisely to counter such a notion."

Wilde fidgeted, and half rose from his chair as he dug in his pocket and drew out a hip flask. Conan Doyle watched as he unscrewed the cap and glugged a mouthful of brandy. "Ugh," he gasped, "This is all a dreadful nightmare, and it keeps getting worse." He became aware of Conan Doyle watching him screw the cap on the whiskey and raised the flask, offering it up.

But Conan Doyle shook his head: *no*, and cleared his throat.

Wilde clearly guessed he was about to receive another revelation and his eyes widened in alarm. "Oh dear Lord, I was right. It does get worse, doesn't it? Whatever now?"

Conan Doyle traced a thick finger along the spine of his Casebook. "As I told you, last night I enjoyed scant sleep and so spent many hours reading and re-reading the entries in my Casebook. It was only then that I noticed another disturbing peculiarity."

Wilde puckered his generous lips in suspense. "*Peculiarity?* I have never like that word *peculiarity*, particularly when it is preceded by *disturbing*. What *disturbing peculiarity* do you refer to?"

In response, Conan Doyle leaned forward and spread the Casebook wide, so that the spine cracked. "Look, Oscar, at the bottom of the pages. What do you see?"

The Irishman leaned forward and squinted down at the Casebook. "See?" He shook his head. "Nothing. The pages displayed are blank. What do you mean, *peculiar—*?" He stopped short as he spotted something. "Wait. I see a small section of torn paper. As if a page has been torn out."

Conan Doyle nodded slowly. "An astute observation. You are correct: a page has been torn out. In fact, when I discovered it I carefully studied the book's binding with my magnifying glass and was able to ascertain that a great many pages have been removed, excised, deliberately torn out."

"I don't understand. Who would wish to tear pages out of your journal?"

Conan Doyle shifted uncomfortably and shook his head. "I have no idea. At any rate, it is clear that the Casebook has been doctored, manipulated, pages excised. I have no remembrance of journeying to Wyrme-Hallow. No recollection of writing this Casebook. No recollection of any of the events described herein. For some reason—and by some mechanism I cannot begin to fathom—we were induced to forget every detail of what happened on that journey. My theory is that through the medium of this Casebook, I was attempting to send a coded message from myself in the past to myself in the future. A sort of trail of breadcrumbs for us to follow."

"A trail of breadcrumbs?" Wilde mused. "A metaphor snatched straight from Hansel and Gretel, a faerie story wherein a witch tries to push two innocent children into an oven. I hope such a fate does not await us!" The Irish wit's hands were trembling as he fumbled out his silver cigarette case and then remembered where he was and slipped the case back into a pocket. "Whatever shall we do, Arthur?"

"I believe what we need to do has already been done. But just in case I wanted you to become familiar with the story—or at least the story I can reconstruct from my Casebook—in case we ever need to return to Darvington."

"Return to Darvington!?" Wilde mused, "How can we go back to a place we've never been?"

A MOST UNWELCOME
DEVELOPMENT

After their encounter with the Reverend Troutt (with two t's), Wilde and Conan Doyle strolled back into the rectory garden to find a tableaux-vivant awaiting them. Mrs Shepherd sat collapsed on the wrought iron garden bench, dabbing away tears and snuffling into a white hanky. Standing over her, a comforting hand laid upon her shoulder, was a short, squat stump of a man in a dark pinstripe suit. He was around forty years of age with a neckless build and a square head. His jet-black hair had been oiled and viciously horse-brushed to his pink scalp. From his demeanour, Conan Doyle guessed that the man was a ranking officer of the law, and if further proof were needed, he was flanked on either side by uniformed constables: one a thin young lad who probably only needed to shave once a week; the other a roly-poly figure almost as wide as he was tall, with a florid red face and a fiery red moustache.

"I see the local constabulary has arrived," Conan Doyle muttered.

Wilde studied the assembled figures and cocked a skeptical eyebrow. "Local constabulary? They look more like the local cast of a production of Gilbert and Sullivan: fat, thin, and short!"

As the two friends stepped closer, they heard Mrs. Shepherd wail, "Oh Albert, I fear they are gone forever this time!"

The short man patted her shoulder reassuringly and said, "Fret not, Delphinia, I shall find them. Fret not. Nothing in Darvington can escape my eye."

"We have searched the grounds as far as the church," Conan Doyle called out in a loud voice, "I'm afraid we found neither hide nor hair of the girls."

The short man visibly startled and jerked alert. He hurled a furious look at the two friends and bawled out, "And who the devil are you two?"

"Oh, dear," Mrs Shepherd said, looking up in surprise as she wiped tears from her flushed cheeks, "I had quite forgot. These gentlemen have come from London."

"From London?" the short man snarled.

Conan Doyle raised his boater and stepped forward to shake hands. "My name is Doyle. Doctor Doyle." Something in the short man's dyspeptic manner made the Scots author reluctant to immediately reveal his public identity, which proved prudent. Conan Doyle was a keen sportsman with a manly handshake, but the shorter man had the grip of a bone-crushing Minotaur. When the Scots doctor finally extricated his hand from the handshake, he massaged his mangled digits and indicated his companion with a nod. "And this is my friend, Oscar."

Although this time the short man offered his hand for a handshake, Wilde, having witnessed the grimace of pain flash across his friend's face, guessed at the ferocity of the handshake and instead raised his boater and nodded a quick bow. "A pleasure to meet you, Mister . . . ?"

The man removed his hand from Delphinia Shepherd's shoulder and raised himself to his full height, which was still a full head lower than either of the two authors.

"I am Albert Lawless, Chief of the Darvington Police Force." The short man's face was untroubled by even a rumour of friendliness.

Wilde drew the cigarette from his lips and blew a jet of smoke. "I'm sorry, but you said your name is Lawless and you are the chief of Police?" He barked a smoky laugh. "Surely you must see the humour in that?"

Lawless's beetling expression argued that he was well aware of the irony but found little hilarity in it.

"I must ask what is your business here?" the Police Chief inquired, thrusting out his chest and tucking his thumbs behind his lapels.

"We came in response to a letter from Mrs Shepherd," Conan Doyle explained. "A letter about the Shepherd girls and faeries. Which, ah, which turns out she claims she did not write. The letter included a rather convincing photograph as proof."

Lawless turned his scouring gaze upon the supine Reverend's wife. "Whaaaaaaaat? Faeries? What's all this about, Delphinia?"

The police chief's familiar way of addressing the curate's wife suggested to Conan Doyle an obvious degree of familiarity between the two.

The Reverend Shepherd's wife recounted her assertion that the letter was the work of her eldest daughter and proof of the wickedness that had possessed the children of late.

Lawless pondered upon this news for a moment, but then he swivelled the glare of his attention back to the two friends. By now his expression had hardened into solid suspicion. "And who are you, sir, that a young girl should write you such a letter?"

There was no way to dodge it now, and so Conan Doyle confessed, "My full name is Arthur Conan Doyle. Although I am a fully qualified physician, you might better know me as the author of the Sherlock Holmes mystery stories. I also have some repute as an investigator of the supernatural."

The police chief's expression wavered between amazement and scowling doubt. "Conan Doyle? The Scottish fellow who writes those absurd detective yarns?"

The Scots author ground his molars at having his most famous works belittled as "absurd yarns," but struggled to remain civil.

"I am one and the same," he replied, "the creator of *detective* fictions." Although Conan Doyle had killed off his most famous literary creation some time ago, he continued to receive hate mail from an aggrieved public and was anxious to avoid the topic.

Lawless shifted his abrasive gaze to Wilde, who was casually standing with a cigarette in one hand, his other resting upon his hip. "And I suppose this chap is Doctor Watson?"

An incensed Conan Doyle considered several possible replies, each of which would likely result in their immediate arrest, but instead said mildly, "This is a colleague of mine, Oscar Wilde."

The police chief's mouth fell agape. "Oscar Wilde? I know that name. It is famous, or rather should I say, *infamous!*"

The remark was clearly intended to provoke, but Wilde made the Police Chief wait as he languorously exhaled a deep lungful of smoke and then replied. "So long as the description contains the word *famous*, I am happy to be either."

Lawless's face visibly reddened. "You're the chap who wrote that . . . that . . . *obscene* book."

Oh, dear, Conan Doyle, thought. *Now we're for it.* He looked away, and his eye happened to fall upon the picnic blanket and the abandoned remnants of the girls' tea party. For a moment he puzzled at the square black box sitting at the edge of the blanket. And then he realised what it was: the Midg quarter plate camera. The fact that it was no longer in the picnic basket where he had first glimpsed it suggested the camera had been moved; moreover, that the girls had moved it. And then he flashed back on the image glimpsed from the parlour window of the Shepherd sisters running past the window clutching something.

The camera.

Suddenly all he could think of was gaining access to the camera. If the girls had indeed managed to snap a photograph or two, it might well provide a vital clue as to their whereabouts. For a moment he considered sharing the information with the Chief of Police, but Lawless was such a blustering buffoon, so full of himself, that Conan Doyle quickly rejected the idea. He discretely tapped his friend's elbow. When Wilde looked, Conan Doyle jerked his head in the direction of the blanket. Wilde screwed up his face in puzzlement but then followed the nod to the blanket and saw the camera in plain view. The Irish wit's eyes lit up and he gave a subtle nod of understanding—his task was to keep the Police Chief preoccupied.

Wilde dropped his cigarette and ground it into the grass with a swivel of his polished black boot. He made a show of drawing out his silver cigarette case, carefully removing another of his piquant Turkish cigarettes, scratching a match, puffing the cigarette to life and tossing the match away into the grass before he jetted smoke out both nostrils and asked in a throwaway manner: "Tell me Mister Lawless, which work of mine has so upset you?"

"You know full well what I am referring to," Lawless snarled. "That exercise in moral turpitude, *The Portrait of Dorian Grey.*"

With all attention focused on Wilde, Conan Doyle took a step backwards, and then another, and yet another until the back of his heel bumped gently into the camera. It was now within his grasp. He just had to kneel down.

Wilde's large face creased with puzzlement. "I'm afraid I've never heard of such of work unless . . ." He grinned knowingly. "Ah yes, I think you misremember and mean to say, *The Picture of Dorian Grey.* A common mistake."

Conan Doyle dropped to a crouch and pretended to be fiddling with his shoelace. Confident that all attention was focused upon the fracas, his fingers fumbled . . . and found the camera. He chanced a look up. All eyes were riveted upon the two combatants. Most likely, no one would see anything.

"Whatever the title," Lawless continued, the cords of his neck straining, "it is a vile piece of filth. The lowest form of depravity!"

Since the release of *Dorian Grey*, Wilde had become used to being traduced in print and to his face, and so was unaffected by the police chief's scorn.

"Tell me, Mister Lawless," Wilde purred, "which parts struck you as particularly depraved? I have no doubt you dog-eared those pages and smudged the type with your sweaty thumbs reading them over and over to verify just how scandalised you were."

In one quick movement, Conan Doyle snatched the camera, jammed it into the leather portfolio next to his Casebook, and stood up again. The camera made an alarming bulge in the narrow satchel, but the exchange between Wilde and Lawless had grown so heated he hoped no one would notice.

"Why, you scurrilous—!" Lawless sputtered, his face purpling. "If I had my way creatures such as you would be publicly flogged. I know your type, Wilde. I know it only too well. I imagine you are also one of those Irish home rule agitators?"

Wilde paused to pick a fleck of tobacco from his tongue. "It is true I am Irish. I believe in ruling my own home. And I am frequently agitated—usually when I run out of cigarettes."

Lawless's face turned black with rage. "I warn you, Wilde, I am a man prone to violence."

"Really?" Wilde replied, "I am a man prone to violins . . . or cellos . . . pretty much any stringed instrument now that I come to think of it."

The police chief made a strangling sound, like an overinflated balloon creaking ominously just before it burst.

Conan Doyle quickly strode up and clapped a hand on his friend's shoulder.

"Oscar, I think there's little point in bothering a busy man like Chief Lawless with esoteric arguments about literary merit. He has a case to solve. Nothing should delay his investigation into the disappearance of the Shepherd girls." He turned his attention to the police chief. "Chief Lawless, it is clear our presence here is hampering your diligent efforts. We are both tired from our journey and my friend's nerves are excitable. We will leave you, the professionals, to continue the search. Should you require our assistance, Oscar and I will be staying overnight in Darvington. We've booked into the Claremont Hotel." He looked down with solicitude at the Reverend Shepherd's wife. "Dear lady, Oscar and I will pray for the safe return of your beloved girls."

The two had turned their backs and were walking away, toward the rectory, when Lawless lassoed them mid-stride with a bellowed: "STOP!"

The two friends stumbled to a halt. *That's torn it.* Conan Doyle thought. *He's spotted the huge bulge in my portfolio.*

Reluctantly, both men turned to face the Police Chief.

"Be on tomorrow's train," Lawless spat, and then added in leaden syllables, "Both of you!"

Their scolding over, Conan Doyle and Wilde hurried away without further argument. Despite the gravity of the situation, or maybe because of it, a giddy urge to laugh uncoiled within Conan Doyle's lungs. Evidently, Wilde felt the same, for as soon as they reached the front garden of the rectory, the pair burst into gales of laughter.

"What a buffoon!" Conan Doyle chuckled.

"Lawless by name . . . lawless by nature," Wilde added. He nodded at the bulging satchel. "Is that what I think it is, Arthur?"

Conan Doyle opened the satchel to show off the Midg Camera. "The camera, no less—snatched from under Chief Lawless's nose!"

"Which, to be fair, is not hard to do," Wilde rejoined, "as he does have rather a pug nose."

"And I have no doubt he will continue sticking it into our business." Conan Doyle patted the camera. "Come, Oscar, we must find a photographer's studio in Darvington and have these plates developed. Hopefully, they will contain a photograph or two that may provide a clue as to where the girls have gone. And, if we're doubly lucky, some solid evidence of the existence of faeries."

THE OLDE CURIOSITY SHOPPE

"I may die. I hope you realise that, Arthur. I may well die, and then the blame will be laid at your feet."

"Come now, the exercise will do you good. It's invigorating."

"Ugh," Wilde said. "Even the avoidance of exercise is exhausting. Please slow down. The pace you're setting is excessive. My cigarette keeps going out."

"Come now, Oscar. It's only a half mile or so to town."

"A half-mile?"

"As the crow flies."

"I hope you're not talking about London crows, which weave drunkenly about the sky, blinded by chimney smoke and coughing soot with every caw. If so we will likely never reach our destination."

Just then they heard the slow clop of hooves coming from behind and turned to see the familiar sight of the rag-and-bone man and his horse and cart trundling toward them.

"Ah, here's our friend again," Conan Doyle noted. He glanced at Wilde. "Is it worth the expenditure of sixpence to cadge a ride?"

"A sixpence? I would purchase the man's horse and cart if it would save us the walk on such a sultry day."

Conan Doyle removed his boater and waved it overhead and the horse and cart rattled to a halt in front of them.

"It's us again. A sixpence for a ride back into town?" He made a quick scan of the back of the cart, but the man seemed not to have added nor subtracted anything from his sad jumble of tat.

The rag-and-bone man scratched the white thatch of beard beneath his chin and ruminated, "I reckon a shilling's a fair price."

"But you only charged us sixpence to drive us here," Wilde pointed out.

"Aye, but now you know how far it is, I reckon you'll pay a shilling."

Conan Doyle released a gasp of umbrage but Wilde quickly snatched out a florin and pressed it into the man's wrinkled palm. "Now is the not the time to haggle," Arthur, he said, lifting himself wearily onto the seat. "Not when it is a matter of life and death. My life. My death."

～

After half an hour of clop-clopping, the rag-and-bone cart shimmied and swayed onto the cobblestones of Darvington High Street. Conan Doyle scanned the shop fronts rolling past and spotted exactly what he was looking for. "You may drop us there," Conan Doyle said, pointing with his cane. They alighted from the cart in front of a photographer's studio and Conan Doyle handed the driver another sixpence.

"What's this fer?" The rag-and-bone man asked, looking at the shiny tanner in his grimy palm. "Yer friend done paid me already."

"That's from me, in gratitude for not having to listen to Oscar complain the whole way here."

The rag-and-bone man grinned, showing off the crooked snarl of his four remaining teeth. He shook the reigns, made a clucking sound with his tongue and the sway-backed horse dawdled away, drawing the cart behind.

"Awfully convenient running into that chap again," Conan Doyle said.

"Hardly convenient, Arthur. I am quite certain that our extravagant tipping represents the sole source of revenue is this down-at-the-mouth town."

When they entered the photographer's studios, they found the space jammed with packing crates and a red-faced bald man who was busy harrying two labourers as they loaded photographic equipment into large steamer trunks.

"Sorry to bother you," Conan Doyle addressed the man, who glared back with obvious irritation. "But are you the proprietor?"

"We've shut down!" the man barked, nodding at the jumble of equipment waiting to be boxed. "As you can no doubt tell, Darvington is no place to run any sort of business. Although if it's shop premises you're looking for, you can pretty much take your pick."

Conan Doyle reached into his bulging portfolio and drew out the Midg camera. "Ah, how unfortunate. There were some exposures in this camera I was rather hoping to have developed. I'll happily pay double—"

"All my equipment is packed," The man snapped. "If you need developing the only place left is the *Old Curiosity Shoppe*, just down the road from the train station. Can't miss it." And with that he ignored Wilde and Conan Doyle and resumed telling his removal men how to do their job.

A few minutes later, Conan Doyle and Wilde stood looking through their own reflections in the mullioned window of the *Old Curiosity Shoppe*, which boasted the most unusual window display either man had ever clapped eyes on. Propped up on a wooden stand was a "genuine mermaid" according to the scrawled chalk sign beneath. But unlike the buxom mermaids lusted after by sailors on the briny deep, this one was tiny and seemed to have been sewn together from the leftovers scoured from the studio of an inept taxidermist. The mermaid had the shriveled face and sunken rib cage of a badly-shaven monkey. From the half way point down the torso had been crudely sewn to the trunk of a large fish, and with the years, most of the desiccated scales were yellowing and peeling free of the body. Beside the mermaid stood a large glass jar in which a grotesque solar system of giant gallstones bobbed. Standing upon a short easel at the back of the window display was a framed antique map of Darvington from 1729. Although such a treasure should have been diligently stored somewhere dark and dry, the map had spent years in the shop window and was yellowed and faded from exposure to the sun.

Wilde looked up from the shop window to the Tudor building's half-timbered façade where a wooden sign swung from a pole.

"*Ye Olde Curiosity Shoppe*," Wilde read aloud, and added, "Why are there never any *New* Curiosity Shops? And why spell *Shoppe* with two p's? Is that somehow a guarantee of antiquity?"

"It is an affectation, I believe," Conan Doyle answered, and then pointed at something in the window and said, "But look at that sign. It appears we've come to the right place."

Wilde squinted in the window and read aloud, "Used clothing, antiques, and curios bought and sold."

"No, not that sign," his friend corrected. "The sign above it."

"Photographs developed."

"That's the one," Conan Doyle said slipping his hand into the door latch. "Come, Oscar. And remember, we are here to have some photographs developed, not to browse for knick-knacks"

"I will somehow resist the temptation," Wilde remarked ironically.

A shop bell chimed as they pushed through the door into a gloomy space crammed with large and ugly furniture and a succession of tables cluttered with assorted bric-a-brac. Everywhere the eye turned it alighted upon a stultifying cornucopia of miscellany. In one corner an antique table groaned beneath a burgeoning display of artefacts— old, new, some treasures, but mostly trash: phrenology busts, fake Chinese vases, porcelain fairings, glass paperweights, Toby Jugs, stereographic viewers, moth-eaten fox stoles, flintlock pistols, elephant's foot umbrella holders, quack medical shocking devices for "invigorating the corpuscles", brass sextants, telescopes, geographical globes from different eras and of wildly differing accuracy, and a decidedly suspicious suit of armour, which looked to Conan Doyle as if it had been assembled from the odds and ends of nine different suits of armour in addition to a few pieces filched from someone's kitchen: a sieve, a colander, etc.

Conan Doyle found the shop intriguing and scarcely knew where to look. Drunken columns of books teetered up from the floorboards, inviting an errant elbow to knock them crashing to the floor. The walls were hung with shiny horse brasses and polished bed warming pans, as well as framed maps and etchings, and gloomy oil paintings of varying awfulness. And everywhere clocks and timepieces of all styles and vintages, from pocket watches to grandfather clocks, some housed in cabinets and some in glass domes. Timepieces were ubiquitous, ranging from hulking Grandfather clocks to delicate Coach clocks whose glass sides revealed ingenious silvery mechanisms whirling within. Some of the timepieces were in full ticking life, and some were dead and inert, the hands of each one pointing to a different opinion as to the correct time.

And above it all, on the highest shelves scraping the ceiling, beady eyes peered down from their glass cases—a taxidermied zoo of foxes, pheasants, weasels, pole cats, badgers, owls, buzzards, kingfishers and more examples of practically every creature to flutter, creep, crawl and bound about the woodlands of Britain.

The shoppe's stale air swarmed with a sneeze-inducing miasma of mould, mildew, and dust, combined with the pungent aroma of old books and leather trunks only just pried open after mouldering for years in a dark attic, while a sour chemical aftertaste of formaldehyde still percolated from all the stuffed corpses. The smell was inundating, and Wilde browsed with a scented handkerchief clamped over his nose and mouth to filter the air. Conan Doyle's walrus moustache drooped into a frown as he looked about the place. A large proportion of the items on display (such as a smashed mandolin) were old and broken tat that should have been consigned long ago to the rubbish tip, but here each item was lovingly labelled with a description and a price, carefully scribbled in eye-strainingly faint pencil.

Conan Doyle eventually found a small handbell on the counter beside a calligraphied sign that invited him to "ring for service."

He tinkled the bell loudly and shouted, "Shop!"

After a moment's silence, a thump sounded from the floor above, and then Conan Doyle's eyes followed creaking footsteps as they crossed the ceiling to an impossibly narrow staircase in the corner of the room that spiralled down from the upper floor. Moments later, a pair of legs appeared as the presumed proprietor descended the dangerously worn stone treads in a series of halting steps.

"Welcome, to the old curiosity shop," greeted the apron-clad shop-keeper as he stumbled to the bottom. He was an elderly man (Conan Doyle guessed he was in his late seventies) with shiny, shock-white hair spilling down upon his shoulders from beneath an embroidered burgundy smoking cap. A pair of pince-nez squeezed themselves onto the pointy end of his long and weasley proboscis. The thin face was clean-shaven, which accentuated the knobby cheekbones floating above the sunken cheeks.

"Good Lord," Wilde muttered sotto voce, "The owner is the oldest curiosity in the shop!"

The shopkeeper peered over the top of his pince-nez and proclaimed in a shaky voice, "From the fine cut of your clothes, I see you are city gents. London, no doubt?"

"Yes," Conan Doyle answered and fumbled to remove the camera from his satchel. "We are visiting Darvington, and I was hoping you could develop some photographs for me. It is rather urgent—"

He was interrupted by the jangling of the shop doorbell, and then a character clomped in whose appearance was so outlandish he seemed like another of the shop's curiosities that had momentarily stepped outside for a stroll. The man, who looked to be in his early forties, wore baggy khaki trousers that had been inexpertly hemmed into knee-length shorts with box-shaped pockets front and back. The shorts looked even more voluminous on his painfully thin frame so that the stick-like legs emerging from the baggy shorts seemed to belong to those of a wading bird. The same was true of the jacket, which sported two sets of epaulettes, as well as a multitude of belts, pockets and fasteners for whatever purpose. His feet were shod in enormous leather boots with thick wool socks pulled up to his knobbly knees. Atop his head, he wore a white pith helmet of the type favoured by jungle explorers, and now he tromped across the floorboards straight up to the shop proprietor who greeted him with the warmth of a regular customer.

"Good morning, Professor Squibb." The shopkeeper paused and turned to Conan Doyle. "I must apologise, but I am expecting this gentleman. If you and your friend would like to browse the shop, I will be with you shortly."

The Professor raised his pith helmet in salute to the shopkeeper, revealing hair that had been cropped to a dark fuzz and sallow cheeks bristling bruise-blue with a four-day growth of beard stubble.

"Good day, sah. Good day!" he barked in a military fashion. "I wonder, has my order arrived?" Despite his outlandish appearance, Squibb's voice was that of a cultured and highly educated man.

"Indeed it has," the shopkeeper chuckled, "indeed it has." He ducked beneath the counter, lifted out a large cardboard carton and set it down atop the counter. "Twenty-four, as you ordered, sir. The finest timepieces. British made. Guaranteed quality."

To prove his point the shopkeeper lifted the box lid to show that the container was packed with rows of smaller boxes. He selected one at random and handed it to the Professor who excitedly tore off the box flaps without bothering to open it properly. His fingers probed and drew out a fine brass pocket watch. Even from where he stood Conan Doyle could see that it was an expensive timepiece: much finer than the one currently dangling from its fob on his own waistcoat.

"Capital! Capital!" The odd fellow exulted. "And now the reckoning, if you please?" He returned the pocket watch to its box and the shopkeeper slid it back into the waiting gap in the larger carton.

The shopkeeper told him the amount, which perked up even Wilde's ears. It was a considerable sum of money, more than a workingman's salary for two or three months. Squibb paid in full with a large bank note drawn from an inside pocket.

"Will you be requiring more Professor Squibb?"

"Eh, what? Ah, yes! " he said absent-mindedly. "Two more boxes. I think that should be sufficient. As usual, I shall pay upon delivery."

"Very good, sir."

"Yes, good, good. Jolly good." Squibb parroted.

The Professor strode toward the door, clutching the carton of pocket watches, and when forced to squeeze past Conan Doyle and Wilde in the narrow aisle way, acknowledged them by touching the brim of his pith helmet and offering them a curt nod.

The doorbell jangled as he left the store.

"Doctor Livingstone, I presume?" Wilde quipped.

"What a strange chap," Conan Doyle agreed. "From his clothes, he appeared to have stepped straight from the African jungle. I must say, however, that something about the fellow struck me as familiar—and why on earth would anyone want so many pocket watches?"

His Irish friend chuckled. "With some people, punctuality is an obsession. Fortunately, that is one vice Oscar Wilde does not suffer from. Perhaps the only vice, come to think of it."

"Can I help you gents find anything?" the shopkeeper had abandoned the barricade of his counter and was standing just a few feet away, his hands pressed together in a posture of supplication . . . or possibly prayer for another sale.

Conan Doyle rummaged in his leather satchel and drew out the Shepherd family's Midg Quarter Plate. "I understand you develop photographs?"

The shopkeeper eyed the camera and started to reach for it. "Certainly sir," he fawned. "But it will be a week."

"A week!" Conan Doyle sputtered, snatching the camera back.

"Sorry, sir, but the summer is our busiest season."

"Yes," Wilde agreed. "We witnessed it. You served an actual customer and made an actual sale. You must be exhausted."

Conan Doyle agitatedly combed his moustache with his fingertips. "I'm afraid that won't do. I need the photographs developed as soon as possible." He pondered a moment and ventured. "It's quite urgent. I'll pay triple your going rate . . . " and quickly added, " . . . if you can have them ready by tomorrow morning."

Doubt flickered in the shopkeeper's eyes, but the offer of extra money chased a smile onto the thin, dry lips. "Tomorrow morning?"

He made a pretence of debating the offer. "It will be difficult, but yes, yes I can have them ready by tomorrow morning."

When the two friends stepped from the shop, the salty breeze blowing up Darvington's main street reminded them of just how stale and fusty the air had been inside the shop.

"I think you're right, Oscar."

"I usually am," Wilde replied and then added, "About what?"

"That oddly-dressed chap, he did look like he'd just stepped from the jungle. Or at least he had the kind of tan one only derives from time spent in a tropical clime. But maybe a few months back. Did you notice? His tan? Faded? He's been back in England six months or more."

"A very Holmesian observation," Wilde replied and chuckled at something that had amused him. "Professor Squibb? I do hope his first name is *damp*."

"Squibb, indeed! I thought something about him seemed familiar. I remember reading about a Professor Squibb in *The Times*. Wasn't he involved in some kind of expedition to the Dark Continent? I seem to recall some kind of tragedy befell the group. Something dreadful. If I remember correctly—"

Conan Doyle's next words were drowned out by the sound of a thunderous explosion.

BOOOOOOOOOOOOOOOOOOOOOOOOOOOOOOOOOOOOOM!

Moments later, a blast wave of hot air hit them in the face, knocking off their boaters, and needling their eyes with gritty dust. The two cowered before the rush of sound and wind, eyes squeezed tight, clothes flapping, hands clamped over their ears. When the roar finally subsided, both men stood stunned, mouths agape, ears ringing. Almost immediately, doors up and down the street flew open as the startled citizenry of Darvington rushed out into the road.

"Good Lord!" Conan Doyle exclaimed as he stooped to pick up his and Wilde's boaters, which had been sent skittering across the pavement. As he handed back Wilde's hat, he noticed that several panes of the Old Curiosity Shoppe's window had been blown out.

"More blasting?" Wilde pondered.

Conan Doyle frowned as he settled the boater back atop his head. "No. That was too loud. And much, much too close!"

Summoned by the thunderous roar, the wizened shopkeeper stumbled out of the Curiosity Shoppe's front door, his face white and strained with fear. He pointed to a black pall of smoke rising from the railroad station and, "Oh, dear, not again! Not again!"

By now many of the citizens of Darvington had assembled in knots in the middle of the roadway, where they stood looking about themselves in a state of bewilderment. Then all at once, people began hurrying in the direction of the smoke and the two friends fell in with the crowd rushing toward the train station . . . or as they soon found, what little remained of it.

When they arrived, they found a scene of pandemonium. Navvies milled about. Shouting. Cursing. Many had obviously been closer to the blast, and now they shambled about in shock, their clothes scorched and tattered. The station master, his face set in a mask of alarm, ran up and down the platform, frantically ringing a handbell to summon the local fire department. A pall of obfuscating smoke billowed in the air, momentarily revealing and then concealing the scene. Clearly, the explosion had been extremely close. The blast had blown the small ticketing booth to match stalks and pieces of its wooden structure—still burning—lay strewn across the platform. Miraculously, the employee manning the booth had survived, and now he sat splayed on the platform, head lolling atop his shoulders, his eyes stunned and blank. A navvy ran out of the smoke banging shoulders with Conan Doyle as he hurried to get away, his face contorted with shock and terror. As another navvy stumbled out of the smoke toward them, Conan Doyle seized the man by the arm and urged, "What happened?"

The navvy was a young blond man, his face blackened by soot so that his blue eyes appeared startlingly bright.

"Dynamite cart," he gasped. "Bugger blew up. Just like that. Blew to atoms!"

The two friends looked to where he had run from, but the far side of the platform, where the navvies had been laying the new rails, was lost inside a swirling cloud of dense black smoke.

Then they heard it clearly: a drawn-out moan of suffering.

"There's someone still alive in there!" Conan Doyle said.

He made to move toward it, but the blond-haired navvy snatched Conan Doyle by the sleeve and held him back. "Don't go any closer, sir. Too bloody dangerous. There are sticks of unexploded dynamite everywhere. Step on one and it'll blow yer feckin' legs off."

Conan Doyle threw a troubled look at first the navvy and then at Wilde who said with deep emotion, "Whatever shall we do, Arthur?"

The moaning continued. Louder. Longer.

Conan Doyle snatched his sleeve loose of the Navvy's grip. "There's a man out there who is injured. Suffering. I'm a doctor. I took an oath."

This time Wilde seized hold of Conan Doyle's arm and restrained him. "No, Arthur. You heard the fellow. It's too dangerous. Think of your family. Your wife and children. Think of me . . . I always do. No, I shan't allow you to go."

Conan Doyle gently but firmly prised himself loose of Wilde's grip. "I will venture only a few feet to see what I can see. I promise, if it's too dangerous I shall not risk my own well-being."

And with that, Conan Doyle jumped down from the platform and crunched through the deep gravel, plunging into the swirling smoke and instantly vanishing from sight.

The navvy shook his head and looked at Wilde. "Your Scots friend's a brave feller. Bloody sight braver than I am."

Wilde's mouth puckered tight with concern as he muttered, "Alas, brave men tend to share one thing in common . . . an early death."

As the smoke folded about Conan Doyle, day turned to night. The pleasant Wessex countryside vanished, replaced by a burning vision of hell. The smoke was hot with fluttering ash, and firefly sparks that scorched his lungs and daggered his eyes. He snatched out a handkerchief and clamped it over his mouth and nose, trying to filter the choking air, but his burning eyes were left exposed, and soon tears trickled down his cheeks in rivulets. He took another step and visibility dropped from a few feet to nothing. When the smoke cleaved momentarily, he could see that the long grass at the far edge of the tracks was leaping with flames, and all the nearby trees were on fire. Leaves and burning clumps of grass tumbled in the scorching air. With his limited range of sight, Conan Doyle could make out little more than jagged chunks of wood and other debris he could only guess were fragments of the dynamite wagon. The wooden station sign that had once read *Darvington* had been blown to splinters. Only the jagged stumps of the signposts remained, and even they were in flames. As he inched along in the murk, the Scots doctor stepped over a large stick, which turned out to be a naked human arm, severed at the elbow, the fingers ending at the knuckles in bloody stumps.

For a moment he paused, considering whether or not to turn back. Wilde was right: he did have a wife and family to consider. But then a long, protracted moan came from the smoke ahead. By now his lungs burned like furnaces, and he was sweating through his clothes. At times the smoke swirled so thickly about him that he could not see his own hand before his face. With a stab of fear, he realised that he had lost all orientation and was stumbling blind. He groped helplessly for the edge of the platform, but his fingers closed upon nothing.

The moan of someone deeply injured came from somewhere in the smoke.

"Hang on!" he called out. "Help is coming!"

He took five more shuffling steps, his breathing ragged and laboured, his head whirling. He stumbled on something and nearly fell. He glanced down to see what he'd tripped over: a man's boot. Waves of gooseflesh irrupted across his scalp as he noticed there was a foot still in it. Reflexively, he looked down at his own feet and found to his horror that one of his large size eleven shoes was planted directly on an unexploded stick of dynamite and his full weight was pressing it deep into the gravel. It was a miracle the volatile explosive had not detonated. The smoke swirled and lifted momentarily, and dread surged through Conan Doyle's heart at what it revealed: the ground around him was littered with dozens of sticks of dynamite, both ahead and behind.

He was walking through a minefield.

The words of the navvy echoed in his thoughts: *Blow your feckin' legs off* and now, when Conan Doyle tried to lift his foot off the dynamite, his body would not obey.

With shaking hands, Conan Doyle reached down and seized the knee of his right leg. He then physically lifted his foot and set it down again. He did the same with his left leg, and then his right, and so slowly advanced in a halting gait, one knee-quivering step at a time. Finally, he could make out the slumped hillocks of the dead horses, the ragged splinters of wood attached to the hawsers and the wheelless axle—all that remained of the dynamite cart. A splash of red gore stained the ground to his left, along with a grotesque tumble of amputated legs and arms. A torso. And the thing beyond it the size and shape of a soccer ball. No doubt the head of the driver.

He tarried a moment. His rescue attempt seemed futile. *This is madness*, he thought. *I can do nothing here. I must go back.*

But then he heard the moaning again, close by and dimly perceived a figure lying on the ground. Another faltering step revealed that it was the young lad they had seen waving so cockily from his perch atop the dynamite wagon. Miraculously, he was still alive, but the blast had torn off both legs below the knees. Conan Doyle took in the grievous injuries and realised there was nothing he could do for the boy . . . apart from provide some human comfort in his final moments.

"I'm here," Conan Doyle said. Dropping to his knees on the sharp gravel, he lifted the boy by the shoulders and cradled him in his arms. "I've got you, son. You're not alone."

The boy ceased moaning and gazed vacantly at Conan Doyle, his eyes spilling shock. Given the dreadful injuries and massive loss of blood, the lad likely had only a few minutes to live.

"What's your name, son?" Conan Doyle asked quietly.

"Rory, sir," the boy said in a thick Irish accent. "Rory McEwan. From County Cork."

"McEwan? That's a Scots name?"

"Aye sir, that it is."

"My name's Doyle, an Irish name, only I'm from Scotland."

The boy forced a pained smile. "Seems we're both a bit confused when it comes to names, eh sir?"

A thick fringe of dark brown hair had fallen into the boy's eyes, and the Scots author gently swept it aside.

Rory swallowed, and his eyes pooled with tears. "I'm going to die, aren't I, sir?"

Conan Doyle hesitated. It was terrible to speak the truth aloud, but he could not lie. He opened his mouth to speak, but words could not squeeze loose of his tightly clenched throat. Instead, he smiled sadly and nodded.

The boy looked away into the swirling smoke and then looked back into Conan Doyle's eyes. "I don't wanna die, sir. I ain't never kissed a girl. How can I die when I ain't never kissed a girl?"

Conan Doyle spoke in a voice torn to rags, "Are you in much pain?"

"Me legs. They hurt somethin' awful. Please . . . can ye straighten me legs?"

Conan Doyle looked down. The blast had flayed all flesh, muscle, skin and tendon from the bone and the boy's legs were skeletal from the knees down. Gently, hesitantly, he lifted the leg bones and straightened them as best he could.

"Thank you, sir," the boy breathed. "That's better, that is."

Conan Doyle's mind cast about for what he could do to assuage Rory's suffering, but he did not have his medical bag, which contained a phial of opium for just such emergencies. And then he remembered something else. His thick fingers fumbled in a vest pocket, and he drew out his hip flask.

"Would you share a nip of whiskey with me, Rory?"

A smile cracked the boy's filthy face. "Would a true Irishman say no?"

Conan Doyle uncorked his hip flask and held it to the boy's lips, who took a first hesitant sip and then a second, deeper swig. The young man choked and coughed a little and finally gasped, "Oh that's fine Irish whiskey, that is."

Conan Doyle smiled. The whiskey was actually scotch, but he didn't correct him.

"I saw it," the boy suddenly said out of nowhere.

"Saw what?"

"The faerie."

Conan Doyle stiffened. "Faerie? What do you mean?"

"I thought it was a spark at first, for it flitted about the horses' ears and then it swooped over Tom's head and landed on the crate just behind him."

Conan Doyle held his breath. No doubt the boy was in the final moments of life, but he could not help but ask, "A faerie? Are you sure? What did it look like?"

But the boy's face was earnest, and by the brightness of his eyes, he seemed fully lucid. "It looked like a spark of fire. A small star. It landed atop the crate, and then crawled in through the keyhole. And that's when the dynamite went off."

The words surged through Conan Doyle like an electric shock.

The boy looked away blankly and said in a voice of dreadful finality. "I know it's me time, sir. But I'm scared to die. I'm terrible scared."

Conan Doyle squeezed the young man's hand and said, "Rory, I want you to think of someone you love. Someone who's passed over. Think of a loved one, and they will be waiting on the other side to take you to the Summerland. Think of someone whom you loved and who loved you. Do you have someone like that?"

"Aye. Me Uncle John."

"Good. That's it. Think of your Uncle John. He loves you and will look after you. Think only of your Uncle John." Conan Doyle could feel the pulse in the boy's wrist skipping, faltering, growing weaker.

Rory turned his head, and his eyes focused on something a thousand miles away. He raised a trembling arm and pointed into the smoke. "Look there. He's coming. Can you see him, too?"

Conan Doyle followed the boy's gaze, but could see nothing only swirling smoke.

"Is it your Uncle John?"

The boy stammered, straining to lift himself up. "I see him. I see him—No. No. No!"

"What? What do you see?"

"It's not me Uncle John. I see a tall man. Very tall. Very thin. He has horns on his head."

Conan Doyle's heart jolted painfully. Was the boy seeing the devil? "Don't think of the devil, Rory. Turn your mind away from such thoughts. Think only of love."

"It's not the devil," Rory said. "It's him—the Lord of the Fey. It was his faerie what I saw."

"Who?"

"Right there. Large as life. Can't you see him? The Lord of the Fey? Look, he's smiling at us. He's smiling. He's . . ." Rory's body tremored with a sick shiver. The trembling arm wavered and fell. Never to lift again.

Against his own volition, Conan Doyle's head raised to follow where the finger had pointed, eyes scouring the shifting smoke. Suddenly all sound drained away into silence—the cries and shouts of the railroad workers, the frantic ringing of the handbell—became muffled and distant, replaced with a whirring sound, like the susurrus of insects, as the air gelled about him. For a moment something seemed to appear, or rather, there was something not visible: a void, an absence revealed by the smoke swirling about it. He caught a vague impression of a tall figure, eight, no, nine feet tall. The body seemed to be that of a human, but from the head sprouted a great rack of horns like a stag's. It was there for a long moment, and then the fog swirled, and tore apart, letting in blue sky and shafts of sunlight. Then the din of the world flooded back in a rush: the frantic clanging of the hand-bell. The keening cries of seagulls overhead. The urgent shouts of navvies and railroad workers.

He looked back at Rory, but the boy's eyes were wide and staring, and his cooling hand fell limp when released.

Mercifully, Rory had slipped away.

Conan Doyle tried to close the boy's eyes, but they would not remain shut, as if unwilling to give up what they had glimpsed in his final moments of life. In the end, the Scots doctor covered Rory's face with his linen handkerchief, and then laid the body carefully upon the ground, pillowing the boy's head upon one of the hard iron rails he had probably helped lay. He rose shakily from his knees and trudged back through blinding clouds of sulphurous blackness. Along the way, he passed a gang of navvies crawling on their hands and knees, picking up the loose sticks of dynamite and passing them back to a foreman who gingerly settled them in a small wooden box. The navvies shouted out a warning to Conan Doyle, but he shambled past them oblivious, careless of where his feet fell.

Gradually, the smoke pall thinned and then suddenly peeled back, revealing blue sky, the ruined Darvington station, and Oscar Wilde, who stood waiting with pair of uniformed constables, wringing his clasped hands with worry.

"Thank God, Arthur. I thought for a moment you'd perished. You-your face. It was dreadful wasn't it?"

Confused and disoriented, Conan Doyle stammered, "I . . . I . . . Yes, I . . I am not entirely certain what I just witnessed."

A man stepped forward, blocking Conan Doyle's view of Wilde. Still deeply shocked, it took the Scots author a moment to recognise the stern face of Albert Lawless. The Police Chief's face was set in a mirthless grin as he clapped a hand upon the Scotsman's shoulders and growled, "Arthur Conan Doyle, I arrest you on suspicion of murder."

It was only then that reality registered: Wilde was not wringing his hands; he was manacled in handcuffs, and a moment later Conan Doyle was, too.

A MURDER, A BODY, AN ARREST

"Where are they taking us?"

"To the gallows, no doubt."

"Tell me you're joking, Oscar."

The two friends were jostling about on the hard bench of a Black Mariah that jounced and swayed as it clattered along Darvington's narrow lanes. With their hands pinioned at the wrists by iron cuffs that had been personally over-tightened by Lawless himself, both men were unable to brace themselves and slid bruisingly about on the polished plank seat, slamming their shoulders into the walls and occasionally being hurled to their knees and then struggling to get back up without the benefit of being able to use their arms.

The Mariah's barred window threw stripes of shadow across Conan Doyle's face as he peered out at a framed rectangle of blue sky uglily stained by the squid ink blackness of smoke still purling up from the ruined railroad station.

"Why are we under arrest?"

Wilde fixed his friend with a face of doom: "They have discovered a body. A young girl's body."

Conan Doyle turned ashen at the news. "Dear God, no! Did they say who it was?"

Wilde shook his head. "The body has yet to be recovered. The local doctor has been sent for to make the identification. Lawless is taking us there now. And then no doubt we will be dragged to the police station where he will beat a confession out of us."

Conan Doyle's mind was awhirl with the events of the last few hours and he was at a loss for words.

The bone-shaking ride in the Mariah seemed brutal and endless. Finally, the wagon lurched to a sickening halt, the barred door was thrown open and the two friends manhandled back into the daylight. Conan Doyle was surprised to find that they were not back at *The Old Rectory*, but instead were standing on a winding lane that climbed a low hill. From this height they could look down upon the tiny town of Darvington, the coastal cliffs and the grey-green waters of the English Channel beyond.

Lawless clambered down from the driver's seat on the Mariah and threw a curt nod to his stout constable, grunting, "Fetch them." And then strode away following a foot-worn path that plunged into a thick coppice of trees.

"See here!" Conan Doyle shouted at Lawless' retreating back. "Are we under arrest? What is the charge? You have to tell us what we're being charged with!"

But the only answer he received was a prod in the kidney from the stout constable's truncheon, who growled, "Get along, the pair of ya."

Conan Doyle and Wilde shared a look of alarm. They were being led into dark woods by a police chief who seemed careless of their legal rights. The pair dallied, genuinely afraid of what might happen once they were out of sight in the trees. The constable prodded Conan Doyle in the kidney a second time, even harder. In response the solidly-built Scotsman turned and gave the constable a look that curdled the air between them, leaving the unspoken threat hanging: *Do that one more time . . .* The look was so ferocious that the fat constable actually retreated a step, but then he jerked his head to show the way and grunted, "You heard the Chief."

The bird song that had been constant fell silent as they entered the trees. Lawless led the way along a dirt path vascular with tree roots that veered left and right and then plummeted down a slope. Up ahead, they could hear the mutter of water tumbling over rocks. Suddenly they emerged from the trees to find the River Wyrme in front of them. The waters were wider here than at The Old Rectory, and faster, boiling around large boulders as the rushing waters dropped in a series of stepped waterfalls.

A white haired man stood looking on from the stony bank, and by the suit and black Gladstone gripped in one hand, apparently, the local physician. As Conan Doyle and Wilde took up their position on the river bank, the doctor looked up at them and the Scots author saw a flash of recognition in his eyes. Apparently, at least someone in Darvington knew who they were. Then the doctor's eyes dropped as he went about his grim task. The thin young officer stripped down to his smalls and waded into a pool of waist-deep water. He sloshed toward the nearest drop, where a section of tree trunk had become lodged between two large boulders, creating a funneling crevice in the rocks. Instantly they saw something trapped beneath it.

A small body.

Naked. Ghastly white. A child's thin leg was visible beneath the cold, clear water, undulating with the current.

"Oh, no!" Wilde breathed, "Please, no."

"I prayed this was a mistake," Conan Doyle said.

The young constable ducked low, plunging both his arms under the chill water as he struggled to tie one end of a rope about the small form. And then, slowly, and with the aid of Lawless and the stout officer, the body was pulled free against the force of the current and floated to the edge of the river.

Dear God! It's the darling little blonde girl, Conan Doyle thought, despairing. *Please tell me it's not Philomena!*

The young constable slipped both his arms beneath the tiny body and lifted it dripping from the icy water. Moments later the sodden form had been laid upon a blanket stretched out on the stony bank.

Wilde had turned his back on the grim spectacle. With a quaking voice he asked, "I cannot look, Arthur. Which of the girls is it?"

The local doctor leaned over the dead child and combed the tangle of wet hair from the girl's face with his fingers. It took everything Conan Doyle could muster to allow his eyes to drop to take in her features.

"Dear God," he gasped.

"What?" Wilde importuned. "What? Is it . . .?"

Conan Doyle leaned close to his friend. "Though this is still terrible, I believe it is neither of the girls we met just this morning."

The stout officer let out a pent up breath and muttered, "It's Jenny Dawkins. Jenny vanished a month ago. Now we know where she's been all this time. Poor darling."

The body was naked apart from a frayed length of cord lashed so tight about the neck it cut deep into the flesh.

Some kind of garrotte, Conan Doyle thought.

A moment later, the doctor rose to his feet and shook his head sadly as he confirmed the identification. He took out a handkerchief and wiped his eyes. Conan Doyle had little doubt that the doctor probably attended at the little girl's birth and now, tragically, he would be conducting her autopsy. At the news, Lawless' face contracted in a bitter expression, as if a pellet of cyanide lay dissolving upon his tongue. But there was hatred in his eyes when he looked up, first at Conan Doyle and Wilde, and then turned his gaze to the stout officer. "Remove the cuffs," he grunted, indicating the two friends with curt nod.

When the cuffs came off, Wilde and Conan Doyle stood massaging their chafed wrists, numb fingers tingling as the blood rushed back in.

"Don't leave Darvington," Lawless barked at the two friends, "until the Shepherd girls have been found."

"How are we to get back to town?" Wilde asked.

Lawless could not keep the curl from his lip as he eyed the Irishman and snarled, "You've got legs, haven't you? Walk!"

~

This time the two friends' luck did not hold out and the-rag-and-bone cart did not miraculously appear. So they were forced to trudge all the way into Darvington, where the two had booked rooms at the Claremont Hotel. It had been a harrowing day, and combined with the long hike, both men were physically and emotionally drained when they finally limped into the hotel, footsore and weary. Each man retired to his own room to take a bath and catch a nap before dinner. Conan Doyle finished his bath and lay on the bed, wrapped in a towel. But, enervated as he was, every time he closed his eyes the events of the day carouseled in his mind: the picnic with the two Shepherd girls, Lawless' scowling visage, the drowned body of the little girl, and especially the face of Rory, the young navvy. And suddenly he was back there, kneeling in the gravel of the railroad siding, black smoke swirling about him, Rory's cooling body cradled in his arms. But then something moved through the smoke toward him: a hollow space of nothingness—a towering form with immense antlers sketchily drawn by the smoke curling about it. Suddenly, Rory's cold body jerked alive. The dead eyes flickered open and looked up into Conan Doyle's face. And though the cyanose-blue lips did not move, Rory's voice resonated in his head, "It's him. The Lord of the Fey. He awaits upon you."

THE MEETING OF THE RAILROAD COMMITTEE

C onan Doyle's eyes snapped open as he startled awake. Somewhere knuckles were rapping upon a wooden door, while a man's voice called out, "Sir, your wake up call." He stared about the hotel room, dopy and disoriented, mouth cottony, as his mind grappled to remember where he was. He sat up and looked about him, noticing the open suitcase on the stand, his discarded clothes draped across a chair, the Midg camera sitting on a tabletop. His mind floundered no more as he reacquired his bearings. He had only meant to doze, but at some point he had slipped imperceptibly into deep sleep. He threw a look at the bedside clock. It was just past six o'clock, the time he had agreed to meet Wilde for dinner.

W hen Conan Doyle followed the hotel porter's directions to the dining room's large, high-ceilinged space, he found that the room was being disassembled. Hotel staff scurried about dragging dining tables to the one side of the room and setting out a line of chairs facing the front of the room, where a small table topped by a speaker's lectern had been set up facing the line of chairs.

Thinking he had overslept and missed dinner, he cast a doubtful glance around the empty room, and only then spotted Oscar Wilde sitting at a solitary table in the gloomy back reaches. Wilde had not yet noticed Conan Doyle's arrival, for he was absorbed in reading a letter, shuffling the papers and re-reading, and then sighing and reshuffling them.

Conan Doyle fell into his seat with an "Ooof." Wilde glanced up from his letter only long enough to hoist a bottle of champagne from its ice bucket and charge Conan Doyle's champagne flute. "For once you're late, Arthur, whilst I am on time. I do hope we're not in danger of setting a new precedent."

"Sorry. Overslept." The Scots author lifted his champagne glass and took a sip. "That's lovely. What is it?"

"*Perrier-Jouët*," Wilde replied, never taking his eyes off the letter.

Conan Doyle harrumphed with surprise. "*Perrier-Jouët*? Out here in Darvington? I am amazed!"

Wilde smiled at his response. "Oh, I assure you, Arthur, it didn't come from the Claremont's meagre cellar. That is why I always take the precaution of fetching my own supply when traveling in the provinces."

At the news, Conan Doyle's mouth fell open. "You mean to say you brought champagne all the way from London?"

"A mere six bottles."

Conan Doyle spluttered with outrage, "Six bottles!"

"Obviously, I would have fetched more, but we are traveling and that always demands some sacrifice—you above all people should know that, Arthur."

"Six bottles of champagne! No wonder your sole item of luggage was so confounded heavy!"

"Obviously, I had to leave some room for the brandy and whisky."

Conan Doyle's only response was a strangulated grunt of exasperation. Before he could pursue the matter, a stooped waiter cowered to their table and handed them a pair of menus.

"Kitchen's about to close, gents," the waiter said. "You'll have to be quick—the dining room's been reserved for a meeting."

Wilde recoiled at the man's words. "Be quick?" he said. "Be quick? My man, I can assure you that I have never *been quick* in my life. Oscar Wilde has three speeds: Stroll. Meander. And dawdle."

Conan Doyle was tired and merely wanted some food and a glass or two of wine. His eyes skimmed the menu with a cursory glance. "I'll have the roast beef and Yorkshire pudding," he grumbled and thrust the menu back into the waiter's hands.

"Be quick?" Wilde chundered irritatedly to as he scanned the menu. "Did you hear that, Arthur? Be quick! A command you give to a dog!" He studied the menu as if it were a contract with the devil for his immortal soul. Conan Doyle could practically see the exasperation squeezing from the waiter's pores. "I shall plump for the lamb," he finally announced. "And I'd like it rare."

The waiter nodded while scribbling on his pad. "Excellent choice, sir. How rare?"

Wilde tossed him an insouciant wave. "Just wound the beast and drag it in here."

The waiter paused, pencil hovering over pad, mouth open, but then shook his head and resumed scribbling. "Very good, sir," he replied and skulked away.

The two fell quiet for a time. Conan Doyle tried to relax as he watched the hotel staff finish their preparations—they were clearly preparing the room for a meeting of some kind. But as he drifted into reverie, his mind returned again and again to the faces of the Shepherd girls, and then, more darkly, to the waterlogged corpse of Jenny Dawkins.

He shook the image from his head and sat up in his chair, returning his attention to Wilde. The Irishman was still absorbed in his letter, his soft brown eyes moving left to right. At the end of each line he released an audible sigh. He finished the last page, rapt, and then reshuffled the pages, starting over at the beginning. Naturally, the author of Sherlock Holmes was curious as to the letter's content, but he could see that it was a private letter, not a piece of business correspondence, and so he tightened the straining leash on his curiosity.

But when Wilde finished the letter and began over for a fourth time, Conan Doyle could no longer hold back and asked, "What on earth is in that letter, Oscar? You keep re-reading it and sighing over every other line like a love-sick schoolgirl."

Wilde paused to take a sour-faced sip of champagne before answering, "It is from my young friend, Bosie."

"Bosie?" Conan Doyle said doubtfully and then checked himself. The Scots author spent his days immersed in his own writing and, apart from scanning newspaper headlines for potential story ideas, paid scant attention to gossip or tittle-tattle. Still, even he had caught wind of Wilde's preoccupation with the son of the Marquis of Queensbury, although he could not bring himself to believe the rumours—after all Wilde was a married man with a fetching wife and two young boys—and so he had put the relationship down to one of Wilde's unorthodox manias. But still, it was becoming the source of scorching gossip, and so he broached the subject with the caution of a mountain climber sliding a foot forward to test the stability of a precipitous Alpine ledge. "By Bosie, you mean the young Lord Alfred Douglas?"

"Yes," Wilde said matter-of-factly, "we went up to Oxford together last weekend."

Conan Doyle absorbed that titbit of information for a moment and obliquely commented, "You do spend a lot of time at your old alma mater." He forced a chuckle. "Trying to recapture your salad days? Eh, what? Early triumphs? Former glories?"

Wilde shook his head as his long face drooped, grew stricken, and then he spoke in a tragic voice as brittle as cracked crockery: "I go there to visit the grave of my youth. It is buried there. Walled up like one of Poe's tragic personae behind every brick and stone." He unleashed a heartbroken sigh. "If only I could recapture those days. My brio. My vigour. My ardour for life. Oh, for the passion and purity of youth!"

"You wish to become like your own character, Dorian Grey, who never ages and who is always in the bloom of eternal youth?"

"Ah, if only," Wilde muttered. He grimaced and shook his head.

"But instead I am his antithesis. Instead, I am the portrait of festering morbidity collecting cobwebs in the attic, blemished by all my sins and transgressions and the careless insults age heaps upon us all." He looked across the table at his friend with wet, gleaming eyes. "Oscar Wilde is growing old, Arthur. Once I was young and beautiful. Now I am becoming all that I detest: Fat. Crapulous. Ponderous and bumbling in appearance and movement. An unsightly and decrepit thing that deserves to be shut away from the public eye, locked in an attic for none to recoil at." He suddenly ducked forward and presented the top of his head to Conan Doyle's gaze. "Look at my hair, Arthur. Just look!"

Conan Doyle lurched back in his chair but examined Wilde's hair with puzzlement. "What am I looking at?"

"Note the grey hairs. Each morning I find more . . . and, of course, I pluck them. I found four this morning. And then there are the sagging jowls, the crinkling eyes. I am collapsing into mortality like a ship-wreck sinking into the sea."

Conan Doyle could see that Wilde was settling into a Byronesque funk and attempted to jolt him free of it before he devolved from prose into poetry. He chuckled good-naturedly and said, "Oh, you do so exaggerate, Oscar. Age has its compensations."

Wilde lashed him with a killing look, demanding, "Pray, name one."

"Oh, I can name quite a few: wealth, success, fame. You have achieved all three."

Wilde shook his head morosely. "Pshaw! Age has taught me to understand the triviality of such meaningless baubles. The devil could gladly have my soul. I would sign any Faustian deal. I would give it all up, renounce everything—the world itself—for a second sip from the chalice of youth."

"I too enjoyed my younger days," Conan Doyle countered, "but I am happy with the man I have grown into. And as for past glories, well, they are in the past. I haven't darkened the doorway of my old university in Edinburgh in years. Too many ghosts."

"Ghosts?" Wilde shuddered. "Please do not speak of ghosts when I am very nearly become one. Why the other day, my barber pointed out the many grey hairs in my beard as he shaved me. He laughed about it as if were a source of amusement!"

"We all are growing grey these days."

"But it is nothing to shrug at, Arthur. It is an omen. A portent. An irrefutable sign that Oscar Wilde is hurtling toward an unknown grave. But it's not just me I mourn for. Think of the terrible loss to the Arts. To the Theatre. Think of the voice of Oscar Wilde silenced for all eternity."

"Yes," Conan Doyle muttered, swirling the champagne in his glass. "I'm thinking of that very thing right now. "

Fortunately, Wilde's morose soliloquy was interrupted as their dinners arrived, and a famished Conan Doyle savaged his roast beef and Yorkshire pudding with gusto, knifing great chucks of gravy-dripping beef and forking it into his mouth. And despite his protestations, Wilde devoured his lamb in a lion-like fashion, in between swallowing morose mouthfuls of champagne.

Suddenly the dining room's double doors banged open, and a large group of men surged in. Most were middle-aged, well-dressed business types puffing cigars, and sipping snifters of brandy. A hubbub of blather crowded into the room with them. Then two gentlemen, one short, one extremely tall; one in plush purple robes, the other in a black frock coat and top hat, strode into the room following the main group. They shouldered their way through the crowd and made straight for the two chairs waiting behind the small desk. The top-hatted gentlemen calmly removed his hat, set it upon the desk, and then lowered himself into a chair, where he sat with the grandeur and stiff posture of a giant statue of Zeus in a Greek temple. The gentleman was bald on top with a long, patrician skull, sucked-in cheeks, and a massive square jaw bristling with enormous mutton chop whiskers. Conan Doyle recognised him from a photograph in *The Strand Magazine*.

"That gentleman is Bartholomew Stonethwaite," he whispered to Wilde. "One of Britain's most famous and best-regarded railroad engineers."

The Irish wit squinted at the imposing figure and commented, "I can see that the gentleman is forged of iron and rivets just like one of his bridges."

The short man in the purple robes had been talking to someone standing behind him, and now he turned to face the crowd and raised his arms to call for order. Both Conan Doyle's and Wilde's jaws dropped when they saw who it was—Albert Lawless, wearing the purple robes and gold chain of office that proclaimed him as mayor.

"Lawless!" Conan Doyle grunted in dismay.

"Oh, dear Lord," Wilde exclaimed. "He's both the mayor *and* the chief of police? Is that allowed?"

Conan Doyle shrugged helplessly. "We are in the provinces now."

Wilde set down his knife and fork. "Well, that's torn it. Call me rash, but I am not ordering pudding."

Conan Doyle shot his friend a look. "Lawless hasn't noticed us. We must be discreet and not draw attention to ourselves."

The advice drew a look of umbrage. "Arthur, you are addressing Oscar Wilde. Be discreet? Surely, you must realise you ask the impossible?"

Lawless snatched up a small wooden gavel and banged it down on its block.

"Gentlemen," he called out. "If you would all kindly take your seats then this meeting of the Darvington railroad investor's society can come to order."

The hubbub drained away as members dropped into their seats, one by one—all except for one man who bounced up from his chair and shouted, "Another accident today, Mayor Lawless? Yet another?" The man did not wait for a response and shared his belligerence with the room. "This new railroad route will end in disaster like all the others." He flourished a sheaf of papers and flapped them wildly above his head. "These shares are worthless." He tossed the handful of papers into the air and they fluttered down around him. "We have all been swindled. This new track will never be finished. The train shall never run!"

The man's proclamation was a stick rattled in a hornet's nest and unleashed a roar of protest from the other members. Many surged up from their seats, waving their shares and bellowing at Lawless, who visibly beetled beneath their catcalls.

Finally, the railroad man calmly stood. Once on his feet, his great height was obvious. He towered over Lawless, and must have been six and a half feet tall. He hooked his thumbs behind the lapels of his frock coat and stared down at the seated members like a stone idol before a tribe of benighted savages. One by one the men fell quiet and sank back into their seats. When the room fell totally silent, he spoke in a resonant voice.

"My name is Bartholomew Stonethwaite. If there is any man in this room who does not yet know me, I am by trade an engineer. What's more, gentlemen, I am a stranger to the idea of failure. I have tunnelled through the highest mountains in England, Wales and Scotland, built iron bridges that span the mightiest waterways, constructed giant aqueducts that have joined canal systems across the deepest valleys. This gorge of yours is a trifling matter to an engineer of my experience. Even as I speak, my best surveyor is at work mapping a new route. Mark my words, once the preliminary blasting is complete, it will take less than a year before the first non-stop train from London pulls into Darvington station. In one stroke, it will cut the rail journey by more than an hour. On the day that happens the fortunes of Darvington will change forever."

A short, balding man on the front row was unimpressed. "With respect, sir, we have been hearing these promises for three years now. And yet in that time, we have seen a score of mishaps, accidents and catastrophes. And every time more delay. More expense for the shareholders. And just today the worst accident to date: the Darvington station blown to bits."

Another man surged to his feet. "You are the fourth engineer to make these same promises. And for all their efforts it ended in disaster. The first railway trestle still lies at the bottom of the gorge. And then there have been landslides, rock falls—"

A stout man interjected, "Bogs across which the rails were laid one day and sank without a trace overnight. Always more hold-ups and more costs for we shareholders to bear. For all your skills, Mister Stonethwaite, I fear you will fare no better than the *genius* engineers who preceded you."

And then a man in a rumpled suit, clearly drunk, swayed to his feet and shouted, "It's the fault of the Fey. They don't want us building in their gorge. It's the Fey, I tell you!"

Lawless scorched the man with his basilisk's stare. "Sit down, Jeremiah, you're in your cups . . . again."

The crowd erupted into brays and catcalls.

"There is always a risk when dynamite is involved," Lawless shouted over the babble of the crowd. "Nothing of any great import was lost today that cannot be replaced within a week. The station sign. The ticketing office . . ."

"What about men's lives?" The question, shouted aloud, drove the room to a resonating silence. It was Conan Doyle's voice, and when Wilde looked, he saw to his surprise that his friend was on his feet and in high dudgeon, large hands balled into fists, a vein throbbing dangerously at his temple. "I was there today and witnessed the carnage for myself. Two horses and two men blown to bits and a young man who bled to death as I looked on, helpless to assist. I would hardly dismiss that as *nothing!*"

"Who said that?" Lawless bellowed, scanning the crowd with a manic stare. "I know that voice. Who said that?"

The crowd of shareholders parted before Lawless' scorching gaze, which now fell upon Conan Doyle and Wilde.

"You two!" Lawless roared. "What are you doing here? This is a private meeting. Are you here to spy upon us!"

Wilde remained sitting and calmly raised his hand. "I must point out that Arthur and I were already in the middle of our meal when you gentlemen arrived. So if anything it is *you* who are spying upon us. And, incidentally, I highly recommend the lamb. Quite excellent and very fresh. It was still bleating as I chewed. I shall likely gambol as I leave the room."

Lawless became apoplectic with rage. "Out! Get them out of here!"

A pack of shareholders suddenly descended upon Wilde and

Conan Doyle and, moments later, both men were dragged from the dining room, manhandled through the lobby, and hurled outside by a multitude of hands. With considerable chagrin, the two authors stood in the middle of the High Street dusting themselves off and readjusting their disarrayed attire. Wilde raised an ironic eyebrow at Conan Doyle and remarked, "What was that you said earlier, Arthur? Ah yes, now I recall: *We must be discreet? We must not draw attention to ourselves?*"

Conan Doyle dropped his head guiltily and fussed with his tie. "Yes. I'm sorry. I did say that. It's just that I could not sit there in silence. Not when I witnessed a boy die before my eyes today."

Wilde looked around. It was past twilight. Flames flickered in the gas street lamps and the sun had recently set, leaving only a bloody stain on the horizon. "Well, what now? I was looking forward to an after-dinner whiskey in the hotel bar, but it appears we shall have to enjoy a digestif elsewhere." He peered doubtfully along the descending slope of the gloomy High Street, with so many of its storefronts boarded up and dark. "*If* there is another place in this wretched little town."

"Come along," Conan Doyle said, striking off. "We'll find something. With this latest revelation, we need to discuss strategy. Disappearing girls, the swarm of railroad accidents, all the talk of faeries and the Fey, I somehow feel all these events are connected."

The pair tramped the length of the High Street but found only two abandoned and boarded-up pubs. They were about to give up and turn back for the hotel when a shabbily dressed man tottered out of a narrow alleyway and weaved precariously past the two friends dragging behind him a vapour trail of alcohol fumes.

"Well there you go," Conan Doyle said. "That chap has obviously just left a drinking establishment, somewhere down that alley." They both squinted into the dark maw of a narrow ginnel. A single brazier burned in the distance, but otherwise the way was impenetrably dark. "Looks a bit dodgy, Oscar. Should we risk it?"

"I have no doubt it is a bit dodgy," Wilde replied, "but I am dangerously close to sober. Needs must."

The two friends probed cautiously into the shadowy passage and after a few moments their eyes adjusted enough to make out a battered doorway and a pub sign crookedly nailed above it.

As they pushed through the door a low rumble of conversation and the reek of unwashed bodies, beer slops and pipe tobacco, bowled over them. They tripped down two worn steps to a stone-flagged floor and found they were in a tiny pub whose low-beamed ceiling promised an evening of bumped foreheads and minor concussion. Most of the drinkers were roughly dressed men hunkered around the bar clutching tankards frothing with ale. Nearly all sucked upon clay pipes and jetted smoke from their nostrils so that the cramped space, seen through a roiling haze of tobacco smoke, resembled a smudged charcoal sketch come to life. A pair of lanterns swinging above the bar and a sad scatter of candles sputtered out the only meagre illumination. All conversation stopped when the two authors stepped inside, as every pair of eyes turned to take in the newcomers.

Hunkered against the far wall were three crude tables—empty beer barrels with crooked three-legged stools for seats, the fat stub of a tallow candle guttering in a puddle of wax atop each barrel. Now the two friends made their way toward them, being careful to duck beneath every beam. They drew up their stools, and a moment later the barkeep abandoned his post and hurried over to greet them.

"Are you sure you gents are in the right place?" the barman asked in a low voice as he made a great show of wiping the top of the beer barrel table with a rag. "Only we got a bit of a rough bunch in here tonight."

Conan Doyle eyed the ten or so men crammed shoulder-to-shoulder around the bar. By chance, the two authors had found the watering hole where the navvies building the railroad came to drink away their aches and pains each night. The standard navvy uniform comprised heavy canvas trousers so stiff with filth they could have stood up in a corner on their own, and heavy blouses with sleeves rolled up to show meaty forearms tattooed with cuts and scars and worn-in grime that a soap-less scrub in a bucket of cold water could not wash away. Most wore rumpled hats and greasy caps jammed down over their ears, with dense, untrimmed black beards and mutton chops of werewolfian proportions. Since the friends' arrival, the navvies' conversation had drained to silence, and most stood eyeing the two friends suspiciously. A palpable sense of threat tightened the atmosphere.

"Perhaps we should just have the one drink," Wilde suggested.

Conan Doyle concurred and said to the barkeep, "Two tankards of your best ale."

The barman bustled away and returned a moment later, setting down two greasy pewter mugs capped with foam. The two friends "Cheersed" each other, banging tankards together and raised the mugs to their lips. Conan Doyle took a sip and found the beer to be bitter, sudsy, and heavily watered down.

At that moment, three of the navvies drifted away from the rest and took up position a threateningly close distance away.

"Now how do you fine gennulmen find your way in a place like this, eh?" The words were spoken with disdain by a rough brute who appeared to be the leader. He was taller than his two cronies and had a face like a voracious pike, only with more teeth. Animal cunning glittered in his eyes.

"My name is Wilde. This is my friend . . ."

"Doyle," Conan Doyle quickly put in, "Arthur Doyle."

"Irish, names, eh? Funny, only neither of ya sounds Irish."

"I hail from Dublin. South of the Liffey," Wilde explained," Only I've lived in London for some years now . . . obviously after graduating Oxford."

"Obviously after gratchulating Oxturd," the man parroted in a mocking voice. "Then you'll be here with the railroad bosses, I take it. Come down to see to things, have ya? Lay us all off? Take on another gang of navvies after the latest accident?"

"No, nothing of the sort—" Conan Doyle started to say when he saw a short, stout piece of wood slip from the man's sleeve into his hand. Suddenly all three men ringing their table were similarly armed —shillelaghs, short wooden clubs designed to cudgel the brains from someone.

The instigator leaned over and snatched up Conan Doyle's tankard, made a stomach-turning gargling sound, and then spat in the drink, swilling the white oyster around before banging the tankard down in front of Conan Doyle.

"Let's see ya drink it." The leader demanded.

Conan Doyle looked down at the gooey white oyster bobbing obscenely in the tankard, and then back up at the man, who was slapping the shillelagh in his palm.

"I said drink it," the man repeated and his two cronies echoed the taunt, calling out, "Drink it, ya English scum!"

Conan Doyle threw a quick glance at Wilde, who gave a barely perceptible shake of his head: *NO.* Both authors were big men, physically strong and both had boxed at university. They could handle themselves in a fair fight. But the three navvies facing them down were armed with clubs. They would be lucky to survive the beating.

All these thoughts raced through Conan's Doyle head in an instant. He looked up for help from the barman, but a group of navvies deliberately shifted their position to block his view. No help from there, then. After a moment's pause, Conan Doyle reached forward, slipped his thick fingers through the cold pewter handle and began to lift the tankard from the tabletop. Wilde tensed in the chair next to him, ready to spring up, guessing that Conan Doyle was about to hurl the beer in his antagoniser's face. The pub door was a good ten or fifteen paces away. He hoped the element of surprise would give them a chance to fight their way through the mêlée.

"Brody!" All froze as a voice boomed from somewhere behind the gang of men.

A figure came barging through the crowd, shoving men aside. At first, Conan Doyle did not recognise the young blond man, who was tall and broad in the shoulders.

"What mischief ya up to now, Brody?" the man challenged.

From the way Brody's lip curled, it was clear the men knew each other. "Stay out of it, O'Brien. Me and the lads is just havin' a drink with these two fine Lundun gennulmen."

O'Brien scanned the spit wad bobbing in the tankard, the two besieged friends, and the navvies clustered around and guessed what was going on. His eyes fixed upon Conan Doyle with clear recognition and he nodded at the Scots doctor. "This here is the fella what went to help our poor young Rory."

"So?" Brody sneered.

"So, this is a brave man who walked through a field of unexploded dynamite. And all to ease the suffering of one of our own."

O'Brien's fierce look threw down the gauntlet. "That's the bravest damn thing I ever seen. Where were you hiding at the time, Brody? I noticed you were feckin' scarce while the rest of us were pickin' up what was left of Tom and the horses."

Brody did not answer, but stood chewing the insides of his cheeks, before snarling, "You've got a big mouth on you, Fergal O'Brien. You wanna watch yerself. Been a lot of accidents lately. Be a shame if you got the sharp end of a pickaxe through the back of yer skull, now wouldn't it? Sure yer old mammy would weep to hear that news."

Brody left the threat hanging and slouched away, pushing through the crowd of navvies back to the bar, his two cronies trailing behind.

Fergal O'Brien reached out a calloused hand to Conan Doyle. "Let me shake a brave man's hand, and buy you a drink."

Conan Doyle stood and shook O'Brien's hand and said. "I'm honoured to shake your hand, sir, but I insist that I buy you a drink, as you have just come to our rescue."

Minutes later the uproar in the pub had subsided, and Fergal O'Brien had drawn up a stool at the beer barrel table with Conan Doyle and Wilde. The two friends narrated the events of the Darvington railroad investor's meeting they had blundered into and their prompt removal.

"Before we were thrown out," Conan Doyle said, "Oscar and I heard the story of the many calamities and accidents. Is that all true?"

Fergal O'Brien swallowed a mouthful of beer, wiped the foam from his lips on his filthy sleeve, and leaned in close. "Accidents? Oh, there's been accidents, all right. And more than just a few." He threw a cautious glance toward the bar, where Brody was holding court with his cronies and hurling filthy looks his way. "I've worked the railroads since I was a nipper. It's a dangerous living. Feckin' dangerous. There's always accidents." He crossed himself. "But never like this. The first trestle was near to done when the whole bloody lot give way and fell into the gorge. Then there's the everyday mishaps: lads getting their hands smashed, feet crushed, or catching the point of a pickaxe through a boot. Or a horse of a sudden takes boggarts and drags a man to his death. There's been a dozen or more killed or maimed in the six months I been working the railroad. And we're the second gang to work it. The first gang downed tools and walked off the job after two fellers got killed in one day. And now the dynamite wagon." He shook his head. "It's beyond bad luck. It's unnatural. Ya might say cursed. And it seems to get worse the farther we go into the gorge. There's many a navvy who thinks he'll never live to see this railroad finished."

"What do you think is the cause of all the accidents?" Wilde ventured. "Is it all just bad luck?"

Fergal took another bite of his beer and grew reflective. "We navvies are a superstitious lot, but I been to a few places in Ireland, a few bad places where no one ever lived or dared go. Like I said, bad places. You know what I mean. I think the gorge is a bad place. We hear the locals whisper it. They say it is the domain of the Fey. That the gorge is a place of fairy forts and strange springs where water gushes up out of the ground. Great waterfalls that drop into bottomless drowning pools with whirlpools that can suck a man down to his death."

Conan Doyle fixed Wilde with a meaningful look that said: *the Fey again!*

Hours later, the London authors tumbled out the pub door in the good company of Fergal and two other navvies whose names were Colm and Barry. While Conan Doyle and Wilde were only the slightest bit tipsy, the Irish labourers had taken advantage of their free-spending friends and were pleasantly drunk. The group swaggered to the gas-lit High Street where they paused to say their farewells.

"A goodnight to you grand fellas!" Fergal said. "And mind how ya go now."

Wilde said the traditional Gaelic farewell "Slain abhaile," and the parties split up and went their separate ways, Conan Doyle and Wilde tramping the upward slope of the High Street back toward the Claremont Hotel, Fergal and his friends stomping downslope to the poorer part of town where for three pennies a night they slept on the cold stone flags of an unheated room.

They had only been gone a second or two when three shadows emerged from the gloomy ginnel that led to the pub they just left. Brody led them out and fixed his eyes upon the retreating backs of Conan Doyle and Wilde. He watched the two authors for a few seconds and then made a clicking sound in his mouth. His two cronies fell into lockstep, and they began to follow. As they reached the High Street, shillelaghs were snatched from their hiding places down boots and shaken loose from coat sleeves.

Brody growled, "Let's see how the fine Lundun gennulmen fare without Fergal to protect 'em."

The two authors had a head start so the Irish navvies quickened their pace to catch up, but as they were closing in on the two unsuspecting friends, they heard the clopping of hooves and then a hulking form loped from the shadows ahead.

"Look lively, ladsssss . . . " Brodie started to say but then the words dried to dust in his mouth.

As it stepped into the gaslight, layers of darkness peeled from the form, which proved to be a stag: a male deer of huge proportions. The beast clopped slowly to the centre of the High Street where it paused and turned to face them. Up close they could see just how enormous it was. The stag stood seven feet tall at the shoulder, and the enormous rack of antlers spanned the full width of the street.

"Jaizus!" one of the cronies whispered. "That's the biggest feckin' deer I ever laid eyes on."

The vision froze them on the spot. The stag stood motionless, fixing the men with a baleful stare. The flickering gaslights sparked a liquid gleam in its eyes.

Staring directly at them.

"That ain't nuthin' natural," the other man whispered.

"Shut up, Eoin," Brody growled. "It's just a stupid wild creature what's wandered into town and got itself lost. It's like more scared of us than we of it."

As if to contradict him, the great stag took a step forward. And another. And then the beast snorted, pawed the cobbles with a hoof, *scoof-scoof*, and lowered its great rack of antlers. And then it trumpeted a roar and sprang forward.

The navvies let out a collective howl of terror and took to their heels, running pell-mell down the slope of the High Street. With the drum of galloping hooves close behind, each man vied to outrun his mates. Brody dared not snatch a look behind until he reached the bottom of the hill. But when he finally risked a quick glance over his shoulder, the giant stag had mysteriously vanished.

WHERE IS WYRME-HALLOW?

Conan Doyle spent a sleepless night wrestling the bedclothes into knots and so at first light he toileted, dressed, and left the Claremont to restlessly perambulate the length of the High Street. When the hands on the town hall clock pointed at nine and twelve, he began hammering on the front door of *Ye Old Curiosity Shoppe*. The "Closed" sign still hung in the door, but after five minutes of fruitless knocking a wizened face floated up to the far side of the glass and stood peering out at him like The Ghost of Christmas Past. Finally, a key rasped in the lock and the proprietor of the shop let him in.

"Anxious for your photographs, I see."

"Yes," Conan Doyle blustered. "Are they ready?"

The shopkeeper wandered away into the depths of the shop, and indicated with a wave for Conan Doyle to follow. The old man stepped behind the counter, reached down, and brought up a small rectangular box, which he set on the countertop.

"I try not to look at the images," the shopkeeper explained, "as a courtesy to my customer's privacy, but I could not help notice that many of the images were spoiled."

Conan Doyle's spirits plummeted. "Spoiled?"

"Did you load the camera?"

Conan Doyle shook his head. The old shopkeeper nodded sagely. "I thought not. Whoever loaded the camera did not understand the proper use of a changing bag."

Conan Doyle thought of the two Shepherd sisters. It was likely they did not even know what a changing bag was. It would be lucky if any of the photographs were not light damaged.

The shopkeeper slipped the photographs into a small cardboard envelope which he fastened shut with a stray length of twine. He made as if the hand the envelope to Conan Doyle, but then snatched it back at the last moment. "I must point out that payment is the same for spoiled photographs or good, as the developing costs are the same."

"Yes, of course," Conan Doyle said. He drew out his billfold, removed a large note, and dropped it onto the counter, and then snatched up the envelope of photographs and stuffed it in his leather satchel.

"Wait, sir," the shopkeeper called as Conan Doyle hurried for the door. "What about your change?"

"Keep it," the author yelled over his shoulder as he fled through the shop door. Conan Doyle was in a fever, hoping the photographs would contain evidence of faeries, or at least a clue to the Shepherd sisters' whereabouts.

∿

Oscar Wilde was breakfasting on a plate of Darvington oysters when Conan Doyle rushed into the Claremont's dining room. After the railroad meeting of the night before, the tables had been dragged back to their original positions, and the Scotsman threaded his way through them to Wilde's table.

"I have them, Oscar. I have them!"

Wilde paused in mid-slurp, an oyster shell held to his large lips. He set it back down upon his plate and wiped his fingers on a napkin. "Ah, Arthur. I see you are characteristically ebullient and bursting with enthusiasm. Please remember the hour and my delicate constitution. I am feeling particularly fragile this morning."

"I have them, Oscar—the photographs from the Shepherd girls' camera. Now we might find a clue as to where they've gone."

"What's that? Camera? Photographs? I'm sorry, Arthur, but you really must slow down. As I have observed many times, only dull people are brilliant at breakfast."

The envelope had been secured with a length of twine and Conan Doyle's thick fingers wrestled with the knot to no avail. Eventually he gave up and fishing out his small pocketknife he cut the string. He carefully unloaded the stack of photographs onto the linen tablecloth and began to study them.

"What on earth's that?" Wilde drawled. "It looks like a swirling vortex seen from Alice's point of view as she fell down the rabbit hole."

Conan Doyle pushed aside the clutter of breakfast plates while they both studied the photographs.

"I don't know what it is," Conan Doyle confessed. "It's clearly an image blurred by motion. Maybe one of them was spinning around while the image was taken. At any rate, I must caution you, these photos were taken by young girls hardly proficient in photography. They likely did not know how to use a changing bag to load and unload the film. It is likely many images were spoiled. Hopefully there should be a few that are all right. Or at least that's what I'm praying for."

Hands shaking with excitement, Conan Doyle turned over the next photo. But it too was an amorphous spiral of blurred motion as if the camera had been spun around. He was about to lose hope when he flipped over the third photograph.

"At last!" he cried.

"What is it?"

"I don't know. I was about to ask you."

"I believe it is upside down, Arthur."

"Ah, yes."

Conan Doyle turned the photograph the correct way up and both men studied a sharp image. It was a street scene: a tiny dirt lane meandering through a clutch of thatched roof cottages. No human figures appeared in the photo.

"It appears to be some sort of rustic village."

"It doesn't look like Darvington."

"Not at all. The image seems . . . somehow old, as if the photograph could have been taken a hundred, no two hundred years ago."

Conan Doyle flipped over the next photo and exulted, "Ah ha!"

This scene was of a packhorse bridge spanning a narrow stream. In front of the bridge the stream formed a wide pool upon which a raft of ducks floated. Crouched beyond the bridge was a thatched roof inn of some antiquity with an inn sign hung over the front door.

"Good Lord," Wilde said. "The village looks positively medieval. The only thing missing is a ducking stool for trialing the local witches. What does the inn sign say?"

Conan Doyle squinted. "Hmmn. Can't quite make it out." Suddenly remembering, he rummaged his leather satchel and brought out his magnifying glass. After a few moments study, he handed the glass to his colleague. "Take a look, Oscar. Tell me what you see."

The Irishman frowned doubtfully, but complied, taking the magnifying glass from Conan Doyle and hunching over the table as he peered through it at the photograph. "It looks like . . . the Green Man," he read aloud. "And it has a painted image of a green man made out of leaves." Wilde looked up from the photo. "But all this means nothing. We have no idea if the girls ever visited this place."

Conan Doyle flipped to the next photo and both men gasped aloud. As if in rebuke to Wilde's comment, the photograph showed both of the Shepherd girls standing on the humpback bridge. Wilhelmina, the older brunette girl, was leaning with her elbows on the bridge wall; the shorter Philomena stood beside her, her face barely peeking above the wall of the bridge. But most amazing, both girls were looking up and smiling at what appeared to be a cloud of bright sparks dancing in the air around them. Conan Doyle snatched the magnifying glass back from his friend and squinted at the shapes, releasing a gasp. "They looks like faeries all right." He looked at his friend, his face flushed pink with excitement. "This is our proof, Oscar. I am sure the girls have run off to this village and here is proof positive of the existence of faeries."

Wilde knitted his brows in consternation. 'You cannot be certain of that, Arthur. We have no idea where or when the photographs were taken. They could have been taken a month ago . . . or a year ago."

Conan Doyle stabbed a thick finger on the photograph. "No, you're wrong. Look at what the girls are wearing—the same frocks they wore the day we met them."

"Still, you cannot know that—"

"Look at Philomena's dress. There's the jam stain."

The observation silenced Wilde, who pondered a moment. "But the girls were left unsupervised for scant minutes. How would they have had time to walk to this village, take a photograph and return the camera to the picnic blanket?"

Conan Doyle shook his head in bafflement. "I have no idea, but if that's so then the village must be close to Darvington. Very close." He picked up the first photo and studied it through the lens of his magnifying glass. "We have two clues as to the girls whereabouts. "They are in a small village somewhere—it looks typical of the villages around Exmoor. And the village has an inn—*The Green Man*."

Mad with excitement, Conan Doyle's eyes roved wildly about the photograph. But then he noticed something at the base of the bridge: a rectangular lump of granite with something chiseled into its broad, flat face. "Wait!" he said in a tight breath. "There's a marker stone here inscribed with lettering." The stone was dark with lichens and moss, which made the incised lettering difficult to make out. He moved the magnifying class back and forth to focus and enlarge the image. "I can make out some letters: W . . .Y . . . R . . . M . . . E . . ." He lowered the glass and looked up at Wilde with an exuberant smile. "It says Wyrme-Hallow. At last we have a name for our village!"

"That's half the battle," Wilde conceded. "Now we just need a map."

"Wyrme-Hallow?" The clerk behind the post office counter said in a voice over-brimming with mirth. "Did you say you're looking for Wyrme-Hallow? I'm sorry to inform you that your search for Wyrme-Hallow is likely to be a fruitless one."

"And why is that?" Wilde asked.

The clerk tilted his head and the round spectacles perched on the end of his nose caught the light and hardened into opaque disks. "Because there is no such place! Wyrme-Hallow is a story we tell our children to make them behave. Be a good girl or good boy or the faeries will come and carry you off to Wyrme-Hallow. It's a local legend. A tall tale." The clerk's head swivelled up to the wall clock and back.

"And now it's the dinner hour and we are closed." The man chirruped a laugh and slammed down the frosted glass window. Something about the fellow and his mocking tone struck Conan Doyle as familiar and he wished he'd had time to scrutinise the clerk's fingers.

They could still hear the clerk's laughter as the post office door closed behind them.

They received much the same response at the greengrocers, the butchers, and at the hotel reception. The general consensus was that Wyrme-Hallow was as real as Lyonesse or Camelot.

"Now what?" Wilde asked as they tramped the descending slope of the High Street. "How do we find a place that doesn't exist?"

"It seems we have come upon a dead-end," Conan Doyle said in a voice both tired and deflated. He had placed all his faith in finding a clue to the Shepherd girls' whereabouts in the photograph, and now he was stymied. He looked up and noticed they had reached the dark ginnel that led to the tavern they had visited the previous night. He threw a glance at his friend. "I'm parched," he said. "Drink?"

Wilde looked at him aghast and replied, "You offend me by asking."

The two plunged into the shadowy ginnel and were mounting the steps to the tavern door when Conan Doyle suddenly stopped so that Wilde bumped into him.

"That pub sign," the Scotsman said, pointing to the wooden board hanging beneath the eaves. "I couldn't read it in the dark . . ."

Wilde squinted up at the sign, which was weather-faded and badly in need of repainting. The ghosts of missing letters read: *The Horned Man*. Floating above was a crude and rather child-like depiction of a cross-legged figure with horns sprouting from his head.

Thanks to his classical education, Wilde immediately recognised the figure, "Cernunnos, the Celtic horned god. He typically represents the cycle of life and death. Often depicted as a stag. One of Lady Wilde's favourites. I told you of my mother's love of folklore and faeries."

For a moment, Conan Doyle could not speak. The figure bore an uncanny resemblance to the shadowy form he had glimpsed in the smoke of the burning railroad station.

"What is it, Arthur? You look as if you've seen a ghost."

Conan Doyle looked at his friend with a stricken expression and muttered, "I think I have."

The tavern owner had a similar reaction to the postal clerk.

"Wyrme-Hallow?" he chortled as he finished buffing a pewter tankard with a rag and hung it next to its sibling on a hook above the bar. He wiped his nose on the same rag and said, "Can't go to Wyrme-Hallow 'cause it don't exist, that's why." He smiled, displaying an absence of front teeth.

"Wyrme-Hallow is just a bit o' local folklore—somethin' ya threaten the kiddies with." He assumed a patronly face and wagged his finger at an imaginary naughty child, repeating the familiar admonition they'd heard all over town. "If you don't behave, the faeries will come and drag you off to Wyrme-Hallow."

"I can tell ya about Wyrme-Hallow if you loik," a rustic voice spoke from the shadows. The two friends turned to seek the owner of the voice and finally made out a dimly lit figure ensconced in a narrow cubbyhole. The man, who had a long shabby beard seemed strange at first, but then he leaned forward, the shadows fell away from his crook-nosed face, and both friends recognised the rag-and-bone man.

"Ah," said Wilde after a moment's confusion. "I didn't recognise you without your horse and cart."

The rag-and-bone man sucked at a clay pipe with a gurgling sound, blew smoke up at the ceiling, and then offered, "If you're lookin' for Wyrme-Hallow you won't find it. It was an old, old story back when I was a nipper. I reckon it's just a ruin by now."

Conan Doyle scented a lead. "A ruin? But the village still exists in some fashion?"

The old man made to speak, but then gripped his throat and coughed drily. "Oi can't speak so good, me throat's that dry."

Recognising the old rascal's ploy for cadging a free drink, Conan Doyle waved to the barman who pulled a pint and then carried it over and set it down before the old man. Conan Doyle and Wilde watched as the octogenarian took his first long, swallow of beer and then wiped his mouth on his sleeve and flashed his higgledy grin.

"At's better," he said. "Oi can talk now. Anyway, there's only old folk such as me can even remember Wyrme-Hallow."

"And why is that?" Wilde asked.

"'Cause folk what goes to Wyrme-Hallow don't never come back. Once they seen the village, the Lord of the Fey makes them forget their home. Trust me, you don't wanna go to Wyrme-Hallow."

"So you know where it is?"

The old man shook his head. "No, not exactly. But then I've never been fool enough to go look. If you follow the river upstream, you'll find it."

"How far?" Conan Doyle asked.

The rag-and-bone man frowned. "How far? I dunno. Five or ten miles or so."

"Do you know where we might find a map?" Wilde asked.

"The rag and bone man pursed his lips and looked doubtful. "Mebbe. But the village ain't been lived in for two hundred years or more. It ain't gonna be on no modern map."

As the two authors stepped into the sunlight and the tavern door closed on the rag-and-bone man's guttural laugh, Wilde looked to his companion and asked, "It seems, Arthur, we need a two hundred-year-old map of Darvington. Where on earth would we find such a thing?"

Conan Doyle frowned, pondering a moment, but then a smile spread beneath his walrus moustache.

~

"Welcome again, friends," the shopkeeper of *Ye Olde Curiosity Shoppe* greeted the pair as they stepped into the store. "Back for more photographic developing?"

"Not this time," Conan Doyle said as they strode up to the counter. He turned and pointed to the window display with his cane. "That old map in the window. I should like to purchase it."

The shopkeeper's brows knotted in puzzlement. However, he was a shrewd bargainer and managed to keep his poker face. "I am very sorry to say, sir, that items in my window are for display only and strictly not for sale."

This time, Conan Doyle was not in the mood to haggle. Without a word, he reached into his breast pocket, drew out his billfold and teased loose a large banknote, which he unfolded and dropped on the counter.

The shopkeeper's eyes flew to read the denomination. £5! Five whole pounds, a ruinous amount of money. Although his mouth remained fixed, the corners of his eyes crinkled with a smile as he said mildly, "Would sir like me to wrap it?"

Ten minutes later the map had been carefully peeled from its frame and was spread out upon Conan Doyle's bed in the Claremont Hotel as the two friends pored over it. Like many old maps, this one was simply drawn, with the names of towns, villages and hamlets rendered in the antique calligraphy of the time. Compared to modern iterations, the map had little geographical detail, but the River Wyrme was shown, and Conan Doyle scanned with his magnifying glass following it inland until he came to a name he had been hoping to find: Wyrme-Hallow, which was marked with a strange symbol—a snake swallowing its own tail.

"The Oroborus," Wilde noted, "the oldest alchemical symbol."

"Yes," Conan Doyle agreed, " and a symbol of eternity. I wonder why the map maker chose that symbol? But there is our proof, Oscar," he said triumphantly. "Wyrme-Hallow is a real village."

"Or *was* a real village." Wilde countered. "The old fellow did say it was likely just a ruin by now."

"From the photos the Shepherd girls took, it did look fairly intact." He traced the path of the River Wyrme from Darvington inland. "This old map is obviously not to scale, but it looks to be only ten miles upstream from *The Old Rectory.*"

"Ten miles?" Wilde said doubtfully. "A long way for little girls to run away to. Plus the photos did not show a ruin. The village looked very much lived-in."

"I agree." Conan Doyle chewed the edges of his walrus moustache as he pondered. "But there's only one way to find out. We must make a journey to Wyrme-Hallow."

"This time by a proper carriage, I assume. Since we arrived in this benighted town our sole transit has consisted of a rag-and-bone cart and a police Mariah. I could not possibly survive another bone-shaking contrivance."

"I can assure you, Oscar, we will not be travelling in any such contrivance."

"That's a relief," Wilde said, but then noticed Conan Doyle's face. "Oh. Ah. What, then?"

"No roads run through the gorge. The only way in is on foot. In other words, we shall need to hike."

Wilde's face projected a vision of horror. "Hike. As in walk? Ten miles? Propelled only by our own legs! Could you not just kill me with a gun or a knife like any considerate murderer?"

"Don't fret. I imagine it will be a very scenic hike." He eyed Wilde's immaculate trousers, cummerbund, and white blouse. "But I think we will need to dress and equip ourselves for such a journey."

"Prepare? How so? A team of native bearers? A sedan chair for me to ride in? At the very least a copious supply of brandy!"

Conan Doyle frowned. "I'm mainly thinking of stout boots and heavy walking trousers, with haversacks for food and possibly a change of clothes. Although I second your suggestion about brandy. No doubt a flask of brandy will prove welcome."

"Dash the journey, I need the brandy just thinking about it!"

An hour later the two friends were rummaging through piles of used clothes in *Ye Curiosity Shoppe*. Conan Doyle was pleased to find some stout canvas walking trousers, a cambric shirt, a farmer's wide-awake hat and a worn but serviceable haversack. He was shocked and horrified when Wilde sprang from the shadows of the *Shoppe* wearing leather lederhosen, complete with suspenders and a Tyrolean hat. The outfit had been tailored for a man of average height and girth, but most of Wilde's substantial six-foot-three frame was fleshily bulging out of it. Most concerning was the alarming amount of pale white Irish thigh that the extremely short shorts failed to cover.

"Look, what I discovered in a dusty niche, Arthur, an authentic Tyrolean walking ensemble. I cannot believe my good fortune. It is like new and perfect for our little expedition." Oscar Wilde slapped his bare thigh and danced a Tyrolean jig to show off his new togs. "Isn't it perfect? I believe it's from lower Bavaria."

Conan Doyle could not disguise his wide-eyed look of horror. "It certainly looks to be rather tight around lower Bavaria."

Wilde's smile dissolved. "I see from your expression you are clearly envious. I'm sure you are disappointed that I found it first."

"Yes, I admit I am sorry you found it first. Very sorry."

Wilde stopped and studied Conan Doyle's face. "You don't like it, do you?"

"The lederhosen are somewhat, ahem, revealing, Oscar. You are showing rather a lot of leg."

The Irishman's brows knotted in a look of concern. "You think the sight of Oscar Wilde's manly legs on full display might draw censure from the locals?"

"I'm afraid the sight of your lily white thighs might frighten the horses."

With a huff, Wilde flounced away to change clothes. In the end, Conan Doyle kitted him out in some baggy-legged trousers, perfect for walking, a pair of heavy boots with hobnail soles, and a workman's shirt that he instantly complained would be "far too scratchy for my delicate skin," even before trying it on. The Irish aesthete kept up a steady stream of objections and complaints during the entire episode, but was mollified when he found a large slouch hat, which he drew upon his head at a rakish slant and spent a long time striking dashing poses and admiring his multiple reflections in the many dusty mirrors hanging on the *Curiosity Shoppe* walls.

"Right," Conan Doyle said as they finally stepped out the door of the shop, both arms laden with their newly-purchased walking attire wrapped in brown paper and tied with twine, "Now we're all togged out for walking. In the morning we'll shop for a few provisions, some bottles of water—a few pies or pasties and some apples—and we'll be all set for our expedition into the gorge. Tomorrow we journey to the semi-mythical Wyrme-Hallow."

THE JOURNEY TO WYRME-
HALLOW

It was 9:30 a.m. by the time Wilde and Conan Doyle had shopped the local grocers to purchase food for their journey. Finally, fully provisioned, they tramped up the steep slope of the High Street, but when they reached the train station they were met by a procession coming from the opposite direction.

Leading the way was a glossy black hearse drawn by two coal-black mares with red plumes atop their nodding heads. Two top-hatted undertakers rode shoulder-to-shoulder upon the seat, and two grooms trudged behind, both clutching brooms draped in black crepe. As the glass-sided hearse clattered by, the two authors caught a glimpse of the tiny coffin inside and realised whose funeral it was—Jenny Dawkins, the poor little girl whose body they had witnessed being fished from the river. The Reverend Troutt (with two t's) walked behind the funeral grooms. He was dressed in his clerical vestments; a simple wooden cross hanging from his neck by a stout cord, his hands clasped something—presumably, a Bible (his hands were hidden by the voluminous sleeves of his vestment). Behind the Reverend came the little girl's parents, both broken in grief, clinging to one another like shipwreck survivors, the mother sobbing uncontrollably and the father openly weeping.

"A sight to conjure pity," Conan Doyle muttered quietly as the sad procession filed past.

But then behind the grieving parents trudged none other than Albert Lawless, whose mayoral robes had been replaced by a white clerical surplice with a simple wooden cross dangling from a stout cord instead of his mayoral chains.

"Lawless is apparently also involved with the church!" Conan Doyle gasped in surprise.

A local man standing beside Conan Doyle overheard his observation and commented, "Aye, Lawless is the verger of our church. Such a godly man."

The man's wife was standing close by and now she added. "Such a tragedy, too, with Chief Lawless having lost his own daughter."

At the news, Conan Doyle's head snapped around. "Did you say that Lawless' daughter also went missing?"

The woman nodded sagely. "She was the first girl to go missing. Almost a year ago."

The husband then put in. "And then he lost his wife shortly after."

The woman dropped her voice to a whisper as she leaned forward and spoke in hushed tones. "They reckon she did for herself—found hanging by a rope. I'm sure the grief of losing her little girl was too much for her."

Conan Doyle and Wilde shared a stunned look at the revelation.

As they walked away, Conan Doyle whispered to his companion, "What do you make of that, Oscar? I suppose we should not jump to conclusions."

"Jumping to conclusions is the only exercise I get these days."

"It is a strange coincidence. Our first meeting was brief, but I got the clear impression that Lawless already enjoyed a degree of familiarity with Mrs. Shepherd, as if he were courting her affections."

"A woman apparently abandoned or widowed with two young girls. I wonder how long Lawless has been ingratiating himself with Mrs Shepherd?"

"Slow down, Oscar. We should not allow our suspicions to run away."

"Too late! My suspicions have already jumped on a train and are headed for the next county!"

At the hearse drew level with the train station, even the navvies repairing the station ceased swinging their picks and shovels as they dragged off their caps and bowed their heads in respect. Wilde and Conan Doyle trudged through their midst, picking their way along the edge of the newly-laid tracks, walking boots crunching in the deep gravel. They reached the point where the tracks plunged into the lane cut through the trees at the edge of the station. The funeral procession passed by, the navvies went back to swinging their picks and shovels. But as the two writers passed, one of the navvies stopped as he pushed a wheelbarrow laden with gravel and eyed them closely.

"Brodie!" a churlish voice snapped the navvy from his reverie. He looked around. "We're not paying you to stand around idling," the foreman bellowed. "Shift yer lazy Irish arse."

Brody flung a contemptuous sneer at the foreman. He spat on his hands and once again gripped the handles of the heavy wheelbarrow and lifted. He wheeled the barrow over to where a team of navvies were shovelling gravel.

"Who were those two, then?" one of the men asked Brodie.

"Our fine gennulmen friends from the pub the other night."

"Begorrah. Where d'ya reckon they're goin'?"

"Dunno," Brodie grunted. He tipped the barrow up, spilling gravel onto the ground. "But I know someone who'd be interested to know."

Conan Doyle and Wilde reached the spot where the pathway cutting through the trees forked in two directions. The right-hand fork was the first path cut through the trees, but was subsequently abandoned after the trestle collapse. That had been over a year ago, and already the ground was sprouting bushes and saplings where the trees had once been cleared. The left-hand fork was the new path the engineer had chosen, and fifty feet of shiny iron tracks had already been laid.

Wilde and Conan Doyle followed the right-hand fork until they reached a steep drop where they stood on the precipice of the gorge, looking out. A hundred feet below lay the smashed and broken timbers of the railroad trestle that had disastrously collapsed. Many of the timbers had since been salvaged, but the shattered remnants remained, half submerged beneath the waters of the fast-flowing River Wyrme that boiled around it.

"This is it then," Conan Doyle said. "The gorge." He gazed upstream, "And up there, somewhere, is Wyrme-Hallow." He looked at Wilde, whose face portrayed a premonition of doom. "Come along, Oscar. It can only be a few hours walk."

"*Only* a few hours?" The Irishman released a pained grunt, his face glum. "Ugh, my feet ache already."

A large crow settled into the branches of a nearby tree, fluttered its wings and scolded them furiously, as if issuing a warning. For a moment the words uttered by Rory in his final moments of life echoed in Conan Doyle's mind: *The Lord of the Fey awaits you* . . .

The Scotsman shivered as a chill breeze blew through his clothes. And with that the two friends stepped off the cleared land onto a worn sheep path and began the long plod down the steep descent into the gorge.

"Ahhh!" Oscar Wilde moaned, after only a hundred yards. "Now your true intent is clear, Arthur, you mean to murder me! First the precipitous descent into the pit of damnation, and then a forced route march."

Conan Doyle swallowed a grimace and stood chewing the ends of his moustache as he stared at the forlorn Irishman who had flopped down on a large rock, snatched off his hat, and was furiously fanning his large face with it.

Conan Doyle looked up at the precipitous path they had just marched down. They had barely travelled two hundred yards and already Wilde was whingeing and complaining.

"Come now, Oscar," Conan Doyle wheedled. "You can't be that tired. We have scarcely begun!"

"Look at this body, Arthur" Wilde demanded. "I have only achieved this physique through a scrupulous regimen of diligent idleness and energetic sloth, with a spartan avoidance of all forms of exertion."

Conan Doyle knew it was true. Wilde's unhealthy lifestyle and strict avoidance of any form of exercise was legendary. He chain-smoked, often lighting his next cigarette from the one he had yet to finish smoking. In London he was known to hail a hansom cab if he needed to go but a hundred feet down the road. Now his scrupulous avoidance of any form of exertion was manifesting itself and Conan Doyle began to fear they would not make it to Wyrme-Hallow before the sun set.

$\sim$

Twenty minutes later they reached the *The Old Rectory* where they had first encountered the Shepherd girls and their mother. Conan Doyle spotted a solitary figure sitting on the lonely bench and nodded at Wilde.

"The poor Shepherd girls' mother," he commented.

Wilde shook his head sadly. "Let us hope we can soon reunite the lady with her daughters."

The two friends were on the far side of the river from the rectory and so did not bother to wave or call out to Mrs Shepherd, but left her to her lonely vigil. They moved on, and soon entered the gorge proper, where the River Wyrme boiled over rapids while the stony banks steadily climbed above them. As they proceeded the river grew wider, the gorge deeper, and the current swifter and stronger. Then the walls of the gorge climbed as they reached a series of pools where the river waterfalled down in a tripping series of steps. The final pool was disturbingly familiar to the two authors, for it was the place where the drowned body of Jenny Dawkins had been discovered. Neither man said anything, but they exchanged grim looks and accelerated their pace as the urgency of their mission sunk home.

After another half hour, the gorge had tripled in size such that the river boiling through the stony canyon required them to shout to be heard above its roar. And then the scenery turned from pastoral to formidable, as they passed precipitous waterfalls that cascaded hundreds of feet down the sides of the gorge into catchment pools. Here and there they rested, watching dippers and chaffinches snatching insects liberated from the spray. Conan Doyle exulted in the sensory overload of the gorge, the somnolent din of the cascades, the sparkle and gleam of rushing waters, while occasionally they'd catch a river otter frolicking in the pools or glimpse a fox skulking along the banks.

Wilde, however, was less sanguine about their sojourn with nature, and complained that the spray was making his Turkish cigarettes damp. The next three miles took two hours, as Wilde insisted on resting after shambling only a few hundred yards at best. His complaints especially galled Conan Doyle since they were walking on smooth rock shelves clinging to the river side. Apart from the odd climb, the way had been mostly flat, at the most a gentle incline, with a cool breeze and easy going underfoot. Yet Wilde's complaining never ceased: the heat, the flies (of which there were none), of his feet, of his thirst, of the abrasiveness of the country air (which Conan Doyle found refreshingly silky when drawn into the lungs and which Wilde insisted upon polluting the fresh air by chimneying one of his cloying Turkish cigarettes.

Suddenly, from somewhere up ahead, they heard the shriek and scream of young girls.

Both men froze and exchanged a look.

"Could that be them?" Wilde asked.

"It definitely sounds like young girls at some kind of horseplay. It could very well be the Shepherd sisters. Come on, Oscar, let's hurry!"

Conan Doyle gripped the sides of his rucksack to steady it as he trotted along the stony path as fast as his feet could move, leaving Wilde blundering behind. As the gorge unwound before him, he rounded a bend and discovered an oval pool of water. The rocky sides of the gorge soared higher than before, and the pool was fed by a mighty cascade that dropped eighty feet. Stirred by the tumultuous current, the surface of the pool swirled with multiple whirlpools that formed, spun, and were torn apart by other whirlpools in a constantly forming and reforming battle. This was easily the highest waterfall they had seen yet, and the plunge raised a chilly cloud of spray and mist. Conan Doyle stopped to look frantically around, chest heaving with exertion. His eyes scanned left and right, but there were no young girls to be seen and after a moment's inspection of the pool, with its deadly whirlpools, it was obviously not a place where children would play in the water.

Wilde finally lumbered up, red-faced and panting. As he scrambled up the path to join Conan Doyle, he snatched off his hat and used it to fan his perspiring face.

"Any sign of the girls?" he panted.

At that moment several birds perched on ledges about the gorge burst into flight, squawking and screaming as they flew away.

Conan Doyle nodded at the disappearing birds. "Unfortunately, I think that's what we heard."

Wilde finally turned to take in the scenery and let out a gasp. "Good Lord!" He exclaimed. "What a stunning vista! I could easily believe I had been transported to the Swiss Alps. This looks very much like the Reichenbach falls your Sherlock Holmes fellow tumbled into whilst wrestling with Moriarty!"

The two men stood staring down into the mesmerising maelstrom of churning water.

"I have yet to check the map," Conan Doyle said, "but I believe we have arrived at the place called the 'Devil's Cauldron.'"

THE DEVIL'S CAULDRON

"Devil's Cauldron?" Wilde repeated. "An apt name. It looks like a Doré illustration from *The Divine Comedy*, right down to the infernal whirlpools!"

Conan Doyle spotted a chunk of deadfall wood lying close to the path, a small branch, and now he stooped to retrieve it. He raised the branch high, then flung it with a snap of the wrist so that it *whicker-whiskered* end-over-end. Both men watched it fall . . . fall . . . fall . . . into the boiling cauldron. It hit the water and bobbed for a few seconds. Then a whirlpool snatched hold of the branch and spun it around and around. But then another whirlpool formed, only spinning counter-clockwise, and wrested it from the grip of the original whirlpool. They watched as other whirlpools appeared, snatching the wood back and forth like watery devils toying with their prey until the chunk of wood was finally drawn under the pulverising downrush of the cascade and hammered deep into the depths. They stood watching for several minutes, waiting for the branch to bob back up to the surface, but as buoyant as it was, the branch had vanished forever. Wilde let out a shuddering breath and shouted over the rumble and hiss of falling water, "If you're considering a dip, Arthur, I recommend that you find another spot."

Wilde's comment made Conan Doyle realise just how close he was standing to the edge of the sheer drop, and now he took a prudent step backward.

The spray made it too chilly to linger so close to the edge of the cauldron. Conan Doyle looked around and spotted a convenient flat rock clear from the falling spray. The rock formed a natural table, convenient for picnicking. The two friends flopped down and dug into their haversacks. They lunched on scotch eggs, pasties, apples, and bottles of cold water (which Wilde complained about, although he did provide a post-prandial pick-me-up by handing around his hip flask [filled with the top-drawer scotch purloined from the Reverend Shepherd's darkroom).

Lunch attended to, Conan Doyle pulled his Casebook from his haversack and paged through it until he found the place where he had pasted in the map that contained the route to Wyrme-Hallow. It had pained him to treat an antique map with such disregard, but in truth, the map was sun-bleached, brittle, and as desiccated as a dead leaf— far beyond any hopes of restoration.

"This Devil's Cauldron is one of the few physical features marked on the map," he announced to his companion. "If you look, Oscar, you will find that we are nearly at our goal." He handed the Casebook to Wilde who took it from him and perused the map with a doubting face.

"What is this?" Wilde asked, his finger tapping a spot far above the village.

"Ah yes, I saw that," Conan Doyle answered. "It says beneath it 'anchorite's hut.'"

Both men knew well what an anchorite's hut was. Anchorites were Christian ascetics who withdrew from secular society to live a life of religious contemplation. They typically dwelled in crude huts located in wild and remote places, far removed from the temptations of human society.

"An anchorite's hut, eh?" Wilde remarked wistfully. "That could be handy. Should my next play be pilloried by the critics, it's good to know a bolt-hole I could escape to."

Conan Doyle fixed Wilde with an arch smile. "And how many cases of *Perrier-Jouët* do you think you could drag to such a remote location?"

Wilde pulled a grim face. "Good point, Arthur. Oh well, never mind."

After returning the Casebook to his haversack, Conan Doyle crunched his last bite of apple and strode to the edge of the Devil's Cauldron, where he tossed the apple core into space and watched it plummet into the frothing water and vanish. Failing to repress an involuntary shudder—just the thought of falling into the cauldron gave him the heebie-jeebies—he nodded to Wilde and the two set off again following the rocky footpath.

From here on in, the path pitched steeply upward as the two began to scale the sides of the gorge, which was so steep in places they had to grab handfuls of ferns growing alongside the footpath to help them clamber their way up. Fortunately for Conan Doyle, Wilde was too short of breath to expel any upon complaining at this point, and they finally dragged themselves up to the shoulder of the gorge, where they found a pathway through the woods that was most likely an animal trail. The going underfoot was loamy and provided a spongy and forgiving surface to walk upon. The path veered deeper into the woods so that they lost sight of the river, but could still hear the muted roar of the rushing waters. The two authors found that walking through the woods was like walking back in time, as the forest became untamed, riotous and wild.

"These woods seem as though they have never been felled," Conan Doyle noted. "This must have been what the British Isles were like, thousands of years ago, when the island was still part of the continent and the first hunter gatherers crept silently between the trees, an arrow knocked to their bowstrings."

"I fear it is likely that some of those ancient tribes are still lurking about!" Wilde added, nervously scanning the surrounding trees.

Despite knowing better, it was possible to believe such a pronouncement, as the two authors found themselves overwhelmed by the sight of behemoth trees swathed in thick carpets of green moss, while the forest floor sprouted poisonous-looking red mushrooms and giant eruptions of toadstools. Frequently, they felt the hair-raising sensation of eyes upon them, and glimpsed the feral faces of foxes and deer that peered timidly at them through the trees.

"I have never seen woods like this before," Wilde said in a wondering voice. "I feel like we are in one of your scientific romances, journeying back to the time of the dinosaurs."

"I think we are, Oscar," Conan Doyle replied. "I believe these are ancient woods, never felled, never farmed—pristine and unmolested by humans. I did not know such a forest still existed in England."

Suddenly, something large flashed through the trees to one side of the path, accompanied by a crash of snapping twigs. Wilde froze on the spot, wide-eyed as he asked in a stretched-taut whisper, "There aren't any bears in England, are there?"

Conan Doyle had also glimpsed the shape and heard the thrash of breaking foliage. "I believe there haven't been wild bears in England since Shakespeare's time. You must know the famous stage direction from *A Winter's Tale*: exeunt, pursued by a bear?"

"Ah, good. Then that definitely wasn't a bear I just saw . . . even though its proportions were rather bearish."

The eyes of both men were rigidly fixed on the still-quivering branches where they had just glimpsed a blur of movement.

"No . . . no, it could not have been a bear," Conan Doyle muttered, sounding utterly unconvincing even to his own ears. "Most likely, just a deer."

"Thank goodness. I am greatly relieved to hear that, although I did not know they had seven-foot-tall deer In England."

After sharing a wide-eyed look of concern, both men set off walking again, notably faster.

But they had gone only a few hundred years when Conan Doyle looked up and muttered, "Oh my! Now look at what's coming to greet us!"

When Wilde glanced up at the forest trail ahead, his mouth dropped open.

Moving toward them was a dense white wall of fog surging

through the trees, swirling about the trunks and tangling in the tree tops as it hurried toward them at a hideous speed. The fog was blindingly dense and dissolved the trees, the woods, the sky, so that the entire world was abruptly swallowed up and vanished. Neither man had ever seen a fog move so quickly—it was on them before they had time to react and surged over and around them in a blinding wave of whiteness so dense that they could not see a hand before them.

Suddenly disoriented, both men gripped each other's sleeves and hung on. "What do we do, Arthur?" Wilde asked from somewhere inside the fog. Although the two men were standing side by side, each appeared to the other as only a vague silhouette.

"I believe the fog is spawned by a sea breeze front," Conan Doyle answered. "We're close to the coast. When a cold current of air from the sea moves inland, it can cause these sudden fogs with the resulting drop in temperature. It may pass in minutes, or it may not abate for hours. I think we must keep going, no matter how slowly, and hope we come out of the other side."

Wilde answered in a shaky voice, "I fear that we may come out the other side just as we step off the edge of a sheer cliff!"

"That is a distinct possibility," the Scots author conceded, "so I recommend you keep your eyes on the trail ahead."

Despite the risk, the two men continued creeping along, eyes glued to the trail as it slowly, slowly, unraveled before them. From the moment the fog enveloped them, the temperature plummeted, and they went from balmy summer's day to late autumnal chill. Both were dressed only in shirt sleeves, and had no warm clothing with them. Soon, chilled to the marrow, both men shuffled along, hugging themselves for warmth, teeth chattering uncontrollably.

After ten minutes of this, Wilde asked, "You don't by chance have an overcoat in your haversack do you?"

Conan Doyle laughed despite his chattering teeth. "Sadly no, although—" he was hit by a sudden thought. "Although we do have our hip flasks."

"Ah, capital idea, Arthur!"

The two men stopped to draw out their hip flasks, although they had difficulty stilling their shaking hands as they unscrewed the flasks and quaffed a mouthful.

"Ah, that's helping!" Conan Doyle breathed after a few healthy swigs.

"Yes, it is. Good thinking, Arthur."

Temporarily warmed, the two friends edged on another twenty feet. Suddenly, the swirling fog grew lighter and began to fray at the edges. And then the last tendril of fog tore loose of the trees and the world burst back into view. Conan Doyle and Wilde looked about themselves, squinting at the sudden brightness.. After the fog, the world seemed surreally vivid, incredibly sharp, bright, and bursting with colour.

"Thank heaven!" Wilde exclaimed.

They noticed a sunny patch of ground on the trail ahead and hurried into it, where they stood basking in the sunlight, feeling warmth flowing back into their bones.

"That was very strange," Wilde noted.

"Yes, I agree. But now that sunshine feels absolutely—" Conan Doyle suddenly trailed off. His eye had been caught by the flash of something bright on the forest floor near his boot, and he bent down and picked it up.

"What have you found, Arthur?" Wilde asked.

Conan Doyle perused the object, brows furrowed, and then showed it to his friend.

"A pocket watch!" Wilde exclaimed.

"Yes," Conan Doyle said. "An expensive one at that—plus it looks brand new." He held the watch to his ear, shook it, frowned in puzzlement, and then shook it again. He tried the winder but the watch was already tightly wound. "It seems to be broken," he mused. "Perhaps that's why someone threw it away?"

"Or accidentally dropped the watch and it broke from the fall."

"Yes, that could very well be."

But as they went to walk on, Conan Doyle caught the toe of his boot on something, stumbled, and tripped. When he looked back he saw something sticking out of the ground. He reached down and grabbed it, and with a grunt of effort tugged it loose from the soil.

The object was heavy—a t-shaped iron spike with a circular eyelet welded to the top.

"What on earth this that?" Wilde asked.

"I have no idea. But whatever it is, it's been deliberately fashioned. It was pounded deep into the soil but this eyelet appears to be there so it can be gripped later and pulled out."

"Any idea what it is?"

Conan Doyle shook his head and frowned. "Not the foggiest." After a moment's dithering, he carefully set it down at the side of the path. "I'll leave it here in case whoever it belongs to comes back for it. After nearly breaking my neck over it, I'm not going to leave in the path where someone else can trip on it."

The two friends set off again, but after another half-hour, this time Wilde stumbled over something. When he looked down, the object proved to be another of the strange iron spikes.

"Should we pull this one up too?

"No. Let's carry on," Conan Doyle insisted, "we're burning daylight."

But then Wilde spotted another pocket watch lying close by. He retrieved the watch and handed it to Conan Doyle who studied the time.

"It also appears to be broken," he squinted at the dial. "The first one we found stopped at 2:14. This latest one stopped working at 2:46."

"Thirty-two minutes difference," Wilde observed.

"That's about how long it's been since we discovered the first pocket watch.

The Irishman nodded. "I was about to make the same observation."

The two men stopped walking and looked at one another.

"Is that just an odd coincidence?" Wilde asked.

Conan Doyle shook his head. "I don't believe in coincidences, but . . ." he looked at his friend. "What time do you make it, Oscar?"

Wilde fumbled for his own pocket watch and drew it out. He

squinted down at the watch in his hand, frowning, then shook it and lifted it to his ear. "My watch also appears to have stopped running."

Conan Doyle quickly fumbled for his and his mouth fell open when he checked it. "So has mine! What time does your watch say?"

"3:30."

"Mine stopped working at precisely the same time! About thirty-two minutes ago!"

"How very odd. What does it all mean?"

The Scotsman shook his head, wondering. "I can't imagine what it means. Perhaps there is a large mineral deposit deep underground. Something that creates a powerful magnetic field. Perhaps that's what stopped our watches?"

"And the iron spikes? Who left them there?"

"I admit I am mystified. We are so far off the beaten track, I cannot imagine who left them. Obviously, they deliberately did so, but I have no clue what purpose they serve."

They carried on along the path for half a mile or so, where they came across more broken pocket watches and more iron spikes driven into the ground.

"More pocket watches, Arthur, and more of those iron spike things."

"Yes, how very odd. I can only imagine that someone has been carrying out some kind of surveying. Perhaps there is a magnetic anomaly caused by a valuable deposit of some kind of underground mineral."

This time, they left the spikes in place and carried on walking. The pathway began to slowly descend, and as they rounded a bend, they reached a clearing where the trees fell away, affording them their first view of the gorge and the River Wyrme surging through it, some four hundred feet below. They had reached the highest point of the gorge.

Suddenly Oscar Wilde spotted something below and pointed to it.

"Look, Arthur, a village!"

"That must be it!" Conan Doyle exulted. "That can only be Wyrme-Hallow!"

They walked on, faster now, and at the next large clearing in the trees, they stopped to survey the scene. However, the view proved disappointing.

"Blast!" Conan Doyle said. "The village looks to be in ruins!"

From their new vantage point the two authors looked down on a sad straggle of tiny cottages. Most lacked roofs and were falling to pieces, while others were little more than a slumped pile of stones, with collapsed walls suggesting where a cottage once stood. From this distance the village appeared to be a total ruin, likely abandoned hundreds of years ago.

"It appears we've been on a bit of a wild goose chase," Wilde noted. "Ah well, if we turn back now we should be in time for dinner at the Claremont. I just might have the lamb again. Plus I left a bottle of *Perrier-Jouët*, with instructions for their sommelier to chill it in time for dinner."

Conan Doyle stood biting his lips as he stood looking down at the ruins of Wyrme-Hallow.

"Look," he said, pointing at a footpath that descended the steep terrain in a series of switchbacks. "There's a pathway descending to the village."

Wilde followed his point and scowled in dismay. "Yes, and that footpath looks extremely steep. Remember, once we've gone down we will have to climb back up again. Plus, looking at that pile of rubble and ruins, I can hardly believe the Shepherd girls are hiding there."

Conan Doyle stood staring down upon the scene of ruin, disappointment crouched in the corners of his eyes. He sucked in an exasperated breath and let it out. But after dithering a moment, he said. "Well, we've come this far. I'm going down to take a look around. You can wait here if you like."

Conan Doyle set off striding along the path that plunged down to the village, and after a moment, Wilde released a sigh of exasperation and followed behind. For most of the precipitous descent, the village vanished from view behind a screen of trees.

And then, as they were nearing the end of the descent, both men flinched at a sudden loud, BOOOOOM!. When they looked back up at the top of the gorge, they were in time to see a pall of black smoke rising above the treetops.

"That sounded close!" Wilde said, with panic in his voice. "Could we see that all the way back in Darvington?"

Conan Doyle squinted at the ugly black cloud rising into the blue skies. "No, it's quite a few miles away," he noted, "but it's definitely coming this way."

"Sounds like it's almost on top of us."

Conan Doyle shook his head. "No, that is in the middle of the forest. They must have an advanced party blasting rocks to clear the way for the new railroad tracks."

He looked back at Wilde. "Come along, Oscar. We're just a few strides away. Let's see what's left of Wyrme-Hallow."

They resumed their descent of the switch-back trail. Ahead another stand of trees screened their view, but in the last few strides, the forest fell away and it was as if they stepped through a hidden veil, for as they rounded a final bend in the path the village of Wyrme-Hallow suddenly hove into view.

Both men stopped and stared, utterly astonished.

WELCOME TO WYRME-HALLOW

"**D**idn't we look down upon this and see a village in ruins?"
Wilde looked at his friend, "I agree. I thought there was nothing left but tumble-down walls and roofless cottages."

Conan Doyle and Wilde looked about themselves in utter disbelief: Wyrme-Hallow seemed fully intact and, apparently, very much inhabited. Peat smoke purled from the chimneys of the squat stone cottages. In the near distance, a woman stooped over a small garden, hoeing a row of vegetables. As they walked farther into the village, they saw more signs of life: a man perched atop a crude ladder who was tossing bales of thatch up to workmate busily re-thatching the roof of a cottage. Farther on, they smiled and nodded to a lady sitting in the sunshine outside the front door of her cottage. She was working at a loom, her quick, clever fingers deftly pulling at the strands of yarn. The tapestry spilling out from her loom featured stone cottages with smoke purling from the chimneys, and a flock of clucking chickens swarming the dirt road. Conan Doyle blinked his eyes. It was an optical illusion, but it looked for a moment as if the woman was weaving the village into existence, for it was hard to tell where the tapestry ended and the village began. Finally, they came to the end of the cottages as a village green opened before them—a green which featured some familiar landmarks.

"Look," Conan Doyle said, pointing. "There's the old packhorse bridge that appears in the photo the girls took. And behind it —"

"The *Green Man Inn*," Wilde interrupted. "The same one from the photograph!"

Conan Doyle threw his friend a happy smile. "I think our long hike warrants a well-deserved drink. Shall we, Oscar?"

"Lead on, stout fellow. I will follow you anywhere if alcohol is involved in the final destination."

Just then the door to the Inn opened and a black scarecrow came tottering out.

"Ah, look what we have here," Wilde said cheerfully. "This appears to be the local vicar. How delightfully bucolic!"

"Yes," Conan Doyle agreed. "No doubt on his rounds to do good deeds."

The Scots author frowned as they watched the vicar approach in what appeared to be a drunken stagger.

"Although he appears somewhat the worse for wear."

The clergyman reached the packhorse bridge and wobbled up it, pausing at the top, where he wavered unsteadily, fighting for balance as he see-sawed back and forth. And then, to their shock and horror, they watched as the clergymen fumbled with his flies, pulled his penis out, and with a relieved grunt unleashed a sizzling arc of urine. As he reeled unsteadily, his yellow jet splashed the bridge wall, the front of his trousers, and then he directed it outward, so that Conan Doyle and Wilde had to dodge back to avoid having their shoes splashed. The Vicar's urination was impressively prolonged and just when it slowed to a dribble, the fierce arc started up again. When he finally finished he shook himself dry and was attempting to put himself away when he off-balanced forward, staggered down the steep bridge, and toppled face-first onto the dirt.

Conan Doyle and Wilde rushed to assist the vicar and dragged him to his feet. He was a younger man, in his early thirties, with several days of unshaven beard stubble. He was dressed in the once-immaculate black vestments of a village vicar—now raggedy, the knees torn out, the white dog collar unbuttoned at one end and dangling loose. He reeked of alcohol and it was clear that he was staggering drunk.

"God bless, ya kind sirs." The reverend said, peering up at them with a wild, unfocusable gaze. "God bless ya, both. It is good to know there are at least two Christian fellows in this godless hellhole!" He waved two fingers at them in an attempted benediction, but his arm got lost during the gesture. "Could you gents be so kind as to point me toward the village?" he asked, squinting up at them.

Conan Doyle and Wilde exchanged a look and then Wilde suggested. "Can you still feel your nose?"

The man fumbled at his snout and said, "Aye, that I can."

Wilde smiled. "Then you must simply follow your nose. It will lead you home."

"God be with ya," the vicar slurred. They released him and watched as he shambled away toward the street of cottages.

"Well," Conan Doyle said, "I think we just met the spiritual leader of Wyrme-Hallow."

Wilde grinned. "The spirit-drinking leader, at least. But on the positive side, that bodes well for our chances of finding alcohol inside. Let us tarry not!"

Together, they strode over the packhorse bridge, which bore a set of ruts where the wheels of innumerable wagons had worn deep grooves over centuries of use. Here, they paused a moment to look down on the glass-clear waters of the stream that ran beneath. Then, spurred by their thirst, they dropped from the bridge and strode up to the front door of *The Green Man*.

Up close, the Inn revealed its great age. It was an ancient, half-timbered building of three stories with an enormous thatched roof that flowed smoothly over the windows and gables as if it had been poured over the structure. Birds which had built their nests in the thatch chirruped loudly overhead. Conan Doyle grasped the rough iron latch and lifted and the two friends stepped inside.

The yeasty aromas of cider and beer washed over them like a kiss and a promise of bliss to come. The tap room was low-ceilinged with a huge fireplace made of large boulders and featured seats on either side to provide a place to warm oneself in the winter. A scatter of small tables and chairs filled the rest of the space, with a grandfather clock propping up one wall. A high shelf ran around the room, just below the ceiling, and it reminded Conan Doyle of *The Old Curiosity Shoppe*, for it also held a collection of glass boxes holding taxidermied animals: foxes, stoats, weasels, hares, badgers, field mice, even a wild cat—all the denizens of an English forest.

Although a bell had chimed as they stepped through the door, no one immediately appeared to answer it. While they waited, Conan Doyle stepped over to examine the grandfather clock. It was very old, but exquisitely elaborate, featuring a clock face containing separate moving discs to show phases of the sun and moon. But to his disappointment, he discovered that the clock did not seem to be running. By a strange coincidence, the hands of the clock were frozen at 2:36, the same time that both his and Wilde's pocket watches had stopped working. He opened the cabinet and his fingers stroked the pendulum which was not swinging, although he could see by the brass weights hanging from their chains that the clock was fully wound.

And then, from behind the bar, he heard footsteps climbing a set of wooden steps and a young woman surfaced from an open trap door. At his first glimpse of her auburn curls, Conan Doyle's heart leapt in anticipation, thinking he was about to come face to face with Wilhelmina, the eldest of the Shepherd sisters. But this was not a girl, but a young woman in her twenties. She was simply dressed in a rustic skirt and blouse, and her spectacular mane of auburn curls cascaded down to her waist.

"Sorry, sir, oi was in the cellar," the young woman's accent was rustic, the kind of accent one seldom heard these days in modern British cities.

Conan Doyle felt himself momentarily tongue-tied as she moved closer and smiled shyly up at him. She was an English rose, all the more perfect for her quaint accent and simple country beauty.

"My name is Arthur," he nodded to Wilde. "This is my friend, Oscar. We were hoping to find two rooms for the night."

The woman smiled coyly. "Very good, sir. Moi name is Shailagh."

Conan Doyle dithered. "Uh, tell me, Shailagh, how much for two rooms per night?"

The young woman looked uncertain, and finally ventured, "A ha'penny?"

Conan Doyle's mouth dropped open. He threw a look at Wilde, who looked equally astounded at the cheapness of the rooms. "Did you hear that, Oscar? A ha'penny a night."

The woman looked from Conan Doyle to Wilde and back, as if uncertain the price was unreasonable

Clearly, Wilde could not resist and smirked, "We'll a little exorbitant, but I suppose needs must."

"Is that all-roit, sirs?" The girl asked hopefully. "It does include all meals."

Wilde winked at Conan Doyle and grudgingly conceded, "Well, if it includes all meals, I suppose we should just have to stay here."

Conan Doyle intuited that visitors from outside were indeed very rare in Wyrme-Hallow. He slapped his hand down on the bar and smiled. "Now then, young lady, we'll take two rooms, but first, we've walked a long way and we're very thirsty. Could you please fetch us two pints of your best ale or cider?"

"Very good, sir. If you and yer friend would loik to find a table, I'll fetch it fer thee."

Conan Doyle nodded for Wilde to secure a table, while he lingered at the bar, watching the young woman. At the back of the bar a number of pewter tankards hung from a line of hooks. Shailagh pulled forward a wooden step stool and then clambered up on it. As she stretched on tip-toe to take down the tankards, the hem of her skirt lifted slightly, displaying shapely calves and soft, round knees.

Wilde noticed his companion's hungry stare and muttered, "Careful, Arthur, you are a happily married man."

"No harm in looking," Conan Doyle replied his face reddening as he flashed a sheepish smile at his friend. "As the saying goes: I'm wed, not dead."

"Oh, to be young again, eh, Arthur?"

Conan Doyle responded with a wry chuckle. "Yes, yes indeed."

"Yes, . . . oh to be young again," Wilde repeated to himself, but this time each syllable was iced with infinite sadness.

As the Inn was rustic and ancient, it had no beer pumps. Instead, the brews it carried were kept in an arched-roof alcove beside the bar where a number of wooden casks rested in cradles. Conan Doyle watched as the young lady approached with her brace of pewter beakers and set one down as she filled the other by a wooden spigot set into the end of the barrel. She then filled the second mug in a similar fashion.

By now, Wilde had settled at a table and Conan Doyle dropped into the chair next to him. Shailagh appeared and set down two tankards brimming with cider. Conan Doyle took the opportunity to casually ask her, "You haven't seen any little girls in the village, have you? In the last few days?"

The young woman blinked at the question. "Little girls? How young, sir?"

Conan Doyle pursed his lips, as if pondering. "Oh, I suppose the youngest would be around 8 years old and the eldest around 13?"

The woman shook her head. "No sir. We ain't got no children in the village. None."

Conan Doyle was surprised, but continued to pursue his questioning. "One was a brunette. Her hair was very similar to yours, only shorter. And the younger girl was a blonde and very fair."

At that moment more footsteps rang up the cellar steps, and then another young woman appeared. She was a redhead with the most astonishing mane of fiery crimson hair. And like many redheads, her face was sprinkled with freckles that spilled down her face and neck and onto her chest.

"This here is Aoife," Shailagh introduced. "Moi cuz. She works with me."

"Ef-fee? Is that how you pronounce it?" Wilde asked. "Aoife, have you seen two young girls wandering about the village?"

The redhead threw a look at her companion before answering. "No, sir, I ain't never seen none. I reckon Shailagh and me are the youngest in the village. We don't get many visitors. You and your friend are the first in ages."

"Most of the people in the village were not born here," Shailagh explained. "They were just folks passing through, but who decided to stay on."

Shailagh threw a look at Aoife, who took the hint, and the two young woman retreated behind the bar.

Conan Doyle hoisted his cider and the two friends *cheersed* one another and clashed tankards. The Scots author took an experimental sip and his face lit with wonder. It felt as if his tongue was swimming in a river of tart sweetness. He closed his eyes and swished the cider about his mouth. He could taste the summer sun kissing the skins of the apples, the warm rain of late afternoon beading on them, the apples trembling on their stalks in a refreshing spring breeze, the apple blossoms droning with bees sipping nectar, and like Keats, he felt the crack and squish of apples in the press, sobbing out the last of their summer sweetness. He swallowed the first mouthful and sat smacking his lips in wonder.

"My word," he exclaimed, "That's not cider, that's witchcraft!—easily the best cider I have ever tasted in my life! "

Wilde chuckled. "Awfully high praise, Arthur—quite unlike you—but I fear you set a high standard for me to agree with." Wilde followed Conan Doyle's lead. But after his first sip, his eyes widened and then he banged the tankard down and hurled a suspicious look at his friend. "Is this some kind of a joke, Arthur? Are you playing a prank on me?"

The Scotsman responded with a look of bafflement. "What? What are you driving at, Oscar? Do you not like the cider?"

Wilde huffed. "Cider, indeed. You must be playing a joke on me!"

"I have no idea what you're talking about, Oscar."

"This, so-called cider? It is nothing of the sort. This is clearly Perrier-Jouët, my favourite French champagne. I know only too well what Perrier-Jouët, tastes like. I've been drinking it for years. Did you somehow smuggle a bottle in your haversack?"

Conan Doyle frowned and muttered, "What? Nothing of the kind!

Might I try a sip of yours?" He reached over for Wilde's tankard, lifted it to his lips, and took an experimental sip, smacking his lips afterward. "It's cider, Oscar. It tastes exactly like mine."

Wilde then insisted upon trying Conan Doyle's cider, and became even more perplexed. "Well, I'll be damned. If it really is cider it tastes exactly like one of the finest French champagnes money can buy. I must speak with whoever brews it and have a dozen barrels shipped to my home in Chelsea."

Conan Doyle chuckled at his friend's consternation and then raised his hand and waved Shailagh over.

"Yessir," the young woman answered keenly, "how is the cider?"

"Heavenly," Conan Doyle replied. "Exquisite. Divine! The best I have ever tasted."

"It is brewed in the village," Shailagh smiled.

"Would it be possible to order some food?"

The young lady nodded. "Yes, certainly, sir."

"Wonderful, we're both starving." Conan Doyle patted his stomach, which had been growling for the last couple of hours. "We just hiked all the way from Darvington," he added.

The young lady smiled shyly and nodded, but did not remark upon his statement.

Conan Doyle looked around the inn. "What do you have on the menu, young lady?"

"We have most things, sir. Just tell me what you'd like."

The response surprised him.

"Oh, well then. I'll just have, er . . . " He pondered a moment and then requested a dish that a simple country inn was most certain to have ". . . cottage pie? Can you do a cottage pie?"

"Yes, certainly, sir. Cottage pie." She smiled and looked expectantly at Wilde.

Wilde elbowed Conan Doyle and flashed a wink, which Conan Doyle intuited that his Irish friend meant to have a little fun with the young lady. "So, let's see. Most anything I like, eh? What a wonderfully expansive promise. Yessss," he drawled. "In that case I think I'll start with escargot sautéed in champagne. Then truffled pheasant with béchamel sauce, fresh leeks and candied Brussel sprouts, aaaaaaaand for pudding I'd like gooseberry crumble with custard."

To the surprise of both men, the young woman never batted an eyelid at Wilde's outrageous order, but simply flashed a smile, muttered, "Very good, sirs," and flounced off toward the kitchens.

Conan Doyle shot his friend a look. "She must know you were joking, Oscar. I'm sure she'll be back in just a moment to take your real order."

But then, scarcely seconds later, Shailagh re-emerged carrying a deep dish wrapped in a red tea towel. When she set it down before Conan Doyle and snatched away the tea towel, steam rose from an enormous cottage pie. He goggled—it looked big enough to feed three large men.

Shailagh smiled at Wilde.

"I'll be back with yours in a tick, sir."

This time, when she re-emerged from the kitchens she was carrying an enormous pewter platter covered by a metal dome. She set it down before Wilde and whisked off the lid.

This time Wilde did not just goggle, he gasped and his mouth fell open. There, spread across a half-dozen plates, were all the dishes he'd ordered, from the escargot to the pheasant. Wilde looked up at the young woman in wonder, which she took as a question. "I will bring your gooseberry crumble when you're ready for dessert."

Both men looked at one another in mouth-gaping disbelief.

Conan Doyle dug his fork into the cottage pie, pulled it free and blew on the steaming pie, then forked a huge chunk of meat and potato into his mouth. As he chewed, a look of ecstasy swept his features.

"How is it?" Wilde asked.

"Heavenly," Conan Doyle replied. And it was not just the deliciousness of the food he responded to. For a moment he was transported back to his youth, for the pie tasted exactly like his mother's cottage pie, and was redolent with the comforts of home, the warmth of a family kitchen, and was baked with motherly love. Each bite tasted like his childhood.

He felt comforted. Cosseted. Loved.

"Once again, the best cottage pie I have ever tasted."

Two more pints of cider arrived without them having to order.

Both men ate ravenously, shovelling their food down. Conan Doyle paused for a moment between forkfuls to snatch a breath and remark to his friend, "Worth the long walk, eh, Oscar?"

Wilde wiped his lips on a napkin and looked at his friend with features fountaining with joy.

"Surely you jest, Arthur. I would walk to China for a meal such as this!"

"How are your candied Brussel sprouts?"

"Exquisite. Delightful! And I didn't even know there was such a thing as candied Brussel sprouts. I thought I just made that up!"

Soon the two friends finished their meals. Conan Doyle mopped up the last of the gravy with a chunk of crusty bread slathered with nicely salted creamery butter, and had to fight the urge to pick up the plate and lick it clean. He was pleasantly stuffed, but even so, he felt deeply envious of Wilde ordering dessert, and wished he had done the same.

A few moments later Aoife and Shailagh bustled up to their table, each carrying an enormous dessert which they set down before the two men.

"I'm sorry, sir," Shailagh apologised to Conan Doyle. "I know you didn't order dessert, but I thought when you saw your friend's you'd regret not ordering, so I brought a serving of gooseberry crumble for you. If you don't fancy it, I can take it away."

"No! No!" Conan Doyle hastened to add, gripping his dessert bowl defensively. I'm sure I shall somehow manage to force it down."

Both girls grinned, bounced a curtsey, and left the men to their dessert.

Wilde took his first spoonful of tart and moaned with pleasure. Conan Doyle followed suit, and as he placed the first spoonful in his mouth, he tumbled backwards into gooseberry rapture. All conversation ended as they seemed to be in a battle as to who could moan the loudest. Conan Doyle felt tart gooseberries bursting upon his tongue like exploding skyrockets, the crunch of buttery crumble between his teeth, as his mouth glazed with a rapture of sweetness. The crumble was drizzled with warm custard—as comforting as a mother's hug—and he parsed every flavour that trembled sublime upon his tongue in a symphony of taste and texture. With the last heart-breaking scraping from the bowl and their spoons reluctantly abandoned with a clatter, both men slumped back in their chairs, a healthy sweat sheening their faces, groaning as they unfastened the straining top button of their trousers.

"That was the most amazing . . . the most confoundedly delightful meal I have ever eaten!" Conan Doyle rhapsodised.

"You damn with faint praise, Arthur," Wilde corrected. "That was more of a religious experience than a meal! I may actually weep. I have dined at the finest restaurants in London and Paris and never had its equal."

"I agree. Now I see why people passing through tend to stay here forever."

Both men were suddenly distracted by the sounds of arguing voices.

"No! No! NO!" I'm still thirsty!"

When they looked up, they noticed for the first time the vicar they had seen earlier in the day. At some time during their meal, he had slunk back into the inn. Dressed in his black cassock, he was sitting in the shadows of the large fireplace, where his clothes rendered him near-invisible. Now Shailagh was standing at his table and trying to wrest the pewter tankard from his grip which he was clearly reluctant to surrender.

"I never saw the vicar come in," Wilde said.

"I have little doubt he is a fixture of the place, much like the grand-father clock."

"And he also doesn't work!"

"Father," Shailagh said. "You are in your cups. I can serve you no more!"

The redhead Aoife, now flew to assist Shailagh. "She rubbed the cleric's shoulders and importuned him. "You've had enough for today, father. Go home and sleep it off. You can come back in the morning."

The man roared with anger and slurred, "Damned harridans. You cause an old man much suffering!" His comment seemed the more ridiculous given the fact that the vicar only looked to be in his early thirties.

Shailagh clearly knew what a spectacle they were creating and threw an embarrassed look at the two authors. Conan Doyle and Wilde shared a look and began to get up from their table, ready to assist the young women, but Shailagh waved them off, saying, "Don't you gents pay no mind. He gets a bit stroppy now and then."

Finally the tankard was pried from the clergyman's hands, and the two women dragged him to his feet. As they guided the tottering form toward the door, the cleric looked to the two friends and drunkenly slurred, "These ungrateful witches do torment me. And I a man with a terrible thirst!"

But the young women prevailed, and the reverend was assisted through the door.

Wilde looked at Conan Doyle and opined. "So even paradise has its share of miscreants."

The Scotsman shook his head and said, "I know only too well. My own father could not control his drinking, which caused much heartache for my family."

The drama over, both men lolled back in their seats, satiated and sleepy.

"I must go up to my room and write to Jean after this," Conan Doyle said, patting his full belly.

"Write to Jean?" Wilde repeated quizzically. "But there's no post office in Wyrme-Hallow—unless you thought to bring a carrier pigeon with you."

Conan Doyle chuckled at the thought. "No, I will have to mail the letter when we get back to Darvington. I often do this when I travel—write to Jean every day. She's always thrilled, even if she receives all four letters in the same post."

The Scotsman grunted up from his chair, but had to grip the table to stop from flying up through the ceiling—he was drunker than he thought.

Just then Aoife arrived at their table and set down two fresh pints of cider. The redhead smiled and winked saucily as she snatched up their empty tankards and whisked them away. Conan Doyle looked at the fresh drinks awaiting them on the table. How many pints had he and Wilde guzzled? Four? Five?

"Well, maybe I'll write to Jean tomorrow," The Scots author said, sinking back into his chair.

Wilde merely laughed and muttered archly, "Tomorrow—the place where all our good intentions live. Come, Arthur, let's drink a toast to Tomorrow."

The two friends *cheersed* one another and had just clinked their pewter tankards when they heard an enormous roar of wind suddenly surging about the inn. Then the door of *The Green Man* sucked open with a gasp and the unruly wind bullied inside lofting a whiff of smoke and a swarm of star-like chimney sparks and green leaves which spun in a tight vortex around the room.

Shailagh and Aoife watched the leaves dancing, and then the redhead rushed forward and struggled to push the door closed against the strength of the gale.

"Well, that was unexpected," Conan Doyle remarked to Wilde and suddenly goggled to see all of the other seats in the inn occupied by what must have been locals—men and women in rustic attire. He had not seen them enter, leaving him to wonder at how drunk he really was.

The villagers were a motley bunch—many of the men in rustic smocks with red or green caps on their heads; many of the women, who were surprisingly comely, wearing bonnets adorned with coloured feathers of a similar hue. The village men all shared a familial look with long, wispy heads of hair and sharp, angular faces, or were clean-shaven with pointy chins. The women were all slender with thin, erudite features and upturned—almost elfin noses—and dark, flamenco dancer eyes, full of witchcraft and male longing. From their facial similarity, it seemed clear that everyone in the village was someone's cousin and not far removed at that, which suggested a fair amount of inbreeding. Conan Doyle expected the locals to be suspicious of two strangers suddenly appearing in their midst and had steeled himself to be treated with deference and suspicion, but just the opposite proved true. The villagers greeted them with hand clasps and back slaps and soon they were treated to yet another round of drinks, which both men felt would have been impolite to refuse.

For the two authors, it was refreshing to be treated as simple travellers, without their celebrity intruding into the conversation. Conan Doyle and Wilde in turn bought rounds for the villagers, many of whom confessed they had never travelled beyond the environs of the village and so were immensely curious about "goings-on in London." At some point in the evening, the light cider they'd been drinking transitioned to scrumpy—a toe-curling cider with a fatal undertow. And so the two journeyers got steadily drunker.

The door flew open as the wind gusted again, sparks and leaves swirled, and more of the locals crowded into *The Green Man*. The latecomers had brought with them musical instruments: fiddles, flutes, whistles and drums and soon they struck up a folk tune both familiar and strange, eerie and cheerful, lachrymose and happy, and most rose to their feet and began to dance.

Both Wilde and Conan Doyle were far too drunk at this point, but the good-natured villagers insisted and gently took them by the arms and dragged them to their feet where they lumbered about the room, sometimes being held up by their hosts as they jigged drunkenly. More tankards of the powerful cider were pressed into the authors' hands and quickly supped so that Conan Doyle soon felt as though his spine was a pivot that had been driven into the floorboards and now the room and all the faces, whirled about him in spindizzy circles. The girls, Shailagh and Aoife joined in during a reel and clasped hands with the men as the floorboards bounced beneath their feet. As their hosts spun them around the floor, the two authors fountained with laughter, hysterically, uncontrollably, even painfully.

Conan Doyle finally begged to take a break, collapsing into his chair and mopping his face with a handkerchief. His eyes were caught by a flash of movement from above. He watched in amazement as the taxidermied fox crept from its glass case and trotted along the high shelf to the badger's case, where the two swapped places and the badger trotted off to take up the fox's empty case. He blinked at the sight, wondering if it was the scrumpy's doing, but then one of the village women seized him by the hand and dragged him to his feet, where she spun him around and pushed him back into the melee of dancing figures.

And then the evening ended as abruptly as it had begun, as the locals shook their hands or clapped them about the shoulders as they bid their goodnights, and then the door burst open as another great wind whooshed indoors, the fire in the fireplace roared higher, a vortex of chimney sparks and leaves whirlwinded about the room as the rabble of locals was sucked out through the door, which banged shut after them.

The two authors found themselves suddenly alone in *The Green Man*, where only Shailagh and Aoife remained, moving about the empty tables carrying trays onto which they collected the many empty tankards and lugged them off toward the kitchens.

Conan Doyle attempted to stand up, but the Inn began to spin around him alarmingly, and he flopped back into his chair.

"I am very drunk, Oscar. In fact, I don't think I've been this drunk since I was a fifteen-year-old schoolboy and snuck out to my first pub when I was a student at Stoneyhurst."

Wilde had hold of his head with both hands, attempting to stop the giddy carouseling of his brain. "I am in the same predicament, Arthur. Although I hope memories are the only thing I bring back. I certainly don't hope I bring back all the cider and scrumpy we drank."

Leaning heavily on Wilde's shoulder Conan Doyle finally swayed to his feet, and stood, wavering unsteadily. "I am far too drunk to go to bed," he slurred. "Perhaps we should attempt to take in the night air on a stroll about the village to clear our heads."

"I'm afraid it is more likely that the village will take a turn around me," Wilde countered, "for my head is spinning."

But despite his complaints, the two finally stumbled out the Inn door, holding each other up as they shambled the darkened lanes of the village. Of course, there were no gas streetlights in the village, but the skies were cloudless and the full moon and starlight so bright, they could see plainly, if a little doubly where they were staggering.

Conan Doyle sucked in a deep lungful of cool night air and let it out. "Just smell that air, Oscar. So clean. So pure. I can only describe it as delicious."

"I would risk a deep breath, Arthur, but after breathing the London air for so many years, I fear I might cough up a several chunks of coal."

As they stood there, gazing up at the twilight sky, the first brightest stars were glimmering to life and they seemed to burn brighter and with more beauty than Conan Doyle could ever recall. Just then a shooting star arced across the sky from left to right, so bright it made both men's eyes water with its brilliance.

After a second, Conan Doyle asked softly, "What did you wish for, Oscar?"

The Irishman chuckled softly. "I did wish for something, but I cannot tell you or it may not come true."

"I've never heard that before. Is that an Irish superstition?"

Wilde was silent for a moment and then burst out laughing. "You know, I think I may have just made that up. So then I'll tell you. I wished to be young again." He looked unsteadily at his friend, his eyes pooled with starlight. "What did you wish for, Arthur?"

Conan Doyle cleared his throat. "Well, this will probably sound silly, but when Touie, my first wife, was in her last stages, she was very ill, often unconscious for days. And then one morning I went into her room to check on her . . . and she was gone . . . " A hitch came into the Scotsman's voice. ". . . and suddenly she was gone," he repeated. "I have always felt like I never had a chance to say goodbye. I wished for anything, a sign from Touie from the afterlife. Ridiculous, I know, but . . ."

His voice broke and failed him.

After a pause, Wilde laid a comforting hand on his friend's shoulder and said, "Arthur Conan Doyle, you are the best man I have ever known. Touie knew you loved her, and that you would never stop loving her . . . in this life or the next. Besides, I believe that love is like the stars above us, something beautiful that burns for eternity. It is something always above us, that can be seen from any point on earth. And so we never have to say goodbye."

Conan Doyle did not respond but stood looking up into the sky, now swarming with stars, which turned suddenly liquid and ran down his cheeks.

When they tottered back into the inn, the two men thought their turn around the town had sobered them up somewhat, but when it came time to stagger up to their rooms, they found the tight circular staircase a challenge. On his first attempt. Conan Doyle made it three-quarters of the way up, but then lost balance and back-pedalled in reverse all the way down to the ground floor. On his second attempt, he tripped on one of the badly worn wooden steps and sprawled face-first on the steps. On his third attempt, he made it all the way to the landing, staggered to his room, barged through the door, back-heeled it shut behind him and then took two reeling steps as he fumbled to pull the shirt over his head. With his arms hopelessly tangled in the sleeves, he face-flopped onto the bed and promptly passed out, fully clothed.

For his part Wilde abandoned the standing-up approach and chose to crawl up the steps on his hands and knees, summiting on his first attempt. He crawled into his bedroom on all fours and eyed the bed from his position on the floor. The bed seemed insurmountably high up, so he curled up on the sheepskin rug, which was surprisingly comfy, and fell fast asleep.

A MOST UNCANNY VILLAGE

When Conan Doyle awakened the following morning he was afraid to open his eyes. He knew how much he and Wilde had imbibed the night before and fully expected the worst hangover of his life. The events of the previous night all had the surreal quality of dream—and as in a dream he could not recall a single substantive detail of the villagers they had met. Instead, his recollections consisted of broken fragments of memory: of the room spinning around him, a woman's laughing face, feet stamping floorboards, nimble fingers plucking the strings of strange instruments, a man's hand slapping the taut skin of a drum, and again and again, the clash of pewter mugs toasting one another. It all had the feeling of a dream—a peculiarly vivid dream, but a dream nonetheless.

Eventually, he had to admit to himself that he was fully awake, and could not burrow back into sleep. He was afraid to open his eyes, but when he cautiously peeked, his vision seemed surprisingly clear. He fully expected that, when he sat up in bed, his head would split in two like a cracked porcelain bowl and his would brains would spill out. But strangely no—no headache, no cottony mouth, no collywobbles in the belly. Instead, he felt rested, invigorated, and refreshed after a wonderful night's sleep.

Just then, knuckles rapped at the bedroom door. He looked up as the door juddered open and Shailagh's comely face poked around it.

"Sorry if I woke you, sir," she apologised. "But your breakfast is waiting downstairs," As if the sight of a beautiful female face first thing in the morning was not arousing enough, the smells of cooking bacon crowded through the door with her, setting him to salivating and rattling the cage of Conan Doyle's voracious hunger.

"Ah yes, I shall be right down."

When Shailagh left, he quickly threw his clothes on and hurried down the spiral staircase, once again stumbling on the deeply worn lower step.

He had just found a seat at one of the tables when, to his amazement, the inn door chimed open and Oscar Wilde entered. He was wearing a gorgeous silk oriental dressing gown with slippers on his feet, so Conan Doyle couldn't help but wonder where he'd been. Wilde noticed Conan Doyle and dropped into the chair next to him.

"Where on earth have you been, Oscar? And so early? I've never known you to rise at this hour."

"Nonsense, Arthur. I am a very punctual riser. Of course, it depends on your definition of punctual. But first, I must share with you what just happened to me."

"Ah, very well then."

The Irishman fixed his friend with an earnest stare.

"This morning, Arthur, I awakened, I admit, uncharacteristically early. The Inn was still in darkness and no one stirred. Yet, I was wide awake having just enjoyed the best night's sleep of my life."

"I did too!" Conan Doyle interrupted.

" Likewise for me also, but shush, let me finish my story."

"Sorry."

"As the dawn was just breaking, I decided to throw on my robe and step outside. The morning was glorious, and so I decided to enjoy a quick amble about the village. Ambling is always a favourite speed for Oscar Wilde. I can, of course, stroll, meander and occasionally saunter. But, if anything, I am built for ambling. And so I ambled my way up onto the packhorse bridge and stood at its apex looking over the idyllic scene: the sheep contentedly grazing, peat smoke curling from the cottage chimneys, geese honking as they flapped their wings and chased one another about the green—it resembled a painter's vision of a bucolic village worthy of Constable. To savour the moment I decided to enjoy my first cigarette of the day. As I was lighting it, I chanced to look down at the stream below and saw the largest trout I have ever seen in my life hovering amidst the underwater weed—"

"How wonderful—!"

"Wait, I have not reached the climax of my tale. So, I stood gazing down at the fish which met my gaze and said, in a very clear and rather erudite voice, 'Good morning, Oscar.'"

Conan Doyle looked stunned for a moment, but then the corners of his mouth twitched up in a smile. "Oh, you are joking . . . pulling my leg . . . are . . . are you not?"

Again, Wilde shook his head. "No, Arthur, I am in deadly earnest. After all, it is not every day that a fish addresses me directly. Of course, I looked about to see if someone was hiding in the shadows beneath the bridge, making fun of me, but there was no one. And that was only the beginning of my strange day. After my encounter with the fish, which I initially attributed to a hangover from the rather wonderful Perrier-Jouët cider they brew around here, I went up to my room, prepared to shave as I felt quite slovenly and looked in the mirror, where I saw the most amazing thing . . ."

"And what was that?"

"Why, me, of course. Only it was a younger, more handsome me. The me of my youth. Look at me, Arthur. Just look at me!"

"Yes, I am looking. You seem refreshed. Did you sleep well?"

"Sleep well? I slept in the arms of the angels. I slept upon the clouds of Elysium! Look at me! I am like a man renewed!"

"Yes, you do look well rested. And you're just in time for breakfast."

"Breakfast! Breakfast? I care nothing for food. Just look at my face. Look closely. Not a wrinkle. Not a blemish. Look at my hair. Not a grey hair could I find this morning. None! Look. Look closely."

Conan Doyle recoiled as Wilde pushed the crown of his head into his face for inspection.

Wilde gripped his friend by the sleeve. "Remember at the Claremont when I showed you the crow's feet around my eyes? The grey strands sprouting in my hair? They're gone, Arthur. They're all gone! My wish last night upon the shooting star has come true. I am growing younger!"

"I'm sure that's a bit of an exaggeration, Oscar. You had a full day of healthy exercise followed by an evening of frolics and relaxation. That's probably the reason—"

"No, you're wrong Arthur. Believe me. You are speaking to Oscar Wilde. I study my face a hundred—nay, a thousand times a day in the mirror. I track every new wrinkle, every grey hair, the newly acquired droop of a jowl, an extra crow's foot in the corner of my eyes, and the traitorous grey hairs I discover snagged in my hair brush. Ten years have been undone in one night. Ten years!"

Conan Doyle ceased to argue. Wilde's preoccupations often transgressed into the manic. But give it a day, and he would return to normal, or at least, as close to normal as Oscar Wilde ever got.

"I will say this," Conan Doyle interjected. "Last night was the drunkest I have ever been in my life, and yet this morning I had not the slightest twinge of hangover. No headache. Nothing.

"Maybe it is the way they brew the cider?"

"It must be magic apples from a magic tree—"

"Do you have a mirror in your room, Arthur?"

"Just a small round mirror. Above the dresser. "

"I have the same. Might I borrow your mirror?"

"Er, I suppose. Whatever for?"

"So I might see the side of my face in profile."

"I, er . . . oh very well then."

Wilde did not need further permission but shouted a "thank you" and bolted from the room. Conan Doyle heard him stomp up the staircase. Stumble. Fall down halfway up. (No doubt on the terribly worn step.) Curse. Laugh. Then thunder the rest of the way to the top. But a scant minute later he heard Wilde's footsteps thunder back down the staircase, stumble on the worn step. Curse. Laugh. Then he ran back into the tap room.

"Arthur, wait! I've had a splendid idea," Wilde gushed. "Did you bring the camera with you?"

"Er yes . . . yes I did."

Then you must take my photograph. You must capture Oscar Wilde in all his renewed youth!"

Conan Doyle made a face but finally acceded to Wilde's importuning before the Irish wit devolved from the obsessed to the manic.

Conan Doyle returned to his room to fetch his haversack and the camera it contained. When he emerged from the inn a few minutes later, he found Wilde standing atop the packhorse bridge striking first one and then another enigmatic pose.

Conan Doyle dutifully shot two photos of him atop the bridge, but Wilde wanted still more.

"A close-up," Wilde cried. "You must shoot me in close up."

The Scotsman flashed a long-suffering grimace but did as he was bid. He climbed atop the bridge and posed Wilde with the side of the Gorge and woodland over his shoulder. But as he was about to squeeze the shutter when a flash of light at the top of the gorge behind Wilde distracted him. He lowered the camera and squinted at the gorge. At first, he thought he had imagined it. But then the flash of light appeared again.

"We're being watched," Conan Doyle muttered darkly.

"What? You are joking, surely?"

"I saw a flash of light up in the woods at the top of the gorge. Someone is observing us through a spyglass or a pair of binoculars."

"What? Could it be that my adoring public has followed us here?"

"More likely we are being observed by someone rather less than adoring. I think we need to confront whoever it is and find out."

DR LIVINGSTONE, I PRESUME?

I t took half an hour for the two friends to scramble back up to the shoulder of the gorge, (ten minutes of actual climbing with twenty minutes of Wilde insisting that he needed to sit down for a rest). When they reached the point of the trail where Conan Doyle had seen the flash of a reflection—presumably the sun bouncing off the glass lens of a telescope or a set of binoculars—upon scanning the forest floor, he once again discovered a stopped pocket watch and an iron stake driven into the ground nearby.

But then Conan Doyle noticed another flash of light from the gloom of the woods farther along the trail. When he looked, he spotted what appeared to be a vaguely human form in the distance.

"Look, Oscar," he said, pointing at the distant shape. "I believe I just saw the person who is spying upon us."

Both men squinted at the distant figure. Although he was a fair distance away, they could make out a surveyor's theodolite mounted atop a heavy wooden tripod. The figure was crouched behind it, one eye to the eyepiece, apparently peering at them. Conan Doyle removed his hat and waved at the man, smiling broadly, while he muttered through his teeth, "I don't know what this chap is up to, but I think we just caught him red-handed."

Wilde sniffed and remarked. "I care not what colour his hand is, but I don't care much for being spied upon."

"Neither do I. Let's be nosy and go confront him, shall we?"

The two friends began to stroll along the forest path toward the figure. As they drew close, they could make out the figure of a man dressed in the most extraordinary outfit: huge jodhpur shorts with clompy boots and knee socks protecting sharp shins and holding up his enormously knobbly knees. He was wearing the kind of shirt one wears on safari: heavy khaki fabric burgeoning with pockets and epaulettes. Completing the just-stepped-from-the-jungle-look was a bone-white pith helmet atop his head.

"Wait!' Wilde said, gripping Conan Doyle's arm to slow him as they drew close. "We've seen this fellow somewhere before."

"Yes," Conan Doyle agreed. "I recognise him now—he's the odd chap we ran into in the *Old Curiosity Shoppe.*"

"The shoppe with two p's?"

"Yes, quite, the shoppe with two p's. If you remember he'd come in to buy a full carton of pocket watches."

"Ah, so he is the chap who's been leaving pocket watches all over the place."

"Yes, and those iron spike thingies. I'm interested to find out what he's up to."

As the two authors strolled up, Conan Doyle shouted a cheery greeting: "Halooo!"

The man raised his pith helmet and flashed them a toothy smile, but up close it was clear he wore the expression and demeanour of someone who's been caught in the act—whatever that act might prove to be. The two friends "Good morninged" him and the explorer "Good morninged" them back.

Conan Doyle affected a casual air as he remarked, "I do hope we're not disturbing your work—whatever that might be." It was an indirect question that begged for an answer, but the pith-helmeted fellow did not immediately volunteer an explanation

Conan Doyle stepped forward and extended his hand for a hand-shake. "My name is Conan Doyle . . . Doctor Conan Doyle."

The explorer's hand was rough and calloused—not surprising given his penchant for lugging about heavy iron stakes which he pounded into the ground everywhere.

Wilde followed next. "And I am Oscar Wilde, playwright, poet, rake and raconteur."

Both men were surprised that the man did not seem impressed, as if he'd never heard of them—or if he did, he did not let on.

"I am Professor Squibb," he replied. "That's Squibb with two b's."

The two authors shared the briefest of glances. Both knew exactly what the other was thinking.

Conan Doyle made a point of examining the theodolite. "So what are you up to on this fine morning, Professor? Doing a bit of surveying? I see by your theodolite that you are a cartographer?"

The Professor hadn't shaved in many days, and his sallow cheeks sported dark blue beard bristle so coarse it could have been used to sand furniture. Now he scratched a bristly cheek with a 'rasp-rasp" sound.

"Cartographer? Ah, well, yes . . . something along those lines," the Professor prevaricated.

"My friend here is a medical doctor," Wilde ventured. "I myself specialised in the Classics. So, Professor Squibb, what are you a professor of?"

The man in the pith helmet chuckled and quickly put in, "Oh . . . many things, really . . . many things. You know what academia is like. One collects so many degrees. I suppose I am a bit of a hodge-podge."

"So you are a professor of hodge-lodge?" Wilde retorted, although Squibb was slow to join with the two authors' laughter.

Something suddenly occurred to the Scots author. "Squibb. A memorable name. I seem to recall that name from somewhere. Were you not part of an expedition to darkest Africa? I vaguely recall reading about it in *The Times*. The expedition came to grief, and you were the sole survivor. Is that correct?"

Professor Squibb was obviously not much of a card player, for his face showed every card in his hand right down to the specific suit.

"Ah, yes, that is, ahem, true. We were there to survey the path of a proposed railway. It would have connected several major towns and brought much prosperity to the region. Unfortunately, the natives believed we were bringing bad juju. Damned darkies. You know what benighted souls they are." The Professor could not repress a sneer. "As Mister Darwin might say, they are barely one step out of the jungle and barely two steps up from the monkeys." The Professor barked a laugh that the two authors did not join in.

"Really?" Conan Doyle said. "As a young man, I was a ship's doctor to African traders. If anything I thought the white traders were the benighted ones—a murderous crew of rough, brawling, drunken savages. By contrast, I found the African natives quite charming and civilised."

For a moment the Professor's expression soured, but then he quietly conceded, "Ah, well, I suppose it depends upon one's personal experience."

Wilde then asked a direct question which Conan Doyle blanched to hear. "So you are with the Darvington railway? Come to help plot the route of the tracks?"

"No, no, nothing of the sort, no, no," Squibb quickly put in. "My explorations are strictly for academic purposes. I am plotting the terrain for a study of . . ." He seemed at a loss for a moment. " . . . for a study of . . . the ancient landscapes around here, which are of great archaeological interest."

"Really?" Conan Doyle said, enthusiasm surging into his voice. "And what might that be?"

Squibb's eyes went blank for a moment, but then he quickly recovered. "What features? Yes. Ah, well, there is an ancient burial barrow—the superstitious locals have dubbed it a 'fairy fort.'" He laughed sneeringly. "Pure nonsense. In truth, it is a chambered tomb built by the ancient druids."

"Really? How fascinating! I love to explore burial barrows. Could you possibly show us?

Clearly, the Professor had not anticipated Conan Doyle's request, and he flustered for a moment. "Well, ah, I suppose . . . I . . . I . . . well . . . yes."

And so Professor Squibb led the two authors on a meandering path through the thrash and tangle of the forest. Conan Doyle tried his best to estimate where they were in relation to the village, but once inside the forest canopy orientation was a challenge. But then it became clear that they were approaching a large, heavily forested hill with trees climbing its sides. They followed Squibb's back until a dark cave opening loomed ahead. Squibb stopped just outside and paused as the three men caught their breath.

"This is it," Squibb panted. "I estimate the tomb is of great antiquity. Possibly three thousand years old, or even older."

Conan Doyle peered into the dark maw of the cave-like opening where the light quickly fell away, revealing only the first few feet of the tomb walls, which were carved with spiral designs and what Conan Doyle recognised as cup-and-ring marks, both designs he'd seen before while visiting sites of great antiquity in his travels around Great Britain.

"Fascinating!" Conan Doyle said. "We must go inside!"

"Uh, I would strongly advise against it," Squibb quickly put in, and then explained.

"The burial barrow is many thousands of years old. The roof could collapse at the slightest disturbance. Plus, such underground places often seep with poisonous gases. One could quickly become delirious . . . overcome . . . suffocate . . . and die!"

Conan Doyle was immediately skeptical of the Professor's first claim—if the burial barrow had survived for thousands of years, it seemed unlikely that it faced imminent collapse. About the second threat of poisonous gas, however, he was less sure of.

"Blast, what a shame," Conan Doyle said. "I would love to have had a poke about inside. I am fascinated by our prehistoric past."

"I know of another cave we might explore. This one is quite safe," the Professor added. "It is not a burial barrow, but it boasts a quite unique and fascinating feature. Would you care to see it?"

Conan Doyle was immediately intrigued. "Yes, by Jove! I'd love to see it."

The Professor glanced at Wilde, who seemed hesitant.

The Irishman quickly put in: "Is this the sort of thing one might explore before lunch? I missed breakfast, and I am feeling rather peckish."

The Professor smiled, "You're in luck. There is a stream close by. I keep my fishing gear there. We might catch ourselves a nice fish lunch."

They followed the Professor through the woods to a trail that descended to the floor of the gorge. This was the headwater that fed the lazy stream that meandered through the centre of Wyrme-Hallow and was composed of several large ponds that Squibb explained were fed by springs. On one side was a rocky outcrop that the Professor led them to. Beneath a dripping overhang of stone, they found a circular pool of bright water from which tiny bubbles rose in a constant stream and burst as they hit the surface. Scattered on the ground about the spring, and dangling from strings tied to the stony over-hang, was a strange miscellany of objects that appeared to be personal effects of the villagers: a glove, a sock, a doll's head, an old teapot. The socks and gloves were knitted from coarse wool, but when Conan Doyle touched the glove, he found that it was as stiff and hard as stone.

"Ah, it's a petrifying well!" Conan Doyle remarked. "Just like Mother Shipton's cave in Yorkshire."

"Good observation!" Wilde agreed. "I have also visited Mother Shipton's."

Both men knew that petrifying wells were rich in dissolved mineral salts. Locals who believed in their healing powers would leave votive offerings hanging close by so that they were covered by spray from the well. Over weeks and months, the accumulation of concre-tionary minerals slowly transformed the offerings into stone-like objects.

"I see the locals still believe in the healing powers of the well," Wilde noted. "Going by all the offerings they have left."

"Pure mindless superstition," the Professor mocked. "But let me show you the well's true power. "Follow me."

Looming behind the well was the small dark opening of a cave.

The entrance was a tight fit, but the Professor led the way, and each man in turn ducked and squeezed through. Once inside, the cave quickly dilated, so they emerged into a gloomy, smooth-walled space which resembled the throat of a great beast. While it had been quiet and peaceful outside, as soon as they entered the cave, they found that the space reverberated to a muffled roar.

"Good Lord!" Conan Doyle remarked as they crouched in the semi-darkness.

"What on earth is that roaring noise?" Wilde asked.

The Professor grinned and nodded. "Press your hand to the cave wall."

Both men followed his instruction, and their jaws dropped.

"My word!" Conan Doyle said. Beneath his fingertips, the entire cave wall vibrated.

"It feels as though there is a great monster just behind the stone," Wilde noted, "fighting to get out!"

"There is a great beast," Squibb replied. "It is another tributary of the Wyrme flowing underground. It forms the large cascade that bursts out of the cliff face at the Devil's Cauldron."

"Just imagine all the ferocious power that is bound up," Conan Doyle commented.

"Yes!" The Professor agreed. "We are in limestone country. The ground beneath our feet is riddled with a network of caves that stretch for miles. Many are flooded—thousands of gallons of water rushing through pitch-black, stony chambers deep underground."

Conan Doyle rapped on the stone wall with his knuckles. From the dull thud, he surmised that the wall holding back the rushing water was, at most, a foot thick. "What would happen if the cave collapsed and all that power of water was unleashed?"

The Professor smiled. "That will eventually happen, but it will take hundreds if not thousands of years. But if it did let go, thousands of gallons of raging water would be unleashed, flooding the gorge and drowning the ruins of Wyrme-Hallow."

Conan Doyle shook his head in wonder. "Good Lord! Let's hope that never happens."

When the three men crawled out of the cave, Professor Squibb led them through a stand of trees where they emerged at a slow-flowing stream.

"Another river?" Wilde asked.

"No, this is simply a tributary of the Wyrme. In fact, it's the same stream that flows beneath the packhorse bridge in Wyrme-Hallow. Professor Squibb dug around in the ferns next to a large tree and produced a fishing rod and a wicker hamper.

"I keep my rod here. This stream produces some excellent trout. I even have a frying pan in the hamper. Let's see if we can catch our lunch."

"Jolly good!" Conan Doyle enthused, while Wilde looked doubtful.

The Professor studied the Irishman. "Have you ever fished, Mister Wilde?"

"Only for compliments," Wilde replied. "Of course, I catch plenty."

The Professor handed him the fishing rod. 'Very good, then. Let's try your luck with the local trout."

Despite Wilde's obvious reluctance, the professor dug in his basket and produced more fishing tackle, and minutes later the Irish wit was togged out in hip-high waders and a fishing hat jangling with shiny lures.

"I haven't fished since I was a young boy," Wilde protested. "I'm sure I no longer have the foggiest notion of what I'm doing."

Conan Doyle could not stop chuckling as he watched his Irish friend bumble about. He pulled the Midge camera from his haversack and made ready to snap a photo. None of Wilde's society friends back in London would believe this without proof.

When Wilde was fully kitted out, Professor Squibb waved to the river. "Now you must wade into the stream, Mister Wilde."

The Irishman looked horrified. "You mean you wish me to actually step into the stream? But it's all wet in there."

"Of course, that is what the waders are for."

With Conan Doyle gripping Wilde's hand to steady him, the Irish wit wobbled from the bank into the stream and took a few shaky steps.

"It seems very unstable underfoot," Wilde complained. "How many people have drowned attempting this?"

"The stream is only two feet deep" Conan Doyle pointed out. "I don't think you risk drowning."

Wilde attempted to cast with a tentative flick of the rod. Most of the line remained sluggishly coiled at his knees. It was undoubtedly the worst cast in the history of fly fishing.

The Professor looked pained. "Sorry, old boy, I think you will have to try again and put some muscle into it. If you could actually get the line more than two feet away from you, you will have a better chance of catching something."

"Oh dear," Wilde said. He brought the rod back, ready to cast again when suddenly the line at his feet snapped taut and his fishing rod bent double as a fish took the bait.

"Oh my goodness!" he cried. "Now what do I do?"

Conan Doyle laughed and shouted, "Reel it in Oscar!'

Wilde fought with the fishing rod. He had no concept of playing the fish, and yet he managed to reel the fish in until the line went taut, the rod bent double, and he hauled the fish out of the water. The trout flailing at the end of his line was enormous.

At that moment, Conan Doyle squinted through the viewfinder of the Midge camera and snapped a photograph to record the event for posterity.

"Quick!" The professor shouted. "Drop the fish on the bank."

Wilde dithered but did as he was told.

The fish flopped a few times but then lay shivered and lay still as if accepting its fate.

"Pull the hook out!" Squibb shouted.

Conan Doyle watched the normally squeamish Wilde take hold of the fish and yank the hook from its mouth. Then Professor Squibb fumbled in his wicker fishing basket and pulled out a club. "Right, hold it still!" He shouted

But as the Professor raised the club, ready to bash the helpless fish, Wilde suddenly snatched up the trout and hurled it back into the stream. Momentarily stunned, it hung transfixed for a moment, but then flicked its tail and shot away.

The Professor was enraged. "What are you doing, man? We had the beast!"

"I'm afraid I couldn't kill the poor thing. It was not just any old fish."

The Professor looked puzzled. "What do you mean?"

"I know the fellow."

The Professor stared at Wilde as if he were mad. "What do you mean, you know the fish?"

"We met just this morning. His name is Ernest, or at least that's what I named him. So I could hardly kill him. It would be most impolite."

"But that would have been our dinner!"

"Yes, I'm sorry. My apologies, but I just remembered that I'm a vegetarian," Wilde fibbed. " That is why I always seem forlorn and despondent. Like all vegetarians, I have lost the will to live." Wilde threw a look at Conan Doyle. "Come along Arthur," Wilde urged, hopping on one leg as he kicked loose of the waders. "I just remembered something we need to attend to. Do excuse us, Professor Squibb."

The Professor looked on open-mouthed and baffled as the two friends hastily departed.

Conan Doyle and Wilde were still laughing about the incident when they stepped back into *The Green Man*.

MAPPING THE VORTEX

"We have been brought here for a reason, Oscar. There is a task we must perform. I fully believe that."

"What do you mean by that? I thought we were here to look for the Shepherd girls?"

"Ostensibly, yes, but I believe there is an overarching reason. I believe we have been manipulated from the very beginning of this affair. First the letter from Mrs Shepherd about her missing girls, who then turn out to be not so missing. Next, we meet the girls for a few minutes, but then they vanish mysteriously and the only clue to their whereabouts are a series of cryptic photographs of a mysterious village the locals believe is nothing more than a quaint faerie story. Finally, thanks to an antique map we arrive at the village but the denizens of Wyrme-Hallow claim they have never seen the girls."

"We've just finished breakfast, Arthur. Must you think so much? You're giving me a headache!"

"Indeed, my head is also aching. And now we run into the mysterious Professor Squibb."

"That's Squibb with two b's."

"Precisely, Squibb with two b's, who claims to be surveying the area for archaeological purposes."

"And then there is the business with the pocket watches and the iron spikes he keeps pounding into the ground."

"Yes. I don't fully understand all that, but I believe the real reason is that he's plotting an alternative route for the Darvington railroad."

The two men were sitting on either side of a table in the tap room, a scatter of plates between them bearing the wreckage of breakfast.

Conan Doyle decided on something and fixed his friend with a look. "You know what I'm thinking of Oscar—our next move."

Wilde frowned at his friend over the pile of egg-scummed plates. "After that enormous breakfast, I'm hoping you're about to suggest a nap—a very long nap."

Conan Doyle chuckled. "Yes, a nap would be most apposite, but I'm thinking that Professor Squibb must be camping somewhere in the woods above the gorge. We need to find out where and see if we can fathom what he's up to."

"Oh dear, from the tone of your voice I intuit this somehow involves my participation?"

Conan Doyle answered with a wry smile.

Wilde pulled a dreadful face and exclaimed, "So instead of a nice restful sleep, you're proposing that we hike back up the Gorge and spend several hours tramping around the wilderness, looking for his base? I hardly think that will be conducive to my digestion!"

Conan Doyle peered through the foliage. An unmistakable human silhouette moved along the forest trail in the distance—a pith-helmeted figure in a jungle outfit.

"Have you seen him yet, Arthur?" Wilde whispered.

"Shhh, Oscar, there's Squibb now. He's coming this way."

The two friends ducked behind a large Rowan tree, whose large lower limbs provided convenient camouflage while allowing them to peek through the branches.

Now Squibb was trudging toward their hiding spot. He had the theodolite and his heavy tripod thrown over one shoulder. The haversack on his back flopped emptily, by which Conan Doyle knew he had used up his supply of iron spikes and was no doubt headed back to his camp to collect more.

Conan Doyle shushed Wilde with a finger to his lips and hunkered down low behind the tree as Squibb passed by.

"What's he up to, Arthur?" Wilde whispered as soon as he passed.

"I think we're in luck. I believe he is headed back to his camp to collect more of the iron spikes. We must follow him, but at a discreet distance."

Wilde frowned. "There's that word discreet again! The last time you used that we were physically thrown from our hotel."

Conan Doyle peeked out from their hiding place. The professor could still be seen in the distance, weaving in and out of sight behind the trees as the trail twisted left and then right.

"Come along, Oscar, but we must be quiet."

"Yes, discreet as you put it! I know. I know."

The two friends slunk along the trail, following, ready to duck behind a tree at any moment.

After several minutes, Conan Doyle grabbed his colleague by the sleeve and dragged him behind a tree.

"He's heading toward some kind of old stone structure—wait a minute! I know what that is. Do you remember seeing the anchorite's hut on the map?"

Wilde shook his head noncommittally. "Vaguely."

"I believe that's where he's heading."

When the Professor reached the hut, he rummaged in the deep pockets of his voluminous shorts, produced a key, and then unlocked the door and stepped inside.

Conan Doyle threw a look at Wilde. "He's gone inside. Here's our chance to get closer."

But as Conan Doyle stepped out from behind the tree, he heard a long, low whistle. Thinking they'd been spotted, both men quickly ducked behind the tree again.

Heart banging, Conan Doyle sprawled with his back pressed against the tree. When he dared steal a look, he peeked out to see the source of the whistle. The Professor stood outside the anchorite's hut, looking the opposite way at three figures approached from the distance. When they got closer, Conan Doyle saw that two of them were carrying a large object between them. And then he recognised the single figure who was humping a heavy load in a haversack.

"The Professor has company!" Conan Doyle muttered to his friend.

"Really? Who on earth is out here traipsing around the woods?"

"Some familiar characters," Conan Doyle threw a look at Wilde, "And not ones I'm anxious to run into again."

Conan Doyle held back as Wilde ducked out and snatched a quick look. "Ah, how regrettable. That nasty Brody chap and two of his fellow ne'er-do-wells."

Conan Doyle took another turn at looking and then ducked back into cover.

"Two of them are carrying a large wooden crate between them, while Brody appears to be carrying a heavy haversack. No doubt it's filled with more of those iron stakes."

The two authors continued to peek at the meeting between the men. Brody did little but bark orders to his two bruisers who loaded the wooden crate into the anchorite's hut, and then Brody ducked inside and came back out minus the heavy haversack of iron stakes. Professor Squibb spoke only to Brody, who communicated chiefly through scowls and morose nods. And then, their business concluded, the three railway labourers turned and tromped away into the woods, presumably heading back to the railway works in Darvington. Squibb lingered long enough to relock the door, and then he turned and walked back toward where Conan Doyle and Wilde were hiding.

"Quick, before he sees us," Conan Doyle muttered and grabbing Wilde by the sleeve and dragging him down to a crouching squat. They heard Professor Squibb's size 12 boots scuffling past on the leafy trail and waited another full minute before standing up again.

" What was all that about?" Wilde asked as the two stood catching their breath.

Conan Doyle shook his head. "I'm not entirely certain, but I take that as proof positive that Squibb is somehow tied in with the railway folk—"

"You mean he's in cahoots?" Wilde interjected.

"Yes, in cahoots to use your newly-favourite word. The Professor is obviously in cahoots with the railway people, which proves the lie to his surveying ancient monuments story."

"So what next?"

So now we need to find out what's in the anchorite's hut."

"But we just watched him lock it up—"

Conan Doyle reached into a breast pocket and once again flashed his set of lock picks.

"Ah, but I see you brought your own key."

Throwing frequent looks over their shoulder, the two authors hurried along the trail to the anchorite's hut. Up close, they saw that the heavy wooden door had been fitted with a hasp and now a huge brass padlock dangled from it. Conan Doyle squatted down and examined the padlock. He took his time and stroked his moustache several times as he inspected the padlock. Finally, he rose to his feet and huffed out a disgruntled breath.

"What?" Wilde asked. "Do you recognise the brand of padlock?"

Conan Doyle's frown caused his moustache to droop comically.

"Unfortunately, yes. Remember the padlock holding shut the door of the Reverend Shepherd's dark room?"

"You made short work of that."

"Yes, only that was a cheap, penny padlock. A child could pick the thing, whereas this is a large brass, mouse-eared padlock manufactured by Henry Squire. Note that it takes a hollow key. Quite unpickable."

"How unfortunate!" Wilde stood pursuing the padlock for several moments and then, to Conan Doyle's surprise, muttered, "Allow me to try."

Conan Doyle looked at his friend askance and laughed. "I'm sorry, Oscar, but unless you have been secretly pursuing a career as a burglar in your free time, there is no possible way you could open that lock."

Wilde looked around at the forest floor, spotted a large flat rock, picked it up, lofted it high, and then brought it down on the hasp and padlock with all his might. The hasp sheared off, and the padlock dropped to the leafy forest floor.

"That's all well and good, Oscar, but now Squibb is going to know someone broke into his hut."

"I solved the first problem, Arthur. I leave it up to you to solve the second."

Wilde and Conan Doyle pushed the door open and quickly stepped inside, peering around in the gloom. The Anchorite's hut had only three narrow slit windows that allowed little light. Immediately inside was a folding camp cot and a haversack filled with clothes and Squibb's personal belongings. Behind that sat more haversacks filled with iron spikes. But something large occupied the middle of the cramped space. In the darkness, neither man could fathom what was sprawled across the floor, but it was large, covering much of the floor space, and the insides of the hut smelled strongly of earth.

They quickly noted a large number of extinguished candle stubs scattered around the hut, nesting in alcoves, atop a chimney breast, and in other places. And now both busied themselves, striking matches and lighting candles. A few moments later, the inside of the anchorite's hut glowed with the soft yellow light, revealing an astonishing sight.

"What on earth is it?" Wilde gasped. "It looks like the Professor has been building giant mud pies."

Conan Doyle and Wilde stepped closer to the shape as both men lofted their candle stubs higher, suddenly making the object clear.

"Good Lord," Wilde breathed, "It's some kind of enormous map! But what is he mapping?"

"I believe it's a type of diorama," the Scotsman finally decided, "a three-dimensional map of the Gorge. There's the anchorite's hut we stand in with Wyrme-Hallow at the bottom, denoted by the scanner of ruined cottages."

Conan Doyle's eye was drawn higher up to the shoulder of the gorge and the animal track they had followed along. Suddenly he let out a gasp of recognition.

"What, Arthur?"

Conan Doyle found a wooden rod which made a convenient pointer. He stepped to one side of the diorama and used the pointer to indicate," Look, Oscar, this is the path we followed in, and notice this wooden x of match stalks. That's where we encountered the first of the broken pocket watches and the iron stakes driven into the ground." He moved the pointer along the trail to the next match stalk cross. "And here's the second one we found."

Conan Doyle stepped back and hoisted his candle as high as he could, illuminating the entire diorama, His eyes traced the other wooden match stalks, and he quickly saw that they made a pattern.

"Look here, Oscar," he said, his voice tautening with excitement. "Look at the match stalk crosses. They appear to make a pattern."

"Yes, I see it now. They form a spiral or vortex. Not quite complete yet. Apparently, many areas have yet to be mapped. Now I understand what the Professor's up to. He's mapping the vortex. That's why he needs so many pocket watches and iron stakes. He follows the trails with a pocket watch in his hand. When the watch stops running, he marks the spot with an iron stake, simultaneously marking the outer edge of the vortex and nullifying it."

Wilde thought a moment and then volunteered. "Perhaps we need to steal the dynamite and hide it somewhere."

"Capital idea, Oscar. And I know just where to hide it. Come along, you take one end of the dynamite crate, and I'll take the other."

A look of horror transfixed Wilde's features. "Oh, dear, I had no idea that this would somehow involve my participation."

SUMMONED BY THE LORD OF THE FEY

The next morning, Wilde still had not come down from his room after Conan Doyle finished a wonderful breakfast of bacon, sausage, fried tomatoes, fried bread, fried mushrooms, fried potato cakes, fried onions sauced with baked beans, followed by two honey-sweetened cups of tea. (Thankfully, the tea was not fried.) After Aoife had cleared the breakfast dishes, and with nothing to do until Wilde appeared, the Scotsman decided to go for a turn-about the village.

Conan Doyle stepped through the Inn's front door into an idyllic morning that he slid his arms into like a warm and comfortable coat. Dew sparkled on the grass. Baaing lambs huddled close to their mother ewes, or gamboled and frolicked about the green, kicking up their newly-found legs. The morning air was clean and fresh and pullulated with birdsong. Conan Doyle strolled to the pack horse bridge and climbed its steep arch. At the midpoint he paused and leant with his elbows on the stone parapet. The stones of the bridge had yet to surrender up the last of their sun-warmed heat from the day before. Conan Doyle breathed in deep through his nose and let it out. There was an autumnal tang to the air, an-end-of-summer aroma of fructification and a ripening harvest yet to be brought in. As he lingered there, the morning sun warmed him through and he closed his eyes and surrendered to the sensation. For a moment a daydream swam up into his mind and he indulged it. Even though Edinburgh would always be his home, he loved London. It was an exciting place to live: the British Library, the scientific lectures, the literary soirees he and Jean attended, the theatre, the bookshops. But London's dark side was always present: the filth, the smoke, the poverty, the crime. He opened his eyes again and the grimy streets of London—poof!— evaporated like a wraith of chimney smoke. He looked about at the village of Wyrme-Hallow. Cotton wool sheep grazed contentedly on the emerald green grass. Ducks quacked and flapped about the ponds. The geese on their nesting boxes craned their necks and plunged their beaks into their feathers, grooming them. The cottages, the bridge, the Inn, the forest—it all formed a bucolic vision of heaven. Who would not want to live in this rustic village with its gentle pace and its beautiful skies and clean air? It seemed like a place a human soul would choose to linger, knowing that it was the best place to be alive. In the best time.

He lowered his gaze to the tiny creek that flowed beneath the bridge. The water below was glass-clear. He paused for several minutes, watching a crayfish silently scuttle between clumps of undulating river weed. And then he saw a leviathan shape cruise out from a thick stand of weed. It was the same enormous rainbow trout that Wilde had tossed to freedom, easily the largest he had ever seen. In his youth he had fished the many ponds and streams around Stonyhurst, the Jesuit boarding school he had attended in Lancashire, but compared to the tiddlers he had reeled in back then, this trout was the size of a whale and must have lived to a great age to have dodged the fisherman's hook this long. The trout's paddle-size tail stirred the waters lazily as it hovered still in the current, and then Conan Doyle could have sworn that the fish looked up, met his gaze, and stared back at him. "Good morning, Ernest," he greeted but the fish did not answer. He threw a quick glance back at the Green Man, sorely wishing that Wilde had been with him to witness this, but of course, he was alone, and when he looked back, the trout had vanished.

He   was   suddenly   startled   by   a   bowel-quaking

BOOOOOOOOOOOOM!!. Once again a plume of black smoke rose above the treetops in the far distance. More blasting by the railroad company, but this looked closer than before. Conan Doyle ground his molars at the sight. Humanity was never happy with the normal balance of nature. How many perfect places had been destroyed in the name of Progress?

His ears suddenly pricked up at the sound of a dog barking. The Scotsman lifted his gaze to see a white and ruddy brown dog crash through the saw ferns at the edge of the forest and vault onto the village green. It bounded with palpable joy across the sheep-nibbled grass, scattering the quacking ducks, and then bee-lined straight for Conan Doyle.

The small hound sprang up the packhorse bridge where it slid to a halt before Conan Doyle and sat back on its haunches looking up at him, held tilted adorably, pink tongue lolling, its stubby docked tail wagging furiously.

Conan Doyle laughed and crouched to pet the dog, which was remarkably friendly. Conan Doyle instantly recognised the breed. It was a Britanny spaniel. His uncle had brought one such dog back from Spain as a surprise for Conan Doyle's twelfth birthday.

"Hallo boy!"Conan Doyle said, patting the dog's head. Why, you look like my old dog, Bandit!"

The words suddenly caught in his throat, for as he looked closer, the dog was indeed the very double of the pooch he had had as a boy.

And as Conan Doyle examined the dog closer, he found the resemblance to his old dog uncanny. The spaniel had the exact same pattern of orange-brown splotches on a snow-white coat, along with the characteristic Brittany mask (the reason he had named the dog, Bandit). Conan Doyle's eyes misted with nostalgia as he threw his arms about the dog's neck and hugged it. His rational mind knew this could not possibly be the dog he had lost in his youth, so many years ago, and yet the dog seemed to recognize him, for it shuddered with happiness as he petted its head and stroked the furry chest.

"This is impossible," Conan Doyle breathed as the dog excitedly licked his face. "You can't be my Bandit."

In fact, Bandit had been one of Conan Doyle's earliest loves and the dog's loss his earliest heartbreak. He had been away at boarding school at Stonyhurst, and when he returned at the beginning of the summer holidays, his mother gravely informed him that Bandit had gone missing. Conan Doyle had wandered the country lanes and the fields on the outskirts of town for days calling out his dog's name, but months had passed since he'd gone missing. And then he began to hear reports that Bandit had been seen chasing sheep at a nearby farm and had likely been shot by the farmer. When it finally became apparent that Bandit was never coming home, Conan Doyle had been devastated and locked himself in his room for days, weeping inconsolably.

It was uncanny, but the dog he was petting now seemed identical.

The Brittany suddenly turned and bounded away, plunging into the forest. It bounded back into sight a moment later, looking back at Conan Doyle and barking; it was clear that the dog wanted him to follow.

The Scotsman laughed as he descended the bridge and trotted across the village green to where the dog waited. It spun around on the spot and barked at Conan Doyle, the stub of its docked tail, waggling furiously.

"You want me to follow you, boy, is that it?" When he reached the dog, it turned and bounded into the forest with Conan Doyle trailing behind. Together they followed an animal trail through the woods. Within the span of just a few feet, the forest grew dense and riotous. Soon the many saw ferns towered monstrously high. Then they passed through a dense grove of oaks. These were ancient trees, their limbs gnarled and twisted. And then, scenting something, the dog started barking and vaulted away into the brush.

"Bandit!" Conan Doyle called out. "Here boy! Here, Bandit!"

But the dog had vanished into the shadows of the forest.

Just then, something snorted, and the bushes shook as something much larger than a dog trampled through them.

Conan Doyle froze. Looked. Listened.

Suddenly, his ears rang as something large and bestial trumpeted—

a deaf-making *BBLLLLLLLAAAAATTTT* squeezed from enormous lungs. And then it lumbered slowly into sight—a stag of monstrous proportions ploughing through the undergrowth. Conan Doyle felt needles of fear tattooing his face. It was a stag all right, but so huge that it seemed prehistoric. It stood seven high feet tall at the shoulder, and its enormous rack of antlers must have spanned fifteen feet. It lolloped closer and then seemed to notice Conan Doyle, the enormous head swinging around as the beast's dark eyes met his. Even from twenty feet away, the air shivered with the reek of its powerful musk as a cloud of silvery flies flitted about the twitching ears. And then, with unhurried inertia, the stag turned and slouched away in the opposite direction.

Despite his initial terror, it was a vision that Conan Doyle felt obliged to follow. He felt as it he were seeing something no living being had ever seen: a living fossil, a relic of something vast, and primeval. And now it seemed as if the stag was leading him farther into the forest, as the dog had done before.

Suddenly the leafy canopy lightened and receded, and in a few strides, he stepped from dense forest into open countryside. There, incredibly, stood an enormous manor house. As he watched in wonder, the giant stag lolloped toward the double doors which had been left thrown wide. Here, it ducked its head, having to twist its great rack of horns sideways to allow the enormous beast to enter. Conan Doyle's mouth dropped open. He somehow needed to raise the alarm, to let the owner of the manor house know that a huge beast had just wandered into his home. He rushed to the open double doors and stepped through into a high-ceilinged, echoic entrance hall. The hall was hung with dozens of ancestral portraits ranging from miniatures to giant canvases. Unbelievably, the huge stag had vanished. But then he heard the distant clop of hooves on marble and peered down a long hallway that led into a great hall in the bowels of the house. He was just in time to see the giant stag saunter past the end of the corridor. The beast's head turned to throw him a casual glance before it clopped on and vanished from sight. Less than a second later a human figure stepped out into the corridor—emerging from the same direction the stag had disappeared—and strolled toward him.

"Good day to you, sir," the man called, his voice friendly. "But are you lost?"

"But, but, but—" Conan Doyle stammered, flabbergasted and gesturing excitedly. "An enormous stag just wandered into your home. Surely he must be in there with you?"

"A stag, eh? You don't say? Well, well!" the man chuckled. He stopped and threw a casual look around. "A giant stag? How alarming."

The man looked kindly at Conan Doyle and extended a hand.

"My name is Finn. I am the local Lord," he said, introducing himself. "These woods and the village are all within my demesne."

Up close the man looked to be in his sixties, with patrician good looks, a touch of grey at each temple, and an enormous salt-and-pepper moustache. He was a big brute of a man with a broad chest and massive shoulders bulging beneath an exquisitely tailored outfit of tweed knickers and jacket, a silk cravat looped about this throat. Although he was the very image of a country squire, there was something decidedly odd about his face, a suggestion of the feral, that Conan Doyle couldn't quite put his finger on, although the man did sport the most elaborate pair of eyebrows he'd ever seen—that bristled like salt-and-pepper shoe brushes.

Conan Doyle was still preoccupied with concern about the giant stag, which he believed could cause great damage. "But sir, the stag. We must attend to him!"

The local Lord smiled, seeming utterly unconcerned, but then he conceded, "Well, I suppose we'd better go have a look for him, then. Come along."

Lord Finn led the way and Conan Doyle followed his back. As they moved along the corridor, Conan Doyle couldn't help but notice the family portraits hanging on either side.

The Lord's ancestors were dressed in costumes contemporary to their period, right back to Tudor times. It was strange, but each of the faces had a decidedly beastial look: here a cleric who resembled a badger; there a woman posed in a chair, her head covered in a medieval hennin, and whose huge round eyes resembled those of an owl.

Finally, they emerged from the corridor into a great hall with a hammer-beam ceiling soaring high above. At the far end of the hall, an enormous carved staircase ascended to a second-floor gallery that circled the room. The hall featured scant furniture: a large throne-like chair with a smaller chair to its left. Hanging behind the throne-like chair was an enormous, floor-to-ceiling tapestry that stretched across one entire wall. The tapestry was evidently ancient and depicted the front rank of a medieval army seen head-on: armoured knights astride their steeds, archers clutching their bows, foot soldiers wielding shields and swords—an army assembled, ready to step out from the tapestry and attack.

Conan Doyle rubber-necked around the hall. No giant stag could be seen and it would be impossible to miss. "I, I, I don't see it," he stammered.

The Lord smiled indulgently and offered an explanation, "I'm sure the poor beast simply wandered out through another door." The man's voice was cultured and aristocratic, although there was a familiar, yet unplaceable, West Country lilt to it. "I'm afraid we are in the habit of leaving doors and windows open in this house. Very often the local beasts of the woods wander in and make themselves at home. We are used to it and find it amusing."

Conan Doyle was alarmed at the Lord's casual response.

"But shouldn't we do something? The beast was enormous! Quite the largest stag I have ever seen in my life."

Again, the Lord smiled, as if sharing a joke with himself. "I shouldn't concern myself if I were you."

Just then Conan Doyle heard the soft neigh of a horse, and, from the corner of his eye, seemed to catch one of the knight's horses at the right-hand edge of the tapestry, tossing its head. But when he looked, it was just the tapestry being stirred by an unseen breeze.

"I am Lord Finn Montcartre," the man said and extended a hand for a handshake.

"Doctor Arthur Conan Doyle," the Scots author replied, automatically stretching out his hand in response, "but please call me Arthur." And although Conan Doyle was a big man with large limbs, his hand was swallowed like a child's by the Lord's enormous hand, so that he was forced to drop his eyes and saw, to his amazement, that the Lord's hands had fingers of such an extraordinary length, that they seemed to sport an extra knuckle joint.

The Lord saw Conan Doyle goggle at the sight and chuckled. "Yes, Dr Doyle, you've noticed my hands. A peculiarity common to those of my ancestry." He seemed for the first time to notice something missing. "But where is your Irish friend, Mister Wilde?"

His words sent a stab of fear through Conan Doyle's heart. "How do you know about Oscar?"

The big man chuckled softly. "As the local Lord, I know of all things that occur in the village. As I said, it is my demesne. I know of you and what you are famous for. After all, I was the one who summoned you."

"What?" Conan Doyle's chest tightened as he began to feel a palpable sense of danger. "My friend, Oscar and I, came to Darvington because of a letter I received from a young girl."

"Yes, Wilhelmina told me about you. About your valour. Your bravery. And your interest in all things supernatural. When I heard of you, I knew there be would be no others . . ." He trailed off suddenly and smiled at himself. "I knew of no others, *in the world of men*, who could help us. And so I had her write to you."

The second revelation stunned Conan Doyle. "You know the Shepherd sisters? Oscar and I have come in search of them. But we have been unable to find them." He looked around himself in alarm. "Are they here? In this house? Do you have them hidden somewhere?"

The Lord raised a hand. "Please, calm yourself. The Shepherd girls are safe. Indeed, they are not within my house. They are close by but hidden. However, I cannot allow them to return to Darvington. They face great danger. There is a canker in that town of men. A worm that is eating the flower. Until that canker is removed, the Shepherd girls are safer with us."

Conan Doyle studied the big man's face. "This is the same danger that led to the disappearance of the four village girls?"

The Lord nodded sadly.

"And you believe the Shepherd girls could suffer the same fate?"

"If I could see into the future—if I had powers of divination—I would say . . ." he paused tellingly ". . . yes."

"You're him, aren't you? The Lord of the Fey? Perhaps I do have a keen mind, but I am not much for riddles. What did you summon me here to do? I am merely a writer. A scribbler."

Amusement played about the Lord's face. "Come, you are much more than that. You have a keen mind, as does your Irish friend."

"If you truly are the Lord of the Fey, then you are responsible for the death of some innocent men. I watched a young boy die in my arms. He was innocent . . . and yet you killed him."

The Lord smiled sadly, but his voice was cold when he spoke. "It is always the innocent who die. We of the Fey are also innocent, but this railway will destroy us." The Lord shifted his feet and spoke in solemn tones. "You have seen Wyrme-Hallow. It is very special. But it is just a part of my demesne. And now all, the woods, the village, the gorge itself, is threatened with destruction."

Conan Doyle thought a moment, and suddenly the answer came to him.

"The railroad. You are afraid the railroad will destroy the village?"

The Lord nodded. "Iron is poison to the Fey. They will run the iron rails straight through the centre of Wyrme-Hallow—an iron dagger stabbed through the heart. We will all perish and our kingdom with us."

Conan Doyle mulled his words a moment and then said, "Surely they will listen to reason. They would not purposely destroy a village."

"They cannot see the village," the Lord interrupted. "It is hidden by faerie Glamour. I allowed you and your friend to see through the Glamour. Most mortals can only see their own greed. The path through Wyrme-Hallow is the straightest path for the railroad. These men who weigh the worth of everything in golden coins know nothing else. They have been trying to build this railway for years. So far faerie magic has thwarted them, but I fear they will never stop trying. That is why I have summoned you. You and your Irish friend must find a way to stop this railroad. And then I will release the Shepherd girls to return with you to Darvington."

Conan Doyle looked thunderstruck at the news.

"But how are we to do that? The railroad is being financed by the wealthiest people in Darvington. They have spent hundreds, nay thousands already. How could Oscar and I persuade them to drop their plans?"

The Lord's smile remained fixed. "Wilhelmina told us you are a clever man. A man who can ravel and unravel plots. You will think of something. Otherwise, the Shepherd girls must remain with us."

Conan Doyle felt all strength drain from him. This was insane. It would be impossible for them to persuade the Darvington railway investors to simply drop their plans.

The Lord of the Fey patted him on the shoulder. "Come now, don't be so down at the mouth. I know a solution resides in that clever mind of yours, Doctor Doyle. You must simply pry it loose. Of course, if required, I can provide a further incentive. Something to goad you into action."

The last sentence was clearly a veiled threat. Conan Doyle swallowed his fear and nearly choked on it.

"But this is beyond—"

At that moment the Scots author was interrupted by the sound of a woman wailing. He turned to look and saw a figure gliding along the upper gallery. It was a tall, willowy woman in a long, moss-green dress that stretched to the floor. Her face was hidden by a veil, although as Conan Doyle looked, the veil more closely resembled a seething fog that purled about her face.

The woman was wailing loudly and wringing her hands.

Conan Doyle turned and stared after the woman, clearly disturbed. "Who is that fair lady? What ails her?"

"That is my wife, the Lady of the Fey."

"Why is she so distraught?"

"She weeps for our future. For the lost girls. For the fate of us all."

When Conan Doyle looked again the woman was descending the stairs to the great hall. She was dressed in a beautiful gown that stretched to the floor and fitted tightly about her ankles so she was forced to take quick, shuffling steps. Despite this, she floated down the stairs and glided toward them smoothly, almost weightlessly. The Lord rose from his seat as she silently approached. As she reached them, she offered her slender hand which the Lord captured in his and kissed, and then turned and presented her to Conan Doyle.

"This is my wife, the Queen of the Fey, our Lady of Dreams. Pray, wife, could you show our guest the missing girls whose souls are in our care?

For the first time, the lady turned her head to look at Conan Doyle.

Even with her face half-concealed beneath the veil of mist, Conan Doyle could see that she was possessed of an other-worldly beauty, with almond eyes of startling emerald green. Meeting her gaze was uncomfortable, for it felt as though his soul was about to be sucked out through his eyes and into hers. Her beauty was so annihilating that he sensed that the misty veil was for his benefit and that to see her face unshielded would strip him of his senses.

"Would you care to see the Lost Girls?" she asked, her voice resounding like silvery chords struck upon a harp.

Conan Doyle, could not imagine what it meant to be introduced to the missing girls of Darvington, but he nodded and said, "Yes! Very much so."

The Lady smiled with her eyes and inclined her head as an indication that he should follow.

She glided away, and he followed, hurrying to keep up as she wafted to the staircase, and then ascended the stairs with the weightless motion of a helium balloon. As she moved, her fluttering gown flowed and reformed about her slender form as though she was a being made of smoke. Meanwhile, Conan Doyle, trudging behind, made the staircase creak and groan with every clumsy step.

They reached the top landing where she conducted him along the gallery until they entered a large room. A single object occupied the centre of the room—a kind of bower, or giant nest covered with arching tree bows from which shimmering silver curtains hung. She reached out with an elegant hand bejeweled with sparkling rings, drew back a curtain, and waved him closer, bidding him to look within. He stepped forward and peered down. The bower formed a kind of giant nest lined with satin bolsters and a scatter of plush pillows. There he saw three young girls curled up together, their eyes closed and their young bodies abandoned to the casual postures of sleep. He reached down a hand to stroke the arm of the nearest girl and found that the arm was hard and smooth and realised, to his surprise, that the girls were actually life-size dolls or puppets made of wood. He threw a startled look at the Lady, who put a long finger to her lips to shush him. Without another word, she let fall the curtain and then turned and glided away so quickly he had to rush to keep up.

"But I don't understand. These are not the real girls. They're just wooden dolls. Why—?"

"The girl's bodies lie within the Lord's demesne," the Lady explained. "We are watching over their souls until they are found. Only when their bodies are found then can they go home and their souls be released."

"I don't understand," Conan Doyle said.

The Lady smiled and spoke enigmatically, "Those who are lost, must first be found."

They descended the staircase together, although it was as if each tread moved up to meet his foot, smoothly carrying him along from step to step. Finally, he stumbled off the staircase at the bottom and threw a look behind him. Although he had been holding her hand on the way down, the lady lingered at the top of the stairs, smiling at him, but then the veil of mist that endlessly formed about her face, thickened, and became opaque, totally concealing her face. Then she turned and glided out of sight, as if moving silently on greased rollers.

In the Great Hall, he looked around for Lord Finn, but found him gone, the room empty. He searched and called out, but no one responded. Again, he heard a horse whinny and spun to look. This time, the opposite corner of the tapestry rippled as if if wafted by a breeze and then stilled. Conan Doyle moved about the house, calling out, but it seemed to be deserted, and so he wandered back to the entrance hall where he had first followed the giant stag.

He stumbled back outside from the great manor house, and as he entered the forest, the gloom fell upon him in the space of just a few strides. When he turned to look back at the manor house, it had vanished. Conan Doyle stopped and looked about himself. The forest seemed strange and unfamiliar, and he remembered that he had blindly followed the stag and now he was utterly lost. He trooped on, retracing the animal trail, hoping to find something that looked familiar, but the forest—a snarl of impenetrable shadow—grew wilder, denser. With no sight of the sky or the sun, he was a rudderless boat sailing into oblivion. For the first time, he felt a sense of rising panic, as he realised just how utterly lost he was. But then he remembered following the dog before he followed the stag. It seemed a remote hope, but he put two fingers to his lips and ripped out the longest and loudest whistle he could manifest. It had been the way he summoned his old dog Bandit back when they were hiking in the Lancashire hills.

He stood still. Listened.

Nothing.

He whistled again and waited. This time, he heard a faint bark from a long, long, long way off, and so he called at the top of his voice: "Bandit. Baaaaaaaandit!" And then he saw it: a flourish of movement in the distance, a thrashing in the saw ferns, and moments later the dog came bounding toward him and crashed to a halt at his feet, barking excitedly.

"Good boy!" He said, kneeling to embrace the dog. "Go on, Bandit, lead us home."

The dog bounded off through the forest, and Conan Doyle hurried to follow. And within a few minutes, they stumbled out of the trees back onto the village green of Wyrme-Hallow.

WILDE MEETS HIS BELOVED SISTER

When Conan Doyle wearily dragged himself inside *The Green Man*, he found Wilde sitting in one of the window seats. The empty tankard in front of him testified that he'd already had at least one drink. He was staring into space, lost in thought, his eyes unfocused. The Scots author sank down heavily onto the bench beside him and then waved a hand at Aoife and held up two fingers to order drinks.

Conan Doyle turned to Wilde, who was uncharacteristically silent, and began, "I must tell you, Oscar, of the most extraordinary experience I've just had—."

But his friend cut the Scots author short by seizing him by the wrist and saying emphatically, "No, Arthur, you must first listen to what I have to say, for I have just had the most extraordinary experience of my life!"

Aoife set down two pints of cider on their table with a wink and a smile. Wilde picked up his mug of cider and took a sip to moisten his mouth. Then he set the pewter mug down carefully and looked at Conan Doyle with a dazed-eye expression, emotions swirling upon his face.

"This morning, Arthur, when you stepped outside, I was enjoying a second pot of tea—it was very good by the way. I highly recommend it. After that wonderful start to the day, I decided I needed an amble around the village. So I ambled, which was fine, but when I arrived back the inn, I still felt restless, and I so I decided to have a short amble into the forest."

"Oh, dear," Conan Doyle said, "and let me guess, you eventually became lost?"

Wilde tut-tutted at the suggestion. "Honestly, Arthur, I know you think I am overly citified and lack any of the manly skills of orienteering and, er, I would have to agree with you. But no, I did not eventually become lost. In point of fact I *immediately* became lost. And though I repeatedly turned back, I always seemed to be going in the wrong direction. Yet courageously I ventured on, hoping to meet a local who could guide me back to the village. Eventually, I ambled out of the forest to find myself in open country by the side of a small lake."

Conan Doyle started at Wilde's words. "Wait? A lake? There are no lakes around here!"

"I thought much the same. But, nevertheless, the lake was there. It was a middling-size lake with rows of Larch trees ringing its edge. I must confess it reminded me of a lake in Ireland I visited in my youth. Although I cannot remember its name."

The Scotsman frowned so that his walrus moustache drooped comically. "And how did you find your way back?"

"I'm coming to that. An obvious path ran around the lake, and so I started walking along it. I reasoned that such a well-trodden path must lead somewhere. Soon, I noticed a figure up ahead in the distance, walking in the same direction. It appeared to be a lady, walking on her own. I hurried on, picking up my pace, hoping to catch up with her. Unfortunately, I was doing anything but ambling at this point. But despite my most earnest efforts, I had scarcely gained upon the aforementioned walker, and so I was forced to greatly exert myself. Slowly, I drew closer to the figure, which by now I could tell was definitely a woman. I redoubled my efforts, but I could not catch up with her. At the end I was practically running—yes, can you imagine Oscar Wilde running? And so, in desperation, I called out to the lady."

"And did she stop?"

"Yes, thank goodness, and turned to look around. I shouted to her that I was lost and asked her if she could direct me back to Wyrme-Hallow. And as luck would have it she said she was going that way.

She waited as I caught her up and we walked along together. The lady seemed to be in her middle-thirties and very fair looking. In fact, I was immediately struck by how familiar she seemed, and had the uncanny sense that we had met somewhere before. I asked if she lived locally. She did not. I then asked if she lived in London. Again, she did not. I asked if she had ever visited Oxford. It was only then that I was struck by what should have been immediately obvious to me—she was Irish. But her voice was somewhat odd."

"Odd?" Conan Doyle asked. "In what way do you mean, odd?"

Wilde shook his head, at a loss. "It was high, ethereal, and some-what uncanny-sounding. But she was very pleasant and warm, and so our encounter was like meeting an old friend or acquaintance. We enjoyed pleasant conversation as we walked and finally we came to a place where the footpath forked in two directions. We stopped, and she pointed and told me that I must take the right-hand fork, which would lead me back to Wyrme-Hallow, whereas she had to take the left-hand fork.

I thanked the lady and took her hand. I was going to kiss it, but her hand seemed strangely cold. So I merely gave it a squeeze and said, 'Slán Agat,' the traditional Irish farewell, and she repeated the same to me. And so we parted ways, and I continued on the right-hand path which soon plunged back into the forest. But at the last moment, I paused and threw a look back at the woman. At that same moment, she turned to look back at me. She smiled and gave a little wave and a smile..."

Suddenly the words evaporated from Wilde's mouth. His lips quivered as he attempted and failed to form words. "It ... it ... it was the smile I recognised. A smile I could never forget. For at that moment, I remembered when and where I had last glimpsed that smile. It was a smile I had seen a thousand times and never thought to see again—a sly look from out the corner of her eye and an impish upturn to her lips. The truth crashed in upon me and I knew at once who the lady was."

By now, Conan Doyle was leaning over the table, eager to hear the climax of Wilde's story.

The Irishman combed a hand through his dark hair and released a shaky breath. "I don't know if I ever told you this, Arthur, but growing up in Ireland I had a sister, a younger sister, named . . . Isola." His voice cracked as he pronounced her name. Conan Doyle had never before seen his friend in such a rush of emotion, Wilde's eyes pooled with tears, and he drew out a handkerchief and dabbed them as he fought to recompose himself. Finally, chin quivering, he stuttered, "Of . . . of all the Wilde family, we were the closest in age, just two years separating us. I was the older brother; she the younger sister. Isola was a golden ray of sunshine dancing about our home. But when she was not quite ten years old she suddenly took a fever. My parents sent her to recuperate with friends in the countryside so as to breathe the clean country air. But then she died of a sudden effusion of the brain." Wilde's voice shrivelled into silence, his jaw quivered, unable to speak, but finally, he resumed, "She was not quite ten years old. My mother, Lady Wilde, was prescient of my sister's death. I heard her say she saw a dark malignancy waiting for our family, and sadly, horribly, unspeakably, her prophecy proved true."

Conan Doyle had been listening intently. Wilde's revelation rocked him back in his chair, and now he spoke in a slow and low voice. "But your sister was only nine. You said the woman you met upon the path was older? A woman in her thirties?"

Wilde looked at his friend with sparkling eyes. "Yes, the woman on the path was in her mid-thirties . . . the very age Isola would have been . . . if only she had lived."

Neither man spoke for a while as a stunned silence settled over them.

Finally, Wilde spoke in a breaking voice, "I met my sister, Arthur. I talked with her. I walked with her. But it was only after we parted that

I recognised the smile, the turn of phrase she used. Only then I recognised her as my sister."

Wilde looked wondrously at Conan Doyle. "What kind of place is this we find ourselves in, Arthur? There is something uncanny about it."

Conan Doyle quaffed a mouthful of cider and set his mug down. "You are correct, Oscar. These woods, this village, it all lies within the demesne of the Lord and Lady of the Fey. I met them today and they set us a task we must perform. And now let me tell you the story of my encounter today, for it is even more fantastic than yours."

Wilde listened quietly as Conan Doyle related his experience of following the dog, then the giant stag, and then the meeting with the local Lord of the Manor, and of the grand house that appeared so out of place in the deep forest, and of the Lady of the house, who seemed to wear a veil of mist and who showed him the missing girls sleeping in a manger—only to then reveal they were merely puppets.

When his story was finished, the two men sat silently watching as the shadows crept from their hiding places in the corners of the room and settled themselves in the chairs around them. After a long rumination, Wilde looked at his friend and quietly remarked. "I now have no doubt where we are. In this strange village where the cider tastes like Perrier-Jouët, and every meal is a heavenly feast and the beds are like sleeping on clouds. When we looked down from the top of the Gorge, we saw an abandoned village in ruins, but as we walked into the main street we found the houses intact and lived in."

"I have no doubt you are right. We have been here two days and have not found hide nor hair of the Shepherd girls. So why do we tarry here? The reason is clear: we have been beguiled by magical food and drink, by beautiful faces, by rustic charm. Our vision is clouded, star-dazzled. Since I was weaned from the nipple my mother, Lady Wilde, regaled me with tales of the Fey and their glamour, which is a magic that casts a delusion over a human mind."

Conan Doyle looked about him. "But this cannot be pure illusion. He slapped a hand against a wall beam, stomped his foot on the floorboards, picked up his pewter tankard and banged it down on the table. This inn, everything, is solid, material. It couldn't just be an illusion!"

Wilde leaned over the table toward Conan Doyle's and spoke in a torn whisper. "If you met the Lord of the Fey, then we are close to the centre of his power, and so the Glamour is strong here. Everything seems solid, but we could be sitting in a pile of rubble. We are guests of the Fey—in the place where the living and the dead intersect— where fish speak, and giant stags wander through the halls of a great manor house. It is no accident that you received that letter and that the Shepherd girls have vanished but only after laying a trail of bread- crumbs that we followed to this place. I believe we have been summoned by the Fey and now they have set us a task we must finish . . . or who knows if we will ever be allowed to leave."

CONAN DOYLE AND THE OAK;
WILDE AND THE WILD BOY

When Conan Doyle went to bed, the Brittany he had discovered lay curled up and sleep at the foot of his bed. But when he awakened the next morning, the dog had somehow vanished. He puzzled how the pooch had somehow escaped his room, and vaguely wondered if the dog belonged to someone in the village.

After breakfast, Conan Doyle wandered about in the nearby forest for a good half hour, trying to rediscover the animal trail that had led him to Lord Finn's manor, but without the dog to guide him, he soon found that he was getting hopelessly lost.

He was about to give up the search when he stepped into a slight clearing in the dense canopy and saw something that snatched the breath from his lungs.

He had entered an oak grove. The grove was clearly ancient, and it was apparent the trees growing there had not seen the glint of an axe blade in centuries. The limbs of the oaks here were twisted and tortured, like witches' hands grasping at the sky with gnarled fingers. He walked slowly through them, senses alert. He knew that oak groves such as this one were sacred to the ancient druids and were the scenes of blood sacrifice and other dark rituals. In the hush of the forest, he seemed to sense their wraiths hovering near. He moved slowly through the sprawl of tortured trunks and limbs, reverential of their great age.

And then he saw it.

It stood alone as if the other oaks had bowed before it and backed away, refusing to crowd it. The oak was enormous. By its size, Conan Doyle guessed it must be hundreds, perhaps a thousand years old. It had likely stood here since the blue stones were dragged from Wales to Stonehenge, the Armada burned, and a crown was lowered upon the head of a young Victoria.

His scalp prickled as he stepped closer. From ten feet up the limbs branched into a confusion of gnarled and twisted boughs, each clawing up at the sky. A clattering tangle of dead limbs crowned its top. As he slowly circumnavigated it, Conan Doyle guessed that the trunk must be close to fourteen feet in girth. The surface was wrinkled and puckered so that imaginary faces surged up from the gnarled bark: here an old man's face; here an old woman's face, and here a monster's face. The trunk contained many hollows, marking places where a bough had once sprouted, only to have flourished and then fallen with the passing of centuries. The remaining limbs sagged beneath a heavy carpet of thick, green moss. And then, as Conan Doyle reached the far side of the tree, he saw something that shocked him.

A small wooden door, set low in the trunk of the tree.

"A faerie door!" he gasped. He immediately felt disappointment that someone had chosen to disfigure this wonderful old tree by nailing faerie doors onto it. But then he looked closer at the doors. Whoever had made them was a skilled artisan, for they featured elaborate scroll work, and the elegant shape had obviously been made by a fine craftsman. He tugged at the tiny brass door handles (they looked like gold dulled and patina'd with moss and the verdigris of decades). The doors swung easily open to reveal a large space within the hollow bole that could easily accommodate two adults. He pushed the doors closed again and continued his circular inspection.

"Hello, gentle old friend," Conan Doyle said, addressing the tree. "Aren't you magnificent?" He laid a hand respectfully on the mossy trunk and then sucked in an astonished gasp as something like electricity flowed from the trunk, through his hand and into him. As the tree spoke not to his mind but to his soul, he heard a familiar voice: "Arthur."

He thought the voice was coming from all around him, but then he realised it was coming from inside his mind. It was a voice he instantly recognised—his first wife, Louise.

"Louise! Louise, my beloved! Is that you?"

Yes, Arthur, it is I, your wife . . . your first wife.

"Oh, my darling Touie. I never had the chance to say goodbye."

I know you love me, Arthur. You proved it over and over. With your every action. Don't think I didn't know your love . . . and your sorrow.

I miss you, Louise, every day. I wish you were here to share, to see what I see."

Know that I am with you always, Arthur. I have never left your side.

It was his first wife, Louise. Grief poured out of Conan Doyle in an unstoppable torrent—terrifying in its ferocity. He fell to his knees as huge, soul-wracking sobs threatened to tear his body in two. He wiped the tears from his face and finally staggered to his feet. He felt emptied, drained, purged of all his grief. His mind was now in a quiescent place where a profound sense of peace and gratitude had the emptiness that had prevailed. He had desperately loved his first wife. He still did. But now he had experienced the sad, final goodbye he had never been able to enjoy in life.

We will be together, my love. We will all be together. All souls dissolve into the One Great Love. I will wait for you there. Until then, love your new wife; she is a wonderful lady. And love and watch over our children. Goodbye, my love. Goodbye . . .

"No, wait, Touie. Please linger a moment longer . . ."

Conan Doyle felt the link break as the ethereal current that had flowed through him suddenly ceased, releasing him. Suddenly his hand was just resting on an old tree bough.

It took him another twenty minutes to compose himself before he staggered from the oak grove, wiping the last of his tears on his sleeve.

~

Wilde entered the forest in a rhapsodic mood. After checking his mirror that morning (as he scrupulously did every morning), he noticed a distinct lack of wrinkles around his eyes. His hair was glossy and dark and seemed to have grown overnight so that it had assumed the length and weight of his aesthete days and fell heavily in glossy waves about either side of his face. Feeling young and desirable (a feeling he had not enjoyed in years) he ambled through the village, nodding to the anonymous rustic types who gawped at him, clearly struck by his radiance. After a circuit of the village, he wandered into the woodland but stopped after only a few feet.

He had come in hopes of finding the footpath that led to the lake where he had met his sister, but one path diverged into many, and he debated which one to follow. Eventually, he selected a path at random and began to walk along it. To his surprise, the woody trail ended abruptly, and he stepped from forest gloom into bright summer farm fields ablaze with golden barley and wheat. The transition was abrupt and stunning. He looked around to see if he could see a farmer he might question.

And then Wilde spotted him.

Not a farmer, but a beautiful youth, a rustic farm boy traipsing through the wheat. He was shirtless in the drowsy summer heat, revealing a slender chest tanned nut-brown by the summer sun. The youth had sun-bleached blonde curls that tumbled down to his shoulders. His slack trousers hung low on a flat stomach ribbed with muscle, scarcely held up by his narrow hips. He was the epitome of lean, beautiful youth, and Wilde felt a hot flash of desire surge through him.

Oh, to be young again. Oh to be beautiful. Oh to be filled again with the sap-ripe promise of youth.

The farm boy shyly chewed a wheat stalk and seemed to be looking straight at Wilde. At this distance, Wilde could not tell the colour of the youth's eyes, but he was somehow certain that they were the clear blue of the azure skies above and sprinkled with golden flecks of summer. The boy now smiled at Wilde and let one hand slide slowly down his bare chest like a coy invitation. Wilde quickened his pace, drawn like a magnet to this vision of Adonis. For the first time in years, he felt himself to be young and desirable again.

Wilde tugged off his hat, waved it aloft and called out, "Haloooo!"

But the boy was a long way off and unlikely to have heard Wilde's call. And now the youth flashed another teasing smile and then turned to walk away.

Wilde called out to him, "Oh, won't you wait, noble youth? We might walk together and talk?"

But the boy walked on another twenty feet when he stopped and threw Wilde a teasing look over his shoulder. When he was certain the Irishman was following, the youth strolled on through the golden wheat.

Wilde hurried after. Almost running now, he reached the field, clambered over the stile and dropped heavily onto the far side. The youth was a short distance away now, and Wilde hurried after him, arms raised as he waded through the waist-high wheat.

By now, a freshening breeze stirred and tossed the crop fretfully around him. Loose straws tumbled in the wind. And then the breeze suddenly strengthened to a gale, flattening the stalks and whiplashing the crop in undulating waves.

Suddenly, the youth seemed to have vanished, and Wilde was alone in the field. The wind ruffled its unruly fingers through his hair. He soon found that the wind had become a whirlwind, flattening a circle in the crop and that he was the centre of that circle. He threw up a hand to shield his face as stalks of wheat and chaff whipped across his face, needling his cheeks. He cowered as the wind pitched to a ferocious roar. And as the winds increased, Wilde felt himself become lighter and lighter until, impossibly, he was lifted off his feet. Wilde cried out, but his voice was drowned in the roar of the wind. Slowly, he was drawn upward, higher and higher into the air. Ten, twenty, thirty feet high. Soon he was looking down on the crop circle forming below him, the field giddily receding. He reached the height of the tallest trees and surpassed them. Soon he was a hundred, two hundred, then hundreds of feet above the ground. He knew that if the whirlwind were to cease suddenly, he would plummet to his death. As his mind struggled to grasp what was happening to him, the farm fields of England receded, shrinking to a patchwork quilt of greens and browns. Gradually, the skies above darkened, and he looked up to see the black, undulating undersurface of a storm cloud above him. And as he cried out in terror, Wilde was drawn up into the base of the towering thundercloud and vanished from sight.

WILDE VANISHES!

Although Conan Doyle waited until six pm, Wilde still did not reappear for supper. He stepped outside the Inn and called for the Brittany, and then toured around the village with the dog following at his side. He knocked on every cottage door and asked about his friend. The villagers were all friendly and tried to be helpful, but none had seen Wilde. So Conan Doyle found a shirt in Wilde's room and then took the Brittany and stepped out into the forest. As a birding dog, he knew the Brittany had a keen nose, and so he gave the dog a good sniff of the shirt and then released him into the woods. Showing willing, the dog gleefully bounded about the trails for half an hour, running this way and that, but eventually returned to Conan Doyle and sat obediently at his feet, panting, pink tongue lolling, stubby tail wagging. Clearly, the dog had found no trace of Wilde's scent. By now, hours had passed. Wilde had still not turned up as the light began to fail and great curtains of gloom hung in the trees. Hurrying against the setting sun, Conan Doyle climbed up to the shoulder of the gorge and repeated the search with the dog, but to no avail. Finally, he spotted distant movement in the forest—a human-shaped shadow drifting between the trees, and he and the dog ran after. But it turned out to be Professor Squibb. He had an empty backpack on his back and had apparently spent the day marking the vortex and pounding his iron spikes into the ground.

"Have you seen my friend, Oscar?" Conan Doyle breathlessly asked. "I believe he's lost somewhere."

The professor smiled helplessly and shook his head. "No, I've not seen him. But if he kept walking in any direction, he would pass through the wood and eventually arrive at a town."

"Yes, I suppose," Conan Doyle agreed, but his worries mounted by the minute. He was about to walk away when the Professor asked, "In the morning, I am hiking back to Darvington for supplies. Could I bring you anything?"

As much as he did not like the Professor, Conan Doyle was touched that the man had the decency to ask.

"Could you inquire at the police station about my friend? I am growing most anxious."

The Professor nodded that he would. But as the professor turned to walk away, Conan Doyle had a sudden thought and ran after him. He dug in his haversack and produced the photographic plates they had exposed on the day Wilde caught the huge trout. He handed the Professor a large bank note and the plates and asked if he could drop them at *Ye Olde Curiosity Shoppe*, which the Professor said he would do.

Conan Doyle and the Brittany continued to search the upper forest for Wilde. But by now, the sun, a bloody eye, had sunk below the far horizon, and Conan Doyle was forced to give up the search and trek back home. As he stepped through the door of *The Green Man Inn*.

O⁰⁻ he had hoped to find that Wilde had already returned, and would be seated at a table, pint of cider in hand, but Aoife and Shailagh had not seen Wilde all day. The look of worry and concern on the young women's faces infected Conan Doyle who now began to despair about the fate of his friend, as his mind began to conjure dreadful scenarios. Conan Doyle imagined Wilde having twisted an ankle and lying lame somewhere in the forest. Or worse, that he had stepped off a hidden cliff and fallen to his death or possibly was lying at the base of the cliff seriously injured. Again and again, he rued the fact that they had not stuck together, blaming himself and resolving that he would not allow Wilde out of his sight in future.

He ate a solitary meal in the empty tavern, morosely chewing the food, which was as heavenly as ever, but which tasted like pablum in his mouth. He stayed awake until late, every half hour stepping outside into the darkness to call out Wilde's name and whistle, hoping he his friend had temporarily lost his way and could find his way back to the inn.

When he finally surrendered and crawled into bed, Conan Doyle had difficulty falling asleep. He awoke often and would tip-toe to Wilde's room and peer inside, hoping to find him snoring peacefully. But each time he found an empty and unslept-in bed his anxiety mounted.

In the morning, he choked down a quick breakfast—expressly so he would have the energy to search for his friend—and then filled his haversack with apples, a chunk of cheese wrapped in cheesecloth, and two bottles of water, and resolved not to rest until he'd found his friend. He thought it unlikely but entertained the hope that perhaps Wilde had uncovered a lead on the Shepherd girls and had walked back to Darvington on his own. He had just scrambled his way to the top of the gorge when he saw a welcome form bounding toward him along the forest trail.

IRISH FIEND RUN TO GROUND!

"Baaaandit! Here, boy!"

The Brittany spaniel raced up to Conan Doyle and jumped up on his legs. Conan Doyle laughed as he crouched and petted the dog who joyfully licked his face. Conan Doyle had saved two sausages from his breakfast and now he fed them to the dog who scarfed them down, licked his lips, and then sniffed his hands for more. Once again, Conan Doyle had fetched a shirt from Wilde's room, and he held it up and let the dog have a good sniff, and then commanded, "Bandit, find Oscar! Find Oscar!"

The dog bounded off into the forest, apparently following a scent trail, and Conan Doyle hurried to keep up.

But the spaniel led him to a place he wasn't expecting to go.

Together they crashed through dense stands of saw fern and gnarled oaks and suddenly stood before the manor house of the Lord of the Fey. Once again, the front doors were thrown wide, and the Brittany shot straight inside. Conan Doyle followed the dog, stepping inside the echoic entrance hall and calling out a "Halooo!" but received no answer.

And then he heard the dog bark from deep within the house. When he followed the sound into the great hall, the Lord and his

Lady sat reclined upon their thrones. Bandit sat at the Lord's feet as he ruffled the fur of its chest and petted its head. The Lady of the Fey sat rigidly on her throne, so still he could not tell if she was breathing, although the eyes of both of them raised when he entered the hall.

"Welcome Mister Doyle," the Lord allowed and nodded. "Have you come to report success?"

Conan Doyle was initially tongue-tied. "I . . . not yet. It is a vexing problem. I am wracking my brains for a solution."

The Lord went on petting the dog and then waved it away. The dog wandered over to the Lady of the Fey and curled up at her feet.

The Lord made a disgruntled noise in his throat and then reached into a pocket and held something up to show Conan Doyle.

"Do you know what this is, Mister Doyle?"

In the Fey Lord's hand, he gripped a metal object—some kind of steel spike.

The Scots author squinted at the object he held up and finally ventured: "It looks rather like a spur."

The Lord nodded and smiled. "Very good. It is a medieval spur, or as they are known by their other name, a goad. I have chosen a goad for you, Mister Doyle. A goad that will encourage you to speed your efforts to stop the railway. Even now, my demesne shakes to the thunder of their explosions. They are blasting through rock formations that are sacred to the Fey, cutting down the trees of our oak groves. Violating all that is sacred and holy to us."

"I don't know what I can do! How to stop them. They have the law on their side."

"The Fey do not care about human laws. Why should you?"

"Because Oscar and I could get into trouble. We could be arrested—"

The words dried up in Conan Doyle's mouth. He suddenly had a terrible premonition as to what had happened to Wilde. "My friend, Oscar. He disappeared. He's in trouble, isn't he?"

The Lord smiled, but it was not a friendly smile. "As I said, a goad. A spur to make you hurry."

"Why don't you just use your magic to stop it? You've done so in the past."

"Because the man you know as the Professor knows how to thwart faerie magic. He is scattering his iron spikes far and wide, shutting down the vortex. Once the vortex has been destroyed, no faerie magic will prevail. The railroad's iron rails will pierce the heart of the Fey domain, and we will be no more."

As if to punctuate the Lord's threat, at that moment, a distant boom marked the resumption of blasting by the railway workers.

With nothing left to say, Conan Doyle went to leave. But then he turned back. "One question. The legends speak of faerie kingdoms that sank beneath the waves—Lyonnesse and such. Do the Fey still live in such downed places?"

The faerie Lord nodded. "Yes. Beneath the waves. Atop a mountain. In a swamp. The Fey are not bound by mortal constraints."

Conan Doyle ran the Lord's words through his head, then nodded. He looked at his dog, who was licking the faerie Queen's fingers. He made a clicking sound. The Brittany leapt to its feet and scurried after Conan Doyle who marched resolutely out of the great house. An idea had formed in his head was gathering substance as he stepped back into the shadows of the forest.

When he neared Wyrme-Hallow, his heart skipped a beat when he glimpsed movement in the distance. A figure was moving toward him along, flashing in and out of sight behind the trees. The figure was rendered anonymous by the distance. Surely it must be Oscar. Where had he been all this time?

But then the figure stepped from behind a tree. Conan Doyle's heart sank when he saw it was Professor Squibb. He was lugging a backpack that was stretched out in a square shape, which Conan Doyle guessed contained another full carton of pocket watches.

Conan Doyle ran up to him.

"Professor Squibb! My friend Oscar. Have you seen him? Any news from Darvington?"

The professor eased the straps of the backpack from his bony shoulders and grunted as the heavy pack dropped to the path with a thump. Squibb paused a moment to lift his pith helmet and wipe the sweat from his face with a handkerchief.

"I've just come from there," he panted, struggling to catch his breath. "Have you not heard the news?"

"News? What news?"

In response, Squibb crouched, opened his haversack and drew something out—a newspaper. With a grim look on his face, he handed it to Conan Doyle, who spread the paper wide. When Conan Doyle's eyes grazed across the screaming black headlines, he was forced to suck in a deep breath.

There, on the front page of the Darvington Recorder, was a pen and ink drawing of a face he knew only too well, while above, in enormous type, read the screaming banner headline: IRISH FIEND RUN TO GROUND!!.

A bitter taste uncoiled on Conan Doyle's tongue. He looked up at Professor Squibb in astonishment. "What on earth is going on?"

Squibb's filthy nails scratched his perpetual three-day growth as he answered. "It's your friend. They found him wandering in circles in the fields outside of town, stark naked and cut to ribbons by brambles and tree branches. Nearby, they found the clothes of the missing Shepherd girls. The dresses were ripped and covered in blood. Your friend has been arrested for their murder."

"Arrested for murder?"

"It appears so. And it gets worse. Everyone in Darvington either knew or is related to the girls. I'm afraid the locals aren't too happy with your friend. He'll be lucky if he lives long enough to be carted off to the assizes at Exeter."

"What do you mean?"

"From what I heard, there's talk of a lynch mob!"

Conan Doyle bit his lip and looked away at the village of Wyrme Hallow far below. Now he understood exactly what kind of goad the Lord of the Fey had prepared for him.

THE BALLAD OF DARVINGTON GAOL

On the hike back to Darvington, Conan Doyle once again had to pass through the strange band of fog. He passed the Devil's Cauldron, and once again could not repress a shudder as he looked down at its drowning turmoil of waters.

He set himself a cracking pace, and so was tired and footsore by the time he slogged into Darvington. It suddenly struck him that he had no idea where the Darvington Police Station was. A pair of Darvington citizens, a burly gentleman in a too-tight suit and a comically tiny bowler and his petite wife were just passing, and Conan Doyle rushed up to accost them. "Excuse me, good folk, but could you direct me to the Police Station?"

"Yes, certainly—" the man began, but then the smile evaporated from his face, and he peered down at the Scots author suspiciously. "Hang on a tick. I know who you are. You're the friend of that Irish monster, ain't ya? That murdering pervert!"

The woman interrupted. "Now, George, we don't want any trouble." The woman grabbed his husband by his brawny arm and attempted to pull him away, but he shrugged her off violently. "Get off, woman, before I give you a backhander!"

The man went nose to nose with Conan Doyle. "Here's what you and your friend deserve." And with that, the man made a revolting hawking noise and then spat in Conan Doyle's face.

Conan Doyle was shocked and taken aback. He snatched out a handkerchief and wiped the spittle from his face as the man and his wife turned to walk away.

Conan Doyle was both a gentle man and gentleman, but now his molars clenched and anger tightened his chest. "Oh, sir, you've forgotten something," he called after the couple.

The large thug spun around and glared at Conan Doyle. "Yeah? What's that, then?"

Conan Doyle calmly walked up to the man, raised his boater, and smiled "Your manners," he said and threw an uppercut that landed squarely on the point of the man's chin, snapping his head back violently. The bully crumpled like a puppet with its strings cut and lay sprawled unconscious on the cobblestones.

The Scots author threw a remorseful look at the man's wife. "Sorry, madam. I am not normally a violent man, but your husband needed to be taught a lesson."

The wife's reaction took him by surprise. "Yes, he did, and gawd bless ya, sir, for givin' him one." The woman patted Conan Doyle on the arm and laughed. "The police station is just down the road a bit, on the right. Ya can't miss it."

Unfortunately, it would not be the last angry encounter Conan Doyle would face that day. When he arrived at the Darvington police station, a crowd of more than two dozen local men loitered outside. The ugly mob was clearly spoiling for a fight. Conan Doyle knew that if things boiled over, he would be facing not just one opponent, and his chances would not be good.

"Here comes his pal now!" someone shouted, and suddenly the Scots author found himself the focus of the mob—a collection of sour-faced, cursing men in flat caps. When they saw where Conan Doyle was intending to go, each man stepped in his way so that he was forced to push his way through their barging shoulders as they flung curses in his face. But despite some shoulder-bruising clashes, he somehow made it to the police station door. Inside he found the roly-poly ginger sergeant resting the overhang of his belly on the front desk. The sergeant looked up when he walked in and sneered. "Thought you'd be along before too long. We got your friend locked up tight. Won't be here for long, though, as he's being dragged off to the assizes in the morning where he's going up before the judge. You'll have heard the name of his famous forebear: Judge Jeffreys. This one's also called Judge Jeffreys and is just as predisposed to hangin'"

Conan Doyle clenched his teeth but ignored the taunt. "Where is my friend? I demand to see him."

The rotund desk sergeant grumbled a curse beneath his breath and threw a surly nod at a plain steel door. He snatched a jangling set of jailor's keys from their wall hook, slouched his belly over to the door, unlocked it, and mumbled, "Ya got five minutes."

The steel door led into a small room with two separate barred cells. The room reeked of despair and the overflowing slop bucket in the corner. The first cell was unoccupied, but the second held an inmate in a prison uniform who was rolled, hunch-shouldered, with his face to the wall.

"Oscar! Oscar, it's me."

When the figure rolled back to face him, Conan Doyle was relieved to see his Irish friend, although he was shocked by his disheveled appearance. Wilde was unshaven, and his hair was tousled and matted. Dark bruises and livid scratches covered his face. Compared to his youthful and vigorous appearance in Wyrme-Hallow, he looked pale and drawn and seemed to have aged ten years.

"Arthur, thank goodness you are here. I've been in this wretched gaol for two days, feeling rather like St Mark as he awaited in his cell to be thrown to the lions."

For the first time, Conan Doyle took in what Wilde was wearing.

"Yes, I know," Wilde said, "I am ashamed to say that, as I had misplaced my clothes, they kitted me out in this convict's uniform. Both the blouse and trousers are a horrible fit and rather itchy around the unmentionables. Although I admit, I do rather like the arrow motif. If I only had a few accessories, say a cummerbund and a colourful scarf, I could actually make something of it."

"Damn your fashion sense, Oscar, we need to get you out of here! I read the account of your arrest in the newspaper, but I want to hear the story from your own lips. What on earth happened? Those bruises and scratches on your face, did Lawless and his bully boys do that to you?"

The Irishman shook his head. "I don't believe so. But let me tell you what I last remember."

While Conan Doyle listened, Wilde narrated his final memories of Wyrme-Hallow, of walking from the woods without transition into open countryside, of spying the golden youth wading through the wheat field (his description left out the erotic aspect of the encounter) right up to the whirlwind forming around him and then lifting him off his feet.

"That's impossible!" Conan Doyle said. "It would require a large tornado to lift a man of your weight and girth off the ground."

"Is that a scientific evaluation, Arthur? Or merely an opportunity to criticise my expanding waistline? If so, I do not need to be chided by you—I have my tailor and my wife to perform that function. I am quite aware that I am growing porcine of late."

"No, it is not a criticism of your girth, although—" Conan Doyle let the word dangle and did not finish his thought. "Although you could weigh as much as one of your boys. It wouldn't matter. A typical English whirlwind would not be able to lift—"

"A fat man like me." Wilde interrupted. "Yes, there's no need to bang on about it. I think you've made your point!"

"And so, after you passed into the cloud—which I am convinced is an artifice of your memory, but let us move on—what next do you recall?"

"I was still spinning around and around. But this time, not in a whirlwind. Instead, I was staggering around and around in circles in a farmer's field."

"This was a different field to the whirlwind?"

"Well, of course; the first was a wheat field. This was a field filled with cows. Apparently, the livestock found my circular peripitations rather disturbing. Their alarmed lowing alerted the farmer and the next I remember, Lawless and his men had seized me and were clamping handcuffs on my wrists."

"Walking around in circles? That hardly seems a reason to arrest you."

I have not fully explained the situation."

"Ah, there's more?"

Wilde made a sour face. "Sadly, yes, a good deal more. It was the condition I was found in which led the farmer to alert the Darvington constabulary."

"And what condition was that? I shudder to ask."

"I was, er, I was in a state of undress."

"How so?"

"I was naked. Nude. Starkers. Au natural—apart from my blushes and the bruises and scratches you see and where I collected those, I have no memory of."

"Your clothes, were they found close by?"

"Ah, now we come to the next unfortunate detail. They searched a nearby copse where they did find some clothes."

"Your missing togs?"

"No, they found two dresses obviously belonging to two young girls. And they were ripped and covered in blood."

"Dear God, no!"

"And then Mrs Shepherd was brought in by Lawless. She identified the clothes as the dresses the Shepherd girls were wearing on the day they disappeared."

"But the bodies of the Shepherd girls have not been found?"

"No, but the picture does not look good for me."

Suddenly a booming voice from behind interrupted their conversation. "No, it does not look good for you, Mister Wilde."

Both men looked around. Chief Lawless stood in the open doorway, a hangman's smile smeared across his face. He addressed Conan Doyle, "And the next step, Mister Detective Fiction, is for your friend to be transported to the local assizes, where he will brought up in front of Judge Jeffreys."

"But this is ridiculous! You cannot believe either of us is involved in any murders of young girls. We only just arrived in Darvington."

"Yes, you only just arrived. And on the same day, both Shepherd girls vanished without a trace. And now we have solid evidence of foul play involved in their disappearance."

"But what of the others? Four girls have gone missing before this."

"And who is to say you and your friend haven't visited Darvington before? You take a train from London, and the next instant, a girl vanishes. Meanwhile, you and your friend are back in London before the hue and cry can be raised."

"That is a preposterous assumption. It would never hold up in court."

"We'll see about that. Your friend goes up before the judge tomorrow. And, believe me, Judge Jeffreys is a man with no sense of humour who is unlikely to be swayed by Mister Wilde's witticisms. And I'm sure that when the judge learns that Wilde is the author of a lewd and disgusting novel, his mind will quickly be made up. Only a sex fiend and pervert could write such degenerate work!"

Lawless snarled a final laugh and left, banging the door behind him.

Wilde looked at his friend, his face utterly distraught. "So if the locals do not lynch me tonight, I have to look forward to facing Judge Jeffreys, the latest in a long line of hanging judges. Oscar Wilde is doomed. Whatever are we to do, Arthur?"

A GOAD FOR CONAN DOYLE

When Conan Doyle slogged back to *Wyrme-Hallow*, he paused at *The Green Man* long enough to quaff a pint of water, and then he clambered up the packhorse bridge where he whistled as long and loud as he could. When his Brittany bounded from the woods, Conan Doyle crouched down beside the dog and hugged him around the neck. Then he whispered in the dog's ear. "Find the Lord of the Fey, Bandit. Find him for me."

The dog's docked tail waggled furiously and when Conan Doyle released him the Brittany bounded away into the woods, with the Scots author rushing after to keep up. The dog led him through a bafflement of trails and finally led him to a place he'd been before. It was not the Lord's Manor house.

Instead, before him loomed the faerie fort and the black opening of the burial barrow Professor Squibb had shown them. The Scots author stepped in through the rocky opening, passing the spirals and cup and ring marks carved into the walls and submerged in the ancient darkness of the barrow. The light from the opening behind him threw a wan circle of illumination on the far wall. He could just make out a crude painting. Two seated figures faced him: the tallest was a figure of a cross-legged man with a rack of great horns on his head. Beside him, a female figure—thin and willowy with huge, owl-like eyes with feathers sprouting from her face.

He ducked as a horseshoe bat skimmed out of the darkness, brushing against his cheek.

"Cernnunos and Áine," Conan Doyle whispered.

At once, a man's resonant voice filled the echoing darkness. "We have many names besides those."

Suddenly the cave began to fill with a glowing light. It grew ever brighter until the walls of the burial barrow melted away and Conan Doyle found himself in the same great hall with its soaring hammer-beam ceiling and the huge tapestry he had visited before. Lord Finn sat in a throne, his lady reposed in a throne beside his.

"Have you come to tell me that the railway is no more?" he asked.

Conan Doyle swallowed. "I . . . I . . . sadly, no."

"Then why do you trouble me mortal, until you have down what I bade you to do?"

"My . . . my friend, Oscar, has been arrested. They are to try him for murder. For the murder of the Shepherd girls."

"Those are human affairs. If I had pity for humans, I might spare some for your friend. But sacrifices must be made. I told you that before."

"In order to prove my friend innocent and free him, I need to produce the Shepherd girls to prove they are still alive. I know you are hiding them somewhere."

This time the lady spoke. "The girls are here under our protection."

The Lord added. "They can only leave under their own free will. We cannot order them to leave."

"But as you said, sacrifices must be made. I just need them to appear in Darvington to prove they were not murdered."

"The eldest girl told us that you are a cunning man who can ravel and unravel mysteries. The answer is clear, then, you must unravel this one . . ."

And with that the light began to ebb away.

"Wait!" Conan Doyle shouted and the light trembled and then grew brighter. The Lord and his Lady reappeared on their thrones.

"A final question. There are many legends of faerie kingdoms that were drowned in the ocean, or at the bottom of deep lakes. And yet the sound of bells are heard coming from the water. How is this so?"

The Lord threw a dismissive wave. "We are the Fey, such things are immaterial to us. Our kingdoms my be at the top of a mountain or at the bottom of the sea. Fey magic is not constrained by human concerns."

Conan Doyle mulled the words over for a long moment. "Yes, that is what I had hoped. If I can find the girls and persuade them to return with me to save my friend, I believe I have a way of stopping the railway."

The light began to fade. The walls of the hammer beam hall, the great tapestry, faded into coloured scratchings on a stone wall, and then the light fled, leaving him, once again, marooned in darkness.

When Conan Doyle emerged from the burial barrow, squinting at the light, the Brittany sat on the path, waiting obediently.

"Come along, Bandit," Conan Doyle said, petting the dog's head. We must return to *The Green Man*. We have no time to spare."

A TEAR IN THE GLAMOUR

On the walk back through the forest, Conan Doyle had had chance to think deeply on the Fey's powers of glamour. He and Wilde had experienced it now many times: seeing a village where only ruins remained, and seeing a grand manor with a great hall and an enormous tapestry that was actually the stony chamber of an ancient burial barrow. He knew now that faerie magic could baffle the senses, so that when stepped back inside the tap room of *The Green Man*, he looked around and wondered what was real, and what was an illusion.

Shailagh and Aoife were nowhere to be seen, but then he heard their laughter and titters coming from the kitchens. He found the vicar sitting at his usual place—the small nook in the shadow of the fireplace. He stepped to the bar and called out for service. When Aoife appeared he ordered two pints of cider. Aoife drew them from the cask and set them down before him with a smile. Conan Doyle picked them up and wandered over to the vicar's table. When he set the pewter mug down before the curate, the vicar looked up at him.

"Join me in a pint of cider?" He asked.

Six empty tankards abandoned on the table showed that the vicar was well along on his journey to inebriation and a slack smile floated to the surface of his face.

"That's right Christian of you, sir. I don't mind if I do."

Conan Doyle dropped into the chair opposite. He took a quick bite of his cider and then sat studying the vicar.

At that moment the vicar had his face plunged deep into his tankard. Conan Doyle watched his Adam's apple pulsing as he poured the drink into him. After a mighty quaff, he set the tankard down, wiped his mouth on his sleeve, then ripped a prolonged belch.

"Good stuff, eh?" The Scotsman smiled.

The vicar grinned. "Aye, that it is, sir. The best!"

Conan Doyle paused a second and finally spoke softly. "You look much younger than in your photograph."

The vicar fixed him with a puzzled frown. "What you mean? What photo?"

"The one in your parlour. Your wife—Delphinia is her name?—showed it to us."

At the comment, the vicar's eyes widened. His mouth dropped open. "I . . . I . . . don't . . . ? I have no wife, sir. I think you are mistaken—."

The denial had no effect on Conan Doyle, who continued, "I assume the girls came here first? You saw them use the faerie door and then followed? Only you found the lure of everlasting drink too enticing, and so you never went back. How long have you been here, Reverend Shepherd?"

The shaky smile on the reverend's face quivered and collapsed. "I . . . told you . . . you are mistaken. That is not my name—"

"Reverend Shepherd, I know who you really are. And now I know where Wilhelmina and Philomena are. They have been hiding in plain sight all along."

Drunk though he was, the reverend had enough wherewithal to try to conceal his lie.

"I think you are mistaken, sir. I am not this Shepherd fellow."

Conan Doyle paused to sip his cider. He set the tankard down and smiled genially across the table at the Reverend. "I finally understand the power of the Glamour. Is it just an illusion? Or are you really as young as you appear?"

"I am who I am, sir." But then his face collapsed in despair.

"How do you know?" he hissed in a voice knotted with despair.

"Of course, I suspected Shalaigh and Aoife from the beginning. You, I had not even considered. In the photograph your wife showed us, you were an old man with a white beard. You seemed far too young to be the same person. But then I overheard Shalaigh upbraid you. She called you Father, but you are a clergyman of the Church of England. By rights, she should have called you Reverend, not Father. I was puzzled by the mistake and the fact that you did not correct her, but then I suspected the truth that you really are her father. Why have you deserted your wife? Your life in Darvington? Your parish?"

The reverend's face grew wretched. "This is my life now. My past is lost forever. I have renounced it all."

And what of your marriage vows ?" Conan Doyle paused a moment and then added, "And what of the vows you made before God?"

Suddenly the man's face contorted into a mask of tragedy. A keening sound squeezed from him. Snot dripped from his nose. He covered his eyes with a shaking hand. His shoulders heaved as he broke into sobs. "Oh, I am fallen. I am fallen," he wailed. He wiped his runny nose on the black sleeve of his cassock. "My sin is compounded by the day. I am fallen and can fall no farther!"

Conan Doyle watched the Reverend's histrionics and then quietly asked, "The missing girls from the village. Did you murder them?"

"What? NO!"

"Are you lying?"

"No!" The Reverend Shepherd's head hung in shame and after a few moments he mumbled, "But I think I know who did. I suspected at the time, but what could I say? I had no proof. Who would believe me? I was a drunk, dishonoured, a sot. And so I took the coward's way out. I fled here. People who come to Wyrme-Hallow never leave. Why would they? It is paradise. The girls came to get me, but I wouldn't go back, and now neither will they. And, yes, I slunk away here and fell into a mug of cider and have never climbed out."

At that moment Shalaigh emerged from the kitchens carrying a tray of washed tankards. Conan Doyle waited until she set them down behind the bar and Aoife began to hang the tankards up before calling both of them over.

"Wilhelmina, Philomena, could I bother you ladies for a moment?"

Hearing their real names called aloud, both of the young women froze. Only Shailagh turned to respond to Conan Doyle's call as the young woman gasped and then forced a smile. "What did you call me? My name is Shailagh."

"I'm sorry Wilhelmina, but your father has confessed everything. I long suspected, but now I know who both of you are." He looked first at one and then the other. "Or should I say, you Philomina . . .' He looked first at one and then the other. ". . . and you Wilhelmina."

The girl who claimed to be named Aiofe looked guilty and dropped her gaze to her bare feet, but Shailagh put on a coy smile and tried to bluff her way through. For a moment an excruciating silence prevailed, but then a laugh trickled out of Shailagh, "Ah Doctor Doyle, that is such a fanciful notion—"

"There's something I must tell you both," the Scotsman interrupted. "Something you may not be aware of. My friend Oscar has been arrested by the police and is in the gaol in Darvington."

Both girls' eyes widened at the news.

"In gaol?" Shailagh repeated. "Whatever for?"

"I'm afraid you girls are the cause, although the Lord of the Fey has played his part. My friend, Oscar, vanished two days ago. I discovered that he was found walking in circles in a farmer's field near Darvington. He was in a state of undress and was mentally baffled. More damningly, when the local constabulary was summoned, they found the clothing of two young girls in a nearby copse. The dresses were torn and covered in blood. Mrs Shepherd was shown the clothes and positively identified them as belonging to her daughters. Naturally, the police concluded that the Shepherd girls had been murdered and arrested my friend for the crime. He is to be transported to the prison at Exmouth where he will stand trial for murder. I fear he may well hang!"

The girls looked horrified; their mouths dropped open at the enormity of the news. Aiofe threw a hard look at Shailagh. "I told you we'd get someone in trouble! Now look what you've done!"

Shailagh's eyes filled with tears. "I didn't mean to get anyone in trouble. I thought they'd find our clothes and stop looking for us. I thought they'd think we'd been murdered like the other girls."

"What can we do?" Aiofe asked.

"What can you do?" Conan Doyle repeated. "You ladies, and you alone, have the power to prove, beyond a doubt, that my friend is not a murderer. Only you can save Oscar's life. I just pray we may still be in time."

Conan Doyle rose from the table. "Now I will fetch my haversack, and then we must prepare some water and food for the hike back to Darvington."

"There's no need for that," Shailagh interrupted.

"Why do you say that?"

Aiofe stepped forward, hands fiddling with her apron strings, and said, "Because we know a quicker way."

Minutes later Conan Doyle and the Shepherd sisters stood before the ancient oak in the forest grove. Shailagh and Aoife walked around to the faerie door on the back of the trunk and pulled it open. "We'll go first," Shailagh said. "Then it's your turn. Get inside and close the door. Wait a moment and then open the door again."

Half incredulous, the Scots author watched as the two young women opened the fairy door and ducked inside. When they had settled into place, Shailagh called, "Wait a moment before you open the door again." And then she pulled the door shut. Conan Doyle waited a moment, expecting to hear a whoosh or some kind of noise, but all was silent. Finally, he felt foolish waiting and began to think he was being pranked. He grabbed at the door handle and snatched it open, "I've been waiting—" he started to say, but the inside of the oak was empty. The girls had vanished.

Conan Doyle clambered through the tiny door into the hollow

trunk with some unavoidable grunting. Finally, he reached up and pulled the faerie door shut after him. He sat there for some time in the darkness, once again expecting to hear a noise or feel a sensation, but nothing.

He finally deduced it hadn't worked for him, so he pushed the door open again.

But when he clambered out he was in the garden of *The Old Rectory*. Suddenly he understood how the Shepherd girls had been able to snap the photos of *Wyrme-Hallow* and then return to replace the Midge camera to its spot on the picnic blanket; for standing before him were the Shepherd sisters, returned to the form of young girls.

THE DEAD GIRLS RETURN!

That morning the streets swarmed with half the population of Darvington, which spilled across the road outside the Darvington Police Station. A police Black Mariah hitched to two brown mares was parked immediately outside and now the front door of the police station flung open as Oscar Wilde, both hands securely manacled, was strong-armed out the door by the thin and fat constables, and pushed through the jeering and booing crowd (some of whom took the opportunity to land a surreptitious punch or two on Wilde). Chief Lawless, smiling grimly, turned a blind eye as he followed behind.

As Wilde was forced to climb onto the rear step of the prison wagon, he resisted for a moment, shrugged loose of the big policeman's grip, and turned to address the crowd.

"At last, an audience!" he cried. "People of Darvington, Oscar Wilde is guilty of many things: a razor-sharp wit, an impeccable dress sense, stylish deportment, but I am innocent of the murder of anyone, expressly of the two lovely Shepherd girls who are angels amongst us."

His words were like kicking a hornet's nest, for a buzz of outrage swept through the crowd of onlookers. Wilde tried to speak further, but shouts, curses, and cries of "hang 'im!" drowned out his voice.

"Will that be your plea when you meet Judge Jeffreys?" Lawless taunted. "I'm sure he's familiar with the infamous Oscar Wilde and his degenerate writings. You might as well tie the rope around your own neck and save us the trouble!"

The stout policeman tried to push Wilde into the Maria, but he clung to the door, resisting. "Wait! You must ask my friend Arthur Conan Doyle. He will vouch for my innocence. Plus he will be able to explain how I am incapable of this murder!"

The Police Chief now pushed through the crowd and the shorter man snarled up into Wilde's face. "It seems as if your friend has run away and sought to save himself. But don't worry, I am about to issue a warrant for his arrest. He will be brought in for questioning and no doubt you will both share a gallows in Exeter."

"LAWLESS!" a man's loud shout vaulted over the heads of the crowd. All heads turned to look, and the crowd saw the owner of the voice. It was Arthur Conan Doyle walking toward them down the centre of the Darvington High Street. He was holding the hands of two small girls who walked on either side of him. Gasps swept through the crowd as they instantly recognised the Shepherd sisters.

As he reached the crowd, it parted before him, and Conan Doyle and the girls walked up to where Lawless stood, his mouth agape.

"Release my friend, Lawless, Conan Doyle demanded. "Here is irrefutable proof of his innocence. Not that you care about proof, innocence, and the rule of law."

"But-but this is a trick!" Lawless stammered.

"A trick? How so? Here the Shepherd girls stand before you in the flesh."

"But we found their clothes soaked in blood," the stout constable complained.

"The blood of a chicken stolen from the kitchen larder," Conan Doyle explained. "A childish prank. The girls ran away from home and pretended to be murdered, but in actual fact, they were camping out in the woods."

The Darvington crowd, which was now all smiles, began to cheer the girls' safe appearance.

Lawless went incandescent, spluttering with impotent rage, but finally, he threw a resentful nod to the rotund ginger constable who stepped forward and unkeyed the cuffs pinioning Wilde's wrists as the crowd began to clap loudly.

"Ah, the sound of applause," Wilde fountained as he rubbed his chafed wrists. "I have heard it often in the theatres of London and Paris, but I confess it has never sounded quite so sweet as now."

"Come along, Oscar," Conan Doyle said, helping his friend step down from the Mariah. "Let's leave before Lawless changes his mind. Plus, we must return to Wyrme-Hallow. I made a promise to secure your freedom, and I must make good on it."

As they walked back through the crowd, Conan Doyle spotted a familiar face and stopped to address him.

"Excuse me, but are you not the attending doctor I saw when Jenny Dawkins was found?"

Lawless was looking on, and the doctor seemed uncomfortable at being addressed publicly. "I am afraid I cannot help you, sir." The doctor said in a loud voice. "And I must be going now. I am a busy man and have appointments to attend." The man tipped his hat to Conan Doyle and then turned and quickly walked away.

"Wait!" Conan Doyle shouted.

The doctor froze as the Scots author stepped up to him. "When Jenny Dawkins' body was pulled from the river, I saw what appeared to be a garrotte around her throat."

The doctor threw an uneasy glance in Lawless' direction in a clear signal to Conan Doyle and then announced in a loud voice that was clearly intended for Lawless and the crowd to overhear: "I'm afraid I cannot discuss my patients with you, sir. Now good day to you." The doctor raised his hat again but quickly muttered, "Number 42, High Street." And hurried away.

Conan Doyle watched him go and then leaned close to Wilde and whispered. "Oscar, you take the girls and wait for me at The Old Rectory. Oh, but don't let Mrs Shepherd see you—not just yet. I will join you later, but first I must consult with the town doctor."

The four of them continued up the curving rise of the High Street, and when they were out of sight of the crowd, Conan Doyle left the others and hurried on, moving into the shadow of the shop fronts. He stopped outside the doctor's office as the others continued on.

When he knocked on number 42, the door opened quickly, and he slipped inside. Moments later, Conan Doyle and the Darvington doctor were alone in his surgery.

"You understand my need to be discreet?" The doctor asked.

"Yes, of course," Conan Doyle replied.

"My name is Doctor Harrison," the man said, extending his hand for a handshake.

"Conan Doyle," the Scots author responded. "I too, am a doctor, although I haven't practised for a while."

"Yes, Doctor Doyle, I am well aware that you are a fellow doctor. I must point out that I am also a fan of your Sherlock Holmes stories. I was quite astonished that day at the river when I looked up and saw you and Mister Wilde together. However, given the rather tragic circumstances under which we met, I could hardly have said anything."

"Yes, I quite understand."

"I think you saw what happened when Jenny was removed from the water?"

"Yes, she had what appeared to be some kind of garrotte around her neck?"

The doctor nodded grimly and then opened a drawer on his desk and removed the very garrotte, which he laid on the desktop. It consisted of a length of thin, stout cord with a piece of wood dangling from it.

"As you say, it was a garrotte. It took quite some time to unwind the cord and pull it from the flesh of Jenny's neck. It was buried very deep in her throat."

Conan Doyle's eyes dropped to the garrotte on the table. "What is the piece of wood from?"

The doctor picked up the garrotte and held it up for inspection. Up close Conan Doyle immediately saw that the wooden "stick" had a precise notch cut into it. "A mortise and tenon joint," he noted and then was hit by an immediate realisation. "It was a cross! A wooden cross hung from a stout cord."

"Hold out your arm," the doctor said to Conan Doyle. "He placed the loop of cord around Conan Doyle's arm and then began to twist the wooden stick, winding the rope tight. "I believe the loop around the girl's neck was wound tight using the cross piece as a kind of capstan. No doubt the great pressure as the rope went taut caused the cross piece to snap off."

By now the rope was tight around Conan Doyle's wrist, and he felt its crushing power. He looked up at the doctor's face. "I know of two people who wear such a cross . . ."

The doctor nodded sadly as he pulled the garrotte from Conan Doyle's arm; He spoke in a thin whisper, "Yes."

". . . the Reverend Troutt and the Chief of Police, Albert Lawless."

The doctor shook his head. "Not just them. The girls who volunteer at the church are all given the same cross to wear."

Conan Doyle recoiled at the thought.

The doctor covered his eyes with a trembling hand. "I wanted to come forward," he said in a quavering voice, "but I didn't know who to approach, and I didn't want to falsely accuse someone. I have been a doctor in Darvington for more than thirty years. I birthed most of these people. Set their broken limbs. Dosed them with medicines for their fevers. Buried some. They're not just patients. They are friends. Family. It is hard to think of one of them being a murderer."

"But one of them is," Conan Doyle said. "He picked up the garrotte and studied it, his face as serious as death. "But I am baffled as to why would a murderer leave their calling card on the victim? Why would they be so careless?"

The doctor cleared his throat and finally ventured. "Jenny Dawkins was smaller and lighter than the other girls. She was missing for a month before her body was discovered in the lower falls, a week after a torrential downpour—several inches of rain in just an hour. The Wyrme ran much higher than usual and overflowed its banks in places. Presumably, Jenny was swept free and carried down river to where we discovered her. None of the other girls have ever been found."

"So you think she was put in the water, where the murderer thought she would never be seen again?" Conan Doyle mulled the thought over a moment and then concluded. "The Devil's Cauldron. I believe the girls were murdered and then thrown into the Devil's Cauldron."

The Doctor pondered morosely and then nodded his agreement, "Where no one who falls in ever comes up again."

TROUTT ALERTS LAWLESS

Conan Doyle caught up with Wilde and the Shepherd girls as they passed the railroad station.

"Oscar, when you return to *The Old Rectory*, make sure the girls aren't seen by Mrs Shepherd, not yet, at least."

The Irishman's face drew into a puzzled frown. "Whatever for? We have the girls. We can just return them to their home. It's time for you and me to jump on a train for London before that horrible Lawless chap arrests us again for something he trumps up."

"We cannot leave Darvington just yet. The Lord of the Fey extracted a promise from me. I must make good on it."

"Whatever now?"

"Remember what young Philomena said to us when we first encountered her in the garden?"

Wilde shook his head uncertainly, "Something about wizards and a dragon?"

"Precisely. We are the wizards and we must fulfil the prophecy. We must release the dragon to save the village."

Wilde screwed up his face in bafflement. "Dragon? What dragon? What are you talking about?"

"I believe it's all connected: the railroad, the murdered girls. I'll explain back at Worm-Hallow."

Conan Doyle started to walk away as Wilde called him back.

"Wait! Where are you going?"

"You go ahead with the girls. I'll explain later. First, I need to rattle the cage of the Reverend Troutt—with two t's."

Wilde let out a sigh as he watched his friend hurry away. He looked down at the Shepherd sisters. "Sorry, ladies, this will all be over some day." As he spoke the words, Wilde reflexively reached for his silver cigarette case. It was only then he realised he was still dressed in the drab gaol uniform. His cigarette case and matches were in the same place his missing clothes had disappeared. He let out a heartbroken sigh, but then he looked up and saw the Tudor facade of *Ye Olde Curiosity Shoppe* just down the road, and a hopeful smile lit up his face.

~

The Reverend Troutt was in his pulpit, preaching to the congregation, when Conan Doyle shouldered through the heavy wooden door into the gloomy church. He deliberately let the door crash shut behind him with a thunderous boom. All heads in the congregation snapped around to look.

The Reverend Troutt paused mid-sermon and looked up, his round eyeglasses bouncing the light back and hardening into opaque disks.

The reverend was clearly startled to see Conan Doyle but quickly recovered.

"Ah, another worshipper," he proffered his best beatific smile. "Late, but all are welcome to worship in God's house."

Conan Doyle noticed Tilly, the carrot-headed little girl, standing beside the pulpit holding an open bible on a red velvet pillow. She wore a simple wooden cross strung around her neck on a stout cord.

Conan Doyle's jaw clenched at the sight. He stepped forward and lobbed something at the pulpit. The broken cross he had borrowed from the doctor hit the aisle and slid along the smooth stones, stopping just before the pulpit. Troutt looked down, and when he recognised it, the sheep's smile vanished from his face, and his lips flattened to a straight line, his jaw tremoring.

"I just came to return your cross, Reverend Troutt," Conan Doyle called out. He made a point of staring at the little redhead. "By now, you must be running short of them."

Conan Doyle stood glaring at the stricken face of the vicar for a moment and then turned on his heel and walked out of the church.

∾

When the Scots author reached the tree with the faerie door in the grounds of The Old Rectory, he was relieved to see that Wilde and the girls had already gone. He opened the door and squatted down, duck-walking into the tight space. It took a few moments to rearrange his feet so he could shut the door after him, but then he managed to squeeze himself into the space and pull the door shut. But nothing prepared him for the horrible sight that awaited him in Wyrme-Hallow.

∾

Chief Lawless was brooding at his desk when the Reverend Troutt rushed into his office, his face white with fear.

"What? What are you doing here?" Lawless hissed in a barely suppressed snarl. "I've told you before—never come to my—"

Instead of arguing, the Reverend held up the broken cross. At the sight of it, Lawless choked on what he was about to say.

"How did that—?"

"The Scotsman." Troutt answered. "The fellow who writes the detective stories, he personally delivered it to me. While I was giving a sermon. He obviously knows—"

"Knows what?" Lawless snarled. "Knows what? Nothing! That's what he knows. And can certainly prove nothing."

"What are we going to do?"

Lawless brooded for a moment, jaws clamped tight, lips compressed, his face purpling. Finally, he muttered, "We need to end this business now before those interfering London gentlemen go any further." He tugged open his desk drawer, took out a small pistol and slid it across the desk toward the holy man. "Take it!"

The Reverend recoiled at the sight of the pistol. "What? I couldn't possibly—"

Lawless reached into the drawer again and drew out an even larger pistol, which he stood and tucked into his trousers. "The two writer fellows are hiding out at Wyrme-Hallow."

"Wyryme-Hallow? But that's just a ruin."

"I know, but Professor Squibb has seen them nosing about the place. They must be camped somewhere nearby."

"What . . . what are we going to do?"

"Silence them, what else?"

"But, but, but no . . . no . . . I can't—"

"We will swing for four murders otherwise. Is that what you want? You'll be defrocked and excommunicated first. Is that how you wish to face your Almighty God?"

"No! I can't. There must be another—"

"There is no other way! Take the pistol, go to the gorge, and start walking. I'll meet up with you at the Devil's Cauldron. When we find them, the two scribblers can join the other girls."

THE FAERIE DOOR

I n the oak grove, the faerie door sprang open, and the two Shepherd girls jumped out first, followed minutes later by Wilde, who had to crouch low and carefully fold his long limbs to fit through the door. When he emerged on the other side, the Irish wit looked around at his surroundings in wonder.

"Good Lord! How is this possible?"

"We are in the land of the Fey, " Wilhelmina said. After passing through the faerie doors, both she and her sisters had assumed their grown-up forms as Shailagh and Eoife.

The Irishman shook his head in bafflement. "I wish we had known about this shortcut the first time around. My blistered feet would have been grateful."

He turned to the Shepherd sisters. "You two must return to the Green Man. You'll be safe there for now. Arthur and I will come and collect you."

Whe Conan Doyle ducked his head out of the faerie door at Wyrme-Hallow, the first thing he glimpsed caused him to recoil and cry out in horror.

"Ugh!" he exclaimed. "Dear God!" His field of vision was filled with ghastly pale and hairy male thighs. When he looked up at the owner of the thighs, Oscar Wilde was looking down at him, a smile on his face

"Yes, I'm excited to see you, too, Arthur."

As he scrambled to his feet, Conan Doyle saw that Wilde's prison uniform had been replaced by the moss-green Tyrolean walking ensemble.

"Oscar!" Conan Doyle gasped, "Your clothes!"

"I stopped by *Ye Olde Curiosity Shoppe* on the way. After all, I could hardly parade around Darvington in a prison uniform—I'd look like a public spectacle. And also grey is not my colour—I looked like I'd been dead for a month. Luckily, they still had the Tyrolean outfit. Can you believe they hadn't sold it? Wasn't I lucky!"

"Yes," Conan Doyle said sourly, "how very lucky for both of us."

"I know you don't like it, Arthur, but couldn't you at least be happy for me? Isn't it bold and provocative?"

Conan Doyle eyed the yards of white Irish thigh exposed for the first time to the rays of the sun. "Provocative is one of the words that leaps to mind. It's provoking me right now!"

"But why did we come back here, Arthur? Surely we should be on a train for London."

"I made a promise to secure your release. I must now make good on that promise."

"A promise to do what?"

"To stop the railway. They mean to run the tracks straight through Wyrme-Hallow. As the girls once predicted—'the Iron Giant is coming.' Iron is poison to the fey, and I promised the Lord of the Fey himself that I would somehow prevent it."

"But how could we possibly stop the railroad? What if we're unable?"

"I have an idea. Remember when we remarked on how many faerie lands are lost beneath the waves?"

Wilde looked puzzled. "Yeeessss? But I hardly see how that pertains. We are nowhere near the coast."

"I've thought of a way. We're going to release the dragon."

"Yes, you keep banging on about that, and I'm every bit as baffled as before. What dragon are you referring to? How do we conjure up a dragon from somewhere?"

Conan Doyle smiled at the question. "First, we'll need some dynamite. Lots of dynamite."

PREPARING THE DYNAMITE

I t took a half-hour slog, with Wilde complaining every step of the
way, for the two authors to clamber back up to the top of the
gorge. After a brief rest, Conan Doyle insisted they hurry with all
haste to the Anchorite's hut, all the while keeping a sharp eye out for
Professor Squibb. The two found cover and lingered in the area
around the hut for five minutes, scanning the pathways for Squibb,
but when they saw no sign of him, they crept up to the anchorite's hut.
The same flat rock Wilde had used before still lay on the ground next
to the hut. This time Conan Doyle hefted it and smashed the hasp off
again. Then, together, they slipped inside.

"How much dynamite are we borrowing?" Wilde asked.

Conan Doyle eyed the stack of four crates in the darkened hut.

"I think all four should suffice,"

Wilde's face twisted into a mask of horror. "Dear God, no, please!"

"Sorry, I was joking. I think just one should suffice."

"One stick?" Wilde offered hopefully.

"One crate."

Wilde's lower lip buckled, but he looked slightly less horrified.
"Well, that's better . . . I suppose. "

Each create was fitted with rope handles at either end.

Conan Doyle, grabbed one of the rope handles and dragged the crate forward until Wilde could grab a handhold on the back of the crate and they lifted it. Wilde immediately gasped at its wait and urged, "Quickly, Arthur, we must set it down!"

"It's heavier than I imagined, are you sure you can manage, Oscar?"

"Yes, of course I can manage. I just needed to get a proper handhold."

The Irishman adjusted his grip and nodded to Conan Doyle.

"Very well, then."

Conan Doyle eyed his friend skeptically. Are you quite sure you have a proper grip?"

"Quite sure."

They hefted the crate between them, but had taken only two steps when Wilde fumbled his grip on the wooden crate which slipped from his hand and his end of the crate smacked down hard on the ground —WHAM!

Both friends froze, staring down at the wooden crate at their feet in horror. From within came a terrifying sound—the hissing and popping of unstable explosive.

"I fear you've woken it up now, Oscar!"

"Oh dear," Wilde said. "And I do so abhor loud, sudden noises."

"I shouldn't worry about that," Conan Doyle corrected. "If it explodes you won't hear a thing . . . because your ears will be a hundred feet away before the rest of your body catches up."

Wilde arched an eyebrow at his friend. "Was that supposed to be a morale-booster, Arthur? Because, if so, it leaves much to be desired." Wilde shifted his grip on the rope handle and lifted his end of the crate. "Dreadfully sorry," he apologised. "I promise I shan't drop it again."

"If you do, you won't need to apologise."

"Yes, point taken, Arthur but perhaps you didn't need to be quite so graphic!"

With many grunts and curse words, they manoeuvred the heavy crate out of the anchorite's hut, this time without dropping it, and set off along the trail, both men shuffling along with the heavy crate banging into the back of Conan Doyle's thighs and the front of Wilde's thighs. After only a hundred feet both were puffing and panting.

"I hope it's not rude to ask," Wilde asked between panting breaths, "but where are we going with this?"

"To the cave where Squibb showed us the underground river."

"But . . . but that's quite a distance from here!|

"Sorry, but it will be a one-way trip. We shan't be bringing it back."

"What are you planning, Arthur?"

"Chaos and destruction."

"Well, that at least sounds diverting."

Wilde kept up a steady stream of complaints as they traipsed through the forest, negotiated the switchbacks to the bottom of the gorge, and then trekked through the lower forest, taking frequent breaks to set the heavy crate down. By the time they reached the opening of the river cave, both men's backs were breaking, their thighs were burning, and their arms were turning to jelly.

When they finally reached the cave entrance, Wilde slumped to his knees before gently lowering the crate of dynamite to the ground.

"Well done, Oscar!" Conan Doyle gasped between heaving breaths. "We did it!"

Wilde knelt on the ground, his arms laid out before him. "My arms are in agony," the Irishman replied, "but it is my tailoring that most concerns me."

Conan Doyle shot the Irishman a puzzled look. "Your tailoring?"

Wilde rubbed at the inside of his elbow joints. "My arms have been stretched a good six inches. The sleeves of all my jackets will now be far too short! You may have to answer to my tailor!"

Conan Doyle allowed Wilde five minutes rest, and then he insisted that they heft the dynamite crate once again. This time they were forced to duck low as they hefted the crate between them as they crawled into the cold and dripping cave behind the petrifying well. Grunting and cursing, they dragged the crate another twenty feet into the cave, where it finally wedged itself tight between the narrowing cave walls.

"That should do, Oscar," Conan Doyle announced. He was forced to gingerly climb over the crate in order to escape from the cave. "There we go," Conan breathed while trying to catch his breath. "Like a cork in a bottle." He placed a hand against the cave wall. Beneath his fingertips, he felt the roaring rush of the underground branch of the River Wyrme—a raging monster which he would soon unleash.

"Thank goodness that's done," Wilde said, mopping his brow with a handkerchief.

Conan Doyle wiped his forehead on his sleeve. "The exercise will be good for us both."

"Exercise? Good for you?" Wilde scoffed. "That is an outrageous lie propagated by doctors and propagandists who know perfectly well what they're talking about. No doubt their arguments are all backed by experience and proven fact, but I think we all know a personal anecdote about some poor fellow who exerted himself, broke a sweat, and consequently died of a chill. These days I vacillate between two conditions: languorousness and torpescence. There are occasions when I grow short of breath buttering a scone."

Conan Doyle now pulled a solitary stick of dynamite from his jacket pocket. Next, he dug into the pocket of his jacket and produced a detonator, which he pushed into the dynamite.

Wilde watched with interest as Conan Doyle busied himself, inserting detonators into sticks of dynamite and then fitting them with a detonation cord.

"However does Arthur Conan Doyle, medical doctor, know how to work with high explosives? "

"Research, for my Sherlock Holmes novels."

"Picking locks and now dangerous explosives? It is fortunate that I specialised instead in drawing room comedies."

After Conan Doyle finished preparing a half-dozen sticks of dynamite with detonators, he placed one in each of the crates.

"I don't need to place a blasting cap in each stick of dynamite, the force of the explosion should cause all of it to explode. At least that's what I'm hoping."

"Those fuses look uncomfortably on the short side. Will you have time to get far enough away?"

Conan Doyle triumphantly held up a reel of something.

"Fortunately, I found this reel of fuse wire. Looks to be about thirty feet or longer. I'm going to wind this about each fuse and then trail the length outside the cave. Once I light the fuse, it should give me plenty of time to get clear."

"But what about Wyrme-Hallow? If you unleash the underground river, won't it be flooded, too?"

"Yes, it will. That's my plan. Remember all the stories we discussed, all the faerie villages that were drowned by the sea, but which you can hear the bells of the church above the waves? I believe the same will be true for Wyrme-Hallow. I intend to save the village by drowning it."

"Arthur, you are unconventional to the last."

"Oscar, I want you to go back to the village and collect the girls and the Reverend Shepherd and then take them to the oak grove. We will use the faerie door to return to Darvington. I'll be along as soon as I have everything ready."

"Should I not stay to help you?"

Conan Doyle looked uneasy. "The dynamite is sweating and unstable. It would be better if only one of us risked his life—in case of a mishap."

"Ah, I see. Once again Arthur Conan Doyle is being brave and selfless. I really hope to break you of that habit someday."

And with that, Wilde got up and limped away, back in the direction of Wyrme-Hallow and The Green Man Inn.

TROUBLE COMES TO WYRME-HALLOW

W hen Wilde stepped back inside *The Green Man Inn*, he found the Reverend Shepherd slumped over the table, apparently passed out. The pewter tankard in his slack hand had tipped over, and a lake of cider had pooled on the tabletop and was dribbling onto the floorboards. The two young Shepherd girls were shaking him and trying to rouse him from his drunken stupor.

"Oh, dear!" Wilde said, taking in the scene. "What's happened?"

The two sisters looked forlorn; both were close to tears.

"Father's drunk and refuses to leave!" Aiofee cried,

"But he must leave!" Wilde insisted. "In just a few hours, the entire village will be underwater."

Just then, the Inn door chimed open, and an unwelcome guest strode in.

Albert Lawless

Wilde and the girls were all struck speechless at the sight of the Police Chief.

Lawless threw a grim smile at Wilde. "Well, well, look who it is— our famous Irish pervert? I was hoping to find you here."

In the sudden silence, floorboards creaked as Lawless strode across the room. He ignored the girls and their father as he first looked at

Wilde, and then his eyes swept about the place, taking everything in and sizing things up.

"This is a very strange village," he continued. "From the top of the gorge, it appears to be a ruin. But when I climbed to the bottom, I was surprised to find that everything is intact." His wandering stopped when he stood in front of Wilde. "How do you explain that?"

"Perhaps you need spectacles," Wilde suggested.

Lawless barked a mirthless laugh at the comment. "Very good, Mister Wilde. There's that famous wit of yours."

Lawless looked around the room. "And where is your Scottish friend? The so-called scribbler of 'detective yarns'? I do hope he's somewhere close."

"Arthur has set off back for Darvington. I am to join him."

"Really? I have a colleague joining me. It's very likely your friend will run into him."

Lawless stopped and gave a lip-curling sneer at the soused figure of the Reverend Shepherd. "A hopeless drunkard—and a man of the cloth, to boot. Not a very wholesome example!"

Now he fixed his gaze on the two Shepherd sisters. "You two ladies seem very familiar. Do I know you?"

"I'm Shailagh," the eldest sister quickly answered, ducking a quick curtsey. "This is Aoifee. We work here."

"We're from the village," Aoifee quickly blurted.

Lawless stared intently at the girls' faces, and Wilde feared he had twigged who they were.

But then he turned on his heel and walked back to Wilde, where he stood looking up at him. Then he casually reached down, produced a set of handcuffs from his belt, and smilingly said, "Give me your hands, Mister Wilde.

"I have just had my innocence proven irrefutably. All of Darvington witnessed the return of the Shepherd girls."

"You, sir, are a self-confessed sex monster. I have no doubt we will find more evidence of crimes you have committed."

"You cannot arrest me, Mister Lawless. I have been proven innocent. You have no authority to do so."

At the comment, Lawless reached into his belt and drew out the large revolver. And now he pressed the muzzle to Wilde's chest. "Resisting arrest? Another crime. Now I can shoot you dead where you stand, or you can agree to come along peacefully."

Wilde said nothing as Lawless cuffed his hand together and then took him roughly by the arm, spun him around, pressed the muzzle of his revolver into Wilde's back, and set him walking with a brutal shove.

The Shepherd girls watched helplessly as Wilde was pushed through the door.

As soon as they had stepped from the Inn, the inert form of Reverend Shepherd suddenly came alive.

"Father!" The girl's cried. "Your not drunk, after all."

The reverend jumped up from the table. It was obvious he'd been shamming drunk all along.

"Quick girls!" Said. "Where is Mister Wilde's Scottish friend?"

"He's gone to the river cave," Shailyn answered

Suddenly the reverend Shepherd was brutally sober.

"You girls stay here. I must find Mr Doyle and tell him what has befallen his friend."

And with that, the Reverend dashed from the Inn, on a mission to alert Arthur Conan Doyle.

INTO THE MAELSTROM!

Conan Doyle inserted a blasting cap in five separate sticks of dynamite and then connected a length of fuse to each one. When he had finished, he evenly distributed the sticks among the crate by pushing the slightly tacky sticks in between other sticks of dynamite. Conan Doyle knew that dynamite exploded by the shock wave generated by the blasting cap—the smaller explosion triggering the larger explosion. He reasoned that the five sticks evenly distributed should send the whole lot scattering to atoms. But as he grasped the reel of fuse wire it felt damp. The cave was a humid place, hardly ideal for storing fuse cord. For the first time Conan Doyle worried that the fuse might be so damp that it might sputter out before the flame reached the dynamite.

Still, there was nothing he could do now, so he trailed the long fuse outside the cave until it ran out, another twenty feet past the cave opening. He reasoned that the length of the fuse wire should give him plenty of time to run clear and start climbing for higher ground. Conan Doyle slipped a box of matches from his shirt pocket. He took out a single Lucifer and was ready to strike it when he seemed to hear a faint voice calling his name. The roar from the underground river drowned out most other sounds, so he stood up and looked around.

He was just in time to see the Reverend Shepherd running toward him. Repeatedly falling down and getting up again, and waving his arms wildly.

The Reverend staggered up to Conan Doyle and collapsed at his feet, gasping for breath.

"Reverend Shepherd?" Conan Doyle asked. "What is it?"

"Lawless!" the cleric gasped. "Lawless. He's here!"

The Scotsman paled at the mention of the Chief of Police's name.

Conan Doyle grabbed him by the shoulders and helped him sit up. "Lawless? What about him?"

The reverend shook his head, his face frantic. "He came inside the *Green Man*! He took away your friend Wilde. He's dragged him off to Devil's Cauldron—at gunpoint!"

Despair swept through the author of Sherlock Holmes. If Lawless had Wilde and was heading for the Devil's Cauldron, it was clear what he had in mind. Conan Doyle's hands shook with adrenalin as he pulled out his box of matches. When he checked the contents, he found he had only four matches left. He removed one match, placed it in his pocket, and then pushed the box of matches into the Reverend Shepherd's hands.

"If I am not back in an hour, you must light the fuse cord and then run. Climb as fast and as high as you can."

"Wait!" The Reverend cried, seizing Conan Doyle by the sleeve. "Lawless is armed with a pistol. What are you planning to do?"

"The Scots author shook his head. "I have no idea. Hopefully, something will come to me."

And with that, Conan Doyle abandoned the task of lighting the dynamite to the cleric and ran off. The only thing he knew for certain was that he had to catch Lawless before Wilde ended up in the Devil's Cauldron.

Ten minutes into his race toward the Cauldron, Conan Doyle developed a crippling stitch in his side. Still, he pushed on, bent over slightly, one hand clamped to his side as he fought to ignore the pain.

But when Conan Doyle arrived at the Devil's Cauldron, he found no signs of Lawless or Wilde. Instead, he recognised an unmistakable figure standing close to the edge of the falls, looking down into the boiling waters. It was the Reverend Troutt, who wore his white clerical robe. His hands, hidden in the long sleeves, appeared to be pressed together as if in prayer.

"Praying for the souls of the girls you murdered?" Conan Doyle shouted as he walked toward him.

Troutt's head snapped around at hearing his name called aloud. And indeed, when the cleric turned to look at him, tears were flowing down his face. "I cannot go to prison," he wailed. "Yes, I have sinned, but my sins must never come to light."

"A little late for that," The Scotsman replied."

The reverend shook his head as if to shake the thought away. "My guilt must be drowned in these waters, where the bodies of the girls rest."

"And how are you going to prevent me from telling?"

At that moment, the reverend hitched back the sleeves of his surplice with a jerk of his shoulders, for the first time revealing his soft, pink hands and the small pistol clutched in them. Now he pointed the pistol at Conan Doyle, although his hands were trembling wildly.

After a moment's consideration, Conan Doyle muttered, "Put the gun down, Troutt. It's one thing to murder a helpless child. Much harder to shoot a grown man in cold blood." As he spoke, the author was steadily inching closer, ready to grapple with the reverend and snatch the gun away.

But then Lawless stepped from behind a tree growing on the very edge of the drop, pushing a manacled Wilde before him. He gave the Irishman a brutal shove so that he stumbled forward and crashed to his knees. Lawless now pushed Troutt aside. He was armed with a much bigger weapon, a Webley revolver, and he held the muzzle of the pistol aimed at Conan Doyle's chest. "I think you'll find that I have no compunctions about shooting either one of you."

As if it could do any good, Conan Doyle reflexively half-raised his hands in surrender.

Troutt now menaced both with his revolver. "Get up!" He snarled at Wilde. "Now, step closer to the edge."

Both men exchanged a look and hesitated. "Do you think he'll really shoot?" Wilde muttered.

"It was him," Troutt whined. "I was merely led off the straight and narrow. I never wanted to murder—"

"Shut up, Troutt!" Lawless snarled. "Say nothing more. In truth, the good reverend is more guilty than me. My daughter's death was . . . " he trailed off as he face contorted with emotion, ". . . an accident. But I had to make sure she didn't tell . . ." So I confessed my sin to Troutt of what I had done to my own daughter. He explained that the fault was not mine. But that certain children, certain young girls, were jezebels, wicked creatures sent by the devil to lead men into temptation. To make us commit terrible deeds. He confessed he had dealt similarly with two such girls in his old parish."

"We must give this up, Albert!" Troutt wailed. "Our sins are coming out. My soul is already burning in hell The killing must stop now!"

Lawless flung a hideous look at the reverend. "It hardly matters, Troutt. They will both be dead in a moment. Besides, you, of all people, should know that confession is good for the soul."

Conan Doyle's jaw clenched with outrage. "And then, the other two girls. You both committed outrages upon them and then murdered the poor angels?"

Lawless's face distorted with hatred. "They were not angels. They were evil incarnate—the pair of them. They led us into temptation. Like all females, they were sluts. Whores. Filthy creatures of the flesh."

When Wilde spoke, his voice was brittle with horror. "And you hung a wooden crucifix about the throats of each girl and then strangled them with it."

Troutt's face contorted with hatred, and he spoke in a trembling voice, "They were corrupt. Imperfect, polluted with sinfulness. We gave them back to God where their sins will be burned away."

Lawless raised the revolver and levelled it at the two authors. "Mister Wilde, raise your hands if you would." Lawless produced a key, unlocked the handcuffs, and tucked them into the top of his trousers. "It would be a shame to waste a good pair of handcuffs." He flourished the pistol again. "Now, both of you, step a step backwards. And again."

Conan Doyle looked behind him. Both of them stood with their heels overhanging the edge of the gorge, behind them a forty-foot drop into the boiling waters of the Devil's Cauldron

Conan Doyle threw a helpless look at Wilde. They were helpless. There was nothing either could do to prevent their imminent deaths. Still, Conan Doyle tried one last attempt to reason with Lawless. "So you're going to shoot us in cold blood and dump our bodies in the river. Is that it?"

Lawless fixed them both with a bitter grin. He moved closer, keeping the pistol trained upon them. "Quite the contrary. I prefer not to shoot you. That would leave bullet holes. But make no mistake, if I must shoot you, I most certainly will. Chances are you will never come up again. Your bodies will be held down by the waterfall—tumbling endlessly in the downforce."

Conan Doyle suddenly knew where the missing girls were and why they had never been found. He nodded at the Cauldron. "That's where the girls are, isn't it? Their bodies held down by the force of the waterfall?"

"Yes, you'll get to meet them." Lawless grinned. "Both of you, tumbling over and over until the rotted meat slides from your bones and sinks to the bottom of the pool. In the unlikely case your remains are ever found, it will look like an unfortunate accident. One of you fell in, and the other went to rescue him. Tragically, both drowned."

Lawless suddenly lunged forward, slamming his shoulder into Conan Doyle's chest and toppling him backwards. Conan Doyle fell, arms windmilling. He hit the water with a huge splash and went under. Wilde grabbed Lawless's arm, and the two grappled, but then the Reverend Troutt rushed forward, and he and Lawless combined their weight, sending Wilde tumbling over the edge.

When Conan Doyle hit the water, the deep chill sucked the breath from his lungs. He could not close his eyes in the glass-clear water and clamped his lips tight as he fought the urge to gasp. He splashed back to the surface a moment later, where he sucked in a huge lungful of air. He was a strong swimmer, but the first whirlpool seized him and he was powerless to resist. A second whirlpool snatched him from the first and twirled him around so that the full force of the cascade crashed down on him, driving him deep beneath the water. As he plunged ten, twenty, thirty feet, his ears popped painfully. The powerful current drove him down to the bottom of the stony pool. He had his eyes open the whole time. Underwater, the cauldron was like a vast cathedral pierced by shafts of light, tremulous and shifting. The water was glass clear, swirling with multiple vortexes of bubbles suspended with dead leaves and sticks and other debris, spinning in watery constellations. The bottom and sides of the pool were a jumble of huge, water-rounded boulders. Here, the clash of whirlpooling currents grabbed him and sent him tumbling. He had managed to snatch a breath before he hit the water, but he knew he could only last a few seconds before his lungs gave out and he would start to drown. He saw a burst of bubbles above as Wilde hit the water and was quickly sucked down to the same depth where the two friends crashed together and then surged apart, battered by the force of the cascade.

After another thirty seconds, both men released their final breaths in a stream of bubbles, and their lungs filled with water as they began to drown.

Then Conan Doyle's drowning brain began to hallucinate. As water poured into his lungs, a droning noise poured into his head—a sound like the singing of angels. Purple clouds swarmed his vision. And then he saw three sylph-like forms swimming toward him through the water. The sylphs took the form of three young girls, their hair flowing in the water, their clothes, long since torn to ribbons, flowed about them. Each of the girls had a crucifix and its stout cord, forming a garrotte around their throats. The girls moved through the water with the speed and grace of dolphins. The girls swam to him and took him by the arms and dragged him along, pulling him free of the down-rushing vortex of water. Together they towed him across the bottom of the cauldron to the downstream edge, where the water had worn a deep groove between the boulders. They pushed Conan Doyle through the groove, where he was snatched by the outrushing current and swept rapidly downstream. A moment later they had done the same with Wilde, and now he barrelled after Conan Doyle.

Both men were swept downstream until they were washed up on a shelf of rock angled into the river. The impact of hitting the shelf gushed the water from his lungs. With his last reserves of strength, Conan Doyle dragged his waterlogged form up the rocky shelf until his head broke the water, and he choked in a breath of sweet-smelling air. Wilde swept up on the same shelf, and now Conan Doyle reached down and grabbed Wilde by an arm looped beneath his chin. Conan Doyle then inched up the shelf, dragging Wilde until his face also broke the surface. Both men lay there for some time, coughing, gasping, choking, until at last, they recovered enough strength to crawl higher up the rock shelf. Finally, legs and arms shaking with exertion, they both managed to scramble up the shelf onto the riverside path, where they flopped like beached seals, coughing their lungs up.

It took a full twenty minutes until both men had recovered sufficiently that they were able to sit up, where they hunkered on the ground, wheezing and shivering.

"What just happened, Arthur? I thought I'd died and was in the afterlife. I saw water nymphs, naiads, mermaids, or whatever they were . . ."

"I believe those were the three murdered girls. We are in a very strange place. We are in the realm of the faerie."

"If it hadn't been for those girls . . ." Wilde gasped, combing the wet hair from his face with his fingers.

"We'd be very dead," Conan Doyle answered, finishing the thought, "and still tumbling beneath the waterfall."

The sun had been sparkling on the waters of the Wyrme, but now the sun dived behind a cloud, and the gorge darkened.

"We have to go back," Conan Doyle announced. "Lawless and Troutt are no doubt on their way to Wyrme-Hallow. We have to get the Shepherd girls before Lawless finds them."

Wilde looked at his friend with horror. "Go back? Are you mad?

Both have guns. Our only weapons are your good sense and my scintillating wit. For Oscar Wilde, escaping certain death once is more than enough for one day. Twice bears all the hallmarks of bravery, an affectation I shudder at!"

Conan Doyle thought for a moment. "Very well. I shall go back alone. You carry on to Darvington and try to raise the hue and cry."

Wilde wobbled shakily to his feet, looked at his friend uncertainly, and then turned to walk away. But after only a few feet, he turned back. "I cannot go." He said. "I must go with you. You'll need my help. Besides, I detest hues almost as much as I despise cries."

TROUTT DROWNS!

B ack at the Devil's cauldron, Chief Lawless and the Reverend
Troutt (with two t's) were debating their next move.

"What now, Alfred?"

"Do not fear, Reverend. Those two meddlers are gone and they're
not coming back. Not ever." Lawless reassured. The Reverend stood at
the edge of the sheer drop peering down into the cauldron. He had
not been able to take his eyes from the boiling white water since
Wilde and Conan Doyle plunged into the waters below.

"How can we be certain, Albert? Jenny Dawkins somehow
managed to float free."

Lawless scowled and shook his head. "A fluke, no doubt. We had
that violent rainstorm. The river was in full flood. You've heard all the
stories about the cauldron? Over the years, many have fallen in but
none have ever been recovered . . ."

"Except for Jenny Dawkins . . ."

A muscle in Lawless' jaw tremored. He threw a look of death at the
cleric and snarled, "Keep your nerve, Troutt. Don't fail me now. After
all, it was you who convinced me we were doing God's work when we
began this business . . . or have you forgotten little Fanny Pryce? It was
you that taught her how to say her prayers . . . around your cock!"

A look of anguish swept Troutt's face. He grabbed a handful of his own hair and pulled at it. "What have I done? I have sinned against my God and my church. This will all come out. We will be found out!"

Lawless said nothing. He was glaring at the reverend, who could not stop staring at the turmoiled waters of the cauldron, his restless eyes scanning the surface as if expecting to see a head surface at any moment.

As Lawless stood gazing upon the cleric, his expression changed. A muscle in his jaw twitched. He swallowed hard and recomposed his face. Anyone watching him would recognise that he had just come to a decision, for now, his eyes burned with a dread certainty. Suddenly, he lunged forward toward the cauldron, peering intently, and threw out his arm, pointing at something below.

"Look! There! Do you see it?"

The reverend responded with an open-mouthed expression of terror and looked from Lawless back at the cauldron, craning to see what the chief of police was pointing at.

"What? What do you see? Is it one of them?"

"It thought I saw a head! Look there, at the base of the falls."

The reverend took a step closer so that he stood on the very edge of the drop, where he ducked up and down, changing angle, straining to see what Lawless was pointing out. "What? Where? What do you see?"

Lawless slowly shifted position so that he was standing directly behind the holy man.

"It bobs up and then vanishes. I think it's the head of one of them. You must see it!"

"No, I don't see it! Where is it again"?

Now Lawless reached out and gently placed one hand in the middle of the reverend's back . . . and gave him the slightest push.

Feeling the pressure on his back, Troutt reared up and tried to back away from the edge, but then his feet shot from beneath him on the slick, spray-soaked stone. He managed a half turn as he fell and was able to grab the ledge.

"Help me, Albert!" He cried as he hung there, feet dangling above the drop.

Lawless looked down at Troutt as he grappled for a better hand-hold of the slippery stones, his arms trembling with effort.

"Well well," Lawless said to the man at his feet. "They do say that God works in mysterious ways. I see that now."

Troutt gasped and grappled for a better purchase. But, bathed in constant spray, the rocks were slick and sharp-edged and soon his hands were also slippery with blood as the stones sliced into the soft skin of his hands.

"Help me, Albert. Help me!"

But Lawless stepped farther away from the edge and watched Troutt's struggles with an odd smile on his face.

Troutt looked up helplessly at Lawless. "No, you cannot do this, Albert." Trout cried. "It is murder before the eyes of God."

A laugh bubbled up from Lawless's throat. "Oh, I think God has seen a lot of murders at this point. What's one more? And, after all, *you* are the only murderer. I will be sure to reveal your secret to the good people of Darvington—that you are the one who has been murdering their daughters all along. I will tell them of how, your conscience-stricken by guilt, you confessed to me before you jumped to your death. "

"God knows the truth and his judgement will be upon you!"

"Yes. No doubt. As it will be upon you, Troutt."

"No, please help me. I cannot die unconfessed of my sins."

"No need. I know all of your sins. And I'm sure you won't be forgiven. Consider yourself damned for eternity. Perhaps I'll light a candle for you." Lawless sneered at the holy man. "But perhaps not."

And with that Lawless stepped forward and stamped his heel upon the fingers of Troutt's left hand, who screamed and pulled his hand away. As Troutt scrabbled to grip the rocks with broken and twisted fingers, Lawless put the sole of his shoe on Troutt's forehead.

"Consider this a benediction," Lawless growled and gave a mighty shove.

Trout shrieked as he fell backwards. His knees smashed into a lower ledge below, sending him toppling end-over-end. He hit the boiling water head-first and plunged from sight. But a few moments later he bobbed back up, spluttering and choking, his vestments ballooned up with air so that he floated buoyant on the water's surface.

For a moment, Lawless looked concerned, but then Troutt was snagged by one of the whirlpools and spun around and around. His screams could barely be heard above the constant roar of falling water. The whirlpools seemed like sentient devils fighting over the soul of a sinner as he was spun in one direction and then the other. But then Troutt was drawn under the thundering cascade and vanished into the spray as the tumult of water smashed down upon his head, driving him deep under.

Lawless stood and watched for a long time, eyes scanning the surface of the water. At some point, he produced a cigar and lit it. He had a long leisurely smoke, and when there was nothing left but a smouldering butt, he tossed it into the cauldron and turned on his heel to walk away. But before he left the cauldron, he reached into his jacket pocket and produced the pistol. He opened the barrel with a flick of his wrist and checked that all the chambers had bullets. He was heading back to Wyrme-Hallow and the *Green Man Inn*, to search for the Shepherd sisters he knew must be hiding there.

A SURPLUS SURPLICE?

"Good fellow," Conan Doyle said, clambering to his feet. He clapped Wilde on the arm and suddenly noticed something. "Your clothes! They're dry."

Wilde looked down at his apparel. "How is that possible?"

At that moment, both men flinched at a loud trumpeting sound. When they looked up at the stoney walls of the gorge around them, they saw an enormous stag standing on the highest ledge, the noble head fixed upon them.

"That's how it was possible, Oscar. I believe that is the Lord of the Fey. I believe that means we are still within the influence of the vortex. We must act quickly before Lawless is able to destroy it."

"Don't forget the Reverend Troutt with two t's."

"Yes, we need to put him on the hook, too, and reel him in."

"Yes, the many must be put in his plaice."

"Ahem," Conan Doyle said. "Let's not pun again until this is all over."

The two set off walking back toward Wyrme-Hallow, but as they reached the Devil's Cauldron, both men could not pass by without an uneasy look down into the infernal place where both had nearly ended their lives.

"Look there," Conan Doyle said, pointing. "What is that swirling around in the whirlpool?"

Both men stared. It was a piece of white clothing the whirlpools were toying with, spinning around and around.

Finally, after intense scrutiny, Wilde turned to his friend and said, "I believe that is an item of apparel, and if I'm not mistaken, it looks remarkably like a clerical surplice."

The two men shared a stunned look.

"The Reverend Troutt?"

"With two t's," Wilde nodded in agreement.

"I have no doubt this was the work of Lawless."

"I agree. One less mouth to blab. I suppose no one heard the good reverend's final confession."

"Not after his unholy baptism. Come, Oscar, let's leave this plaice. We're falling back into punnery."

THE DRAGON UNLEASHED

When they reached Wyrme-Hallow, Conan Doyle insisted
that Wilde remain at the Green Man to protect the girls,
while he carried on to the river cave. He had lost track of time, but
he reasoned an hour must have passed, and he suspected the
Reverend Shepherd had run away rather than light the dynamite
fuse.

Keeping an eye out for Lawless, he crept toward the river cave. As
he got close, he could see the reverend hovering by the cave opening.

"Reverend Shepherd, he called out in a tense whisper, "Why did
you not light the fuse?"

"Because I wouldn't let him," a deep voice answered. It was a voice
that Conan Doyle instantly recognised with a sense of dread. The
voice came from the cave opening, and now Albert Lawless tore loose
of the cave shadows and stepped into the light of day. He had his
pistol in his hand and pointed it at Conan Doyle.

Lawless's eyes crawled up and down Conan Doyle as if he could
not quite believe what he was seeing.

"I must admit, Mister Doyle, you are the very last person I
expected ever to see again. How on earth did you escape the Devil's
Cauldron?"

Conan Doyle swallowed hard and answered. "I'm a strong swimmer."

Lawless snorted with disbelief. "Impossible! Someone must have helped you. Did your Irish friend also escape?"

"I'm afraid not." The Scots author shook his head sadly and dropped his gaze lest Lawless see the lie in his eyes.

"I don't believe that, either," Lawless said, "Is Mister Wilde here, too, lurking about somewhere?" He took a cautious step backwards, throwing a quick look around as if expecting Wilde to spring upon him. His attention returned to the Reverend, and now he threatened him with the pistol. "You!" He sneered. "Get back to the Inn and crawl back into a cider pot where you belong!"

Clearly expecting a bullet in the back, the Reverend cringed away and then broke into a run, never looking back.

Lawless hadn't noticed the fuse cord running thirty feet out of the cave, and one of his feet was actually standing on part of the cord.

"Quite ingenious of you. You meant to blow up the river cave, which would no doubt have flooded this valley, preventing the railroad. Satisfy my curiosity. Why would you do that?"

Conan Doyle had one hand in his pocket, feeling for his spare match. "The gorge is sacred to the Fey. That's why all attempts to build the railroad through here have failed."

Lawless burst out with contemptuous laughter. "The Fey? You are as addled as the drunken curate, which reminds me. I took these from him."

Lawless reached into a pocket and drew something out. The box of matches Conan Doyle had entrusted to the reverend Shepherd.

Now Lawless shook the box, which rattled faintly. He pushed the box open with a thumb and glanced in.

"Only three matches left. What a shame."

Lawless removed a match and scratched it to life on the side of the box. The match flared and lit, but then the Police Chief dropped it at his feet, where the match flame futtered and went out.

"Two left," Lawless teased. He drew out a second match and repeated the act, allowing the flame to die at his feet.

"Your last match, I'm afraid, Mister Doyle, and after this, I really will have to shoot you."

Lawless scratched the last match to life. He teased Conan Doyle by holding the match by the very end so that it burned the longest before dropping it at his feet and allowing it to snuff out.

"I'm afraid you're out of matches and out of time, it would seem."

Lawless began to raise the pistol, but then Conan Doyle held out the match he had secreted in his pocket.

"Four matches," he corrected. "I kept one in reserve."

Lawless looked momentarily concerned but then sneered.

"A fourth match which I'm sure is quite waterlogged after your baptism in the Devil's Cauldron."

In answer, Conan Doyle flicked his thumbnail across the head of the match, which flared and burned. Lawless only had time to register surprise when Conan Doyle tossed the match at the fuse. The burning match bounced off the stone and came to rest, lying against the fuse, which immediately burst to fizzing life.

Lawless looked momentarily stunned but soon recovered. "Well done, Mister Doyle. But unfortunately, it can be easily extinguished, like your life."

Lawless strode quickly over to the fizzing fuse, stomped his foot down and ground it out with a swivel of his shoe.

The fuse extinguished, Lawless raised his pistol again and aimed at Conan Doyle's heart, who stood defiantly, his arms at his side, ready to receive the fatal shot.

But then a firefly spark blew past on the wind, bright as a small star. It captured the eyes of both men, who followed the spark as it dropped upon the fuse and kindled it back to fizzing life.

Lawless threw a surprised look at the fizzing fuse. "What? What the devil?"

Conan Doyle threw a mocking grin at his nemesis. "Now you have a choice, Lawless, shoot me or use the precious few seconds to put out the fuse. You cannot do both. There's a full crate of dynamite stashed in the cave. If it goes off, it will blow a hole in the cave floor, unleashing millions of gallons from the underground tributary of the

Wyrme and flooding this valley. Then your train line will never run, and the Darvington Railway and all its investors will be bankrupt."

Lawless, dithered, torn between shooting Conan Doyle and attending to the fizzing fuse, which was racing toward the cave entrance.

With a growl of anger, Lawless ran to intercept the fizzing fuse, but each time he stamped the sole of his shoe down on the fuse, extinguishing it, the fuse sputtered back to life six feet farther on. He growled with anger and stomped on the fuse repeatedly, which miraculously kept relighting. And so the Police Chief was lured into the cave where the fuse suddenly fizzed to life in a dozen places, so that it was clear he would never put them all out.

When Lawless disappeared inside the cave, Conan Doyle took the opportunity to run for it, and now he sprinted toward the higher ground on the sides of the gorge. Conan Doyle had learned how to rock climb during his school years at Stonyhurst, and had acquired more experience during trips to Switzerland. Luckily, the rock face was abundant with toe, and finger holds, so he scrambled up the face with ease. When he was forty feet up, he hung from the rock face and looked around to see where Lawless was.

Inside the cave, Lawless stamped and battered with his hands at the fuse, extinguishing each newly erupting flame. With the last one put out, he grinned triumphantly, at which point the fuse spontaneously lit in a dozen places, all sizzling toward the stack of dynamite waiting in its crate. Lawless' eyes widened with terror, and with an anguished cry, he turned and dashed out of the cave, running for his life. He made it twenty stumbling feet when the dynamite exploded with a cacophonous roar blasting a gout of flame and smoke from the cave entrance like the erupting barrel of a cannon. The blast caught Lawless in the back and hurled him two dozen feet. He hit the ground hard and tumbled head-over-heels like a rag doll.

Smoke swirled, concealing the scene for moments, and when it finally cleared, Lawless lay as if dead. But then he stirred and staggered painfully to his feet. He tried to take a step only for his right leg to buckle, and he screamed out in pain and nearly fell. It was clear his leg was broken or worse. The blast had shredded his jacket and trousers to tatters. He looked up to see that Conan Doyle having forty feet on the side of the Gorge.

"Pah!" Lawless shouted, shaking an angry fist. "You failed to kill me!"

Remarkably, the policeman had managed to keep the pistol gripped in his hand, and now he raised it, took careful aim at Conan Doyle, and squeezed off a shot. The bullet struck the rock face inches from Conan Doyle's face, spitting stone chips as it ricocheted away. Lawless raised the pistol a second time, fighting to keep the wavering muzzle centered on the Scotsman's form.

Conan Doyle dithered. His position left him helplessly exposed. If Lawless's next shot didn't kill him, it was likely the third shot would. He hugged the rock face, trying to present a smaller target, but then a building roar erupted from the cave opening. The ground around it suddenly slumped, dropping ten feet. The air resounded to a noise like mountains collapsing as the underground Wyrme, released from thousands of years of confinement, broke loose. Lawless turned to stare in wide-eyed terror as a roaring geyser of water erupted hundreds of feet into the air. The tumult struck Lawless square-on and sent him tumbling across the ground. Within seconds he was swept up in a torrent of mud, boulders and broken tree limbs. His head bobbed up once, twice, as the tsunami of debris swept him along, but then he went under again and, this time, vanished from sight.

As Conan Doyle watched the horrific spectacle, he saw how quickly the water level was rising and began climbing as fast as he could. The Scotsman kept fit by playing football and cricket, but soon, his arms and shoulders were burning from the exertion. He couldn't force his limbs to move any quicker, but when he looked down, he found the flood waters surging around the cuffs of his trousers. He saw a momentary respite in the form of a ledge ten feet higher—if only he could reach it in time. A final handheld beckoned ahead, but it was beyond the stretch of his reaching fingers. He would have to chance it and try to leap the gap. He coiled his leg muscles, ready to spring. But then something clamped around his ankle and began to draw him backwards. He threw a look down to see Lawless. His face was bruised, bloody, and smeared in muck, although the bloodshot eyes burned with hatred. It was clear the policeman had refused to die until could extract his final revenge. Now his crushing Minotaur grip was fastened on Conan Doyle's ankle and was trying to drag him down into the maelstrom. Conan Doyle kicked down with his free leg against Lawless's fingers, who howled with pain, although his grip never slackened. Conan Doyle kicked a second and then a third time. Each time Lawless bellowed with pain, but his death grip never relented. Conan Doyle decided that fair play and chivalry had their place on the sporting field, but not when he was engaged in a life-and-death struggle. The next time he drove his heel down with all his might—straight into Lawless's face. Cartilage cracked, and the lawman's nose heeled over at a sickening angle. Conan Doyle drew his leg back and then kicked a second time. This time his nose heeled over to the right. Conan Doyle gathered all his strength and then kicked down with all the force he could muster. Lawless's head snapped back under the blow. Conan Doyle kicked a second time, and finally, the minotaur grip slackened as Lawless tumbled backwards into the roaring tsunami of mud and water and was swept away.

Conan Doyle pulled himself higher, but by now, his arms were shaking with lactic acid. He rested a moment and sprang for the next hand-hold . . . but his grasping fingers fell a full foot short, and he began to fall backwards . . . only to see another hand reach down and seize him by the wrist. When he looked, he found himself staring at a pair of naked male thighs scarcely concealed by a pair of obscenely short shorts.

Oscar Wilde, of course. Who else?

Now Wilde seized Conan Doyle's wrist with a two-handed grip. He was bending in a deep squat, thigh muscles trembling as he leaned back and pulled with all his strength.

Despite his abhorrence of exercise, Wilde had actually put on a few pounds of muscle, and at well over six foot, the large Irishman hoisted his friend onto the safety of a ledge.

As Conan Doyle lay on his side, gasping to catch his wind, he looked up at his Irish friend and laughed with gratitude.

"Thank you, Oscar, I've never been more happy to see your pale Irish thighs."

Wilde raised a bushy eyebrow and replied, "No one has ever spoken those words to me before, but oddly, I will take it as a compliment. I was here in time to see the long-anticipated demise of Mister Lawless. What now?"

"Now we must hastily return to the Green Man to collect the Shepherd girls and their father—if he'll agree to come—before the village is inundated."

A KISS FOR FORGETTING

B y the time the two authors got to Wyrme-Hallow, shallow waves of flood water were sweeping along the village streets and breaking against the stone cottages and the sides of *The Green Man*.

"Where are the girls?" Conan Doyle asked.

"Waiting for us at the oak tree," Wilde explained. "Why are we here, then?"

"I must retrieve my Casebook and then endeavour to persuade Reverend Shepherd to come with us. However, I am not sure he will listen."

The water level was rising visibly by the second. Conan Doyle waded through the knee-deep water to the Inn and heaved the door wide against the weight of the water.

He sloshed his way into the tap room and looked about the place. Already wooden bowls and other debris floated about the room. And then he spotted the Reverend sitting at his usual table by the fireplace and waded up to him.

The Reverend had filled a half dozen tankards with cider and was methodically working his way through them.

"Reverend Shepherd. The village will soon be underwater. You must come with us."

The reverend finished draining his tankard, then banged it down on the table and sighed with contentment. He looked up at Conan Doyle as he dragged the next tankard forward. "I have lived long enough with the Fey. I have no need to leave."

"But what about your wife? What about your young daughters?"

"I am a drunkard. It is my calling in life. No one will miss me."

"We're leaving by the faerie tree before it is underwater. I beg you to reconsider. Come with us."

The Reverend hefted his tankard as a rebuttal. "This is all I need, and here my tankard will always be full—even at the bottom of a lake."

Conan Doyle looked around. The water level was rising rapidly. He shook his head in dismay as he waded to the staircase and gingerly climbed the steps. He paused in his former bedroom only long enough to find his precious Casebook and toss it into his haversack.

Wilde's face fell when he saw his friend emerge from the Inn . . . alone.

"Our friend, the reverend, won't come then?"

Conan Doyle shook his head bitterly. "No, but we must hurry before the water submerges the faerie tree and first I must visit the Lord of the Fey. I promised that I would stop the railway. I must tell him that I kept my word."

When they reached the faerie oak, they found Wilhelmina and Philomena waiting. With the girls following, they set off into the woods but quickly became lost. Conan Doyle put two fingers to his lips and blasted a piercing whistle. Moments later his Brittany bounded up, stubby tail wagging."

Conan Doyle shared a crafty look with Wilde. "Fortunately, Bandit knows the way to the Lord's manor house."

Wilde frowned doubtfully. "A manor house in these dense woods? Highly unlikely, I should think."

The four of them followed the Brittany as it bounded away along the forest trails, occasionally dashing back to ensure they were following. Soon they came to the fairy fort and glimpsed the dark opening of a burial barrow.

"There it is, Oscar."

Wilde fixed his friend with a frown. "The cave opening? That's the Lord's manor? Surely you jest, Arthur! I had something rather more resplendent in mind."

"Come, you'll see."

They reached the cave opening and peered in.

"We need a lantern," Wilde pointed out. "It's pitch black inside."

"I'm out of matches. We'll have to use yours."

Conan Doyle looked back at the Shepherd sisters. "Come along, girls, and stay close.

As soon as the group stepped inside the barrow, they felt the temperature plummet. Oscar Wilde scratched a Lucifer to life and held it high. The faint illumination lit only the walls on either side, which were carved with cup and ring marks and elaborate spirals.

"I kept my promise," Conan Doyle spoke into the darkness, his breath fogging in the subterranean air.

Suddenly, the cave grew bright from a glow that seemed to emanate from the air around them. The barrow had a high ceiling. On the far wall, two grotesque figures had been etched—a depiction of two thrones had been carved, and something monstrous occupied them.

The first appeared to be a carved effigy of a hybrid creature: a giant hind mixed with a human form, as though the two had somehow melted and flowed together. The eyes were almond-shaped like a deer's, and the gleam in them showed they were squeezing up into three dimensions and were looking straight at the two friends. Sitting beside it was a thinner creature with the round eyes of a giant owl.

The first being, whatever it was, finally spoke.

"So, you kept your promise?"

"Yes, Conan Doyle answered.

"But I see that you are disturbed by my true appearance. Perhaps I should assume a more familiar form?"

The figure on the throne casually waved its furry hand. The stony walls around them shivered and dissolved, and they found themselves in the great hammer-beam hall Conan Doyle had originally visited.

The huge tapestry once again hung behind the throne the silver-haired man occupied.

"Is this better?" the Lord of the Fey asked.

"An infinite improvement for me," Wilde answered.

"You have stopped the railway?" The Lord asked.

"Not completely," Conan Doyle admitted. "I believe that work will continue. A new route may be found, but the iron rails will never run through the gorge. Wyrme-Hallow will soon be covered by a lake. In order to cross it, they would have to be a viaduct or a railway trestle. The cost would no doubt bankrupt the scheme."

The Lord nodded sagely. "You are a clever man, and you were wise to choose a clever companion. I did well to summon you."

"I rather like this chap," Wilde whispered to Conan Doyle sotto voce.

Conan Doyle stepped forward "I must now ask you a favour. The Shepherd girls. They must be returned to their mother."

"They are welcome to stay with us in Wyrme-hallow, but if they wish to leave, I will permit it."

Conan Doyle shot the two sisters a questioning look. "What do you say? You have had this experience, but your life is waiting for you back in Darvington."

Both girls looked dismayed at the prospect. "But we can't go back," Shailagh protested. "We are no longer little girls. We have lived in Wyrme-Hallow for two years. Time passes differently in the village. A year in Wyrme-Hallow only lasts a day in Darvington."

Aoife added, "I don't want to go back to picnics and playing with dollies. I like my adult body. I like being free. I won't go back!"

Conan Doyle and Wilde shared a look. Wilde paused a moment and then addressed both girls. "There are others to be considered. Every day your mother sits on the park bench in her garden, staring out at the river, hoping and praying that her little girls will come back to her. It is heartbreaking to see her."

The two sisters shared a despairing look.

Wilhelmina stepped forward and addressed the Lord. "Might we come back from time to time? For a visit?"

The Lord slowly shook his head. "No. That cannot be permitted. Once you leave Wyrme-Hallow, you must let go of this part of your life. If you return to childhood, the memory of this place will fade, and one day you will believe that this was all just make-believe, a story you made up together, the childhood fantasy of young girls."

Shailagh's eyes overflowed with tears. "But . . . but I never want to forget Wyrme-Hallow!"

The Fey Lord shook his head sadly. "But that is the faerie way. No mortals can keep their memories. All this must appear as a dream. And you, Mister Doyle, I believe you have kept a journal. I ask now that you surrender it."

Conan Doyle hesitated for a moment, his expression stunned, but then he dug into the haversack and drew out the Casebook. He was loathe to give it up and hesitated. To lose the proof of the existence of faeries and of the kingdom of the Fey was a disaster. But when he looked up, the Lord of the Fey extended his hand, waiting.

The Lord took it from him and paged through it, smiling to himself.

"Yes, I'm afraid that proof unequivocal of the existence of the Fey would confound human understanding. And, of course, it would lead to endless intrusions of the human into our world. And as you know, there are already so few places left to us." He waved his hand, and the brass bowl next to his throne burst into flame.

"But we Fey have never been clumsy and guileless in our dealings with humans, and so . . ." The Lord smiled craftily as he flipped the casebook open and began tearing pages out, seemingly at random, and tossing them into the air so that they fluttered into the fire and burst into flames. When he had finished pruning the book, he handed it back to Conan Doyle.

Conan Doyle's frown showed that he was greatly aggrieved at the savage editing of his Casebook, but the Lord merely chuckled at his concern. "I think that will do nicely. It will provide you with some tantalising clues. Some evocative but unprovable hints. As you are a bard, a scribbler of tales, I warrant you will find a story in what I leave you."

Conan Doyle gripped his Casebook to his chest. It was notably thinner now. He was crushingly disappointed but knew it had to be so.

"Ah," The Lord suddenly added. "But there is one thing I must return to you before you leave. Something I borrowed that I believe will serve as the centrepiece of any story you concoct."

The Lord reached into his top pocket and drew out a large and heavy card. When he pressed it into Conan Doyle's hand, the Scots author's mouth fell agape.

It was the photo of the Shepherd girls with the faeries attending their picnic. The photograph that had originally led the two friends on this chase to Wessex.

"But how shall we forget all we have experienced?" Wilde asked. "I ask only for Arthur, who has a mind like a steel trap, whereas my memory is more like a sieve."

The Lord smiled and looked at the beautiful lady sitting at his side. "Forgetting begins with a kiss."

The Lord gestured toward his guests and said, "Sweet lady, our friends must leave us. Please kiss them goodbye."

The Lady of the Fey rose from her throne, the caul of fog swirling about her face. She paused first with the girls and she bent over and kissed them both, first on the forehead and then on the lips. Next, she moved on to Wilde, who moved by her beauty and majesty, seized her hand and kissed it. Her pleased smile was the only part of the woman's face visible as she bussed him on the lips. Then she moved to Conan Doyle. She leaned close, and her lips met his. To the Scots author, the kiss was like a sip of honeyed wine, the sweetest he had ever tasted. As she drew her face away, he caught a heart-ripping glimpse beneath her veil at the most beautiful face he had ever beheld.

The Lord spoke again. "Having received the Kiss from the Lady of the Fey, from this moment on, your memories of this time will diminish, ebb away, until they take the form of a waking dream that lifts from the mind and evaporates quickly. And although you would fain hold onto it, the dream will elude you, save for an inexpressible echo in the soul. And so, I bid you humans, adieu . . . adieu . . ." and as he spoke, the great hall began to dim, and the walls shimmered and dissolved as darkness poured in like a liquid. Suddenly they were back in the burial barrow, and the Lord and Lady of the Fey had flattened back to little more than scratchings upon the stone walls.

The four of them stumbled toward the barrow opening until they finally stepped out into the light of day.

As they walked back to the faerie oak, Conan Doyle hoped they could yet persuade the Reverend Shepherd to come back with them, but when they reached the village, only the very uppermost chimney pot of *The Green Man Inn* remained above water.

At the sight, tears flowed freely down the girl's faces.

"I never want to forget this place," Shailagh sobbed.

"Me neither!" Aoife echoed.

The two girls turned to one another and hugged.

But as they all silently looked on, they heard a strange chiming sound.

Wilde threw a puzzled frown at his colleague. "What on earth is that?"

For a moment, Conan Doyle looked mystified but then smiled sadly and said, "I believe those are the chimes of the Grandfather clock. It's finally working."

At the news, Wilde dug out his pocket watch and studied it. "My watch is working!

"Mine too!"

"What time do you make it, Arthur?"

"Time to go home."

The girls were still wiping their tears when they reached the faerie Oak. Wilhelmina opened the faerie door, and they both scrambled inside and pulled the door shut. A second later, Conan Doyle snatched the door open again. The girls had vanished.

Conan Doyle held the door open for Wilde, who had considerable difficulty folding inside his six-foot three-inch frame, all the time flashing yards of lily-white thigh as he turned, twisted, and struck contortionist poses as he tried to squeeze his body through the door, forcing Conan Doyle to avert his eyes.

"See you on the other side, Oscar", Conan Doyle said and closed the door, then muttered to himself. "And I soon hope never to see those thighs again!"

When he opened the door again, Wilde had vanished. Now he looked around for his Brittany, which was sitting a dozen feet away, its head tilted to one side, pink tongue lolling.

"Come on, Bandit!" Conan Doyle beckoned, patting his leg. "Are you coming home with me? My children would love you, and we have a nice warm fire for you to lie down in front of."

But the dog did not move.

"Come on, boy—!" He started to say again, but when he looked a second time, the dog had vanished. In its place stood a strange creature barely three feet in height. It could have been a goblin or a wood sprite. It had translucent wings on its back and globular, protruding eyes. For the first time, Conan Doyle realised that his dog had just been a bit of faerie magic.

"Thank you," he called to the creature. "Thank you for letting me spend some time with my beloved dog."

At his words, the creature bent from the waist and threw Conan Doyle a courtier's bow. But then the wings began to flutter. It rose several feet in the air, where it turned into a bright spark of light. And then it vanished.

With no reason to tarry, Conan Doyle grunted his bulk into the hollow of the tree and pulled the door closed behind him. When he pushed the door open again, Wilde and the Shepherd sisters, now returned to the childish form of Wilhelmina and Philomina, were waiting for him in the garden of *The Old Rectory*.

∼

B ut back at Wyrme-Hallow a man had been lurking in the shadows, watching as the four had used the fairy door to escape. Now he stepped forward from the gloom of vegetation. It was the Reverend Shepherd. His white collar dangled loosely from a single stay, his thick black hair was disheveled and he sported a four-day growth of beard. As always, he was drunk, and he gripped a whiskey bottle in one hand. For a moment, he lingered and threw a glance back toward the village. He could hear but not see the encroaching water hissing through the undergrowth. It would be a matter of minutes before the fairy door and the ancient oak were submerged. Now he paused to raise the bottle to his lips and took several Adam's-apple-bobbing pulls at it, then regarded the bottle with the forlorn look of a man saying goodbye to an old friend. Then he hurled the bottle away into the depths of the trees. He ducked down, yanked the fairy door open, and folded his long limbs inside before pulling the door shut after him.

A TEARFUL REUNION

As was her daily ritual, Delphinia Shepherd spent most afternoons, a solitary figure reposed upon the bench in the garden, her vacant stare fixed upon the empty grass lawns that stretched down to the glistening waters of the River Wyrme. In the days since the girls had vanished, she had kept a solitary vigil here each day hoping against hope to see her bairns come running up the slope to greet her.

But as the months passed, a single chilling thought surged up into her mind again and again: Wilhelmina and Philomena were never coming home again—just two more Darvington girls vanished and overtaken by a terrible fate. So in her solitary watch, Delphinia Shepherd sat on the park bench accompanied only by her sorrow.

Today, Delphinia's pretty blue eyes were glazed like a porcelain doll's as her unseeing eyes fixed upon the downslope of grass. For a moment she thought she heard the voices of her girls, their childish giggles and laughter, shrill with excitement, but then she told herself it was just the cry of birds from the gorge. Just then something moved into her field of view and she lifted her head as her eyes refocused.

Four figures moved toward her, climbing the ascending slope of the garden. She squinted her eyes into focus (vanity prohibited wearing the glasses she had been prescribed). The two taller figures were grown men and each was holding the hand of a young girl.

She tried to examine the girls more closely but her eyes were starred with tears.

Delphinia tried to stand up but all strength fled from her body in a dizzying rush and she collapsed to her knees. She could not speak, could not scream, but her mouth opened and emitted cries of distress. All she could do was extend her arms to her girls and beckon them toward her.

The two girls, upon seeing their mother, dropped their grip on the two men's hands and ran toward their mother. "My angels!" She cried as the girls' flew into her arms and she rained kisses on their faces and could not hug them tightly enough.

Conan Doyle and Wilde strode up a moment later, both men chuckling at the exuberant display of filial happiness.

"We have returned your girls as promised, ma'am. Conan Doyle said. "I am sorry it took so long. We were ... ah ... " He trailed off, lost for words as he felt his own throat constricting with emotion. He threw a glance at Wilde, a man who famously was never lost for words.

"We risked life and limb," Wilde added, scandalously, "and suffered many hardships, but in the end, we found your two angels lost in the woods."

"You have my undying thanks, gentlemen. I can never repay your kindness, for I—" Delphinia Shepherd suddenly stopped short, and her eyes widened at something moving toward them.

When Wilde and Conan Doyle looked behind them, they were surprised to see a male figure trooping up the sloping lawn toward them. It took each a moment to understand who the strange figure in the black clerical surplice was, but finally, they recognised the figure of the Reverend Shepherd. The youth he had enjoyed in Wyrme-Hallow was gone, and now he appeared as he had done in his framed photograph: a stoop-shouldered man of advanced years, with a wild vortex of shock-white beard spilling down his chest.

"Oh, oh!" Delphinia gasped and pressed a hand to her heart,

suddenly seeming to have difficulty breathing. "It is my husband. He has returned to us. Surely my heart cannot withstand this sudden rush of happiness."

And then she swooned to the ground.

It was a scene from a Victorian Melodrama, and at first, all truly thought that Delphinia Shepherd's heart had given out. But then Conan Doyle, the doctor, stooped over her and felt for a pulse at her throat.

"Dear lord, is she?" Wilde asked breathlessly.

Conan Doyle looked up and smiled reassuringly. "She has merely swooned, as before."

Conan Doyle and Wilde then carried the prostrate Delphinia Shepherd back into her house and arranged her on the leather Chesterfield as once before. As the father and daughters fussed around her, Conan Doyle and Wilde used the family reunion as an excuse to quietly slip away from the rectory unobserved.